TECH-HEAVEN

LINDA NAGATA

BANTAM BOOKS

NEW YORK TORONTO LONDON SYDNEY AUCKLAND

TECH-HEAVEN
A Bantam Spectra Book / December 1995
SPECTRA and the portrayal of a boxed "s" are trademarks of Bantam Books,
a division of Bantam Doubleday Dell Publishing Group, Inc.

ISBN 0-553-56926-0

Published simultaneously in the United States and Canada

Bantam Books are published by Bantam Books, a division of Bantam Doubleday Dell Publishing Group, Inc. Its trademark, consist-
ing of the words "Bantam Books" and the portrayal of a rooster, is
Registered in U.S. Patent and Trademark Office and in other countries. Marca Registrada. Bantam Books, 1540 Broadway, New York,
New York 10036.

PRINTED IN THE UNITED STATES OF AMERICA

RAD   0 9 8 7 6 5 4 3 2 1

For Dallas
Who Likes to Speculate

ACKNOWLEDGMENTS

Special thanks to Richard Curtis for insisting that I re-write this, and for showing me how. A warm thank you as well to Jennifer Hershey for her invaluable guidance in the final revision, and to Mark Voelker, for his detailed critique of the suspension procedure.

Part I
FUGITIVE

L.A. FLOW—LIFESTYLES
"Parent-Child Dialogue #1, Version 17"

CHILD: *Daddy, Why do people get old?*
PARENT: *Aw, that's just the little fee nature charges for all those wild birthday parties.*
CHILD: *Why do people have to die?*
PARENT: *Hmm. Because nobody's figured out a way to live forever, I guess.*
CHILD: *Why not?*

1

To Live Forever

Katie Kishida rode into the little Andean village of La Cruz on the back of a bony black steel mannequin. Through her VR suit she directed each crunching step along the mineral soil of the village's lone street. A freezing wind whistled through the mannequin's external joints and soughed past the rim of her VR helmet. She clung to the mannequin's back, studying the helmet's video display, anxiously searching the village for signs of life. But there was nothing—not a wisp of smoke or a scrounging bird, or even a cat slinking through the cluster of worn, wood-frame buildings.

She commanded the remotely controlled unit to stop. The village made a neat frame for an imposing line of white peaks supporting a heavy ceiling of storm clouds. Bass thunder rumbled there, arriving almost below the range of hearing, a deep vibration that set Katie's slight, sixty-four-year-old body trembling, and snapped the brittle tethers she'd placed upon her fear.

The Voice cops had forgotten her.

She didn't want to believe it. Certainly in Panama

they'd tried to stop her. Failing that, they'd seized her holding company, Kishida-Hunt. They'd confiscated her assets, declared her a criminal, and then . . . nothing. She'd journeyed south for weeks with no sign of pursuit, and that worried her most of all, because the Voice cops wouldn't give up unless they thought she was dead . . . or disarmed. Maybe they knew about her bootleg copy of the Cure. Maybe they'd seized it before it could be shipped to La Cruz. Or maybe the life-extension schedule was a fraud, and there had been no pursuit since Panama because there was no Cure—and no way to restore life to the cryonic suspension patients hidden in a clandestine mausoleum in the mountains above La Cruz.

Fear had become her default emotion.

She shut down the remote, then slid from her perch on its back to stand on her own stiff legs. Her lean muscles ached and her ass was forever sore. She lifted the video helmet off her head. The wind streamed past her cheeks, its bitter touch oddly familiar. She thought she could feel Tom's presence in the mountains' unremitting cold. Tom had been dead thirty years. Or maybe he'd just become a crystalline life-form when his heart had stopped, his body and their marriage both immersed in liquid nitrogen, $-196°$ C, a cold that had haunted her life.

A child's laughter suddenly broke through her reverie. Katie looked up quickly. Motion caught her eye, drawing her gaze up the street to a single-story building slightly larger than all the others, with a hand-lettered sign by the door declaring *Provisiones*. Katie remembered. This was the same store where she'd bought a cup of hot coffee fifteen years ago. Back then, the building had been painted a shade of blue that matched the sky. But time had bleached and chipped away the paint until now there was only a hint of color left between the cracks. The walls were further abused with rusty staples, a few still clenching the tattered corners of handbills that had long since blown away. A little girl was peering past the partly opened door, bouncing up and down in excitement as she exclaimed in lilting Spanish over the skeletal aspect of the remote.

In her eagerness, Katie dropped the helmet in the

street, forgetting it before it hit the ground. She hobbled toward the battered building, fighting muscle cramps in her legs. If the Cure had been successfully shipped from Vancouver, then it would be here, in the village store. She could claim her package and push on, higher still into the mountains, to the hidden mausoleum where Tom waited. If she could get to that quiet place, with the Cure in hand and no cops on her trail, then perhaps she could finally confront the ghost that had haunted her for thirty years.

The little girl smiled at her. From inside the store, a woman shouted. The girl glanced over her shoulder, then turned back to Katie with a grin. She opened the door wider. *"Hola, Señora. Entre usted, por favor."*

Inside the store the air was warm with electric heat and light. Katie began to perspire under her many layers of clothing, even before the door had closed behind her. She felt disoriented as she pulled off her gloves and stuffed them in a pocket. The physical comfort of the store's interior seemed alien, bold and fragile at once. Outside, the frigid wind gusted hard past the roofline. The building seemed to inflate, and then it shuddered. It was only a matter of time, Katie thought. The wind would penetrate this bubble of warmth, cool it, slow it, stretch it out in time, arresting the process while preserving the structure.

There wasn't much left in the store beyond structure anyway. Most of the shelves and ceiling hooks were bare, as if the owners had already finished their going-out-of-business sale. Near the back though, Katie discovered a couple of beautiful woven blankets, and some food and modern camping supplies. Behind a yellowed linoleum counter an old woman, dressed in native woolens, watched with stern eyes.

Katie browsed self-consciously through the meager selection, gathering a supply of food—beans and rice and aseptic juice cartons. A blanket. A pair of heavy woolen socks. Her heart raced; her pulse felt thready. Was the package here? Was it? She piled the items on the counter, then produced a false ID.

Her jaw worked for a few seconds as she tried to introduce saliva into the terribly dry cavity of her mouth. If the package wasn't here then it was over. All over. And she could climb up into the mountains or wander down to the sea and it wouldn't matter. Tom would remain on ice. And she would have to endure his ghost every time she closed her eyes.

She passed the old woman an ID card bearing the fictitious name of Theresa Myers. Then she asked, in Spanish, as if it were something of small importance, "Do you have a package for me?"

The woman squinted at the ID. Then her eyebrows shot up. She looked at Katie with a kind of awe. "Theresa Myers? Theresa Myers? Ah, you have come. At last, at last." And she ducked down under the counter and pulled out a cardboard box that was no larger than a briefcase. "All the other villagers have gone to Arica or even beyond. But I swore to remain until you came. My granddaughter and I. Now we can follow." She took Katie's ID and entered it on her phone while Katie cautiously touched the box. The woman handed her back the card. "I'm a wealthy woman now, Señora. I'll buy a home in Arica. This village has always been my home, but now the mountains are at war with the sun and people are no longer welcome here. . . ."

Katie nodded, only half listening as she used a knife to open the package. Inside was an unlocked ceramic case whose top slid back, curving, to disappear into the liner. Nested in the padded interior was a collection of nearly two hundred sealed ampules and a cyberbook.

She ran trembling fingers across the ampules; touched the buttons on the cyberbook, scarcely breathing. This was supposed to be a general rejuvenation therapy, developed in her own European labs. It hardly seemed possible.

The Cure.

Be young again. Raise the dead. Neat and easy.

The market value of this kit would be incalculable . . . if it worked.

Where were the Voice cops?

She wondered again if she'd gambled away her life and fortune on a fraud.

Then her lips set in a stubborn line. Silently, she chastised herself. She'd come so far, given up so much. She

was not going to succumb to pessimism now. The Voice
cops were not omniscient. It was still possible to move beneath their gaze without being seen.

She reclosed the case, then pulled on her gloves. Nodding her thanks to the old woman, she tucked the case
under one arm, grabbed the sack of groceries with the
other, and went outside.

The wind had grown in strength. It tugged angrily at
the hood of her parka, and as she watched, it unbalanced
the remote, sending it toppling to the unpaved street,
where it lay humped around the supply pack strapped to
its chest.

"*Shit.*" Not an auspicious sign.

She tramped over to it, and set her booty on the ground.
The bipedal remote unit had been designed to function
as a full-body prosthesis. Its legs and arms were slender
and well-braced at the joints, like reconstructed bones. Its
torso was narrow, sitting in a swivel joint on the pelvic gir-
dle. Its head was a smooth model of a human skull, with
glass lenses where the eyes should have been and a blank
surface instead of a mouth and nose. It was controlled
through the VR, giving its user a physical presence in remote locations. But it required constant guidance.

Picking up the helmet, Katie dusted it off and set it
back on her head, pulling it down over her hood. She
flicked it on. A video image appeared on a screen just
inches before her eyes. She frowned, then realized the remote was looking straight up into a roiling ceiling of heavy
gray clouds. Well. At least the satellite eyes of the Voice
cops wouldn't be witnessing this scene.

A finger-width plug dangled from the helmet. She
grabbed it, then felt beneath her collar for the socket.
Close to the skin, beneath her many layers of clothing, she
wore a wired suit. Sensors in the suit's fabric picked up every flexion, every muscle twitch of her body. Processors,
working from experience, weighed the validity of the motion, culling the random stretches, the cramps, the sighs,
the farts, while sending the purposeful signals on to the
steel body of the remote unit. In the process, the scale of
motion was amplified. A tiny twitch in Katie's thigh and

calf translated into a four-foot stride for the mannequin. A
slight shift of her weight caused it to turn.

Now she guided it carefully to a standing position, feet
set wide and torso leaning slightly into the wind. As always, its metal hands were locked behind its hips, palms
spread flat to create her seat.

She felt a lull in the wind and switched out of the remote's sensorium. Grabbing the case that contained the
Cure, she stuffed that and her groceries into the pack on the
remote's chest. Then she hurried around to its back and
climbed on. She could feel it rocking under her as a gust of
wind shot down the village street. Quickly, she switched
back into the remote, and suddenly she felt balanced, strong.
She lifted her head; looked with glass eyes toward the peaks.
Lightning played there. Thunder grumbled. A wholly appropriate setting for bringing the dead back to life. She grinned,
and started the remote unit running up the road.

Fifteen years ago, the cryonics company, Forward Futures, had established a hidden mausoleum high in the
Chilean Andes. They'd chosen a nineteenth century copper mine for the site. Katie had been part of the team that
had come down from California to settle in the cryonic
suspension patients, set up the compact distillation facility
that would manufacture liquid nitrogen from the atmosphere, and finally, to help seal the mausoleum.

The abandoned mine had been situated at the bottom
of a steep slope laden with snow. The crew had concealed
the entrance behind a huge slab of rock that had flaked off
the mountain. The activity generated a small avalanche,
leaving the slab half-buried—a natural-looking stone
lean-to that shielded the outer steel door from casual observation. A scree-slope facsimile netting, manufactured in
California for landscaping purposes and guaranteed for
twenty years of use, had been hung over the door as further camouflage. Finally, the crew had closed the road behind them with a few sticks of dynamite.

Fog shrouded the slope as Katie clambered over the
rocky debris that blocked the road, and then walked the
remote past the mine's huge pile of tailings. Using her
video display, she gazed through the streaming mists,

straining for a sight of the tiny mining village that had already been abandoned when she'd made her first visit here. At last she saw the bell tower of the church, a dark edifice in the fog. A few steps more, and she was saddened to see that the weight of snow and time had caused the church roof to collapse, though the walls still stood. Three other structures had been part of this village too, but all now lay crushed on the ground, like detritus found in the footprint of a mountain god.

She looked around. There was not a scrap of vegetation. Patches of snow lingered on the leeward side of every tumbled rock. The air was dry and thin and bitterly cold and the only sounds were the rush of the wind as it curled past her helmet and the crunch of the remote's worn feet against the sterile ground.

She passed the church and wandered another half mile, around the foot of a ridge that flanked the village. The abandoned mine had been used as a mausoleum even before Forward Futures took it over. Fifteen years ago there had still been a cross fixed over the entrance.

She rounded the last rock outcropping. A natural terrace fronted the mine. She saw the slab just beyond. Carefully negotiating a field of tumbled rock, she worked her way to the slab and squeezed behind it. Her remote eyes immediately adjusted to the semidarkness and she caught her breath in concern. The cross was gone. And the facsimile netting had been pulled off the door. It lay crumpled on the frozen ground. She stared at it a moment through the remote's camera eyes, and then she disconnected herself from the machine and dismounted, removing her helmet with arms stiff from the cold. How long ago had the vandals been here? Years? Or days?

Her gazed turned to the door. It was still intact. She crouched in front of it, studying the lock, her breath coming fast and deep in the thin atmosphere. The lock's protective cover had been torn away and the keypad had been bashed with rocks or bullets. But when she pushed on the door, it held. That brought her momentary relief. Probably the vandals hadn't gotten inside.

She worked at the broken stubs of the buttons, running the combination through while thunder boomed and wisps of fog swept past on a bitter wind. She completed the combination, but the door failed to open. She stared at the lock in consternation. The day was starting to fade. Though she had a tent and a sleeping bag and heating rods, the thought of camping at this elevation, in this weather, frightened her. She suspected it wouldn't be hard to fall asleep and never wake up again.

So she ran the combination again, going slowly this time, pressing each button hard. Still the door failed to open. She stripped off her gloves and ran the combination again. Four times. Five. Cursing. Fingers fumbling; really feeling the altitude; hardly able to think. Six times. Or was it eight? And then she had it. Something rumbled inside the steel door. She pushed. The door gave a little. She pushed harder, and slowly, the heavy panel swung in on its hinge.

Inside was a dark passage through the native stone, no more than six feet long, and then another door. Slowly, carefully, she entered the second combination, grinning in overdone triumph when she got it right the first time.

She shoved the door open, releasing a puff of supercold air bearing a faint earthy smell. The interior was pitch-black. But it wasn't silent. A soft machine whir filled the air like an ethereal hum. She could hear the drip of liquid, the click of automatic equipment, the distant howl of wind as it clawed through turbines mounted in the air shafts that ventilated the caverns of this former copper mine.

She put her gloves and helmet back on, then reestablished the electronic link with the remote. Its skeletal body became her body; its steely hands, her own. She walked it into the mausoleum, making it turn and close the doors behind it. Then she slipped the helmet off, blinking into the frozen darkness. "Hark: Lights on," she said softly, and the primitive AI that resided here obeyed.

Fixtures deeper in the cavern flicked on. The light spilled out over the chiseled rock of the first chamber, revealing niches that held frail human figures wrapped in colorful woolens. These were the Indians who'd been interred here after the mine played out.

Forward Futures had secured its own dead in the second and third chambers. They'd brought them here, seeking to protect them from the turbulence of politics as well

as the assaults of time. But the patients were owed more
than protection. Katie's hand slipped into the pocket of
her parka, tightening around the cool weight of the pistol
she carried. Forward Futures had an obligation to bring
their suspension patients back to life . . . even in defiance
of the law. She didn't trust them to do it. Her fellows on
the board of directors were a cautious lot. They would
have told her to wait. As if waiting were a safe option.
Hesitate now, and their only chance to revive the patients
might be sealed permanently in the past. So Katie had
made her own decision. She'd refused a political appointment to the Voice colony on Mars to come here herself.

    She left the gun in her pocket. Turning back to the re-
mote, she opened the chest pack and retrieved the sack
that held her groceries, and the satchel that contained the
Cure. Leaving the remote to stand sentinel at the door,
she set off across the rough stone floor of the first chamber. The walls narrowed, then expanded again into the
second chamber. Here, fluorescent light fixtures shone
down on silver-bright steel cylinders, twin rows of them,
standing shoulder to shoulder and more than man-high.
They lined both sides of the passage, towering over her
head like crowded columns in some futuristic temple. On
the ceiling, the glowing fluorescent light tubes were inter-
spersed with ceramic tracks that crisscrossed the rock. A
small robot rolled slowly along the tracks. It had two ma-
nipulator arms and camera eyes and it looked like a crab
as it moved stolidly from one storage cylinder to another,
monitoring the levels of liquid nitrogen in each. These
were the cryogenic habitats of the new dead. No colorful
woolens for them. Their bodies were wrapped in plastic
and immersed in liquid nitrogen. All biological processes
stopped at −196° C.

    She passed under a ventilation shaft. The howl of the
turbine grew louder. Cables dropped out of the shaft like
a tree's black roots. They hugged the ceiling, and she followed them to the third chamber. Here there were cylinders on only one side, and a vast collection of black-boxed
batteries on the other. She counted carefully down the
line of cylinders, two, three, four, five from the door.
There. In the front row. That one had Tom.

With her gloved hand she touched the steel surface. Traced the stenciled number. It had been so long.

She turned, and with her back pressed against the cylinder, slid to the ground. Her legs bent reluctantly, and she winced against a dull ache in her hips. She was sixty-four and could no longer deny that age was catching her, despite the rigorous diet, the constant exercise. Her eyes closed, and again she felt the clutch of fear, like a black-hooded figure rattling the bars of her rib cage, warning her that she was running out of time.

Suddenly, the howl of the turbines rose in pitch as the wind outside heightened, and she distinctly heard Tom's voice calling her, distant, almost angry. Her eyes snapped open. Dry and gritty eyes, accustomed to facing unpleasant scenes.

Tom does not want to come back.

She could hear his spirit twisting through the turbines. Staring straight ahead at the stacked black boxes of the batteries, she tried to ignore the cold howl of his demands. "It's not like I'm offering you a choice," she muttered. "So shut up."

She pulled the satchel onto her lap and opened it. Amid the vials was a spindle of clear plastic, longer than her hand but no wider than her little finger. She picked it up and held it to the light. The soft plastic squished a little within her grip.

Embedded inside the transparent spindle was a glittery white shaft, as fine as a human hair. She tipped the spindle back and forth and watched the shaft sparkle like a thread of fresh snow. It was a hypodermic needle, encased in protective plastic. Six inches long, the ceramic needle was sharp enough to penetrate a human skull—even a skull that had been frozen for thirty years.

"See this, Tom?" she asked softly. "I'm going to use this to drag you back—whether you want to come or not. Because you owe me. Dammit, Tom, you owe me plenty, and I'm going to collect."

She looked up expectantly, waiting to hear the roar of his protest in the humming voice of the turbine. But there was nothing beyond the mindless howl of the gale.

Part II
LIQUID
NITROGEN

EARLY TV COMMERCIAL: MARS NOW!
(excerpted dialogue)

The time is now.

In the first decade of the new century the United States of America will take a bold step forward. We'll expand the horizons of all the world's people by establishing a permanent human presence on Mars. And what's more, we'll do this without rending the pocketbooks of the American people. Using available technology, we'll launch an unmanned mission to Mars that will use automated and robotic equipment to establish a habitat on the planet's surface—a habitat that will be put to use by a manned mission scheduled to follow twenty-six months later.

We'll do this, if we choose. Mars Now! Because the future won't happen until we make it.

2

The Future Won't Happen
Unless We Make It

Katie Kishida had been thirty-four years old when Tom's surgeon informed her in hushed tones that she would soon become a widow. "You understand. His internal injuries are just too extensive."

Katie tried to understand. Tom had been alive when the rescue team pulled him and his crew of firefighters from the wreckage of the forest service helicopter. Alive. And she'd been allowed to hope. Now ...

"Oh, Katie!"

Katie turned to see quiet tears on her mother's crepe-paper cheeks. Belle Schiller had arrived at the hospital during the hours Tom had been in surgery. Now her arm went around Katie's waist as she hugged her daughter close. "Oh, Katie, I'm so sorry. This is just so *wrong*. So wrong."

The surgeon hovered over them, his hands half-raised as if he wanted to contain any sign of hysteria they might exhibit. Katie tried to nod. Tried to assure him that she *did* understand, that she was all grown-up, in control. But her voice broke. "What am I going to tell my children?" Joy was twelve, Nikki was ten. Daddy had two little princesses.

The surgeon had no answer for her. From the look on his face, Katie knew he wanted to leave, that after years of dealing with grieving relatives, he still had no idea of what to say. But something held him back.

He said, "I know it's difficult for you to hear this at this time, but we'd like you to consider an organ donation. Your husband's heart is still strong, and his corneas could—"

"No." Unlike most people, Katie and Tom had actually talked about their own mortality, had debated the possibilities in late-night sessions, his voice coming to her out of darkness as he lay next to her in their bed. He'd been skeptical, frugal. She'd been insistent. Now he would soon be dead. Katie glared at the surgeon, revitalized by sudden anger. "You won't take any part of him!" she snapped. "And you will keep him alive as long as you can."

"Katie . . ." Belle soothed. "Come sit down. You don't have to decide right now."

"The decision's made, Mom." She gently removed Belle's hand from her waist, and patted it softly. "Excuse me, now. I have to make a phone call."

"Mrs. Kishida," the surgeon insisted. "There's no easy way to say this, but I want to strongly advise you to reconsider. We can't help your husband. But by donating his heart, we could save somebody else's loved one; you could give somebody else another chance at life. And your husband did indicate on his driver's license that he wanted his organs donated."

"But it's my decision now, isn't it? And I say no."

"Katie—"

"No, Mom." She adjusted her purse on her shoulder and turned to leave.

"Mrs. Kishida," the surgeon said again, this time with a tinge of sarcasm in his voice. "You can see your husband now. Or don't you want to be with him?"

She glanced briefly over her shoulder. "There's nothing I want more in all the world."

Tom had never wanted to spend the money. But Katie was a stockbroker and she had real estate dealings and the money was far less important to her than Tom. She fumbled in her purse for her wallet, shuffled through the assortment of plastic cards until she found the one bearing the emergency number of Forward Futures, Inc. She held that and her AT&T card in one trembling hand, staring at them, willing this moment to be part of a nightmare. This could not be real. She struggled to open her eyes, to wake up. When that failed, she started punching numbers into the telephone.

It rang only once before a woman answered. "Forward Futures. You've reached the emergency line."

"This is Katie Kishida," she said, and gave her member number. It was the same as Tom's. They were on the family plan, along with their two daughters. "My husband, Thomas—" Her voice broke, and for the first time since the accident, she began to sob. "My husband Thomas is not expected to live through the night. . . ."

The woman from Forward Futures was solicitous as she recorded Katie's information. But she couldn't hide the eagerness in her voice; the cryonics company didn't perform more than one or two suspensions a year, and each one was a learning experience. She assured Katie they would have a suspension team at the hospital in Bakersfield within three hours, and then she hung up.

Katie could smell the stench of burning forest. The scent cut across her consciousness as she returned the phone to its cradle. She looked quickly over her shoulder, fearing . . . fearing some supernatural assault, perhaps, she didn't know. Then she saw the firefighters. Four men in smoke-stained flight suits, milling silently in the waiting room outside the ICU, their cheeks taut, their gazes carefully fixed on the floor, on the walls, Katie's mom among them, her strong hands massaging a white tissue, the bearer of bad news. Belle looked up as Katie approached. The firefighters looked too, for a moment anyway, their eyes darting nervously while heartfelt banalities filled the air: "Let's not stop hoping." "It could have been anyone." "Damn, what a tragedy." "Why Tom?"

Katie hugged each one of them, though she could find nothing to say. Then she turned to her mother.

Looking on Belle, Katie saw much of herself—the same petite build, the same golden blond hair and lightly tanned skin, the same meticulous nature—offset by a quarter century. "Who's with Tom?" she whispered, knowing the answer even before she asked.

"Roxanne," Belle said. "She came in off the fire line to see him. She said she wanted to be alone with him for a minute."

Katie nodded stiffly. Emergency personnel liked to help each other out. She wondered which nurse had bent the rules to let Roxanne Scott into the ICU. She exchanged a lingering glance with her mother, then pushed cautiously past the door.

The rooms on the intensive-care ward were glass-walled. A few were draped. Most were open, the patients clearly visible. The air trembled with the rush of ventilators, the pulse of monitors, a chaotic night song of struggle. A nurse caught sight of her and started forward with an angry glare, but before she could reach Katie another caught her by the elbow and whispered something in her ear. "He's in the third room," one of them said gently.

But Katie had already seen Roxanne through the glass wall. She hurried forward, only to pause in the doorway.

Roxanne stood beside the bed, her gaze downcast, one hand resting lightly on the hose of a ventilator that whooshed beside her. Katie could not yet bring herself to look at the figure in the bed, so she studied Roxanne instead.

Like the firefighters outside, Roxanne still wore her forest service flight suit. But there were bloodstains on the sleeves and chest. With a start, Katie realized it was probably Tom's blood. Roxanne was the EMT who'd brought him in. She was also Katie's oldest friend—or at least her surrogate sibling rival. They'd been next-door neighbors—two only-children who'd long ago adopted the testy relationship of sisters born too close.

Katie must have made some sound then, because Roxanne looked up, quickly removing her hand from the ventilator's hose. Her face was dirt-streaked, her dark brown eyes framed with smeared mascara. The scent of burning forest haunted the room. When Roxanne spoke, her words were low, but clipped with fury. "If he's dying anyway, why don't you get him off this ventilator? You know he hated this shit. I've been on more climbs with him than you have, Katie. I've seen him on the fire line. He was no life-grubbing coward. He knew who he was and where he was going and he wasn't afraid to die. *Please*, let him die clean."

Katie listened to the rhythmic pulse of the ventilator, so similar to the rhythm of her own breath whenever she worked through her fear on a sheer rock face, climbing behind Tom. Roxanne liked to lead. Could she be thinking of taking matters into her own hands? Katie lowered her chin defensively, a gesture that echoed old backyard conflicts when Roxanne would try to tug her over the line. "His family hasn't even seen him yet. Why are you in such a hurry?"

Roxanne's eyes narrowed. She leaned forward slightly, her fist cocked near her breast. "My old man was left to rot on a ventilator. You remember what that did to him."

Katie felt herself grow stone cold. Roxanne might have been her friend. She might have been Tom's friend. But she wasn't family. She had no rights here.

But Roxanne wasn't through. "My mom loved Dad *too much*," she said. "She didn't want to let him go." Her gaze seemed to take Katie's measure. "I heard you told the doctors to keep Tom alive as long as possible."

"That's right."

"And do you think a man like Tom would want to live like this?" Roxanne jerked her chin at the figure on the bed.

Almost unwillingly, Katie followed her gaze.

Tom lay with a sheet pulled up to his bare chest, his hands slack at his sides. He had a plastic mask strapped over his nose and mouth, his eyelids looked bruised, and his cheeks were swollen with edema. An IV had been inserted in his neck, and his weathered bronze skin had

taken on a sallow hue. Katie felt her hands start to tremble, so she quickly stuck them in the pockets of her
blazer. "Listen, Roxanne," she said softly. "No matter
what you say, no matter what you believe or what you
think Tom believed, I'm *not* going to let him die. Not
now. Not ever."

The stinking scent of smoke that accompanied Roxanne
taunted Katie, rousing perilous memories of nights in the
wilderness and the hot feel of Tom's skin against her own.
She squared her shoulders. "Just stay out of my way,
Roxanne, because I'm not letting him go."

Katie heard a step behind her. Roxanne looked to the
noise. Her eyes went wide in shock, then immediately
clouded in confusion. Katie turned to see Tom's brother
edge into the room, his brows pulled down in a dark scowl
that was a sure sign of uneasiness among the Kishida men.
Harlow was a little taller than Tom, a little huskier, but
the resemblance was close enough that she could understand Roxanne's moment of dismay. Harlow studied
Roxanne suspiciously, then turned to Katie. "Has something changed? Is he improving?"

Katie shook her head. "They say he won't make it
through the night." She glared at the surprise on
Roxanne's face. "But it's not over," she promised. "It's not
over."

Harlow had brought his mother, Jane Kishida, up from
L.A. Jane was a slight, slender woman, her black hair
styled in a wavy permanent laced with dignified gray. After Roxanne left, her Buddhist prayers filled the room
with a warm mutter of hope. Tom had never practiced her
faith. He'd been more or less a Christian, but Jane had
never seemed to mind.

Later, Katie's mom brought the girls in. Joy was twelve;
Nikki was ten. They both clutched hankies, their eyes already swollen and red with crying. Katie comforted them
for a while, then she told her mother to take them home.
"They're too young for this," she said.

When they were gone she kissed Tom's mother on the
cheek. "I have to go meet someone, Jane. I'll be back."

She went down to the lobby, saw that it was empty,

then checked with the front desk to see if the team from Forward Futures had arrived yet. They hadn't. She waited just inside the glass doors of the hospital, staring pensively at the circular driveway and the road beyond. A security guard seated at a desk near the door asked her if she needed help. She shook her head. "Just waiting for someone."

A few minutes later an ambulance turned off the roadway and onto the hospital grounds. As it came up the driveway, she made out the Forward Futures logo on the side and sighed in ambivalent relief. They were here. She was thankful for that, and yet at the same time their approach dispelled the last bit of doubt she'd held about the doctors' diagnosis. Hope that she hadn't even been aware of harboring blew out of her like a last breath. Cold swept into the resultant void, a kind of frozen determination. She straightened her shoulders and raised her chin as the ambulance rolled to a stop before the glass doors.

A single man got out. He was dressed in street clothes and as he strode across the foyer, a rust-red Mars pin on his lapel glinted in the artificial light. Katie's gaze fixed on it. Tom had worn a pin like that, every day he wasn't in his forest service uniform. The pin was a political statement, an open vote of support for Mars Now! and the troubled mission to Mars.

The glass door clacked open under the cryonicist's hand. The security guard looked up from behind her desk, her suspicious glance taking in this latest visitor.

The cryonicist looked young—too young to be dealing in death—his dark Mediterranean skin still as smooth and unworried as a child's. Katie stepped forward. In her peripheral vision she noticed the Forward Futures ambulance pulling away toward the parking lot. "Hello," she said, thrusting her hand out. "I'm Katie Kishida."

He accepted her hand. His skin felt hot, vital, alive. Her fingers basked in the electric warmth. "Hello, Mrs. Kishida. My name's Gregory Hunt, and I'm the suspension team leader. I'm sorry we had to meet under these circumstances. Is your husband's prognosis still the same?"

She nodded. "But at least you're here. Now he'll have a chance." She reached out hesitantly and touched the pin on his lapel. "Tom wore one of these. He talked about Mars a lot. A new frontier, and all that."

Gregory smiled. "He'll get there. It's important that you believe that. Your husband's not going to die tonight. He's going to deanimate, and that's a temporary condition. Death isn't the relentless power it used to be."

"I do believe that." Katie studied him with narrowed eyes. He looked to be only in his early twenties. But obviously he shared her indignation at the prospect of Tom's death, and for that she forgave him his youth. "I don't like being defeated," she told him, as they walked together toward the hospital's administrative offices. "I'm not ready to give up on Tom. How could I? How could I let him die now from something that may be survivable in ten years? *He's my husband!*"

That was her mantra. *He's my husband.* Beyond love, beyond hate, beyond death, that connection would remain. She could see herself loving another man, visualize Tom with another woman. But any such bond must be temporary because between Katie and Tom there was a *connection* that must always exist in defiance of time or the logic of the perceivable universe. They were mated in a way that was permanent and irrevocable. No matter how far apart their paths should wander, if there was to be a last day of the universe, they would enjoy it together.

From time to time Katie had tried to explain these feelings to Tom in the dark of their midnight discussions. "Wow, that's deep," he'd say, and she could imagine his eyes rolling in a silent *Oh, brother*. But the way he held her let her know that deep inside, he believed it too.

She looked up at Gregory Hunt. His eyes were dark and narrow. Not at all handsome, yet lit with a riveting intensity that would be hard to forget. His thick black hair was cut short in the front, long in the back, tied in a neat ponytail behind his neck. He had a righteous certainty about him that in other circumstances might have been annoying, but in this moment it played perfectly to her mood. "I don't like giving up," she said again. "If the Good Lord wants Tom now, as my mother says, He's going to have to fight me for possession."

The corners of Hunt's lips turned up in the faintest of

smiles. "The team's ready," he said. "And Forward Futures has an agreement in principle with this hospital, so there shouldn't be any problems. We've already notified the administration, and they've agreed to allow us to begin suspension procedures in the ICU. As soon as a physician declares your husband clinically dead, we can take him."

Around midnight, Katie's mother returned to the hospital. The girls had finally gone to sleep, so she'd left them under the watchful eye of a close friend. Katie nodded. "I'm glad you could come back." She looked around the little hospital room at Tom's mother, Jane, and his oldest brother, Harlow. She wished his sister, Ilene Carson, were here. Ilene was the oldest of the three Kishida children, a transplanted Californian who'd made herself into a hot East Coast politician, winning a seat in the U.S. Senate in the last election. If Katie had a mentor, it was Ilene. For sixteen years she'd stood beside Katie whenever life got ugly. In an age that discounted the value of an elder generation, Katie had come to think of Ilene Carson as the head of the family. But Ilene wouldn't be coming tonight. Bad weather had delayed her flight from Washington, D.C., and she wasn't expected to arrive until noon tomorrow.

On Katie's side of the family there was only herself and her mother. So everyone who could be expected tonight was already here. It was time. Katie took a deep breath.

"I have something to say." Faces turned to her, eyes wide with sympathy. She suspected they wouldn't stay sympathetic for long. "A few years ago Tom and I made some . . . unusual preparations for our . . . ultimate deaths. We signed a contract with a cryonics company called Forward Futures—"

"Oh, Katie—" Harlow interrupted.

"Just, listen. Please," she said. "We made arrangements for ourselves and the children to have our bodies suspended in liquid nitrogen in the event of our deaths. We never dreamed we'd need the service this soon."

"Katie, what are you talking about?" Belle asked. "I don't understand. . . ."

Harlow stepped in with an explanation, saving Katie the

burden of composing an answer. But as he spoke, he looked at her, not at Belle, and doubt was heavy in his voice. "Cryonics is the practice of freezing human remains . . . in the hope that some new technology will allow an eventual cure."

Jane's face registered open disgust. "Harlow, you can't be serious. I *have* heard of that stuff. But it isn't real. Even the supermarket tabloids make fun of it. Tom would have never, never—"

"Mom—"

"You won't make a joke out of Tom's death!" she cried. "I won't allow it."

"This is not a joke," Katie said, her voice more harsh than she intended. "This is a last resort and no one's going to stop it. My personal physician will be here soon. *She* doesn't think cryonics is a joke. If Dr. Ruiz agrees there's no hope for Tom's recovery, then she'll wait with me. When Tom's heart finally stops sometime tonight, she'll declare him legally dead, and the suspension process will be started. The team from Forward Futures is already at the hospital. The sooner his body is frozen, the less deterioration his brain will suffer."

The two older women stared at her in shocked silence. But Harlow was nodding slowly. He came around the bed; slipped his arm around her waist. "I'm with you on this," he said.

Katie nodded, shivering, feeling suddenly faint inside.

Belle started shaking her head. "I don't understand," she said. "When Tom . . . *if* Tom dies, his soul will go to God. How can you—? How can you expect to—?"

"I don't know anything about souls, Mom. You know I've been an agnostic since I learned what the word meant. I do know that a person in cardiac arrest can be revived through CPR, but a hundred years ago a person in that condition would have been declared dead."

Jane stirred. She looked at Harlow with angry eyes. "Cryonics!" she snapped. "I've seen those strange people on talk shows. Do you really believe them, Harlow? What do you know about this?"

"I've looked into it," he said cautiously. His gaze

shifted sideways toward Katie. "Haven't signed up for anything yet."

"It is strange," Katie admitted. "And troubling, because it changes the definition of death.". She bowed her head, feeling a deep pain behind her eyes. "We should have told everyone before, I can see that now. The company advised us to, but we didn't want hard feelings."

"Yes, you should have told us!" Jane cried, her delicate little hand closing into a fist. "Oh, *why* am I so angry? If there's any chance of saving Tom, I want to take it. But . . . but *this*! Is he going to be dead, or not? Should I grieve or should I hope? Will there be a funeral? There won't be a body. Oh, Tom, I'll never live long enough to see you again." She broke down sobbing. Harlow left Katie, to kneel at her side.

Katie gazed at them, mother and son, while Jane's questions echoed in her mind. But she had no answers.

"Katie?" Her mother's voice whispered near her ear. "I want to speak to you alone, Katie."

"All right, Mom."

She let herself be led outside the room. Somewhere down the hall another patient moaned. A nurse barked a command in a harsh voice. A cart clattered past. Belle set her hand on Katie's arm and looked into her eyes. "I know how much you love Tom, darling. And I know you'd do anything to save him. But have you thought about what this is going to do to you?"

Katie blinked in surprise. "It's going to give me hope."

"But what kind of hope? That someday, hundreds of years from now, Tom will wake up into a world full of strangers, his family long gone?"

"I hope to be there," she said. "I hope to have the children with me. That's all. It's a chance. Better than giving up on him."

"Will you be a widow? Or a wife with an absent husband?"

"I don't know, Mom. I haven't exactly had a lot of time to think about it."

Belle gave her a quick hug. "I know, darling. And I'm sorry. But I'm so worried about you. Hope can carry people through the worst of times. But it can also poison lives.

I don't want you to waste your life hoping for something that will never happen."

"I really don't want to talk about this now, Mom. Later, all right? But not now. The cryonic suspension will take place whether I change my mind or not. Tom signed contracts. It was his decision. But I'm not going to change my mind."

Belle nodded. "All right. Then I won't say anything else. If this is what the two of you really want . . ."

"It is, Mom. And thank you for understanding."

Harlow was still explaining the procedures involved in a cryonic suspension when the attending physician looked into the room. "Mrs. Kishida," he said. "Could I speak with you, please?" Katie nodded, and stepped out into the hall with him. He looked at her, his dark eyes angry. "I've just been informed you're planning to place your husband in cryonic suspension. I guess the doctor's always the last to know. Is that why you're unwilling to approve an organ donation?"

Katie was at a loss for words. Before she could find something to say, or even decide on her emotions, the doctor plunged ahead with his opinion. "Cryonics is a fraud and you're wasting your money. There's no way to repair the physical damage caused by the freezing process, and even if there were, there will never be a drug to cure your husband's injuries."

Katie discovered her mouth open in amazement. She closed it firmly. "I don't agree," she said, and turned back to Tom's room, in no mood to deliver a tutorial now on predicted advances in cell repair technology. But then she hesitated, glancing back over her shoulder. "My personal physician will be taking over Tom's case," she said. "So you needn't concern yourself further."

The doctor arched one eyebrow skeptically. "And he approves of this?"

"Yes, she does," Katie said. "And yes, Dr. Ruiz has hospital privileges. Everything's arranged."

He seemed surprised. "Then you've planned ahead for this?"

"Of course. Forward Futures won't accept patients on a

last minute basis. They consider that unethical." Yes, Katie had planned for this. Katie had planned everything in her life. She firmly believed that lasting joy was not achieved by happy accident. "Tom's chances of eventual recovery will multiply if we get him under quickly."

The physician shook his head in open contempt. "Zero times anything is still zero. And as far as I'm concerned, the whole business of cryonic preservation is unethical. Those shysters have convinced you to spend a whole lot of money for nothing, while the people who might have been given life through your husband's organs are left to die." He turned and stalked off through the ICU. Katie stared after him, her teeth tightly clenched.

"Katie?"

She turned to see Gregory Hunt. He'd changed his street clothes for surgical garb. Now he leaned against the desk of the nurse's station, a tall man, with a thin, muscular build. "Sorry," she said. "I didn't see you there."

He studied her with cool curiosity. "Just came in. I wanted to let you know we're all set up. We'll be able to begin cooling procedures within minutes of your husband's clinical death. And Dr. Ruiz is here. I've already explained the procedure to her."

Katie nodded. "Thank you."

He inclined his head in the direction the staff doctor had taken. "I'm sorry you had to be subjected to that, but it's a pretty common reaction."

"I know."

"Then you haven't changed your mind?"

"Of course not."

"But you're feeling guilty, just the same."

She sighed, her gaze sinking to the floor. "Don't you ever repeat this to anyone waiting in that room," she said, her voice so low that Gregory had to lean forward to hear her. "But Tom never really wanted to do this. He signed the contract just to make me happy." She looked up, to meet Hunt's gaze. "But he belongs to me. I have a right to do this. No one else has any claim on his body. And *his* life is just as important as anybody else's."

*   *   *

Tom expired in the wee hours of the morning. His heart had been beating erratically for several minutes and Dr. Ruiz advised everyone present that it was time to say their good-byes. Katie waited in a corner of the room while one by one, the family performed whatever rites they felt were necessary. Then she stepped forward. She stood for a moment, gazing down at Tom, silently cursing the oxygen mask that perched like a parasite over his mouth and nose. There seemed so little left of him. She bent and kissed his forehead, her eyes half-closed as she drank in the familiar scent of his skin. Blinking hard, she ran her fingers across the graceful curves of his brows and cheeks. His long eyelashes were encrusted with blood. Forty-six years old, and still as beautiful as the day she'd met him. "Bastard!" she hissed through her tears. "How dare you do this to me?"

The cardiac monitor ceased its nervous pulse and wailed a flatline. "Tom!" Katie cried. She fell forward, her forehead pressed against his shoulder while the world seemed to burn around her. Then Harlow's arms enfolded her. He pulled her gently away. "Clear the room," Dr. Ruiz said sharply. "Except you, Katie," she amended, with a sympathetic glance.

"I'm going to stay with Katie," Harlow said, and Dr. Ruiz nodded.

"Mr. Hunt," she called. "Get your team in here." Then she commenced her examination and moments later declared Tom legally dead.

Katie stood with her back pressed against Harlow's comforting bulk while Gregory Hunt and an assistant guided a long, wheeled cart into the room. The cart's lower deck was loaded with medical equipment and oxygen cylinders. Locked onto the top was a man-sized canvas cradle supported on a steel frame. Katie knew enough to identify the Forward Futures life-support cart. She'd seen articles on it, skimming the text with only academic interest.

A second assistant pushed a dolly loaded with ice chests into the room. Ben. That was his name. A young man like Gregory. And the middle-aged woman who'd helped Gregory with the cart was Connie.

The team of three worked with determined speed. Con-

nie started disconnecting the hospital monitors. Gregory
stripped off the oxygen mask and smoothly inserted an
endotracheal tube into Tom's throat. "We'll work with the
hospital's IV," he announced. "Let's get him moved."

With Dr. Ruiz helping, they transferred Tom to the canvas cradle on the life-support cart. Katie shuddered at the
body's limp posture, and again, when the white sheet
slipped off, exposing a ragged net of sutures across Tom's
swollen abdomen. Then they had him on the cart. He almost disappeared behind the high canvas sides of the cradle.

The bed was pushed out of the way. Ben slipped into
the gap with one of the coolers. He set it on the bed and
opened it. It was crammed with bags of crushed ice. He
hefted one, tore it open, and began packing raw ice
around Tom's head and neck. Dr. Ruiz stepped up to help
him. "We want to cool the surface blood," he told Katie.
"Minimize cellular degradation as much as possible."

She nodded, feeling empty, hypnotized by a ritual she
didn't want to understand. Her focus shifted to Gregory
and Connie where they worked on the other side of the
cart. "That's the heart-lung resuscitator," Ben said as he
ripped open another bag of ice. "We want to continue
circulation—keep the tissue oxygenated."

Gregory maneuvered an arm of the machine out from
under the cart. He raised its elevation, then swung it
around again, settling the cusp against Tom's chest. He
glanced up, and his gaze met Katie's. She could feel her
hope pour into him. He seemed to feel it too. His expression grew darker, more grim. "We're ready," he muttered.
And Connie turned a valve.

Pneumatic sounds filled the room: a harsh suck-and-
release rhythm as the HLR started a compression sequence against Tom's chest. Connie attached an oxygen
line from the cart to Tom's endotracheal tube.

Unexpected motion drew Katie's attention. Her eyes
widened as she watched Tom's right hand start to clench,
then open slowly. A shudder ran through his body. His
mouth opened, and she could hear air wheezing past the
tube, into his lungs. *"He's alive!"* she whispered. "You said
he was dead. But he's alive."

"One point five grams sodium pentobarbital!" Gregory barked, as he rigged a new IV line to the catheter already in Tom's neck. Connie yanked open a storage drawer in the cart. Tom was breathing in and out now, in slow noisy gasps as if fighting the rhythm of the machine.

"What's going on here?" Harlow shouted as his arms tightened around Katie.

Dr. Ruiz stepped toward them, her calming hands outstretched. "It's the machine. It's revived him. But just temporarily." She looked over her shoulder as Gregory readied a syringe. "If we took Tom off the machine, his breathing would stop again. He looks like he's functioning now, but on his own he's *not* functional."

Gregory administered the sodium pentobarbital. "You're poisoning him, aren't you?" Katie asked.

"It's a barbiturate," Gregory snapped.

"To secure anesthesia," Dr. Ruiz explained. "He's dead, Katie. He's not coming back."

But he was alive. Katie could see that. He was breathing on his own. She shook her head, not understanding the vagueness of this death. She wanted to run to him, shake him, make him wake up. But she didn't want to interfere. This was the treatment Tom needed.

But what was Tom thinking?

What did he feel? What did he dream under the ministrations of the machine? Was he aware at all of what they were doing to him? Did he know that they were forcing him to die again?

Then the drug took effect. Tom's twitching movements subsided. His attempts at breathing faded back into the ugly rhythm of the machine. "He's gone," Harlow whispered.

"More ice!" Gregory shouted. Connie scrambled for another cooler. Gregory's gaze cut across the room to Katie as he helped Ben and Dr. Ruiz pack ice. His expression was hard, half-accusing. "We'll be giving him a series of drugs on the way into Los Angeles," he said in clipped syllables. "They're intended to support his brain against damage from reduced blood flow." He accepted a bag of ice from Connie, ripped it open, and emptied the contents across

Tom's chest. "All right, let's go. We'll finish packing ice in the ambulance."

He took the head of the cart; Ben took the foot. Together, they wheeled Tom out the door. Katie followed them, Harlow supporting her arm.

Outside, she had a brief glimpse of her mother's anxious face, of Jane, red-eyed and crying. Of Roxanne Scott. So Roxanne had finally come back. Huge, dark circles framed her eyes as she glared at Katie.

Katie stumbled past them. The world had begun to buzz around her. She could hardly feel her feet or hands. Maybe this really was a dream and she was about to wake up.

The doors of the ICU snapped aside. There was an elevator ride. Gregory asked her something. She couldn't develop an adequate answer. Then she was sitting in a chair, in a corridor somewhere, her head between her knees. Harlow was rubbing her back and her mother was kneeling in front of her, whispering reassurances the way she'd done when Katie was a little girl.

This is real, Katie thought. *And I'm not going to wake up.* She studied the stains on the embossed pattern of the vinyl floor. Listened to the hum of air-conditioning beyond her mother's voice. Observed the flickering shadows cast by a defective fluorescent tube. Her skin was damp and cold, as if her body had just broken a fever. Head still down, she slid her wrist between her legs so she could check the time. Three A.M. And twelve minutes.

Slowly, very slowly, she sat up. She rubbed at the dampness on her face, ran her fingers through her long blond hair. Not yet daring to examine the hollowness beneath her breast.

"Hey," Harlow said. "Better?"

"Let us take you home," Belle urged.

Then Roxanne spoke up. She stood across the corridor, her arms crossed belligerently over her chest, her dark eyes hard with anger. "I can't believe you've done this, Katie. You lived with Tom for years, but now I'm starting to wonder if you ever really knew him. You always sat out the tough climbs, but Tom never did. You were afraid of dying, but Tom wasn't. Why are you torturing him like this? He has his own destiny. *Let him go.*"

Katie studied her for a moment, wondering—not for the first time—who Roxanne Scott really was. Roxanne had been close to Tom for years, in an odd relationship that seemed more man-to-man than man-to-woman. Competitive. Macho. Not that it mattered now.

Katie's gaze shifted to Harlow. He looked flustered, struck dumb by Roxanne's display. "Where's Tom?" she asked him.

"In the ambulance. They're going to finish packing him in ice before they transplant. Hunt said it would take a few minutes."

Roxanne stepped forward. "Think about it, Katie," she warned.

"Shut up!" Harlow snapped. "Just leave her alone."

But Roxanne wasn't the kind to be put down easily. "You want to play God, Katie? You think you can take chance out of your life? Well, it won't work. Tom has a right to his destiny. He was my best friend. And I know that he was *not* afraid to die." She nodded her head in a short jerk of affirmation, then she turned and stalked away down the hall.

Harlow stared after her, swearing softly under his breath. "Where'd you pick up that airhead?"

"Roxanne's a very spiritual person," Katie said, her voice as flat and detached as her soul.

She looked around. There weren't any friendly directional signs, so she guessed this was not a public area of the hospital. But across the hallway was a bulletin board, and pinned to it, half-hidden behind lecture announcements and sheets of paper detailing the latest revisions to hospital policies, was a poster of Mars emblazoned with the logo Mars Now! Katie blinked in confusion, rocked by an odd sense that the poster hadn't been there a moment before, that somehow it had suddenly materialized in her field of vision as a kind of icon of hope.

He'll get there. It's important that you believe that.

She stood cautiously. Brushing off a flurry of helping hands, she shuffled to a nearby water fountain. She drank the icy water; splashed more on her face, then looked back at Harlow. "I want to go into L.A. with him."

"Oh, Katie, no!" Belle said.

"I want to go with him," Katie repeated, wiping her face on her sleeve. "I want to see this through."

"No, Katie. It would be a mistake," Belle said. "Stay home. The girls need you. And you'll want to remember Tom the way he was."

"No. I have to know what I've done to him." Guilt was beginning to eat at her. Tom had died twice, but both times they'd caught him, pinned him in a state somewhere between life and death. But what if Roxanne was right? What if he really *needed* to die? What if there really was a soul? What if he needed to make the final journey and he couldn't . . . because she'd bound him to this life. *I need you, Tom. And I won't let you go.*

It was selfishness, pure and simple. She could see that now. And she could accept it. She wanted Tom back. For herself. For the children. Damn the consequences.

She looked back at her mother, determination running like a cold liquid metal through her blood. "Tom's helpless now. He's depending on me."

Harlow sighed. "I'll drive you, Katie. You know where this place is?"

"Yes. I've been there before. Tom and I. We looked over the facilities before we signed up."

"Come on, then," Harlow said, taking her arm. She kissed her mother good-bye, then followed Harlow to the ambulance bay.

Wedged Time—
Alternate Landscapes

Time stretched. Thought proceeded with glacial slowness, as if his mind had grown vast and diffuse so that each electronic signal required hours to reach its destination. The condition made his pain exquisite. He could follow each long, slow, deep, and relentless wave of it across the entire field of his awareness. *I . . . should . . . not . . . be . . . like . . . this.* The thought took long years to form. He already knew he was dead. He knew he should be blissful, secure in the house of God. Yet he was not. A familiar essence had been stolen from him, teased out of his body cell-by-cell by the dividing hand of God. Something that was not him, yet was part of him, just the same. All gone. Even the memory of it. He couldn't name it; he couldn't visualize it. He could recognize it only by the amorphous emptiness left behind inside his chest, a wound that ached with the fierce pressure of vacuum.

"You're confused," God said. "There's nothing more of you than this. I've brought you out of the world whole, just as you went in."

Liar! His anger erupted simultaneously around the periphery of his nebular awareness. It acted as an imploding shock wave, driving his diffuse self inward. He began to contract, and as his span shrank, time quickened.

God shook his head in mild disgust at this childish display. "Oh, stop it. Temper tantrum or no, you can't go back."

But there's more. You've forgotten something. A part of me . . . so familiar. I'm not complete.

God failed to understand. "Earthly attachments don't mean anything now. You'll get over it."

But his pain didn't ease. And he continued to contract. Not only himself, but the universe that housed him, so that he soon found himself imprisoned in a warm, moist, dark womb. The belly of God. The environment was suggestive. For the first time he recognized the shape of the emptiness in his soul, saw it for the familiar dark outline of another wound throughout the substance of his body. He grasped at the shadow, but there was nothing there. *What have you done with her?* he asked in horror. *My familiar. . . .* He groped for the proper title of this other who was part of himself and yet different. *My familiar—*

"You're alone," God insisted. "Always have been."

My Familiar! he cried. *You've taken her out of me. I want her back! Give her back to me or let me go.* He thrashed furiously, twisting and kicking, trying to break through the walls of the womb. He had no use for God. God couldn't fill the emptiness inside him. Only she could do that. *I love her more than you. Let me go.* He thrust his head back, dealing a harsh blow to the body of God. He kicked with his feet until God cried out in pain. He thrust with his head again, and this time a shudder ran through the walls of his prison and a moment later he felt as if the weight of the world had collapsed upon him, as if he'd been suddenly incarnated into the center of the earth and all that rock pressed down upon him, forced him into a channel that was much too small to pass his body. Then he was through.

Falling.

He screamed in terror as his body plummeted into night. There was nothing above him but stars and distance, the air so thin it was almost impossible to breathe. The lack of it set his head and heart on fire. He curled into himself like a falling spider, sensing the presence of ground somewhere far below. *Forgive me!* he cried to God. *Take me back.*

But God refused to hear him. God had vanished into the starry void, pouting, feelings hurt.

Anger issued from the active boundary of the empty places. It gave him strength of will, if nothing else, and he decided: *I will fly.*

He forced his body to open. Deliberately, he spread himself against the wind, belly down, arms and legs wide, head up. Little good it did him. He fell faster, plunging through thicker and thicker layers of atmosphere until the wind screamed in his ears and he grew so hot he thought he would ignite.

Then abruptly, the stars vanished. Nothing but inky blackness all around. The air that flowed to his lungs was thin, icy. Tasting of snow. His fiery body glowed with a faint red light, human meteor plunging through cloud. What lay below? What difference? Ocean hard as land at this speed. His eyes rolled back in his head. He would never be filled. Her shadow would languish inside him. He would die an absolute death, for God wouldn't have him now. *"Why?"* he roared, but the wind tore the word away before he could hear it.

So he prayed—not to God, but to her, forming silent words with freezing lips, *Save me, save me, save me. . . .*

The roaring in his ears grew louder. The wind seemed to be sweeping up past his face at impossible speeds. Something struck the outstretched tips of his fingers. He lunged at it. The impact shattered his fingernails. He reached out again, more slowly. A smooth, frozen surface raced past his groping fingers. He clawed at it, and came away with bits of ice lodged in his ruined nails. The wind bellowed like a river caught in a narrow gorge. The gale was being channeled upward by this wall of ice! The wind bounced him around. He felt like a bird in a storm. The wind tossed him into the ice wall. He hit it with his shoulder, and for a moment his fall almost stopped. Then the wind eased and he plunged downward again. But now he had an idea. Maybe it was not too late to fly. He spread his arms wider. The wind caught him and tossed him up. He spun, and fell, concentrating on the irregular buffeting of the gale against his body. Flying. Bodysurfing the storm. He learned quickly. If he held himself just right he could float, bobbing up and down only a few feet, his hand upon the wall to mark his position.

He drifted slowly down, and slowly, the darkness began to ease. A diffuse light radiated through the fog around him, to be caught and amplified by the white face of the icy wall. The sight heartened him. But his lips were cracked and frozen, and his nose and toes and fingers had lost all feeling. He looked down, but all he could see was a dimensionless gray. He was trying to decide if the surface was only a few feet away or several thousand when he slipped below the gale zone. He plunged, screaming. He could hear the gale roar on above him, but he was beyond its aid. He dropped feet first into a bank of soft snow, sinking to his shoulders. His body rang with the impact. He groaned. He could still hear the distant roar of the gale, but closer, he could hear the soft crunching of the snow as his head rolled against it, the terrified wash of his breath, the *boom boom* of his heart.

I'm alive. He regarded his existence in a state of incredulity. "My Familiar," he whispered, closing his eyes. A smile played on his lips, cracking the frozen flesh, sending rivulets of cool blood washing down his chin. He didn't care. He was alive. And he could feel the presence of his Familiar in this world like the pressure of sunlight on a summer's day.

L.A. FLOW—NEWS AND INFORMATION
Flash Call Line Anonymous Message—
Recorded 3:17 a.m.

"Here's one for you. You know Senator
Ilene Carson, that East Coast hotshot on
the National Health Care Committee?
You know—'Cost-cutter Carson'? Well,
her baby brother's about to be cryonically
preserved here in L.A. You might want to
ask her how she feels about that when she
arrives at the airport today. A hundred
fifty thousand dollars just to put a dead
man on ice...."

3

Dead Man on Ice

Corvette. Beemer. Porsche. Jaguar. Lamborghini. Lexus. Z-car. The names rolled together in a potent chant as Katie counted the company on the freeway. Even at 4:00 A.M., I-5 was busy. A lot of fine cars out in the night. And why not? Traffic flowed at 4:00 A.M. It was a great time to drive.

"I do it sometimes," Harlow said. His voice touched her like a searing light in the darkness. She flinched; glanced at him. She could see his face . . . just barely. Lit from below by the dash lights, which he'd turned way down. She hadn't even realized she'd spoken out loud. Must be tired. She touched her forehead, as if she could feel brain burn. Funny, she didn't feel tired.

"Sometimes I get up in the wee hours," Harlow went on. "And I drive for a hundred miles or more . . . in any direction. It doesn't matter where I go, 'cause I just turn around and come right back. It's the driving. Gives you a chance to lose yourself for a while. Zen meditation."

"I'm not tired," Katie said.

"It'll hit," Harlow promised.

"Look at the cars." Thousands of cars. So much power.

White lights coming, red lights going, lanes of life flowing forward, back. A landscape utterly transformed from its primeval design. Nothing here as nature intended. Nothing at all. No. This great freeway was a human thought, rolled out smooth and laid across the countryside, the uppermost sedimentary deposit of time. So much power. Nature didn't have a chance.

She chuckled in grim satisfaction. Nature had designed Tom's body so that it couldn't heal the injuries he'd suffered. Nature had decreed that he should die. So Nature was the enemy now.

"Katie, you all right?"

She stared past the flow of traffic to the lights of the ambulance almost a hundred yards ahead. "Did you know that every day the average American consumes two hundred fifty thousand calories in food and fuels used to produce that food? That's equal to one hundred eighty quarts of Häagen-Dazs ice cream a day." A mirthless chuckle rolled past her lips. "Now that's power."

"Do you still see the ambulance?" Harlow asked, an edge to his voice.

Katie nodded. "Three ahead," she said, as a motorcycle passed them on the right. Thoughts slid round and round inside her head, as if caught on the rim of a whirlpool eager to pull her consciousness under. One hundred eighty quarts of Häagen-Dazs ice cream. The freeway seemed fantastical, alien. Threads of thought flowing between the oceans and the mountains. California's cogitation. Nature remade.

I love you, Tom. You belong to me.

A light snapped on overhead. She leaned against a lamppost, chomping on a smelly cigar, the cold weight of a readied gun heavy in her pocket: a Hollywood-issue New Jersey hood, doing bad Jimmy Cagney. *You want to take him, God? I won't let you take him.*

Tomorrow she would consume two hundred quarts of Häagen-Dazs ice cream, and the day after that, two hundred and fifty. And her power would grow. The spectacular thought that had made this freeway would be nothing but an infant's first analysis of the difference between *smooth* and *rough*, compared to the thoughts that *would* be, when the thinker learned to command the disposition of individual molecules.

Nature didn't stand a chance.

She grinned like a death's head, her empty hands closing on a dream. Nanotechnology. An ugly, ungainly word. But the dream spun bright in the long night on the freeway. Nanotechnology: the promise that one day thinking machines could be built on the scale of bacteria. Acting machines. Working on command to reshape the world. To raise the dead. To rewrite the limits of life. To make the universe her playground. A child-safe playground. And she and Tom utterly safe there. "They're heading for the off-ramp," she said.

"I see them."

Dawn began to pale the light show. Bright signs advertising motels and all-night convenience stores faded. Headlights winked out. Traffic thickened at once on all sides as commuters left early to beat the rush. Harlow slowed, squinting worriedly as the ambulance made a left turn one block ahead. "It's all right," Katie said. "I know the way."

She guided Harlow the last few blocks, instructing him to pull into a crowded parking lot in front of a squat gray building almost unnoticeable in its basic ugliness. "Forward Futures," Katie said with a grin.

"So I see," Harlow responded, nodding at the sign done in letters drawn to look as if they'd been swept by the jet stream.

The building was three stories high, basic cinder block, remarkable only for its scarcity of windows. There were offices on the second floor. A few lights showed through the windows there. Otherwise the building might have been the proverbial black box, smooth-walled, contents unknown. "The ambulance will pull up to a bay in the back," Katie said. She could feel Harlow's measuring gaze, and smiled to herself. He didn't feel the power yet. Not yet. But he would.

"You sure you're up for this, Katie? How about getting some sleep first?"

"I'm not tired." She opened the door and stepped out, stretching, breathing the sour Los Angeles air. She wasn't tired at all; she was feeling downright giddy. She slammed the car door with an eager *crack*! "We made it, Harlow!" She stomped the ground for emphasis, then turned to him with a grin. "So many things could have gone wrong! Tom could have died at the crash site, and then some coroner might have wanted to autopsy him. He could have died at the hospital hours before Gregory could get there. He could have had massive damage to his brain. He could have had impaired circulation. Someone in the family could have made a stink about this whole thing.

"But none of that happened! Ha! I won this round, Harlow. *I won*. And I'm going to fight fate every step of the way to get my Tom back."

Harlow carefully locked the car. "How do we get inside?"

As if in answer, keys rattled in the glass door fronting the building. Katie looked up as a young woman pushed the door open from the inside; she beckoned to them. Katie didn't hesitate. She started up the steps, hearing Harlow follow close behind. "Hi. My name's Maryann," the young woman said as they approached. "I'm so sorry to hear about the accident." Maryann had wide sympathetic eyes, short blond hair, a bold nose, and wore no makeup at all.

Katie swept past her. "Have they unloaded him yet?"

"They're just starting. But he's received all his transport medications, and his temperature's already down to twenty-two degrees C."

"Is that good?"

"Yes. The sooner we can get his temperature down, the less ischemic damage he'll suffer."

"Ischemia . . . lack of blood flow?"

"Yes." She locked the door behind them. "Most of the staff is here, and we've already prepared the perfusate. Your husband is relatively young and has experienced general good health, so we're hoping surgery and perfusion will proceed easily."

Maryann led them through a lobby equipped with three obvious security cameras, past the entrance of a small auditorium, to a heavy steel door. Again the keys. She unlocked the door and let them through. Harlow was beginning to look nervous. "Tight security," he muttered.

"A lot of people object to what we do here," Maryann responded, tension in her voice. "We have a responsibility to protect our patients." She looked over at Katie. "Gregory said you wanted to observe the surgery and perfusion. You realize it'll take several hours to complete."

"I want to see it," Katie said. Because to see it was to be part of it. To know that everything that could be done for Tom *was* being done.

"And I'm sticking with Katie," Harlow added, almost belligerently.

Maryann had them change into surgical scrubs, then she led them to a surgical unit. "He's in here," she said, indicating a table, only half-visible past the medical team surrounding it. Katie craned her neck to see. The HLR had been removed. The body was packed in ice and draped in surgical cloth. It might have been anyone under there.

She recognized Gregory behind one of the surgical masks. He eyed her doubtfully. "You doing all right?" he asked.

"Fine." She moved closer. Uneasy. Determined not to get in the way.

"We're going to perform surgery on the femoral artery to connect a heart-lung bypass," Gregory said. "We'll use a perfusion pump to remove his blood and replace it with a perfusate that'll better support his tissues and inhibit edema. The fluids will circulate through a cooling bath, and that'll keep his body temperature dropping. We want to get him down to a few degrees above freezing, and then we'll introduce the cryoprotectants."

His tone was optimistic. But Tom's injuries slowed the process. There were mutters of concern over the next forty minutes, but the staff worked efficiently, the team did its job. Katie started to get wobbly on her feet and Harlow found her a chair. Finally, Tom's body temperature reached 5° C. A stainless steel hand drill was used to open a small burr hole in Tom's skull. Katie came over to watch. She felt uneasy about it, as if she were trespassing, illicitly viewing a part of Tom that should never have been exposed to her vision, that never would have been exposed if somehow she'd managed to protect him.

Guilt, she thought, was not a logical emotion.

Gregory showed her the brain. It looked white and shiny. The blood in the cerebral vessels had been completely replaced with the clear perfusate. "Looks good," the chief surgeon said with an air of satisfaction. "Let's prep him for the heart-lung machine."

Tom's chest was exposed, and the surgeon cut a line down its center, slicing through the breastbone, and finally, carefully exposing the heart. Tubes were placed in the aorta and the heart, and then connected to a larger, more complex heart-lung machine than the one that had been used in the hospital. And once again, Tom's circulation was restarted. Now cryoprotectants were gradually added to the perfusate solution, mostly glycerol and mannitol, to minimize ice formation and reduce freezing damage. It was a long process. The concentration of cryoprotectants could not be allowed to rise too quickly, or osmotic pressures across the cell membranes would further damage the body's tissue.

Four hours passed. Harlow had finally gone home, promising to be back before the end of the day. Katie found herself sitting in the building's lunchroom, across the table from Gregory, an untouched sandwich on a plate in front of her. "Eat," he said.

She picked up the sandwich and took a small bite. It seemed tasteless. She drank some skim milk. The morning's euphoria had faded, but she still felt a strong undercurrent of happiness. "It's going well, isn't it?" she asked.

"Quite well," he agreed.

They returned to surgery just as the cryoprotectant perfusion was judged adequate. Katie stood aside, watching, while Tom was taken off the heart-lung machine. The surgeon closed the incision in his chest. Then, using the burr hole in Tom's skull, the surgeon placed a temperature probe on the surface of Tom's brain. He closed that incision. Another temperature probe was placed in Tom's throat, and a third in his rectum.

Then the ice packs and protective wrappings were removed. For the first time since the hospital, Katie could see Tom's face. It had a yellowish cast beneath his tan, and its texture seemed stiff, almost waxy. Like an artificial copy, she thought. Exact in detail, but unquestionably inanimate. She felt something give way inside her: a strut snapping beneath her emotional architecture.

Tom was gone.

Then two large plastic bags were wrestled over his body, eclipsing her view. She stared at a white wall until her breathing had steadied and her composure had self-repaired.

Finally, Tom was submerged in a tank of silicone oil. Wire leads from the temperature probes in his body were connected to a computer. "The Silcool bath is at minus ten degrees C," Gregory explained. "We'll be adding dry ice to it over the next day and a half to slowly bring Tom's temperature down. After that he'll be transferred to liquid nitrogen storage."

"I want to see that too," Katie said.

For the first time since she'd met him, Gregory really smiled. "Somehow I expected that. But right now you must be about ready to collapse on your feet."

"Really, I'm not. I am so glad I came here ... but I should be going home. The girls will need me. I've already stayed away too long."

"Let's go out and get something to eat first," Gregory said. "You haven't had anything all day. Unless you get something in your system, you're going to get the shakes when this adrenaline high finally wears off. After we eat, I'll drive you back."

"Oh no," Katie said, shaking her head. "I'm not riding with you. You haven't had any more sleep than I have."

"I've had catnaps," he said defensively.

"I'll take the shuttle."

"Well at least let me take you to dinner."

Katie was surprised to see that it was already dark outside. She sat in the passenger seat of Gregory's old Toyota as they drove about six blocks to a vegan restaurant situated on one end of a convenience mall. He was wearing his Mars pin again.

The restaurant was dimly lit. Indian music played softly in the background. The dining area was about half-full, mostly with yuppie clientele. Katie stopped at the pay phone to call Harlow. His wife answered. She said Harlow was still asleep, but that he was determined to drive Katie home as soon as she was ready. Katie gave her the address of the restaurant, then called home. She talked to her

mother and then each of the girls. "I'll be home in a few
hours," she promised. "Wait up for me." They said they
would.

She found Gregory in a booth at the back of the restaurant. He'd already ordered for both of them. She sat down
across the table from him, and suddenly felt as if she
might never move again. Gregory quickly shoved a basket
of crackers toward her, and she ravenously devoured four
packs. The waitress brought a glass of milk, and she drank
half.

"This does not feel real," she said after a minute.

"Be thankful for that," Gregory said.

She shook her head, confused at her own dispassion. "I
can't accept that he's gone."

"He's not gone. He's just away for a while."

"A long while."

"Maybe." He picked up his fork aimlessly; set it down
again. "When were you born?"

She gave him a scowl of mock suspicion. "Why?"

"You're still young. But I'd be willing to bet that when
you were born your parents didn't own a color TV, nuclear
war was expected at any minute, spaceflight was limited
to a few hours in orbit, any pregnant, unmarried teenager
was shunned, computers were found only at elite universi-
ties, the idea of blacks in elected office was controversial,
commercial jet travel was only a few years old—"

"All right, all right. So I'm an antique."

He grinned. "The point is, you're not. You're only in
your thirties, and yet the world has undergone immense
technological and social changes in your lifetime. And the
rate of change is accelerating. Thirty years—"

"Thirty-four."

"If we can hold this world together that long, who
knows where we'll be?"

"Mars?" she teased.

He frowned disapprovingly, as if she'd made a sacrilegious joke. "Yes," he said quietly. "That's exactly what I
mean. We could be on Mars. You. Me. Tom. With bodies
that won't easily succumb to injuries. With bodies that we
can control precisely, and shape to suit our needs.

"Thirty years. Maybe fifty. Maybe more. But it will happen. You need to keep a perspective on time, all the immensity of time that's available to us."

"If cryonics works."

He shook his head. "No. If *nanotechnology* works. And why shouldn't it? Our bodies are already maintained by molecular machines, naturally occurring. When we've developed artificial analogs, we'll have won."

"What are you going to do on Mars?"

He looked startled, as if she'd caught him at play in a children's romance. Then he leaned across the table. This was not fantasy; not to him. "I want to see Mars transformed into a real world. Add an atmosphere. Find water. Design life-forms, plant a forest. Make it live."

"Paradise found."

"Paradise *made*. The human need for creative action satisfied."

"And to go where no one's gone before. How long do you plan on living?"

"As Gregory Hunt?" He shrugged. "I doubt I'll last more than a thousand years before my own growth and change makes that identity meaningless. But something new will come of me. Evolution in the individual, rather than the species. A thread of life stretching, changing through the eons. Different at every point from what has gone before, yet all the points connected through time. In time anything can happen. And it will all have started right here—" He rapped the table.

"In southern California. Yes." She smiled. "You dream fine dreams, Gregory Hunt. I need a dose of your confidence. I do."

They talked more—about cryonics, about Mars, about Tom, and what he'd meant to Katie. The food came, and Katie found that her appetite had been restored in full. They were finishing a last course of herbal tea when Harlow arrived. He came hulking up out of the restaurant's dim aisles like a stiff-legged bear. She stood up to greet him. He hugged her and kissed her on the cheek, then shook hands with Gregory. "Ready?"

"Yes." She reached out a hand to Gregory as he stood up. "I'll call you tomorrow." Then she hugged him. "Thanks for everything."

Out on the street, the traffic seemed uncommonly noisy; the air smelled foul. A panhandler accosted Harlow. Harlow told the old derelict to shove off. "Gregory wants to live forever," Katie said.

Harlow raised an eyebrow. "A bit ambitious."

Katie tried to imagine the old panhandler endowed with immortal life, with the kind of control over nature that Gregory envisioned. She frowned, speculating, then suddenly turned back. "Hey! Old man!"

"Katie! What are you—" Harlow started after her, but she ignored him.

"Hey, old man." She positioned herself squarely in front of the man and waited until she was sure his gaze had focused on her. His eyes were blue, bleary and red-rimmed, almost hidden under his sagging eyelids. He had a good growth of salt-and-pepper beard, a ragged ski cap, and the usual odd assortment of cast-off clothes. He smelled of tobacco, body odor, and alcohol, and his face was inflamed from scratching. It suddenly occurred to her that he probably wasn't much older than Tom.

"Can you spare a quarter, fifty cents?" he asked. He nudged a guitar case with his foot. "I usually sing for a living, but I've only got five strings. This is a six-string guitar."

"What would you do if you could live forever?" Katie asked.

The man stepped back suspiciously. "You from the devil?"

"I'm not offering. I'm asking. Ten dollars for an answer. What would you do if you could live forever in good health?" She dug around in her purse and pulled out a bill while the old man hemmed and hawed. "Answer?" she wheedled, holding it out for him to see.

"I'd fuck women like you." He snatched at the bill, but Katie quickly yanked it back. Her eyes narrowed.

"Okay. You just spent a hundred years fucking women like me. Now what?"

"Hey!" he whined. "I answered your question."

"It was a boring answer. What would you do next?"

He took another step back. "I—I'd like to have a sailboat," he stammered. "I lived one year in Tahiti, back in

'69. No one believes me, but it's true. I'd ... like to go back there."

"And do what?"

He shrugged, the set of his body telegraphing a growing resentment. "Just live. That's all. What's it your fucking business anyway?"

Katie nodded. She gave him the money.

Harlow waited a few feet away. He shook his head at her. "I don't know you, Katie," he said.

She craned her neck to look at the stars overhead. There weren't many visible past the city's glow. "You're interested in astronomy, aren't you, Harlow? Where's Mars?"

He sighed. "You know, I think it's below the horizon right now."

"Oh." The disclosure carried more weight for her than it should have. She looked down at the sidewalk; scuffed her feet. Took a first tentative glance at the void in her heart that she'd studiously ignored over the past day. She shuddered. "I don't think I want to live without him," she whispered.

Harlow quickly put his arm around her. "Come on. You're tired. The car's right over here."

But it was too late. She'd already started crying and she didn't think she'd ever stop. Harlow settled her on the front seat of the car. He shut the door and the seat belt slid home. When he got in on the other side, he hugged her and kissed her and handed her a box of tissues. "I'm getting you out of this city."

Somewhere on the way up I-5 she must have begun to doze, because she woke with a start as Harlow shut off the engine outside her own house. The lights were on. She wiped her face with a tissue, then blew her nose. Harlow opened the door for her. In the house, petite hands lifted aside the curtains. A young face peeped out. "It's Mom!" Nikki shrieked. And suddenly the front door slammed open and Nikki and Joy bolted out and into Katie's arms, squirming and crying, until they were all three sitting on the driveway. Harlow seemed to pick them up as one, herding them into the house with disapproving noises. Belle stood just inside the door. She patted Katie's shoulder and smiled sadly. Tom's mom was waiting just behind her. It was difficult to read any emotion on Jane's face. Then Tom's sister, Ilene, swept into the room from the direction of the kitchen.

"Katie dear!"

Only two little words, but Katie immediately felt some of the gloom begin to lift from her heart. Ilene had always known how to make things better, had always been ready to help. This petite woman of fifty-five had been elected to the U.S. Senate only four years ago, but already she'd earned national stature. Tonight she was dressed in beige satin pj's, her hair neat as ever in an easygoing perm, and wire-rim glasses on her flat nose. It was the first time Katie had seen her without makeup, and she was struck by how vital and forceful her expression was even without the emphasis of cosmetics. "Ilene, I'm so happy to see you." And she meant it.

"Katie, darling," Ilene said. "I'm so sorry. I didn't get in until this afternoon. I would have picked you up in L.A. if I'd known you were there. As it was, I wanted to drive back for you, but no one knew quite where you were." She slipped between the girls to kiss Katie deftly on the cheek.

But as she pulled away, Katie caught a look of warning on her mother's face. Belle's throat bobbed nervously. "Katie ... we've tried to explain to Ilene the, ah ... *arrangements* you've made for Tom. She's not entirely happy about it."

Not entirely happy? Katie felt a hint of uneasy warmth cross her cheeks. She didn't want to deal with controversy. Not now.

Belle glanced anxiously at Ilene before continuing: "Katie, I'm afraid the situation has gotten a little more ... *complicated* since you left the hospital last night. Have you seen the news reports?"

"News reports?" Katie echoed, looking between her mother and Ilene.

Ilene nodded, allowing just a touch of a frown to darken her face. "When I arrived at the airport, I was accosted by a reporter and cameraman from a local newspaper. They wanted to know how Tom's cryonic suspension could be justified, given my views on the economics of extraordinary medical procedures. I had no idea what they were talking about. Cryonics? At first I didn't even recognize the term. Then I recalled hearing about this crackpot idea of freezing dead bodies. I thought the reporter must have gotten her facts wrong and I told her so. It never occurred to me that you and Tom had really involved yourselves with—" She interrupted herself, a hurt expression on her face. "Why, oh why didn't you warn me what was going on?"

Katie blinked helplessly. "I let everybody know last night, in the hospital. You weren't there. I couldn't wait." She hugged the girls closer to her sides, wanting only to disappear with them into her bedroom.

"You could have shared your intentions with me years ago," Ilene said. There was no anger in her voice, only hurt—that Katie could have left her so vulnerable. "*Why* did you never mention it? Does the whole idea embarrass you as much as it embarrasses me?"

Katie felt her cheeks go crimson. She shook her head, uncertain just how she'd earned this reproof.

"Lighten up, Ilene," Harlow growled. "Katie's had a rough twenty-four hours. This can wait until tomorrow."

"I'm sorry," Ilene said. And she really did sound distressed. "But we have to talk about it tonight. Katie, we've been friends for years. So I have to tell you that I think what you're doing is sacrilegious. I also think it's immoral on secular grounds. It needs to be stopped now. At once."

"Ilene!" Jane cried, in a voice fully mortified.

"I'm sorry, Mom. But I can't just stand by and let this atrocity go on. Tom is dead. We need to have a funeral, commend him to God. But where's the body? Being used for medical experiments by an organization of crackpots!"

"You should have stayed home!" Nikki blurted. Joy began to cry.

"It's all right," Katie said. "It's all right, it's all right." A mindless, motherly drone to soothe the children. She'd already withdrawn from the moment, encased herself in an imaginary bubble that diverted the angry words around her. "I'm going back into L.A. tomorrow," she told Ilene. "Why don't you come with me? We'll talk about it on the way."

EXCERPT FROM SPEECH BY
SENATOR CARSON:

"... *before national health-care reform, one
quarter of all children in America lived
beneath the poverty line. One quarter of
all children never saw a doctor outside
of a public hospital emergency room. National
health insurance changed this. But national
health insurance can't do everything.
Some have asked us to include funds for
artificial hearts or experimental organ
transplants in our program. And I
sympathize with those in need. But funds
will always be limited, and it's impossible
to overlook the fact that for the cost of one
artificial heart we can provide a full
vaccination series for thousands of
children. The choices are harsh, but we
have to make them. ..."*

4

Choices

Katie awoke to a brilliant glare of afternoon light pouring in through her bedroom's western window. The light ignited a pounding headache right behind her eyes. She groaned in protest and rolled over—to discover Nikki watching her from Tom's half of the bed.

Nikki lay on her side, her head propped up on her hand. Her plain brown eyes—showing just a bit of an epicanthic fold to mark her father's heritage—held an expression as calm as Mr. Spock's. Soft wisps of short brown hair framed her serious face. Katie smiled at her, and reached out to touch her tanned cheek. A fleeting smile twitched across Nikki's thin lips, then disappeared.

Katie lay back against the pillow with a long sigh. She pressed the heels of her hands against her temples. "Oh, I think my head's going to crack ... what time is it, anyway?"

"Almost two," Joy said.

Katie raised her head in surprise, to see her older daughter sitting cross-legged at the foot of the bed. Joy was twelve, and the changes of puberty were already showing. Her breasts were budding beneath a pink sweatshirt that suddenly looked too small. Her face was thinning, giving up its girlish roundness for the more defined lines of a young woman. But her eyes were the same: wide eyes, with the iris so dark the pupil was lost in it; warm eyes, like a dark body emitting heat in the infrared. Magnetic eyes that had won her a court of boyfriends from the age of four. Her father's eyes. "We're sorry we woke you up, Mom. But we needed you."

"They're talking about Daddy on CNN," Nikki added.

Katie shoved herself up on her elbows. *"What?"*

Joy made a disparaging noise. "They're just trying to embarrass Auntie Ilene. You know how the media is."

"Like dogs chasing cars," Nikki explained. "They snap and growl and try to bite your tires, but drive on a block and they'll never think about you again."

Unless they make you crash, Katie thought. She studied her younger child, this ten-year-old who'd somehow come to possess a deep-set self-assurance that most women couldn't manage until they'd reached a successful middle age.

Nikki's probing gaze seemed to observe her thoughts, but she made no comment on them. "Somebody from Forward Futures has been trying to call you," she said. "At least he was this morning. But we unplugged the phones."

Katie frowned in confusion. Her headache was beating in time to her pulse now, and she desperately wanted a cup of coffee. "Who was calling me? Did you take a message? Why'd you unplug the phone?"

"Too many newspeople trying to get in touch with Auntie. You know how it goes. They were driving us crazy."

"I sure never thought it'd go this way." Katie lay back on the pillow again. How had things gotten so out of hand? "Dammit!" she said, sitting up suddenly. "This is nobody's business but ours."

The girls said nothing. But through the silence Katie could feel their expectation. She was the mother and it was up to her to somehow set things right. She sighed, her fingers moving softly against Nikki's arm. She looked at

Joy, inadequacy hanging like a weight around her neck. "I'm sorry I haven't been here for you."

"It's all right, Mom," Nikki said, sitting up. "You had more important things to do. But I want to go with you when you go back to see Daddy."

Katie's lips parted in sudden concern. How much had they been told? What did they understand? "Nikki, Daddy's not in a hospital anymore."

Nikki rolled her eyes. "I know, Mom. I know. He's supposed to be dead. But we know better. Someday we'll have him back." Joy nodded her agreement, even as tears welled up in her eyes.

Katie looked from one to the other, wondering again at the wisdom of what she'd done. They were only children, clinging desperately to a promise that most people would consider irrational and irresponsible. What did they really believe?

She chose her words carefully. "Nikki. Joy. I want you to understand, right now, from the beginning. We're not getting Daddy back. At least not within our lifetimes. He isn't going to be here for you. Not when you graduate from high school, not when you get married, not when you have children of your own. He won't be here. Maybe, in another time. . . ." She shook her head. "But not now."

Nikki swallowed hard. Her lips began to tremble. "I know, Mom. I know all that. But I want to go with you to see Daddy."

Katie shook her head slowly, sorrowfully. "No. It's too ugly, Nikki. I don't want you to remember him like that."

"But it's okay for *you*?" she said. The hurt in her eyes seemed boundless. "You think you love him more than I do?"

"I don't think love can be measured," she said. Joy started weeping softly. "Oh, Joy," Katie whispered. She gathered them both in her arms. What was this doing to them? she wondered. What would this do to *their* lives?

After she showered, she had Nikki reach behind a nightstand to plug in a phone, then she called Forward Futures. "The news media's all over us," Gregory said. "I didn't know you were sister-in-law to a senator."

"It's been the same here. How's Tom doing?"

"Fine. We're still bringing him down to dry ice temperature, minus seventy-nine degrees C. We're scheduling the transfer to liquid nitrogen storage for tomorrow afternoon."

"Okay. I'll be there."

She hung up and looked at the girls. "Guess it's time to face Auntie. Has she cooled down any?"

"Nope," Nikki said. "I took a lot of stuff from your cryonics file this morning and gave it to her to read, but she hasn't changed her mind. She still thinks we're nuts."

Joy blew her nose into a tissue. "I don't understand why she wants Daddy to die."

"She doesn't *want* Daddy to die, honey. She believes that he already *is* dead, and that he'll never be alive again." But then she hesitated, thinking about what she'd just said. Was it true? Ilene had ignited a national controversy last year by maintaining that some medical procedures were simply too expensive for society to support—even if they proved effective. Was Ilene applying those same principles to Tom? How could she?

Katie's thoughts flashed on the first time she'd met Ilene. She'd been eighteen years old, Tom was thirty, and Dad was furious. Nobody had thought it would work—except Ilene. She'd come west for a visit and inside an hour she'd plumbed Katie's soul, given her approval to the affair, and offered Katie the encouragement a woman-child needed to smother her own self-doubts.

Then she'd worked her magic on Dad, convincing him that the situation was really not so awful after all. Ilene of the silver-tongue, a born politician but never a phony. Without Ilene, Katie and Tom might have come to nothing.

And her influence had continued through the years. Though childless, Ilene had understood how Katie felt when her first daughter had been born two months premature. And later, she'd used her influence to bring the whole family back from a vacation in Europe in time to say good-bye to Katie's father when he'd suffered a massive heart attack.

These special deeds stood out in Katie's memory, but

they weren't what made her love Ilene. No. It was the constant, undemanding nature of her interest, the humanistic content of her thought, her unflagging allegiance to the simple and ancient concept of *family*.

So how could she abandon her brother now? Katie sighed. It was time to find out.

She found Ilene in the living room, curled up on one end of the couch. The coffee table in front of her was strewn with pamphlets, booklets, and magazines, all dealing with cryonics, while balanced on her lap was the book-length contract that was Tom's suspension agreement. But she wasn't reading. Her attention was fixed on a picture of Tom and the girls that rested on the mantel. She had a faraway look in her eyes.

"Ilene?"

Ilene's gaze shifted. The fatigue lines around her eyes hardened when she saw Katie. But her voice was soft with sympathy. "Katie darling." She glanced at the pamphlets on the table. "I've spent the last few hours reading, as you can see. I wanted to understand. And I think—"

She drew a deep breath, then let it go in a sigh. "Oh, Katie. I know how much you loved Tom. And I know how much he loved you. You had one of the finest marriages I have ever encountered, and you did not waste your days together." She looked again at Tom's photo on the mantel.

In the brief pause, Katie struggled to find a few words that might turn the conversation. She didn't want to talk about these things. She wanted to kick herself free of this room and float away, above it all, and never connect with the tumult in her mind.

But Ilene had other plans. While Katie was still floundering, she leaned forward and took aim at her emotional core. "At times like this we all operate on instinct. And I know your instinct is telling you to *do anything* to get Tom back. Do anything. But he's gone, Katie. You have to accept that. For your own peace of mind. For the children. None of us gets to choose our fate."

Katie felt the blood rush to her face as her earlier doubts returned. She pressed her hot cheek against the doorframe, grateful for the cool, hard pressure of the wood.

"I'm not going to change my mind," she whispered, feeling the words like an oath.

Ilene looked at her over the gold rim of her reading glasses. "You know this isn't just a private disagreement."

Katie nodded miserably. "I know you're being hounded by the media. Did you give a statement?"

"I've explained my opposition to . . . the method you've chosen for my brother's interment."

"*He* chose it, Ilene."

"Katie, I don't want to hurt you any more than you've already been hurt. But we've always been honest with each other. I *know* that Tom only wanted to please you when he signed this contract with Forward Futures." She tapped the document on her lap. "He would never have chosen this end for himself. He was too generous, too much in love with the world."

Katie found she couldn't meet Ilene's gaze. Because Ilene was right. Tom had signed the contract only to please her. Nevertheless, he'd signed it willingly. "His eyes were wide open. And so was his mind. He is in love with this world. And he's not ready to leave it."

The senator was shaking her head. "You've put me in a terrible position, Katie. I've always maintained the conviction—against great opposition—that this society cannot afford extraordinary medical efforts. We have to know where to draw the line on treatments or we're going to bankrupt ourselves. This is even worse. How is it going to look if a fortune is spent to preserve my brother's body? Not his life, mind you. Simply his *dead body*."

Katie frowned. She'd always figured that what she did with her own money was her own business. Certainly it was not the business of Ilene's constituents. "The funds are coming from an insurance policy. Not from any government. And we paid for that policy. Tom and I. Out of our own moneys."

Ilene picked up the contract, setting it on the coffee table with a loud thud. She sat up a little straighter; leaned a little bit closer to Katie as she asked: "Do you think everybody's entitled to this service? Should cryonic suspension be part of our national health insurance plan?"

Katie sighed and looked away. What did national health

insurance have to do with Tom? "I'm not here to decide for everybody," she said. "Just my family."

Ilene's frown was grim. "Unfortunately, I *am* here to decide for everybody. That's part of the job of United States senator. And I'm telling you there's no way this country can afford it."

Katie let her anger boil off through a slow count of ten. "I don't want anything from the government except the freedom to choose for my family," she said. "If you'd like to witness Tom's transfer to long-term storage, it's scheduled for tomorrow afternoon. You're welcome to come with me and observe. If not . . ." She left the sentence unfinished, though her eyes shifted toward the front door.

The gesture didn't escape Ilene. "Yes," she said stiffly. "Yes, I'll go with you. I'd like a chance to pay my last respects."

Driving into L.A. the next day, Katie felt as if she'd endured two deaths in the family. Tom's end was a physical reality. The demise of her friendship with Ilene was only a cerebral adjustment, but it still hurt. She could hardly believe this person beside her was the same Ilene she'd trusted for so many years.

She flinched as Ilene's voice broke her train of thought.

"Was Tom actually dead when those cryonicists started pumping poisons into his body?" Ilene was driving her rental car, her sharp gaze scanning rapidly between the traffic on the freeway and Katie's face. "I've heard that cryonicists were accused of murdering an old man a few years back. That they killed him with an overdose of barbiturates so they could get on with their procedures."

Katie blanched. It hadn't been like that, she told herself. But she remembered the case Ilene referred to. The patient had been legally dead, just like Tom. She shivered, remembering Tom's brief resurrection in the ICU after Gregory connected him to the heart-lung resuscitator. Tom had started breathing on his own. He'd been alive. Anyone could have seen that. *What had he been thinking?* And had she been an accomplice in his murder?

But she held her questions close to her heart, hoping fervently that Ilene would never learn the bitter details of

Tom's last moments. She paled to think what mischief Ilene could make of that. "He was dead. Dr. Ruiz said so."

She felt drawn into herself, like a snail in its shell. She didn't want to talk to this stranger who looked like Ilene.

Where had her old friend gone? Had she ever really existed outside Katie's mind? A whiff of Ilene's sophisticated perfume reached her, and she trembled with fear. Ilene had always known how to influence people, how to wield power. She'd developed that talent generally described as force of personality long before she'd obtained any political clout. It was within her reach to isolate Katie within the family. Oh, sure, she'd never turn Harlow, but their mothers . . . what did the two older women really think of what she'd done to Tom? Katie knew they both held reservations; that they'd said nothing much against it only to avoid hurting her.

She saw again what a mistake it had been for her and Tom to keep silent about their intentions. If they'd let the family know from the start, they'd have had that much longer to explain, to convince. But they hadn't wanted to *upset* anybody. . . .

Guess everybody was plenty upset now.

Her fist thunked the armrest in a sudden spurt of anger. "What do you want from me, Ilene? You've looked over the contract. You know there's no going back. Tom's suspension can't be reversed even if I wanted that."

Ilene's gaze fixed on the traffic; her stern expression didn't waver. "I want a statement from you that this was a mistake. That it's wrong and greedy to seize more life than our natural span. That we should put our resources into the welfare of our children and our world, not into ourselves."

Katie stared at the road ahead of her. Two deaths. Two deaths in two days. "I'm going to miss you, Ilene."

A light rain seemed to have inspired an early rush hour that day. It was only one o'clock, yet the city's streets were clogged with bumper-to-bumper traffic. They were still six blocks away from Forward Futures when Ilene finally gave up. They left the car in a mini-mall parking lot, bought two umbrellas, and started walking. The fumes from the creeping traffic seemed more pungent with the rain. Boom cars competed with each other for mastery of the street. Suddenly, traffic ceased moving altogether. "Look," Katie said, craning to see past the young trees that lined the street. "There must have been an accident. I can see police cars on the sidewalk. Their lights are flashing. Hey, wait a minute."

She blinked her eyes hard and strained to see through the rain. The sidewalk up ahead was crowded. Crowded with people holding signs. Protesters. Katie felt her heart skip in sudden anxiety. She hurried forward, holding the umbrella as a shield against the slanting raindrops, lifting it every few steps for a visual update.

After a block, she was certain the protesters were congregating in the parking lot of the Forward Futures building. Another block, and she could hear shouted obscenities overlaid against an unintelligible chant. She could see only one police officer. The others must still have been in the patrol cars that had been driven between the trees and parked on the sidewalk. Still a block away, Katie came to a sudden and undignified halt. What should she do?

"If you want my advice," Ilene muttered in her ear, "you'll find a back entrance."

Katie looked down at the shorter woman as she huffed and puffed under her umbrella. Ilene's expression was cool and firm as she studied the congregation. "And ... you?" Katie asked tentatively.

Ilene turned to her. "Into the breach," she said. "I'd rather go head-to-head with the mob than be caught *sneaking* into a place like that." And she strode forward purposefully, leaving Katie to follow or not.

There must have been more than two hundred people occupying the Forward Futures parking lot, though very few of them seemed concerned with the actual business of cryonics. White Supremacists! accused one sign, held by a black man arguing heatedly with a leather-booted skinhead, whose T-shirt was emblazoned with the prediction: The Future Belongs to the Aryan Nation.

Money for the Living, Not the Dead was carried by a frail young woman with two small children clinging to her skirt. That seemed to be a popular sentiment. Katie also made out:

No Greedy Geezers.

Put Our Resources in Babies, Not Corpses.

Poor People for a Better Life Now.

Shelter for Five Homeless Families or $ One Body Preserved $.

And of course the religious right had representatives present: You Can't Dodge Hell in a Freezer brought a brief smile to Katie's lips as she followed Ilene.

Beyond the protesters, a woman on the stairs argued with the lone police officer. Katie recognized Maryann, whom she'd met the day Tom was brought in. Apparently, whatever she was saying failed to sway the cop. He shrugged disinterestedly and turned to look out upon the crowd with an air of smug satisfaction.

Then two bored-looking reporters on the edge of the crowd recognized Senator Ilene Carson. They perked up immediately. Beckoning to the cameramen who'd been standing under the eaves of a neighboring building, they started forward to meet her.

The first reporter was a young man with black hair and a thin mustache. "Senator Carson!" he shouted, before his cameraman was even ready. "Are you going to enter the enemy's camp?"

"Has your position on cryonics changed, Senator Carson?" asked his female counterpart.

Ilene drew herself up in an official attitude. She suddenly looked much taller than her five feet two. "My position has not changed. I'm here primarily to view my brother's remains, but I've also scheduled an inspection of the facility. . . ."

Katie started to edge around them, but the second reporter saw her and stuck a mike in Katie's face. "Mrs. Kishida, do you really believe your husband will live again?" Katie eyed the mike suspiciously, wondering if they could get electrocuted in the rain. "Mrs. Kishida?" the reported pressed.

Katie's gaze shifted to the reporter's face. "I believe he'll live forever."

She left Ilene to the reporters and pushed her way through the crowd until she could climb the stairs to the front door. Maryann, the Forward Futures staffer, looked at her with a helpless frown. "Can you believe this? And we used to have such a nice, quiet home." Katie mumbled something sympathetic while the door was unlocked, then she stepped inside.

The smell of coffee and wet clothes washed over her. The lobby that had been so empty yesterday was packed today with news reporters and Forward Futures members. "That's her," someone said, and suddenly a pocket tape recorder was thrust in her face. "Mrs. Kishida, have you changed your mind about your husband's suspension?"

"Of course not." She pushed her way forward, leaving questions in her wake.

"Katie!"

Craning her neck to see past the crowd, she glimpsed Gregory waiting by the inner security door. She waved to him, and darted through the pack. "There's Senator Carson!" someone shouted, bringing Katie's fifteen minutes of fame to a premature end as Ilene entered the lobby. Gregory held the security door open, a pained expression on his face. "Sorry about all this. I didn't—"

Somebody pushed Katie hard from behind. She stumbled into Gregory, knocking him back against the doorjamb. The raw thunk of fist against flesh reached her ears as pain blossomed in her back. Swearing, she turned to see a little man in a blue-and-green tie-dyed shirt racing down the corridor into the working heart of the facility. His black skin glistened in the overhead lights. His buttocks worked like a gazelle's. *"Security!"* Gregory bellowed. He lunged after the intruder. Katie slammed the door shut behind her and sprang after them.

The rubber soles of her wet shoes squeaked as she pounded down the corridor. She could taste fear in her mouth. Tom was here and he was helpless. Who was this stranger? He was skinny as an AIDS patient in his last days, but oh, so strong. What did he intend? She could not believe it was good after the violence she'd felt in his hands.

She saw him hesitate at the door of the surgical unit. Gregory was almost on him when he leaped away again, ducking into a cross-corridor. As she rounded the corner, she heard a fire door slam open. An alarm went off. Footsteps pounded down a stairwell to the basement vault where the patients were kept in storage. Tom was down there, in a cold room just outside the sealed vault. He was scheduled to be transferred to the vault in a few weeks, when his body temperature had been brought down to that of liquid nitrogen. But now he was exposed and vulnerable.

Gregory got to the fire door ahead of her. He slammed it against the wall and leaped down the stairs. Vaguely, Katie was aware of other people appearing in the corridor, shouting at her. But she ignored them. Half flying, half falling, she followed Gregory down the stairs, her feet hardly touching ground until she hit bottom. Then she grabbed the slowly closing fire door at the base of the stairs and flung it open in time to see Gregory make a diving tackle around the intruder's hips. The two men hit the floor with a thud and rolled, crashing into three large steel cylinders of liquid nitrogen. The tanks skidded on their dollies. "Look out!" Gregory shouted. He let go of the man and rolled away as one of the cylinders crashed over, square in the spot where he'd just been. "You son of a bitch!"

The intruder was already on his knees. His head swiveled, brown eyes afire with determination. Then he focused on the coffinlike tank that held Tom's body packed in dry ice. He scrambled over to it. He kneeled at the side of the tank, his hands poised just over the rim as if he wanted to touch the body but the cold held him off. For an instant the scene metamorphosed in Katie's mind: vital, colorful life praying at the white tomb of death. Then she hit him. Drove her shoulder against his and sent him skidding once more into the floor. She raised her fist and slammed it into his face. Sudden pain burst through her knuckles and she drew back in shock. She'd never hit anyone in her life. Then she closed her fist and struck him again.

To her surprise, he didn't try to fight back. He twisted and flopped as if the only thing on his mind was to get away, run away, as if there were some possibility of escape from the facility. He grabbed the carry handle of the fallen cylinder and pulled against it, trying to extricate himself from her grip.

Then Gregory had his hands. And suddenly the room was full of people in white coats. "It's all right, Katie, we've got him now." She released her grip on him and turned away. She found herself sitting on the floor next to Tom's ice coffin. She scrambled up to it; peered over the side. She could see nothing of him under the white layers of ice. Her breath tore through her throat in harsh gasps, and the cold burned her lungs.

"What did he want?" Ilene asked later, when the police were conducting their investigation. She stood with Katie beside Tom's body while the staff brought up the equipment for the transfer. There was a tension in the room Katie hadn't felt two days before. Words were issued, not spoken. Each one sharp and to the point. Movements were rapid and brusque. No joy of camaraderie today. A hostile army was waiting outside the door.

"He wouldn't say what he came for," Katie said. "But he called us white supremacists. He figured we were trying to time travel to an age when AIDS will have wiped out the African people."

"Does he have AIDS?"

"Who knows?"

"Is this organization racist?"

Katie's eyes shifted in sudden humor. "They took Tom, didn't they?" Ilene's expression hardened into a scowl. Katie looked away. "Besides, I've been introduced to several Hispanic names," she added uneasily.

"Too much money for too few people," Ilene muttered.

Katie frowned at her. "Since when did you become a Communist?"

Ilene stiffened. "I'll write that one off to the stress of the day."

"Gee thanks." The "stress of the day" had left Katie in a nasty mood. She wanted to get Ilene out of here, wanted the cops out, the reporters out. Wanted to restore the easy sense of unity and mutual support that had carried her through her first day here. But things weren't going to work out that way.

"What's that?" Ilene asked, as a huge, more-than-man-sized metal cylinder was rolled into the room. They stepped aside, and it eclipsed their view of the tank that held Tom.

Katie said: "That's Tom's storage vessel. It's made like a giant thermos bottle. He'll be placed in it and cooled some more, and eventually the vessel will be filled with liquid nitrogen and that's it. Long-term stor—"

She dropped to the floor before she knew what had happened. Only as she pressed her forehead against the cold linoleum was she conscious of the explosion that ripped through the room in a deafening pulse of pressure and sound. Something hard struck her on the shoulder and hip. A supple weight fell across her legs, then rolled away. Her ears were ringing, but beyond that—only silence. As if the force of the explosion had driven all sound out of the room.

Then somebody shouted, shattering the moment of calm. "Get out! Get everybody out! One of the cylinders is cracked. We've got a spill."

Fog started billowing through the room, bringing with it a sepulchral chill that set Katie's teeth to chattering. She raised her head and looked around. She saw Ilene on the floor behind her. Her eyes were closed. Her glasses were twisted, one side shoved up over her forehead. Amid the salt and pepper of her hair, Katie could see blood oozing from an injury just above her ear.

Katie twisted around. Through the fog she saw an over-turned nitrogen cylinder wedged beside Tom's tank, its end torn open, curled teeth of shattered metal where the valve should have been. The valve was gone. A clear, glassy liquid boiled from the wreck, spreading across the floor with alarming speed. It swept across her outstretched fingers as she scrambled to get away.

Liquid nitrogen could only exist at $-196°$ C—a temperature more than cold enough to freeze living flesh. Yet its touch didn't hurt. The contact was almost soothing, like the calming breath of a very cold fog.

Still, Katie lost no time scrambling to her feet. In the suddenly frigid atmosphere her body quaked with cold. Water vapor crystallized on her hair and eyelashes. She danced backward on shaking legs to avoid the expanding spill.

The liquid caught Ilene. It boiled against her feet, her legs, generating a white fog that obscured her body. Katie reacted instinctively. She jumped forward, grabbed Ilene under the arms, and pulled her toward the door. Supporting Ilene's head on her forearms, she brought her out of the room and into the stairwell.

A crowd of people clogged the way. Suddenly there was nowhere to take Ilene, so Katie stretched her out on the floor, just outside the open door. She kept a careful eye on the spill, but its progress had halted. Drains in the floor were carrying some of the liquid away, while the rest boiled off into harmless gaseous form.

Slowly, the air in the room cleared and she could see the shattered equipment, the dented cylinders, the fallen chunks of concrete that had been knocked off the ceiling.

"What the hell happened?" somebody shouted.

"One of the nitrogen cylinders ruptured. It must have been defective."

"No," Katie said. "It was a bomb."

Gregory dropped to his knees beside her and started examining Ilene. "It was a bomb, all right. And thankfully the storage vessel shielded us from most of the blast. Breathing. Heartbeat. Looks like concussion. Must have been hit by flying debris." He looked up the stairwell. "Got an ambulance on the way?" he shouted.

From somewhere upstairs, somebody shouted yes.

Katie took a deep breath to calm her racing heart. Then she leaned back on her heels and looked around. The stairwell was jammed. People sitting on steps, others milling around. The predominance of white coats made the few spots of blood more prominent. A cop at the top of the stairs was shouting for everybody to evacuate.

"We're damn lucky," someone said, "that no one was killed."

"He had a bomb," Katie muttered, shaking her head in disbelief. "I didn't see it."

"He must have had it hidden under his shirt," Gregory said. He was still crouched over Ilene, taking a second measure of her pulse.

Suddenly Katie's head jerked up. She looked again into the cold room. The bomb had been planted on one of the nitrogen cylinders by Tom's coffin. The cooling tank that held his body hadn't been sheltered behind the huge storage cylinder. It had been fully exposed to the blast. When she saw the metal debris that lay across the tank, her eyes widened in horror. She darted into the room, unmindful of the cold now. She started to grab at the debris, but suddenly Gregory was with her. He caught her hands. "It's too cold. You're going to hurt yourself." He used his shoes to kick the debris aside. She followed his example. Even so, the cold penetrated her feet like a lance. Her chest ached with it.

When they had the surface of the ice cleared, she leaned over the tank. More metal fragments were buried in the ice. How many had reached Tom's body? "His head," Gregory muttered. "That's all that really matters. Has he had any damage to his head?"

A man in a white coat stepped up. Katie recognized the surgeon who'd worked on Tom. He had thick white gloves on his hands. Reaching into the ice, he drew out a curled, triangular piece of metal. Then some shards of glass. He removed a few chunks of dry ice and threw them on the side, then he reached down to run his hands around the plastic bags that encased Tom's head. A look of relief broke across his face. "I can't feel any debris this deep," he said. "I think he's all right."

Nobody laughed at the irony of the statement.

Katie stayed at the facility until Tom's transfer was finally underway. It was night when she left. She went to the hospital to visit Ilene. The senator had remained unconscious for only a few minutes. She'd been awake by the time the ambulance personnel arrived, but the emergency-room doctors had insisted on keeping her in the hospital overnight. "They just want to bill my insurance company," she grumbled. Then her dark eyes met Katie's. "I heard what you did," she said. "I want to thank you for getting me out of there."

"If I hadn't done it, someone else would have," Katie said, pulling a chair up to the bedside.

"Can't have a senator die on the premises, eh?"

Katie smiled. "You've already given us enough trouble, Senator Carson. Dying would have been just too much."

Ilene sighed, her head and shoulders resting on the pillow, one side of her head heavily bandaged. She seemed older tonight than Katie had ever seen her. Her eyes were red and the worry creases on her forehead were white. "Do you get the feeling you've suddenly been slipped into a different world?" she asked.

"I know I have been," Katie answered sincerely.

"You poor child. It's been a rough couple of days, I know. Probably the roughest you'll ever have. And I added to it. I'm sorry for that, Katie."

"We've always been friends."

"We always have been," Ilene agreed. Her powerful gaze locked onto Katie's. "But I don't know if that can go on. Most people today try to overlook their philosophical differences, as if philosophy weren't important. But I'm not like that. I'm not afraid to talk about politics or religion or death or responsibility. And I still don't like what you're doing to Tom. I shouldn't have attacked you the way I did, but my feelings were honest. Those ... *cryonicists*—" Her jaw muscles went tight when she said the word. Katie could hear her real meaning behind the attempt at politeness: *those nuts, crackpots, ghouls ...*

"They're just people like you and me, Ilene. Maybe a little more optimistic."

"Or selfish."

Katie stood up to leave. "I'm sorry you feel that way—"

"Katie, I just don't understand *why* you're doing this."

Katie's eyes flickered wide in surprise. "Oh, Ilene, that's so simple. I love Tom. And I'm not willing to give him up."

Wedged Time—
Alternate Landscapes

Snow. It surrounded him, held him, cushioned him. A deep snowbank. He could almost see the presence of his Familiar in the white sparkle of the crystals. He could feel her touch against his unclothed body. Her spirit ran through him, warming him, denying the cold.

He lifted his head. Was she near? He thought he should try to crawl out of the snowbank, but his arms worked sluggishly. He pushed with his legs, and managed to move a few inches before he fell back. He lay still, staring up at the whitening sky, enjoying the warmth. He turned his head. There were peculiar, bright red traces in the snow. He followed one of the broken smears until his gaze settled on his hand. His fingertips were bleeding. Strange that he couldn't feel it. He squinted, peering closer at his fingers. Tiny crabs made of snow were walking across his nails. Six-legged, with minute eyes on stalks and pincers tenderly exploring his skin. A dozen of them could fit on the nail of his smallest finger. They crawled up out of the snow and onto his hand, his shoulder. He could feel them working at his torso, his groin, his legs.

They weren't hurting him. At least, he felt no pain. He watched one remove an egg from the cluster under its abdomen. Holding the egg delicately in one pincer, the crab inserted it into a pore on his forearm. He felt a twinge then, a peppery sensation that seemed to break out at once all over his body. The crab reached under its belly for another egg, adjusted its feet slightly, and inserted it into another pore. *Food for the crabs,* he thought, and laughed grimly. A bit of sun broke through the clouds, starting little rainbows dancing in his eyelashes.

He slept. When he awoke, the sun had fallen behind the cliff of ice that towered over him, its summit lost in fog. The crabs had left his body. If he gazed into the snow, he could make out their shapes, but they were utterly still—their eyestalks folded flat, their legs huddled under them—a frozen army. He closed his eyes, and the blackness inside him took the shape of his Familiar. "Where are you?" he whispered. He could still sense her presence . . . somewhere. In the air? In the light?

He struggled to get up. The snow felt cool and pleasant against his body. *Is that right?* he wondered. But then, he wasn't the same man he used to be.

He held up his hands to the fading light. He no longer had skin on his fingers. Instead, a hard, bony gray shell had grown over each phalanx. The skin on his hands was gray, thick, slick, and hairless, like dolphin skin. His whole body—

—had thickened. He could feel the smooth, hard, insulating fat beneath the streamlined surface. He ran his hands up and down his torso, not displeased. His penis was protected in a prominently displayed pouch. His testicles had retracted into his body. He lifted one foot and looked at it. Uttered a short laugh. Big. Gray and smooth on top, gray and rough on the bottom, the sole divided into thick pads, dense gray fur in between. His toes looked thick and short.

He reached up to feel his face. His fingers were remarkably sensitive. He felt a flat face, a thick layer of fat hiding all evidence of the detailed structure of the bones beneath. His nose was flat, his nostrils small. His browridge seemed to be protrudent. His head was hairless and dolphin-smooth. He grimaced, searching out needle-sharp teeth with a thin, dry tongue.

He sensed the presence of his Familiar in this transformation. She'd brought the wind to slow his fall and the crabs to change him. But where was *she*? He could feel her in only the most diffuse way, and he began to worry that she was dead or disassembled, her spirit torn into a thousand parts and scattered between the wind and the creatures in the snow.

But if she was dead, why had she bothered to save him? There could be no life for him, alone.

He clambered out of the snowbank onto firmer, icier footing. His feet held the surface easily. The wind still roared above him. He was in a shallow bowl, like a pool that had been carved by a waterfall before winter came to this land. Snow flurries showed him the cleft where the wind raced in, before striking the cliff of ice. That was the direction he would go.

L.A. FLOW—TRENDSETTERS
"A Glimpse of the Other Side"

*". . . I was moving rapidly through a dark
tunnel toward a brilliant white light. I felt
no fear, no concern at all. I was happy.
I knew I was dead, but that wasn't a
problem. I was on my way to God. . . ."*

5

Arrested on
the Way to God

"How do you feel?"

"How do I feel?" Katie echoed Gregory's question, her mind playing over possible answers as she guided the Audi down the dark highway. Tom had been on ice almost six months, and the media bluster had long since died away. Her life had taken on a regular beat, and she didn't dwell too much on the past.

"I feel all right. I feel like the worst is behind me." Her hands rested easily on the steering wheel as the car sped past an almond orchard, spring blossoms burning like white fire in the headlights. "I can feel Tom out there. He's not absolutely gone. That helps, you know. It helps a lot." She glanced at Gregory. In the dim green light from the dash his face seemed a collage of shadows. Strange, how she could admit things to him that she could never have admitted to anyone else—not even Tom. She teased him about it sometimes: *Father Gregory ...*

"You know, sometimes I think he can feel *me*. That he's trying to get back to me." She'd been an avid materialist for so long that this confession drew a blush to her cheeks. She laughed to cover her embarrassment. "Quick, save me! I'm becoming a spiritualist!"

She caught a flash of white teeth in the dark and knew that he was grinning. She smiled herself, quietly happy in his company. Gregory was a kid, just twenty-three, yet she felt more comfortable with him than with friends she'd known all her life. In the months since Tom's death she'd come to depend on him like a brother. Like a brother . . .

Did other women treat him this way? She hoped not, but she suspected it was so. Some men had a knack for putting women so at ease that the women would confess anything to them, confide anything. Father Gregory. It was cruel to tease him that way, yet the tag seemed to fit. His face was too rough to be handsome, his nose too large and harsh, his dark eyes too narrow. But his masculinity was never in doubt and Katie admired him—just as she might admire a priest, or a hypothetical brother—someone whose sexuality had nothing to do with her. "Thanks for coming tonight," she said.

"Hey, I'm honored."

She snorted. "Oh, I'm sure Roxanne will shake you free of that misconception in the first three seconds. She didn't invite you over because she likes you—"

"I know, I know. She intends to have *me* for dinner. I'm honored that she considers me important enough in your life that she needs to barbecue me."

Katie laughed again.

They left the orchards behind and entered wooded foothills. Shortly, they turned off on a side road, then Katie slowed until she found the start of a long, winding driveway overhung with trees. "This is it." Roxanne's house was set in a clearing at the end of the drive, surrounded by a carefully tended lawn and garden. It was a large two-story structure with a huge deck in front and amber lights glowing by the door. Katie parked on the lawn, at the start of a flagstone path lit with footlights.

"Forest rangers earn this much money?" Gregory asked as they stepped out of the car.

"Roxanne's an only child with a large inheritance. Kind of like me."

"Ah."

"I can't remember a time when I didn't know Roxanne. We were always together as kids—except when we weren't speaking." She chuckled softly. "This scene over Tom's suspension isn't our first falling-out, you know. Guess we've gotten in the habit of forgiving." She gazed thoughtfully at the house. "Roxanne's a real unusual person. Love her or hate her, she'll never bore you."

"And she lives here alone?"

Katie shrugged. "Oh, she's had live-in company from time to time, but last I heard she was going solo." She looked up at the house. Soft yellow light glowed through the curtains and blinds in the front room. "She and Tom did a lot of climbing together. His death really hit her hard."

"And the suspension."

"Yeah. We hardly talked at the funeral and not at all since . . . until she called this week. But she's been talking to someone, because she knew all about you. She was very interested in you."

A door opened on the deck. Three black Dobermans charged out, barking a fearsome warning. Gregory started. But Katie walked around to the front of the car, clapping her hands together. "Cass! Julie! Ember!" The dogs surrounded her, still barking and growling, but their tone had gentled. "Girls, this is Gregory. He's going to visit tonight."

Gregory stood stiffly as the dogs sniffed him, their suspicion a soft growl in their throats. One of them nipped his hand. "Get away from me!" he snapped, flinging his arm out over their heads. They bounced back a few feet, then stood their ground, staring at him with unfriendly eyes.

"They just don't like some people," Roxanne called. She stood on the deck, leaning on the railing, dressed in tight-fitting blue climbing pants and a knit tank top that showed off her slender, muscular body. She'd traded her brown curls for a short boy's cut. Katie wondered what she'd been doing with herself the past six months. When Roxanne had called a few days ago she'd said very little, just a hello, how are you and hey it's been a long time, why don't you come to dinner? Oh, and bring your friend Gregory along. . . .

"Better call off the dogs, Roxanne," Katie said. "Or your reputation as a hostess is going to suffer."

She turned her palms up helplessly. "Hey, is it my fault they can smell his occupation?"

"Medical student?" Katie asked acidly.

"Undertaker."

Gregory edged gingerly past the dogs. "Yeah, I can see it's going to be a fun evening," he muttered. He followed Katie up the garden path.

Roxanne met them at the top of the stairs. She took Katie in a great bear hug, her skin smelling of baby oil and a subtle perfume.

Katie pulled back in surprise. "You've done something." She stared at Roxanne's face. The early pouches and lines of pending middle age that had been barely visible around Roxanne's mouth six months ago were gone. Gingerly, she touched Roxanne's cheek. "You look beautiful. Did it hurt?"

"Some. Worth it, though." She slipped her strong arm around Katie's shoulders and kissed her on the cheek. "I'm back in balance."

Her skin was hot, and to Katie's surprise, she felt her own body react with a roseate glow that she hadn't felt in—

She shifted uncomfortably, glancing over her shoulder at Gregory. "Roxanne Scott," she said in belated introductions. "This is Gregory Hunt."

Roxanne glanced back at him, her teeth flashing in a mocking smile. "So I gathered." She didn't offer her hand. Instead her gaze fixed on the Mars pin on Gregory's lapel. "Mars, huh? Tom was into that—though I doubt you two had anything else in common . . . except maybe Katie?" She cast an inquiring eye.

Katie extricated herself from Roxanne's arm and scowled. "At least the mission to Mars has finally been approved."

Roxanne chuckled at that. "You figure the world will

hold together long enough to let it happen? From the headlines, it sounds like Mother Earth is going to hell."

"I've never been the pessimist you are."

"So true," Roxanne admitted. She rubbed her hands together like a spider spinning silk. "Won't you come inside? I've made some changes. I think you're going to like it."

"Brace yourself," Katie warned Gregory. "Roxanne's always had unusual taste."

"Somehow that doesn't surprise me."

The door opened onto a foyer with a hardwood floor and shoe racks on either side. Murals done in classical Japanese style had been painted on both walls. One depicted an *oni*, a blue man-monster with a build like a stocky wrestler. He had horns on his head, a lecherous grin, and three evil eyes, all focused on a cowering maiden. The other mural showed the emaciated ghost of a fallen warrior haunting his disloyal wife. This much Katie had seen before. She explained the murals to Gregory while they removed their shoes.

"Kind of grim," Gregory said. He set his shoes on the rack. "I think I'd prefer mountains or flowers."

"Oh come on," Roxanne said. "You're not afraid of death, are you?" But before he could answer, she turned and stalked off into the living room.

He glanced at Katie, one eyebrow raised. She gave him a little smile of encouragement, then together they followed Roxanne. But they'd taken only one step into the great room when Katie stopped in astonishment. "Good God, Roxanne."

Most of the room was as she remembered it: two stories high, with a stairway on the left wall leading up to the bedrooms, and a wide passage on the right side that led to the dining room and kitchen. There was the danish sofa in front of the wall-sized window, now curtained against the night. The persian rugs laid out across the white padded wall-to-wall carpet. The climbing ropes neatly coiled and hung like multicolored sculptures—purple, red, blue, gold—against the honey-colored wood of the left wall. Life-sized photos of climbers on the right. The granite hearth and fireplace, a stack of kindling needing only a match to make a friendly fire.

But the wood paneling that had covered the two-story-high wall around the fireplace had been replaced with ugly squares of artificial rock, fitted with modular handholds. The result was a climbing wall, like the ones some fitness clubs in the city offered their clients. But it wasn't the wall that had drawn the exclamation from Katie.

The artificial stone ended three feet below the peak of the ceiling. In the triangular space between rock and roof, Roxanne had fitted a portrait of Tom. The poster was three feet high at the center and almost nine feet long. It had been printed from a photograph. It showed Tom's face and bare shoulders, his muscular arms stretched out to either side. He seemed to be leaning on a wall or perhaps the back of a sofa and he appeared to be looking down on everything that went on in the room. The photo was black-and-white.

Katie stared at the picture. It captured perfectly Tom's wide dark eyes, so unusual in Japanese families that they'd joked about a smear of Dutch trader in his ancestry. And there too, the half-smile that would sometimes grace his lips when he looked at her. What was Roxanne doing with a picture like this? She turned away, fighting to still the anger that was slowly building in her throat. Her gaze fixed on Roxanne. "Was he your lover?" she croaked.

Roxanne chuckled. "Never. Never. As hard as I tried."

Katie glared at her, wanting to cut Roxanne, to hurt her, for placing this doubt in her mind. But Roxanne seemed oblivious to her. She sat on the persian carpet in front of the fireplace, pulling on climbing boots. "Then why?" Katie asked. She could feel Gregory move up beside her. He touched her arm in a gesture of support.

Roxanne looked at them, her brown eyes sparkling with satisfaction. "*Why* is a question I don't handle very well."

"Cut the crap," Katie snapped.

Roxanne sat bolt upright. Anger flooded her eyes. "All right. You see those gentlemen over there?" She pointed to the three head-to-toe life-sized photos of climbers mounted on the far wall. "Tom almost joined that gallery. Each one of those gentlemen was a friend of mine, and each one is dead. Frank there, on the left, bought it on the

San Diego freeway, when a drunk slammed into his motorcycle. Cary pulled an OD. And Richard fell."

Katie had seen the portraits before, but she'd just assumed they were decor. Now she studied them, puzzled,
still angry, wondering who the hell Roxanne Scott really
was. She turned on her suddenly. "So you collect pictures
of dead men? You invited me here to tell me that?"

"No. I invited you here to climb." She launched a pair
of boots at Katie's chest. Katie's hands flew up, catching
them out of reflex. They were extremely light, with low-
cut blue leather uppers and a brown sole. Brand-new. And
just her size. "I'm not dressed to climb."

"So go in my room and grab some clothes. Come on,
Katie. You're not going to get pissed at me and leave first
thing after driving all the way out here, are you? And I bet
your squeeze is hungry. He'll be disappointed if you don't
let me feed him."

"Gregory's not my squeeze," Katie muttered. She
looked up, to exchange a glance with him.

He appeared wary and uncomfortable. She didn't blame
him. He hadn't asked to be caught up in her nasty personal affairs. "Whatever you want to do," he said softly.

She didn't know what she wanted.

Her gaze shifted to the climbing wall, and Tom's portrait overhead. Then she asked Roxanne the question
foremost in her mind. "Why's Tom different?"

"He's the only one I never laid." Roxanne let that settle
out in the air for a moment, and then she started laughing.
She rocked back and forth on her butt, laughing too hard.
A phony laugh, loud and harsh and suddenly extinguished.
Her gaze met Katie's. There was no humor in her eyes.
Only a cool glint of pain. "Let's climb," she said. "And
touch my captive angel."

Alone in Roxanne's room, changing into climbing pants
and T-shirt, Katie's anger slowly dissolves like the walls of
a fortress washing away under a heavy acid rain. She's left
feeling isolated/emotionally detached/fated—like a patient
being prepped for a necessary surgery. All lies in readiness.
Katie must only dress for the operation and present her-

self. Already she can feel Roxanne's fingers inside her mind.

She knows that Roxanne is set to dissect her, and she tells herself to go home, that she doesn't have to go through with this. Then she pretends not to hear. Tonight Roxanne has become a magnet, a beacon that burns in her mind like a flare against an ocean of night. It's almost as if Katie can see her through the walls of the house, sprawled on the sofa in the living room, engaging Gregory (a lesser light) in baited conversation. Roxanne is half-reclined, one smoothly muscled arm resting on the back of the sofa. Katie can visualize the subtle terrain of that arm with startling clarity.

Downstairs:

There are no ropes. Katie makes mention of this fact as she studies the wall, but Roxanne's not concerned. "It's easy," she says. "And not even two stories high."

Just high enough to hurt.

Gregory watches from the couch. There are four different approaches. Katie selects one near the chimney, because it seems easiest. Roxanne nods in approval, standing by as Katie reaches for the first handhold, just slightly over her head. She finds a dimple in the rock that will hold her toe and she pulls herself up far enough to gain another handhold. She feels awkward. Her chest is pressed against the rock, and she can't see her feet. Roxanne's fingers brush the inside of her thigh and she flinches. "What's a matter?" Roxanne whispers. She takes Katie's thigh in both hands and guides it away from the rock. "You're too close to the wall. Sit back. That's right. *Find* your balance. Let your legs carry the weight. Don't fight the rock."

"Right. What's wrong with me tonight?"

"Nothing I can't fix."

Katie frowns. She wants to open up the distance between herself and Roxanne, so she settles her stray foot and looks up for the next hold. She climbs slowly and deliberately, past one square of artificial rock and then the next. Gradually, her body warms to the activity. She begins to feel graceful, and confident, though she keeps one eye on the carpet below in case she has to come off the wall.

Roxanne is climbing on another approach, only a few feet away. Katie's startled at this realization. She tries to concentrate on the job at hand, but her mind won't focus. Her eyes keep glancing at Roxanne.

Climb. Fingertips explore the next hold, search out the curves and dimples of the cement sculpture that pretends to be wind-worn rock. She listens to Roxanne's boots shifting upon the wall. Hears her soft breathing only a few feet away.

It doesn't take strength so much as balance. And a focused mind.

Her fingers stiffen. She pulls herself higher. It's time to find a new toehold.

"You climb gracefully," Roxanne says, her new face flush with light exertion and very beautiful. "Better than me."

"No." Katie shakes her head emphatically. She knows who she is. On the rocks, Roxanne's always her superior.

"You *could* have been better than me," Roxanne whispers. "If you had any confidence in life beyond the technosphere."

Katie's boot turns up a hold, but it's a stretch. She's not well-balanced and is reluctant to release her hand. Fear starts building in her chest, a cold, spiraling wave rolling over and over upon itself. She draws a deep breath; tries to blow the fear away. She can smell Roxanne's perfume. There's no discernible scent to her sweat, though it shines upon her arms and face and chest like oil. "Hot up here," she says. She wonders at the logic of houses with high ceilings. How in the hell are they supposed to be heated?

"Relax," Roxanne urges. "It's a stretch, but you can do it. Focus your mind on the *now*."

So easy to say, Katie thinks, imagining Roxanne's body suspended on a rope against a real cliff. "You're a bit distracting to me tonight," she mutters, hoping Roxanne won't hear.

" 'S okay. I don't mind."

"Climbing." She eases her fingers off the hold. Looking up, she sees a crevice in the artificial rock. She reaches for that, her hand steady, though she's shaking inside as she feels the weight taken up on her awkwardly set legs. But it *is* okay. It's a good hold . . . so long as the rock doesn't snap under her fingers. She knows that things happen that way sometimes. The rock is rotten but doesn't look it. A little pressure, a little more, and—

She pulls herself higher, grinning in triumph as her boot leaves the lowest hold.

"You're flying, kid," Roxanne assures her.

Her grin widens, because Roxanne's right. She's found a way around her fear. She climbs because she's afraid of falling. But being afraid, each step becomes an exhilarating triumph of will, a celebration. *"I'm alive!"*

Roxanne purrs deep in her throat, a sweet sound that makes the skin on Katie's back tingle. "You're coming out of limbo, you know?"

Katie presses her temple against the rock as she turns to look at Roxanne. "What's that mean?"

"You know: *limbo.* A state between. To be part of the world, and yet not take part in it. To be not dead, but also not alive. The spirit a captive, the body . . . dissatisfied."

Katie doesn't like this talk. It makes her too aware of a dark curtain that's been hanging across her mind for months now, hiding herself from herself.

Her toe slips. She drops against the wall. Her chest slams into the rock. Suddenly, the only fact that seems relevant is the distance that separates her from the floor. Her heart hammers inside her chest. She hears Gregory's exclamation but is unable to respond to it. Her fingers are growing slick with sweat.

" 'S all right," Roxanne says, her voice soft and confident, soothing, like a cool breeze across Katie's cheeks. "Your hands are still in balance. Your body loves the rock. Search it. You don't need tech to find the way. It's all inside you. There. . . ."

Katie finds a purchase with the toe of her right boot. She hugs the rock in relief, her thigh pressing against it like an iron band. Her arms are starting to shake from fatigue.

"Balance," Roxanne reminds her. "Not strength."

Katie eases away from the wall, thinking *I wanna fuck somebody.* She finds a hold for her other boot. *I wanna fuck somebody.* There. It's out in the open. *I wanna fuck.* Any

warm, hard body will do. She almost laughs at herself, she's
so desperately horny. How could Roxanne know it would
go this way?

She reaches up with an exploring hand, but there is no
more wall. Only a smooth gloss of poster paper under her
fingertips. A flush of warmth envelopes her. She leans
back in surprise and looks, eager to meet Tom eye to eye.
This is what she was climbing for.

But it's not as she expected. The portrait's too large.
She's right in front of Tom's face, and she can't take it all
in at once. Her eyes pan back and forth. She leans farther
out from the wall.

"Easy," Roxanne says. "He don't bite."

He's chewed out a place in my soul, well enough. And she's
suddenly angry. The prize is not as promised. Roxanne's
cheated her. She wants a rope, so she can drop down like
a spider and be done with this.

Later, alone in Roxanne's bedroom, where she'd come
to change back into her own clothes, Katie sat down on
the edge of the bed and bowed her head, resting her forehead against her hands. She hadn't done drugs since she
was a kid, yet she felt like she'd just come down from a
bad high. A deliberately engineered rotten revelatory experience. She felt like the synapses in her mind had been
transformed into cold metal, clacking efficiently as she explored openly now the hungerings in her body that had
nothing to do with food. She thought of Tom and the gentle touch of his rough, calloused hands between her legs.
She shivered. Then she stood up, stomping her foot in a
sudden bout of rage. *Damn Tom! Damn Roxanne! And damn
life!*

She pulled off Roxanne's T-shirt and threw it in a corner
of the room, then she stripped off the climbing pants. She
stood in panties and bra, her hands coiled into fists. Her
heart pounding under the influence of adrenaline. It's not
so bad, it's not so bad, she told herself. A lot of people are
far worse off than you. But she could draw precious little
comfort from other people's misery. She wanted to hit
something, something safe, something that could take her
anger and remain unharmed. Turning, she caught sight of

Roxanne standing in the doorway, leaning against the doorjamb, her eyes doe-soft with sympathy.

Roxanne.

Katie breathed a soft sigh of disappointment. She'd half hoped it would be Gregory. Father Gregory, come to hear her confession/confusion and to give her the absolution she'd never sought from him before. Roxanne came into the room. Her gaze was wired to Katie's. Her bare feet glided across the plush white carpet. She didn't look down. If there'd been anything on the floor she would have tripped over it and fallen. She touched Katie's cheek with the back of her hand. Then she leaned forward and kissed Katie on the lips, an interlocking kiss so Katie could taste her mouth and feel the warm probing of her tongue. Katie didn't resist. Indeed, she openly participated, like an angry adolescent out to prove she could not be shocked, or even touched in any meaningful way.

Roxanne seemed to measure the violence of her mood. She pulled back, her gaze thoughtful. "Dinner's ready," she said.

Katie almost spit in her face. Then Roxanne was gone, as silently as she'd come. Katie was alone. She turned to look for her clothes, her hands shaking in rage. How dare Roxanne attack her peace like this! What was she doing? What did she hope to accomplish?

Katie dressed, then went into the bathroom to splash water on her face, waiting a few minutes for her rosy cheeks to cool before she went downstairs.

There was a fire in the fireplace now, and set in front of it, a low black lacquer Japanese table set with three pairs of honey-brown chopsticks resting on tiny blue ceramic koi. Gregory leaned against the hearth, sipping a near beer from the bottle. He looked bored and unhappy. Katie wondered again why Roxanne had invited him, what his role was to be this evening. He smiled in relief as she came down the stairs. "Thought you'd abandoned me."

"I considered shinnying down from the bedroom window, but I've had enough wall work for one night."

He said nothing, but his offer reached her clearly just the same. *If you want to leave now, we can.* She shook her

head slightly. Perhaps it was self-punishment, but she
wanted to see what else Roxanne had planned.

"We're to be seated on the floor," Gregory said. "You
there, me here." He pointed to opposite sides of the table.
Roxanne would be sitting between them, facing the fire.
"She doesn't want anybody in the kitchen, so don't bother
offering to help."

"I never do," Katie said.

"Never do what?" Roxanne asked as she swept into the
room, bearing a large silver platter.

Katie took one look at the contents, and wrinkled her
nose in disgust. A sudden sadistic impulse took her. "I
never do eat those things. Roxanne, you can't be serious."
The platter held oysters set in ice, garnished with lemon
wedges and salsa. "You won't eat beef, but you eat that
stuff? *Filter feeders?* They're probably loaded with toxins or
heavy metals. Bet you don't even know where they were
harvested."

She glanced at Gregory. He had a wide grin on his face.
Roxanne looked at him in irritation, then her gaze shifted
to Katie. "They're from an aquaculture farm outside San
Diego. Thirty-two dollars a pound and real clean. Come
on. I know you and Tom used to eat these things when
you were in college." Katie stiffened against the expected
blow. "What was it you used to tell me? That oysters enhanced one's ... *vitality?*"

"So do rest and exercise," Katie snapped. But she
picked one up and slurped it down.

After the oysters, there were stir-fried noodles and vegetables, mandarin pancakes and steamed yams, and a final
course of fresh fruit and frozen yogurt. The food was perfect, and by the time they were done, Katie's anger had
ebbed. She lay back on the carpet, eyes closed, enjoying
the heat of the fire against her skin. She listened to the
liquid splash of coffee as Roxanne poured three cups, and
then the too-casual tone of Roxanne's voice: "You've participated in a lot of cryonic suspensions, haven't you,
Gregory?"

Katie's eyes opened. She felt a flash of tension, sus-
pecting the next act had begun. By the tone of his voice,

Gregory seemed to sense it too. "Only five," he answered warily.

Roxanne set the coffeepot on the table. "Were you standing by waiting for them to die? Like with Tom?"

Katie sat up. She watched Gregory blow thoughtfully on his coffee. After a moment, he answered: "Sometimes."

"But you don't get called out until people are on the edge," Katie said.

"Sure."

Roxanne nodded. "Do they always die?"

Gregory shrugged. "Not always."

"So you've seen people recover from near death."

A cold smile of understanding flickered unexpectedly across his lips. "You're looking for near-death testimonials," he accused. "Well, forget it. The white light's a hallucination of the dying brain, nothing more."

Roxanne looked amused. "And an answer like that's just denial." She turned her measuring gaze on Katie. "The white light is real."

Katie felt fear climb her spine. "You don't know that."

"I do." Roxanne tapped a nail against her coffee cup. "I was in a coma once for four days and I'm telling you, there *is* another side."

"Oh, that convinces me," Gregory said. "Not a chance that you were just getting high on oxygen-starved brain tissue, right?"

Roxanne ignored him. "I *know* what's waiting for me. What's waiting for Tom . . . if you'd only let him go."

"Rot?" Gregory suggested. "Worms? Oblivion?"

Roxanne turned on him. "You blind son of a bitch! We're part of nature. Why shouldn't our bodies return to the earth? But our souls move on. Tom's soul *needs* to move on."

"Oh Roxanne shut up!" Katie cried. "You don't know anything about it. You don't know anything."

Roxanne leaned over the table, her gaze hard. "I'm just warning you. If you ever do manage to revive Tom's body, you may find there's nobody there. He may take that moment of freedom to continue his spiritual journey—" Gregory made a noise of disgust, but Roxanne ignored him. "He may be gone."

The fire still flickered: evanescent orange fins, in existence for a moment, then gone. Katie suddenly realized that Roxanne had left the room. She looked at Gregory. *Father Gregory.* Canyons of doubt splayed open in her mind.

"Know what?" she whispered. "Tom told me once that when he was real little, like four or five, he became aware of death. He started asking questions about it, all kinds of questions, about graveyards, and souls and gods and bodies. And he didn't like the answers. They made him angry. And he swore he would never die. And that his mother and father and brother and sister would never die. And then his father was killed in a car crash. And after that he knew someday it would happen to him too; death would come and take him. And he was terrified. Until one day his sister, Ilene, explained to him that death meant going back to the earth, giving your body back to the earth from which it came. And after that he wasn't afraid anymore, because the earth was his mother." Her gaze fell, to the fading water rings on the table. "But Roxanne's right. We haven't let him go back to the earth. And we never will."

Wedged Time—
Alternate Landscapes

A ceiling of clouds heavy with snow rolled ponderously past the peaks that girded the cleft, while in the pass itself, strands of fog ran like damned souls being carried to hell on the tearing fingers of the wind.

It was late in the day and the light was fading as he climbed the steep approach. His sheathed fingers gripped the frozen surface with remarkable strength; his great padded feet never slipped. He climbed eagerly.

Was she watching him? He wondered. Was she waiting for him somewhere close by? He could sense something . . . in the air, in the blowing snow. Some hint of a presence. Was it her? *My Familiar.* He reached out, pulling himself up through the last step until he could actually look out into the cleft.

The wind almost slapped him off the ice face. He ducked quickly. In his brief glimpse he'd seen a small saddle of curved, wind-sculpted ice. If he tried to stand on it, he'd surely be blown down. So he decided to crawl.

Keeping his head low this time, he pressed his fingers against the ice, and slid onto the cleft, edging across on his belly until he could peer down the other side.

His eyes registered a scene. His brain accepted their input, perused it, and rejected it as utterly absurd. But the eyes were insistent. They forced the brain to reconsider, and suddenly what had appeared to be a white textured simulation of infinity was revealed as a vista of snow-covered mountainous slopes that plunged for miles below him, white on white on white, unrelieved even by a protruding rock face until finally, at a distance that seemed impossibly far, the snowy slope disappeared into a forbidding gray wall of fog that reached upward to infinity like a veil raised to hide the very end of time itself.

A crushing darkness engulfed his heart as he looked out upon the vastness below him. There was no sign of her, no sense of her in all that great space. He'd come the wrong way.

A hoarse sob sawed its way through his throat.

"Bloody awful winter wonderland, isn't it?" someone shouted in his ear, in a coarse voice barely audible over the wind.

Every muscle in his body seized up in surprise. He almost sent himself skittering over the edge, but at the last moment he threw his hands out, fingers spread and pressing hard against the ice to arrest his motion.

The blue-furred hand of a giant reached out to clasp his arm and steady him. "Whoa! I know we've changed, but we're not quite sleds, now are we?" the creature shouted, its breath cinder-hot against the membrane sealing his ear. He stared at the fingers that held his arm. They were twice the length and girth of his own, and covered with smooth, short fur, sky-blue in color. He counted only two fingers and a thumb, but that was enough to wrap his arm like a steel band. His gaze followed the thick, stubby, densely furred arm up to a monstrous face that grinned at him with a mouth large enough to eat an infant's head whole. The teeth inside were huge, sharp-edged chisels, gleaming white and widely spaced. The tongue winked red. The lips were black as a dog's. The nose was fat and bulbous, the eyes were widely set, and the creature had two bony horns protruding from the top of its head. It sported a long mane of thick black ringlets that stood out on the wind like a headdress of writhing snakes, and its earlobes had been cut and stretched into huge, grotesque loops by the weight of dozens of gold rings that had somehow been threaded by the living tissue.

It wasn't a giant, he realized. It was really no taller than he was, but so powerfully built that its limbs seemed too big even for its stocky frame.

And it was female. He realized this with a start of surprise. Though it wore a ragged gray loincloth made of some kind of dried skin, and a brown mantelet around its shoulders, it had made no attempt to hide its shapely, blue-furred breasts. On the contrary, it seemed to thrust its chest out proudly, as if to be sure he didn't miss this feature. It was standing in a trench dug into the snow on one side of the cleft, and despite the harsh wind, he could smell a musty scent rising from its body that stirred in him feelings he at once reviled.

But he couldn't get the scent out of him. It touched some addled memory, and at once he recognized the thing as a demon oni. Somewhere, long ago, he must have heard tales of such creatures, or perhaps he'd encountered them. Oni. Evil things that preyed on the real people of the world. He searched his mind for details, but there were no details. With a start he realized there was nothing. His past was as blank as the great fog bank beyond the mountain. His memories were as slippery as ice. Already, he could recall in only the vaguest way his fall, the assault of the cold, his transformation. What came before that he didn't know. And he fretted that even these memories would be gone soon. And the Familiar? Would she leave him too? He bit his lip in slow anguish. It would almost be a mercy if the abandoned shadow inside him could be forgotten.

The demon oni leaned closer to him, her red tongue darting out to touch her black lips. "Why'd you come up here?" she asked. "What are you looking for?"

"My soul."

The oni tilted her head back and let go an ugly peal of laughter. "She dumped you, huh?" Her hand squeezed his arm even harder, causing him to wince in pain. "Wicked of her to leave you so far from anywhere. But I'm here now. And you're a handsome one, aren't you?" Her eyes were a bronzy color. He felt acutely uncomfortable under their intent stare. "Hungry?" she asked. He realized that he was. "Want to come in out of the cold?" Suddenly he felt the chill, as if the temperature had plummeted in anticipation of the approaching night. "It'll soon be all blackness out here, but in the warrens you'll find bright fire, fresh meat, warm company. Come on." She tugged at his arm and he felt his smooth gray belly slide across the ice.

He quickly stabbed at the ice with his fingers to try to hold himself back. "Let go of me."

"Oh, I can't do that. All of us here are in it together." She reached for him with her other hand. He tried to twist away, but he was almost helpless on the ice. Catching him under the armpits, she pulled him toward her with all the effort of a mother lifting a baby. He tried to get his legs under him, to scramble away from that lolling mouth, but he slipped on the ice. She pulled him against her breast, crushing his face into her harsh blue fur. Her odor filled his nostrils and shot through his bloodstream like a volatile drug, straight to his brain, igniting in him a sudden, horrible pang of hunger that was at once a desire for sex, for food, a gut-wrenching, grasping need for power. "We're in it together," the oni crooned, as one hand groped at his genitals. "In it for a long, long time."

In a clumsy, horricomic move she backstepped and toppled them both into the snow. He was on top of her, and suddenly he was humping her, his penis risen from its protective sheath, ramrod-hard as it drove into her body. She gripped it with tiny muscles that he'd never felt before, as if her vagina were filled with minute, pressing hands. She cackled in pleasure under him, her red tongue vibrant, her breath sickly sweet. *"No!"* he screamed, horrified at such contact, such collusion with a monster. He reared back. Slammed his fists against her face. Her smile vanished. Her teeth came together, lips rolled back like the snarl of a predator. She caught his hands in an iron grip. And all the while his buttocks were moving up and down, up and down, as if they obeyed her will, not his. And when he came he thought he would never stop, that his body would melt and spurt into hers along with the semen he ejected with a scream of utter agony.

L.A. FLOW—LIFESTYLES
"Multiple-Choice Quiz"

Question 1: What is a dream?

a. *the mind at play*
b. *a mental exercise aimed at honing the brain's efficiency in processing sensory information*
c. *the world's oldest form of virtual reality*
d. *all of the above*

6

What Is a Dream?

Katie awoke, shaking with fear, her heart hammering in helpless panic. *"Oh, Tom,"* she moaned. She reached out to the nightstand and switched on a soft light, then lay back against her pillow, staring around at the familiar room. *It's only a dream*, she told herself. Only a dream.

A dream that had occurred again and again since that dinner with Roxanne almost a year and a half ago. Something had happened that night. Her confidence had been shaken, or her doubt had been exposed. And the result was the dream.

The dream was always different, yet always the same. Sometimes there were images to accompany the terrible emotions. Sometimes, like tonight, just sensation, an impression of ice and cold and a horrible feeling of emptiness inside her, as if her body had been forcefully aborted of a child.

But the child was still alive. She could hear him in the frozen wilderness, calling to her for help. But try as she might, she could never rescue him, could never even find his trail.

"Oh, Tom," she whispered again. She closed her eyes, and deliberately tried to slow her breathing, calm her heart, telling herself silently, over and over again, that Tom had no consciousness, no brain activity, that he was not suffering. But his last moments in the ICU had scarred her. To see him come to life like that . . .

What had he been thinking? What had gone on inside his head during those moments after circulation had been restored, before Gregory injected the anesthetic? She'd never experienced telepathy; didn't believe in it. Yet she knew Tom very well. He'd always had vivid dreams and he was proud of them. He'd bragged that he lived a second life at night, "wedged time," he called it, because he could wedge days of adventure into a few hours of sleep. Gregory had assured her that Tom couldn't possibly have been dreaming during the time he'd come alive, that dreaming was part of a normal sleep pattern and didn't occur during true unconsciousness. But she wondered. Many times comatose patients had awakened to report magnificent and enlightening visions.

No one really knew how the brain worked.

"But he's not dreaming now," she muttered. There could be no metabolic or biochemical activity at $-196°$ C. His brain couldn't be functioning anymore. Yet in her own dream, she could still hear him calling her.

She sighed. Experience had taught her there was no point in trying to go back to sleep after the dream. She checked her clock. Five-thirty. Throwing back the covers, she stood up and pulled on her sweatpants. This house was cool in late winter.

Her mother was in the kitchen making coffee, already dressed for her morning walk. The dogs huddled at the door, worried that they might be left behind, although they never had been. "You're up early," Belle said.

"Ummm." She sat down at the kitchen table, and gratefully accepted a cup of coffee. "I had another dream about Tom."

"Ah."

She started to sip at the coffee, but it was too hot. "Maybe we shouldn't have sold the old house," she said suddenly.

Belle looked at her in surprise. "What? Sweetheart, it's a bit late to think about that now."

"I know. And I don't really mean it." She sipped the searing coffee, so she wouldn't have to say more. But her gaze roamed unhappily around the kitchen. It was large and country-rustic, with wood everywhere and great window-walls looking out over an empty pasture. She loved this house.

But it wasn't Tom's house.

Katie had sold the old place last year. She'd found a new home outside of town, a "gentleman's farm," with several acres of land. There was an orchard, and a pasture because she thought that someday she might like to have horses. The pasture was slowly changing into forest. The girls caught a bus to their school in town. Katie worked the stock market via computer from an office off the kitchen. Half her waking life seemed to be spent on the telephone. "I keep playing this scene in my head," she said.

With a sigh, Belle pulled out a chair and sat down across the table from Katie. "Tell me about it."

"It's silly, but it really scares me." She stared into her slowly swirling coffee. "I see Tom coming home unexpectedly, producing a key to the old house out of a pocket, going into the house only to find it occupied by strangers."

"That's easy. You feel guilty about going on with your life. Maybe you feel guilty about Gregory."

"Gregory's my friend, Mom. He's not my lover."

"He loves you."

Katie flinched. She didn't want to face it, but she knew it was true. Her lips pressed together in a tight line, while her thoughts danced in constricted circles. Gregory? It was absurd. Gregory was a kid. But all right, sometimes she was tempted. Father Gregory? Huh. He didn't feel so untouchable anymore.

They sat quietly for a few minutes. Joy's cat came padding down the hall. Katie clucked at it, and it jumped up on the table. She stroked its back, listening to the coffee machine steam and fantasizing about Tom coming home. The phone rang. They both flinched at the unexpected noise: 5:43 by the microwave clock. Katie sprang out of her chair, catching the phone before it could ring again and wake the girls. "Hello?" she said, her heart hammering on the burst of adrenaline.

"Katie," Gregory answered. "Sorry to wake you, but I've been up all night and I needed to check in with you before I sleep."

"That's all right. I was already awake." She struggled to keep her voice steady. "Were you on a suspension?"

"No. I've been working the emergency room." She kept forgetting—he was now *Dr.* Gregory Hunt, M.D. "Have you caught the morning news?" he asked.

"At this hour?"

"It's always later in D.C. Katie, we've got legal problems. The cryonics industry, that is. Hell. The whole field of biotechnology is being threatened. Listen, Katie, I don't know the details. I just heard of it myself a few minutes ago when Maryann called me. The board's scheduled a meeting for ten o'clock this morning. I think you need to be there."

In a dead-flat voice hiding mounting misgivings, Katie asked, "Why?"

"So you really haven't heard." Of all things, he sounded relieved. "I told them there was no way you could be part of it. But you know Maryann. She worries."

"Gregory, what's going on?"

"I'm wandering, aren't I? Sorry, I've been up all night. It seems some Big Brothers working under the name Generational Challenge are trying to put the brakes on biotech—and one of the specific targets on their hit list is the cryonics industry."

"Oh?" She tried to treat the statement skeptically. She was used to hype from Gregory. Like Maryann, he too was a bit paranoid when it came to threats against the practice of cryonics. Katie was more concerned about why anybody would suspect her of working against the company. "Why's my name involved in this?"

"Well, uh—you're sure you haven't heard?"

"Gregory!"

"Look, Katie, there's no easy way to say this, but Senator Carson is the movement's political ringleader."

"*Ilene* . . . ?" She felt a sudden chill on the back of her

neck. Somewhere, far off, she thought she heard a faint
voice crying her name.

Katie hit the interstate with the rising sun at her left
hand. She clicked the radio on, scanning for news. Her
search turned up bursts of commercials, classic rock, raun-
chy radio yak ... then finally, the cultured, masculine
voice of a respected media icon. He'd been around as long
as Katie could remember and she recognized him instantly.

"—explore the senator's notion of generational rights,"
he was saying—and by the bent of his voice, Katie could
tell the idea impressed him. "Very simply, the concept that
each generation has the right to its time in the world—"

She reached down to turn up the volume, but touched
the wrong knob and the radio scanned over to the next
station. The Stones, still no satisfaction after all these
years. She swore and scanned back.

"—its roots in natural law. The last time natural law was
brought into national debate was in the context of the
abortion issue. If you'll recall, proponents of the theory
propose that because of our natures, some things are in-
herently immoral, like destroying a fetus or manipulating
genetic material ... or continuing a life span beyond its
natural range."

Her cellular phone rang. Katie picked it up as a station
wagon passed her in the left lane. Three blond-haired
children stared at her out the back window. None of them
had a seatbelt on. "Hello?"

"—look forward to a time when genetic engineering will
have conquered the aging process—"

It was one of her clients, a woman her own age, twice
divorced. She wanted to get Katie's opinion on a company
that owned a chain of upscale coffee shops. For years the
number of adults living in households without children
had been growing. Those same adults would presumably
have more time, and more money for luxuries like
gourmet coffee, right?

The voice on the radio continued:

"—Senator Carson has proposed a new series of regulations, akin to our present environmental regulations. They

demand that companies intending to market technological innovations be required to prepare in advance a sociological-impact statement, analogous to an environmental-impact statement, to determine whether or not the new development will be detrimental to society as a whole."

"Society?" Katie echoed softly into the phone. She flashed on a scene with a lot of lonely old fogies sipping java in a fancy shop. Saw herself in there among them. The new environment. A debit card for gourmet coffee; untraceable cash for biotechnology. A cold sweat broke out across her cheeks. She remembered the phone, and muttered a promise to research the company and call back with an answer by the following afternoon.

"—economic implications," the radio insisted. "Loss of American competitiveness in the global marketplace would seem a given. But the senator, in her far-sighted manner, has addressed this. Generational Challenge has sibling groups in democracies around the world. There are even rumors of alliances with fundamentalist countries—"

The sun flared in Katie's eyes. Past the glare she glimpsed the station wagon with the unrestrained children now stopped on the side of the interstate, a highway-patrol car behind it, lights flashing. Then Katie was past, staring stolidly at the traffic ahead. She could feel her palms slick with sweat. She reached down, to pop the radio back to scan. On the next station over, the Stones had been replaced by CCR. On the station after that it was the Police, and then the Beatles, for God's sake, ten thousand times "Revolution." Twelve stations over she finally found something new. A steely, formal sound that seemed to linger from song to song, with a lot of dopey kid-lyrics but some thoughtful stuff too. At least it was novel. She listened to it all the way into L.A.

Since Tom's death, Katie's social relationships had changed. Many of her old friends had become distant, obviously uncomfortable in her presence . . . as if widowhood were contagious.

Katie let them go. In her own mind, Tom's death stood out as a geological discontinuity—a boundary marking the end of one phase of her life—and much of what she'd been and done and dreamed had been left behind.

The old era belonged to Tom. The new era she named in honor of Father Gregory. Now she took a seat beside him, round a conference table at Forward Futures. The company's founding brass were all present (anyway, those who weren't yet on ice), and every current member of the board of directors. They treated her politely, but in their surreptitious glances she could read their doubt, the unspoken sentiment that *she* had brought this catastrophe down upon them.

Well, maybe she had.

The current CEO was a fellow named Harrison Simms, a short, balding, bespectacled gent whose every move reflected the crisp efficiency of a skilled bureaucrat. He sat at the head of the table, carrying on a low-voiced debate with blond-haired, plain-faced, and perennially worried Maryann.

On his other side sat Dr. Morales, the surgeon who'd worked on Tom. Dr. Morales was a kindly man, with a deeply tanned face and receding hair that was going to gray.

Katie could put names to most of the others around the table, but they were more acquaintances than friends. Finally, her wandering gaze settled on Gregory. He was watching her, his eyes cold, his mouth set in an angry line. "Have you caught any news?" he asked.

She looked away guiltily. "Just part of an analysis."

"They're coming after us."

She forced a lame smile. "Hey, at least they're taking us seriously. You know most people view us as harmless crackpots—but not Generational Challenge."

Gregory stared, as if unsure that it was a joke. He must have decided to go along, though, because a thin smile broke through his reserve. "Okay," he agreed. "I guess that's a kind of progress."

At the head of the table, Simms spoke in a soft yet commanding voice: "Well, I guess we've all heard the news by now." There was a brief titter from around the table. "You know, I've been a fan of Senator Carson's ever since she entered national politics. She's always struck me as hardheaded, practical, and honest. I don't think it's going too far to say that she saved the country's health-care system during her first term in the Senate." His attention fixed on Katie. "But she's the enemy now."

Katie let go a breath of relief, glad that Simms was willing to speak candidly in front of her. "I think we've all known that for a while."

Harrison Simms laced his hands on the tabletop and nodded. "So can we assume family influence isn't going to count for much?"

Katie laughed softly, self-mockingly. "I think I've pulled all my influence ... in the wrong direction." She shook her head, wondering about possibilities untried. "It never occurred to me to keep Tom's suspension a secret. But maybe I should have. Maybe—"

"Forget it, Katie," Dr. Morales said. "It's not your fault. Generational Challenge is more than one person, and cryonics is a small part of their wider concerns. They're sniffing at every field dealing with life extension. But their focus is going to be a ban on bioengineering."

"And that's a technology we desperately need," Gregory said. "How are we going to fight this?"

"Play the publicity machine while our lawyers work on the case," Simms said. "And call in all the support we can get. But we've got to move carefully. If we can be painted as a godless, power-hungry elite, then we've lost."

Katie slipped out of the strategy session near noon, ostensibly to visit the loo, but she found herself drawn to the stairwell. She turned the knob of the heavy fire door, pulled hard to get it open, then stepped through onto the landing. The door closed behind her with a loud *snick* that echoed against the concrete walls. The air here was warmer, more moist than in the hallway. She walked down the stairs, her footsteps reverberant. She knew the door at the bottom would be locked. She didn't even try it. Instead, she sat down on the bottom step, thinking of Tom on ice, somewhere in the vault, two locked doors away.

So many radio stations played the same old music, years-old music, over and over again. Generational Challenge would be against things like that. Make way for the new.

The door at the top of the steps clunked open. After a

moment of hesitation it shut again, and footsteps descended behind her until Gregory crouched at her side. She could feel his gaze, though she wouldn't turn to meet it. "You're crying," he accused.

She rubbed quickly at her eyes. "I am not."

"Hey, don't let them scare you."

"I'm not scared!"

He slipped his arm around her shoulders. "But . . . ?"

She sighed. "Strategy sessions are fine, but there's one thing no one upstairs is discussing. What if Generational Challenge succeeds? What if *we* lose?"

"We won't," he said firmly.

"But if we do. Will they be able to reverse Tom's suspension?"

Gregory shrugged. "Who knows what they intend to do? But even if they leave the suspension patients alone, they'll never allow us to revive them, or even to do the research that would make that possible."

Katie stared straight ahead at the locked door. "Then I'll take him out of the country," she said softly. "We'll take all of them, if it comes to that."

She felt Gregory stiffen. "Assuming there's a place to go," he said. "Assuming they'll let you out. Remember, dead bodies have no rights. And I, for one, have no intention of being run out of my own country."

That was a sanctimonious answer. She pulled away from him, shrugging out of his embracing arm. She had to wonder if this was a game to him, a way to play the young visionary, and nothing more. "Principles might get to be a luxury, Gregory. I'll do what I need to do. I'll do whatever has to be done."

She stared at the locked door, thinking of classic rock tunes playing over and over again. She shuddered, wondering if old fogies really could change.

That evening, she walked into the house just as Ilene's Senate speech was being replayed on C-Span. Wordlessly, she dropped onto the sofa beside her mother.

"Generational Challenge is not against technological change," Senator Carson was explaining. "Technology will evolve; society will evolve, and we will all benefit. There

will come a day—not so far off—when we will heal the
earth and move out into space. There will come a day—
not so far off—when the people of the world will grow
closer to one another through globe-girdling virtual realities. There will come a day—not so far off—when the
knowledge of our species will be available to every individual through hypertext. But knowledge is not wisdom,
and there will also come a day—not so far off—when a
brilliant young genetic engineer will attempt to create
a child who is more than human. There will also come a
day—not so far off—when nanotechnology will allow the
rich and the powerful to erase from their bodies the bur-
dens of old age. And there may also come a day—not so
far off—when the present generation decides that it will
be the last. That there will be no more ordinary children
born to ordinary people. That those who exist in the present will continue to exist for all time, never yielding the
resources and wonders of this world to a new generation,
greedy geezers unto the end of the earth. When that day
comes, we will no longer be human. And I submit to you
today that there is something profoundly valuable to being
human. Our human-ness is worth preserving. That is the
creed of Generational Challenge. Let us move into space.
Let us heal the earth. But let us always remain human."

"How can she do this?" Katie muttered. "She loved
Tom. I know it."

"I don't think she's aiming at Tom," Belle said.

"But she'll hit him anyway. What does she think this is
going to do to Joy and Nikki?"

"She must feel this as a deep responsibility."

Katie nodded slowly. Her mother had a way of quickly
cutting to the heart of things. Despite their differences,
Katie had never thought of Ilene Carson as anything but a
dedicated, responsible woman. If she was taking this stand
now, knowing how it would hurt her own family, then she
must feel a sound motivation. And that frightened Katie.
What if Ilene was right? What if Roxanne was right?

And what if I am wrong?

She sat unmoving, staring at the TV, long after the news
was over.

WHAT IS PROGRESS?

1. *Traditional hunter-gatherers worked only twenty to twenty-five hours a week to feed and clothe themselves. A modern family of four will probably spend a hundred hours or more ... when they can find jobs.*

2. *In tribal societies everyone had a place and everyone was important. Today most people don't know where they belong, or why.*

3. *Traditional societies saw themselves as part of the web of life. In the modern world people rend at the web in their frantic efforts to fill their shallow hearts and insatiable hungers.*

THIS *IS PROGRESS.*

MORE, PLEASE.

7

The Modern World

Generational Challenge: It sounded like a game show, but overnight it became the most talked-about subject in the country. For the first few days of the media blitz, Katie kept hoping the whole thing would fizzle as people learned more about the issues. But gradually she began to understand the realities. Immortality was not going to be cheap—not any time soon, at least. People on the street knew that, and sentiment was running hard against life-extension technologies.

Harrison Simms called her on the morning of the third day, shortly after the girls had caught the bus to school. The CEO of Forward Futures sounded tired. And no wonder. Since Ilene's announcement he must have appeared on every talk show and news program in southern California—plus several satellite feeds to New York. "I need volunteers," he said. "Sal Greer's doing yet another show with a segment on cryonics. But he's tossed out the experts. Now he wants suspension members with relatives on ice."

Katie felt a weight suddenly settle in the pit of her

stomach. All the controversy that had accompanied Tom's
suspension seemed to be closing in on her again. "When?"

"Can you be in L.A. by noon? Katie, we really need you
on this."

Sal Greer's show wasn't just a local phenomenon. It was
seen across the U.S., by an audience numbering in the millions. A voyeuristic audience. They would want to know
how Katie felt; what she dreamed. That was human nature.

"Give me the address," she said softly. "I'll be there
early."

She called Nikki and Joy's school and arranged to pick up
the girls. When she got there, Nikki was standing outside
the principal's office, her always-serious face locked into a
scowl. Her brown hair was bound high on her head in a no-
nonsense ponytail, and she hugged a stack of books under
her arm. Joy waited beside her, her great dark eyes worried,
a little pout on her lovely face. At fourteen, Joy already had
a host of boyfriends. In a common sibling opposite reaction,
Nikki, two years younger, pretended not to want any, prefer-
ring books and study. Or maybe she wasn't pretending.
Nikki was wise beyond her years. It was possible that in that
young, reflective, stubborn mind, she'd already worked out
the cost/benefits of love at such a tender age and had decided to forgo. That would be like Nikki.

Katie had always found her younger daughter a bit in-
comprehensible. More so since Tom's death. The two had
been confidants, in the way that mother and daughter usually are. Tom's death had wounded her, perhaps more
deeply than Joy. A chill had fallen on her already-cool nature. She'd made it her business to know all she could
about cryonics and the theoretical science of nanotechnology that might one day save her father. She studied hard at school, taking all the advanced classes. And she
ran track and cross-country and insisted on a vegetarian
diet. But she rarely made time to play with other children
and so had few friends. Not that she ever complained.
And once, about a year after Tom's death, she came to
Katie late one night and thanked her for having the fore-
sight to put her father on ice.

Katie pulled into a parking stall and unlocked the doors.

Joy slipped into the front seat. Nikki dropped her books on the backseat and pulled on the shoulder harness. "I had a physics experiment set up for today," she said. "Now I'm not going to have a chance to do it."

"I'm sorry," Katie said as she backed the car out.

"What's going on, Mom?" Joy asked. "Something wrong?"

"I'm going to be on a talk show this afternoon. I thought you two should know. We'll be discussing cryonics . . . and your father."

"Generational Challenge," Nikki muttered. "It's those geeks, right?"

"I don't know who'll be there," Katie admitted as she eased the car into traffic. "But this is our chance to show we're just ordinary people."

"We?" Joy asked, looking straight ahead. She'd always been so calm, so capable of happiness.

"Cryonics people in general," Katie explained.

"Will me and Joy be on the show?" Nikki asked.

Katie smiled. "No. It's going to be rough, Nikki. I wouldn't put you through that. You could be facing a bad time at school tomorrow already."

"Oh, come on, Mom. Everybody in school knows about Dad. When somebody tries to throw a bomb at a senator, word gets around. Anyway, most of the kids think it's cool. So let us go with you, okay? I want to tell people what I think."

"So do I," Joy said softly.

Katie glanced in surprise at her older daughter. Joy had never said much about the suspension. And it was in her nature to soothe controversy, not court it. Still, she kept a portrait of Tom at her bedside, with the hand-written caption Once and Future.

"I was going to take the two of you home."

"No way, Mom," Nikki said, and Joy shook her head. "We're at least going to the studio with you."

Katie smiled, pleased at the depth of their support. "All right," she said, despite her reservations. She picked up the phone and handed it to Joy. "Call your grandmother and tell her what we're doing."

*   *   *

Sal Greer's producer almost entered a state of rapture when she met Joy and Nikki. "They have to be on the show," she insisted. "We'll feature the three of you first, as a family. Such lovely girls! The audience will eat it up."

"Do it!" Nikki said.

Katie raised a hand of protest. "Now wait a minute—"

"Come on, Mom. We're here to be exploited. So let's go all the way. We have to show people that two grieving kids getting their Daddy back is not wrong."

It's that simple, Katie thought. She studied Nikki's eager face, then looked questioningly at Joy. Tears glistened in her elder daughter's eyes. "You don't have to," Katie said.

"I want to, Mom."

Katie turned to the producer. "All right. But if things get too rough, I'm taking them out."

"Don't worry! Sal loves kids. He's not going to let anything happen!"

They found themselves seated in an arc on stage, Sal Greer standing beside them as he studied the audience. Even motionless, his tall, blond-haired figure seemed charged with sheathed energy.

Abruptly, the introductory music began to play. Katie braced herself against a sudden bout of nerves as the camera panned the studio audience. She followed its sweep on the monitor, noting the individual faces: mostly white, forty and over, with a midwestern feel—tourists come to Hollywood to watch a live show.

Her breathing accelerated. She'd never been a public person. She treasured the privacy of her personal feelings, her familial relations. But Sal Greer made his living by exposing private lives.

The camera finished its circuit and zoomed in on Sal. His sharp voice snapped into the mike:

"Over the last two days we've featured the opinions of experts on the implications of the Generational Challenge, the upstart political movement that is demanding social accountability from scientists. . . ."

Katie forced herself to relax as Sal commenced with the introductions. She listened to his brief discussion of Tom's suspension, using the time to bury her inner feelings as deeply as she could, resolving that while she would happily discuss the morality and ethics of cryonics, she would not allow Sal access to her own inner life.

Sal might have sensed her resistance. He turned to her with a cutting gaze. "Katharine. Your husband's suspension was accompanied by bitter family objections, public protests, even a bomb assault. Yet none of this deterred you. Why?"

Katie drew in a deep breath. She tried to see beyond the studio audience, to the millions who would view this show later in the day. "My husband and I made the decision to seek cryonic suspension long before his death. We made promises to each other. I wasn't about to be put off by crackpots."

Greer smiled indulgently, and the audience tittered. *Let one crackpot call the other black.* "How do you feel about the lobbying efforts of Generational Challenge?"

She kept her gaze steady. "Their stated intention is to ban life-extension technologies and to outlaw the practice of cryonics. As far as my family's concerned, they're attempting to kill my husband."

A scandalized mutter ran through the studio audience. Hands popped up. Sal's eyes narrowed. "But Katharine—legally your husband is already dead."

She nodded, feeling herself on firm ground now. "That's true. But medical technology's continuously changing the definition of death."

"Do you think of Thomas as dead?"

She flinched, startled at this intimate swerve in his interrogation. This was what she'd dreaded. But suddenly she *wanted* to answer the question. For herself.

Looking down at her hands, she groped for words to describe feelings she'd never pinned down. "I think ... I think of him as *waiting*. Not dead. Not alive. Not accessible. But there, just the same." She looked up at Sal, surprised at how easily the answer had come.

But Sal wasn't satisfied with the level of her exposure. "You must have loved him a great deal."

The question inspired an unexpected gush of emotion. Her voice went husky. "Yes," she answered, feeling as if that single word has been forcefully pulled from her.

"So do you intend to remain loyal to your husband?" Sal

asked this question in a voice so casual he might have been asking for the time of day. "Or will you take lovers? Marry again? Remember, Mrs. Kishida. It could be decades before your husband's revived, if ever."

Katie stared at him, struck speechless by the depth of his intrusion. Not so for Nikki. She leaped to her feet. "You leave her alone!" she shouted. "How can you be so cruel?"

Sal Greer seemed stunned. "My apologies, young lady. No one here wants to be cruel, or to bring more hurt on your family than you've already suffered." He turned back to the camera. "But I need to ask the questions that are on everyone's mind. What is the legal relationship between Katharine Kishida and her deceased husband? What obligations does she owe him? To judge the social impact of cryonics, we must apply these sorts of questions, however uncomfortable they make us feel."

"He'll always be my father," Nikki said defiantly. And Katie smiled, knowing the bad moment had passed.

Sal Greer turned to Nikki, his brows raised in interest. "Now here's a point we haven't considered. Thomas Kishida left behind two daughters, lovely young women who must face the most difficult part of their lives without a father to guide them. What is wrong, *what is wrong*, I ask you, if these two girls are allowed to dream of a time when they'll have their daddy back?"

The studio audience responded immediately, hands popping into the air. Sal Greer leaped forward, sticking a wireless mike under the chin of a thin, overly made-up woman in the first row. "I lost my father when I was six," she said. "He died in the Vietnam War, *serving his country*. But no one offered to bring him back."

"So you think the practice of cryonics isn't fair?"

The woman looked suddenly flustered. But with a visible effort, she gathered her indignation and leaned forward into the mike, so that Greer had to yank it back. "I think death is just part of being human. These cryonicists are a lot of irresponsible airheads playing at being God." She sat down with a proud look that said she'd made her point.

The audience mumbled uneasily. Katie leaned forward. She'd regained her balance. Now she was determined to seize the moment. Softly: "I think that what it means to be human is bound to change over time. Death *does not* have to be part of that definition."

Hands went up all over the audience, but Sal ignored them as the show's musical theme began to waft from the speakers. "Our next guest is here to address that very point," Sal said. "When we come back we'll be joined on-stage by Senator Ilene Carson, the driving force behind Generational Challenge, and, coincidentally, the sister-in-law of Katharine Kishida."

Katie was on her feet before the fadeaway was complete. She turned on Sal, sparked by a sense of betrayal, which she recognized at once as being foolish. It was Sal's job to set people up, and if he weren't a master at it, he wouldn't have such a highly rated show. She let out a sharp breath between pursed lips and looked at Nikki. Her younger daughter was standing at her side, mumbling something nasty under her breath. "It's all right," Katie said. "We've been wanting to talk to her."

"On national TV? No tact."

Sal Greer came over and patted them both on the shoulder. "You're doing great. We're going to give the spot to Senator Carson for a few minutes, then we'll bring your family in. Or should I say the rest of the family?" He chuckled and walked away. Katie resumed her seat, leaning past Nikki to whisper a few words of encouragement to Joy.

The cameras rolled and Ilene walked out in a blue business suit, her hair perfect, her expression calm. She shook hands with Sal and acknowledged the applause from the audience, then sat down and immediately took control of the dialogue. "Well, Sal, you've pulled another coup. From the look on Katie's face, I'd say she was just about as surprised as I was to discover the identity of her fellow guest."

Sal smiled innocently. "My condolences on the loss of your brother, Senator. And no one is here today to try to dissect the levels of your private grief. But perhaps you could tell us—"

Suddenly Nikki was out of her seat again. "Perhaps you could tell us why you want my father dead?" she barked. The cameras swung wildly to bring her on-screen. Katie started to reach for her, to pull her back down to her seat.

Then she thought better of it. She leaned back, wickedly delighted at this sudden turn.

The audience was gasping. Ilene looked shocked, then hurt, then—for only a moment—annoyed. Katie turned at a motion in the corner of her eye. Joy had risen to stand beside her sister.

"Nikki, dear. Joy. This issue is complex and—"

"We're not simpletons," Nikki interrupted.

Katie bit her lip to stifle a grin.

"Of course you're not, dear. Nikki, I loved your father, just as I love you. But we have to recognize that in the wider perspective, death is good for our society—"

"That's sick!"

"Nikki," Katie said, feeling it was time. "Please sit down." She exchanged a look with her daughter, and reluctantly, Nikki returned to her seat. Joy accompanied her, looking stricken.

"It does sound sick," Ilene was saying to the camera. "But death is the only force that allows our society to renew itself with every generation. . . ."

Watching her, Katie felt a reluctant admiration for this skilled politician. But she couldn't let this go on. As soon as Ilene slowed for breath, she interrupted.

"You talk about perspective, Ilene. About society, about generations. But you make no mention of *people*. Real people die. And no matter how much faith we claim to have in a personal God, who could look at their dying husband or brother or parent or child and say, 'We love you, but we're going to let you die now, for the good of society, even though we know it's in our power to continue your life.' How many people would make that choice? Senator Carson has. I know she loved Tom. But she's made the choice to let him die because she has *perspective*. And she wants to make the same choice for each and every one of you."

Ilene started to rebut, but Sal interrupted her. "*Are* we going to let Senator Carson make that choice for us? Back after this."

Katie stood up after the fadeaway and crooked a finger at the girls. "Come on. I think it's time to go."

Sal Greer was suddenly there, blocking her way. "Wait. We're just getting into the meat of the issue—"

"You mean the dessert, don't you? A little blood spilled on the stage? No thanks. We've said everything that's relevant. I'll leave Ilene the spotlight to defend herself." And she pushed past him.

Ilene glared up at her with sullen eyes. "This isn't personal, Katie."

From Katie's throat came a noise that was not quite a laugh. "Oh yes it is, Ilene. It most certainly is."

"Gee, Auntie," Nikki said, in a voice laden with teenage sarcasm. "If we'd known you were on the coast, we would have invited you to dinner. Next time why don't you call and let us know what you're doing."

Joy dabbed at her eyes with a tissue and murmured, "Auntie, I wish you'd try to remember who Daddy was."

Then they were backstage, Katie hustling them toward the exit, fired by a sense of exhilaration. She and Nikki traded a grin and a smooth five as they burst past security. "Nobody's going to believe I didn't put you up to that," Katie said with a laugh.

Nikki shrugged. "Who cares?"

The tape-delayed show was broadcast late that afternoon. Katie watched it with the family, and all agreed that things had gone well. The audience had been almost hostile toward Ilene after they left. She worked hard throughout the rest of the show to win them back, with questionable success. The closing credits were rolling when the telephone rang. "Bet that's Gregory," Joy called.

Katie smiled and reached for the phone. "Hello?"

"Caught you on TV today. You bitch. You think you can take us down. But we're not stupid. We know—"

She switched the phone off.

"Mom, what's the matter?" Joy asked.

"Crank call." The phone rang again. Katie stared at it suspiciously before she picked it up. "Hello?"

"Hi, this is Paula Waylan, *Pulse of Los Angeles News*. I'm trying to reach Katharine Kishida."

"That's me."

"Caught you on TV today. . . ."

Katie shivered at the unwholesome echo. But she answered the reporter's questions as best she could. This was her role now: publicity hack. The reporter thanked her and Katie put down the phone. The phone rang. Joy groaned. Nikki ran out of the room screaming. Katie grinned and picked it up again. "Hello?"

"Hi, this is Yvette Sanchez, Associated Press. . . ."

"Hi Katie, It's Gregory. You did great on the show today. . . ."

"Hi, this is Rick Touchard. I write for the San Diego—"

"Hi, Katie. It's Jane. My, your phone's been busy."

"Jane! Yeah, it's been ringing off the hook."

"You were wonderful on TV today. I called Ilene and told her so. . . ."

Riinng. "Power-tripping whore! We're not going to let you screw us out of—"

Katie switched off the phone, a sour feeling in her stomach. She stood up and stretched.

"Want some coffee, Mom?" Joy called from the kitchen.

"Sure. I'm going out to the front porch to get some air."

"Okay. I'll bring it to you."

She took her jacket from the closet, slipped it on, and stepped outside. Dusk had fallen across the orchard. Bats wheeled through the air. She gazed down the long, curved driveway toward the country road, almost a quarter mile away and half-obscured by a line of tall pine trees planted on the boundary of her land. In the evening stillness she could clearly hear the engine of a car accelerating away, but she could make out no headlights on the road. She squinted, puzzled. Then her chin snapped up in alarm as a dull roar and crackle reached her ears. A moment later, billows of black smoke began to waft up among the pine trees. She spun around, colliding with Joy. Coffee sloshed across the farmhouse porch. "Mom!"

Katie turned her around and shoved her into the house, following close on her heels. "Call 911! The fire department!" she shouted as she slammed the door behind them. "Somebody's torched the weeds out on the road." She grabbed a fire extinguisher from the kitchen and a shotgun from a closet. Dropping a box of cartridges into her pocket, she raced for the front door.

Nikki suddenly appeared in her way. "Mom, what's the matter?"

"Stay in the house," she ordered. She burst through the door, crossing the porch in two strides. The dogs suddenly appeared, leaping and cavorting about her as if this were a game. They escorted her as she ran out into the slow dusk.

She was breathing hard by the time she reached the road. The air was thick with smoke, though the flames were still small—an angry orange line cutting slowly through the sparse weeds and lapping at the trunks of the old pine trees. She cursed, viciously and loudly, when she saw the blackened skeletons of the climbing roses that had graced the entrance wall. There was no one around, so she set the shotgun on the ground and went to work, using the fire extinguisher first against the flames that threatened the old trees.

Nikki showed up a moment later with a shovel.

"I thought I told you to stay in the house!"

"This is my home too!" She began scooping up shovelfuls of dirt from the burned areas and throwing them on the flames. Katie growled in frustration as her fire extinguisher guttered empty. Then her mother was there, with another fire extinguisher and a shovel. At almost the same moment a neighbor arrived with his fire extinguisher, and by the time the fire department showed up, the flames were almost out.

Katie stood by the road, shaking with rage as she watched the firefighters finish their mop-up. The fire truck's headlights glared through the gathering twilight. Its emergency lights flashed red and flares burned incandescent on the road. The tense light splashed across graffiti scrawled on the entrance wall. Not Money Enough, it screamed on one side. And on the other, To Keep You Out of Hell! And on the road itself, with an arrow pointing to her driveway, she could just make out the epithet Life Hog!

She turned as a car approached from down the road. It slowed as it drew near, then pulled off to the side. As the headlights winked out, Katie recognized Roxanne Scott's Toyota pickup. "Looks like you're living in the fast lane now," Roxanne said as she walked over, still in her forest service uniform. She surveyed the minor damage with an amused smile. "Everybody in the office watched the show. You and Nikki were real cute."

Katie felt a bit of the fire blaze up in her gut. "So what brings you by, Roxanne? Or do you just have a nose for disaster?"

Roxanne grinned. "Disaster's my job, remember?" Then her grin subsided. She looked down sheepishly. "Sorry. You know how hard it is for me to resist a bad joke." Katie grunted noncommittally. "I'm here on impulse," Roxanne said. "I think about you a lot."

"Come on, Roxanne. It's hardly the time."

"Hey! What better time? We may not agree, but I figure I'm still your friend. We go back a long way, Katie. I don't want to see you drift away."

Katie's nose wrinkled. "Man, I can still smell the gasoline even over the stink of the fire. Those *bastards*! How the hell did they find my house so fast?"

Roxanne shoved her hands in the pockets of her jacket, looking suddenly uncomfortable. "I've got to get going, Katie. But hey. Call me sometime. Let's go climbing. Use it or lose it, you know. You're not getting any younger."

Katie stared at the point where Roxanne's hands had disappeared into her jacket. The smell of gasoline was much stronger than it had been only a few minutes ago. She glanced at the bed of the truck, a bit of doubt festering in the back of her mind.

Roxanne stepped in front of her. "You and Gregory made it into bed yet?" she asked.

Katie's gaze shifted thoughtfully, to linger on Roxanne's face. "No." She started toward the truck, wanting to have a look, but Roxanne moved quickly to block her.

"I know some guys. They've heard about you. They want to see how you climb." Katie started to brush past her, but Roxanne yanked her hand out of her pocket and set it squarely against Katie's shoulder. The smell of gasoline was very strong. "Come on, Katie! Take a look at your life. It's no fun. What are you going to do for the rest of your days? Be some kind of geek talk-show heavy?" Her face reflected her contempt. "Man, I don't know what's happened to you. You would never have let yourself be used like this in school. Can't you see that the phony media slavers are out to own you? They love your pain, your angst, your futility. They're going to pin you like a fucking butterfly in a fucking glass-topped box and ooh and ah over you until they find the next geek-more-pitiful. Save your dignity. Run away. Let it go now, while you still can."

A puff of evening wind stirred Katie's hair and swept the ugly, sweet stench of the fresh burn past her nose, where it mingled with the scent of gasoline. The fumes seemed to trigger a new blood vessel to come on-line in her brain. Capillaries nourishing some new neuronal inter-connectedness were suddenly flooded. Certainty struck her like a frigid wind off a glacier. She looked into Roxanne's eyes and knew the truth. "You started all this, didn't you?" she said. "God, I was so overwhelmed I never even bothered to ask who brought the media in that night Tom died. But it was you, wasn't it? You knew Ilene was flying in. You set the media dogs on her."

Roxanne's hands disappeared into her pockets again. She backed off nervously. "Wake up, Katie. You're wasting your life."

"Did you really think a little pressure would turn me?"

Roxanne had her hand on the truck's door. "What's with you?"

"You really stink, Roxanne. Did you spill some gasoline on your jacket?"

"Man, you're over the edge."

"Do you think if I looked, I'd find a torch and a can of spray paint in your truck?"

"Fuck you." She yanked open the truck's door and slipped inside, cranking the key over in the ignition. The engine roared to life.

Katie took a step after her, fists coiled. "Nobody's got me pinned!" she shouted as Roxanne slammed the door. "I'm anchored. Anchored solid. And I'm no fucking ephemeral butterfly."

Roxanne gunned the engine and the truck jerked backward onto the road, its fat tires spitting gravel. The flashing red light of the fire truck highlighted the twisted fury on Roxanne's face. Katie flipped her the finger as she shifted into first and roared away.

Wedged Time—
Alternate Landscapes

My Familiar. Through the darkness he strained to sense her, but her shadow had gone fragile and thin, like the shadow of a strand of fog on a cloudy day. He felt her fear.

A sudden slap like red fire across his face woke him from his reverie. He blinked, and the last trace of her vanished.

He lay on the hard rock floor of a cave lit by foul-smelling torches. The atmosphere was oppressive, heavy with heat and moisture. The blue oni hunched in front of him, her mouth leering, droplets of milk poised on her breasts. Behind her, a crowd of other oni gathered, their pelts red, pink, gray, or blue, their toothy mouths hideous, their bronze eyes full of suspicion, and hate.

"He's different," one growled in an ugly, gravelly voice, its three-fingered paw pinching painfully at the smooth, furless flesh of his shoulder.

"Not one of us," another agreed. It had a torch in its hand, which it held so close to his face that the heat singed his skin.

He reared back, but another, a red-furred one, grabbed his hairless head and forced his face to the unsteady light. He struggled, but it might have been a vise enclosing his skull. "Look at him, look at him," it sneered. "Smooth as a fish out of water. What are you doing on a mountain, fish? Want me to send you home?" And it slammed his head against the rock of the cave floor. Darkness wound like smoke across his mind, but through the clouds he saw the red oni, standing now, aiming a kick at his side, the claws of its three-toed foot glistening in the torchlight.

A gurgle of rage erupted from his throat. With his palm stiff as a hatchet, he hacked at the creature's ankle, knocking its foot out from under it and sending it tumbling down on top of him. For a moment he thought the sheer weight of it would snap his ribs. He tried to thrust it away, but it twisted around on his chest until he was looking into its bronzy eyes. Its maw opened. It snapped at him. He grabbed at its hair and yanked its head back just before the teeth closed on his face.

Then the blue-furred oni reached out and slapped her companion on the head with the flat of her hand, sending it tumbling against the cave wall.

The crowd of demons hooted and laughed and suddenly exploded in an all-out brawl. Claws raked at furred flesh and heads cracked against walls with enough force to break flakes off the slick rock. Horrible growls filled the narrow passage, in hellish harmony with the scent of blood. And for the moment, at least, he seemed to have been forgotten.

He tried to get to his feet, driven by some half-formed notion to flee. But his body was weak. He couldn't make himself stand upright. He found himself knuckle-walking, one step forward, when suddenly a dirty child loomed in his vision. He glimpsed pale skin, wild eyes, tousled hair. And he realized with a start that this was no oni child, but something more fragile, more dear to his fading memories. A being, as he had once been . . . or known.

Driven by a vague sense of kinship, he reached out to the little one. But in the child's gaze he saw only a vacant kind of fury. Then the little one sprang into the air, planting the ball of its foot against his cheek in a blow that snapped his head back and knocked him off his precarious balance. He went down. The child darted past him. The oni melee ceased.

He twisted around as a concerted howl rose from the pack of

demons. "No!" he screamed as they sprang after the wild child, and within three bounds a pink-pelted female caught it. She seized it by the hair and shoulder and bent its head backward, exposing the smooth, hairless, pale skin of the neck. Then she sank her teeth into its throat, ripping half its neck away.

He cried out in anguish.

The oni ignored him. They mobbed the little body. He could no longer see the corpse. He didn't have to. The pop and crunch of bone told him all he needed to know.

Desperately, he pushed himself to hands and knees and began to crawl in the opposite direction. Then he was on his feet and running. The passage went down, down, twisting and branching but always down, the air growing heavier and hotter with every step. He could hear the oni far behind him now, hooting and growling, and he knew that at any second their attention would leave the poor slaughtered child and return to him. He wept in shame as he ran. He was running from those who had murdered a child. But he didn't slow down.

Now the passage widened. It opened into a rounded chamber dimly lit by scattered torches. Steam smelling strongly of sulphur billowed from walls draped in a thick growth of black and purple slime. Embedded in the slime were glassy cells that varied from the size of a fist to the size of a man's chest. The smallest of them were opaque; the largest quite transparent. He paused beside one, staring through the sheer purple hull of the cell at the coiled body of an imprisoned child who watched him in return with dull, frightened eyes. The child was grotesquely obese, so that though she had the height of a toddler, her swollen proportions made her look like an oversized infant in a bedraggled wig. He reached out to touch the membrane. It felt crisp and fragile beneath his fingers. He pushed harder, and his fingers punched through the membrane. He quickly yanked his hand back, leaving a hole. The child kicked weakly, her jaw trembling as she snapped at a black teat inside her cell.

He turned away, sickened. But almost against his will his gaze was drawn to another cell. This one was small and opaque, and when he touched it, it felt more substantial than the first. He couldn't see inside it, but on its purplish-black surface he could make out the raised silhouette of an infant. When he laid his palm over its chest, he could feel the rise and fall of tiny breaths.

A wave of dizziness swept over him. He staggered away from

the wall, oppressed by the heat and the stench and the horrible purpose inherent in this nursery. And yet he couldn't bring himself to leave. He made his way slowly around the room. There were hundreds of cells attached to the curved walls, and as he examined them he could see that each one contained a child somewhere in development between a fetus and a toddler. An entire generation growing in the walls, the future's treasure, waiting to be consumed by the demons of the present. Was this what he'd asked for? Was this what he'd asked for when he'd called out to his Familiar to save him? Had she *sent* him here? He bellowed in anger, a deep, ugly, animal sound that reverberated in the chamber and set the babies twitching in alarm.

With a start, he recalled the demon oni. He listened sharply, but he could pick up no sound from them, no hoot or howl or growl. He found no reassurance in that. Perhaps they were moving on him in stealth. He chewed on his lips, wrestling with a horrible dread for his own life that urged him to run as fast and as far as he could—and an equal horror at abandoning the helpless inhabitants of this stinking nursery. His fists clenched in rage. He wanted to smash every pod in the room, release each little victim from this obscene parody of the jungle laws of nature. But his violence would kill them. He knew it. There must be another way. He needed time, to think and to learn a way around the oni masters of this place.

Reluctantly, he cast about for another way out of the chamber, and found a small passage half-hidden behind a spur of rock. He entered it, relieved to leave the steaming, stinking nursery behind.

After a few steps the passage widened into a second chamber. This one seemed minutely cooler than the first, though its walls also steamed beneath a thick curtain of dark slime. A net made of tiny bones bound together with what looked like strips of dried flesh hung from the ceiling to the floor, dividing the chamber into a large pen and a narrow passage. He touched the curtain of bones, peering through the small apertures at a herd of thin, dirty children, much like the child he'd seen in the upper passage. Their hair was matted, and their eyes were dull. Some picked obsessively at the orifices of their naked bodies. Some fought with their mates, in slow-motion tussles accompanied by little animal growls. One girl was throwing dirt in her own face, over and over, her red, puffy eyes never blinking. Another scratched continuously at a forearm already drenched in blood. A boy pounded his toes with a loose rock. His feet were a bloody pulp, but he continued to raise the rock and bring it down hard against his own body. He made no cry of pain, and his dull, frozen face never changed expression.

"Trespasser!" The shriek exploded only inches from his ear. He jumped, twisting one hundred eighty degrees in the air, landing with feet spread, legs crouched. The blue oni glared at him with her bronze eyes, her black lips still rouged with blood. *"Trespasser!"* she screeched again. "Who sent you here? Who sent you? You're not one of us!"

He backed away from her, past the curtain of bones. "Run away!" she screamed at him. "Run away, you coward, you wimp, you pansy, you weakling, you sissy, you spineless, marrowless, namby-pamby, sentimental fool . . . before I feed you to the pen of ghosts." She seized the curtain of bones in one fist and shook it hard. The clacking, rattling sound sent the children cowering against the walls . . . except the boy practicing self-mutilation. He continued at his task, unperturbed.

He stared at her, as insistent words pushed past the tightness in his throat. "You eat . . . these children."

"That's right. And I'll eat yours too, that's shaping here in my belly. It's that or die. There's no room for all of us, and I don't plan to get out of the way."

He looked at the children in the cave. They gazed back at him with angry, resentful eyes. *Greedy, gluttonous, voracious, rapacious thief of time and space. Where's our turn?*

"Who sent you here?" the oni hissed, taking one step closer to him. "Do you remember? You do remember. She's one of us, you know. One of us. She doesn't care about them"—she gestured contemptuously at the children in the pen—"she cares about you. About you. . . ."

She stepped closer still, her three-fingered hand suddenly seizing his arm. The children began to moan and cry. "The ghosts aren't like us, you know. They're stupid and dull. They haven't even been born. We're not eating them so much as their heritage, you see? *Our* heritage, 'cause we never gave it up, never intend to give it up. She sent you here, didn't she? So it can't be so bad. Or do you really want to die?"

Revulsion had been building up in his chest until suddenly it ripped from his throat in a fiery scream. *"I won't do it!"*

His rage seemed to energize the penned children. They raced about the enclosure, striking the walls, throwing rocks, rattling the bone curtain, climbing it and howling.

He grabbed at the curtain and pulled on it. The oni saw what he was about and leaped on his back, trying to wrest his hands away. He pulled harder and felt the curtain begin to give. The shrieks from the children were shrill and deafening in the chamber. The oni sank her teeth into the back of his neck, her jaws working furiously to snap his spinal cord. He screamed and threw himself back against the wall, delighting in the crack of her skull against the rock. She fell off him and he lunged at the net, yanking it hard. It was filled with children now. They covered it from floor to ceiling and their combined weight helped him bring it down in a great clatter of bones and shrill screams of terror.

He jumped back, staring in horror at what he'd done. The net was filled with children. Crushed children. Entangled children. Bloodied children. Only one remained free of the trap he'd sprung on them. But the boy with the crushed feet continued to raise his rock and slam it down on the remains of his toes, taking no notice of the confusion around him.

The blue oni was lying on the floor and laughing loudly, hysterically. The chamber was suddenly filled with demon oni, their sweet breath mingling sickeningly with the sulphurous fumes. They mobbed him. He punched and kicked and bit at random, and they slapped him about, laughing. Then they caught him and took him down. A great gray male rested one knee on his head, grinding his cheek into the floor while the others wrapped his body in strips of thin leather, like undertakers preparing a corpse. His arms were lashed to his sides, his legs were lashed together, and then they lifted him over their heads in a great hooting torch-lit parade of triumph and carried him from the chamber, down a new passage, periodically slamming his body against the ceiling for the sport of it, and he began to black out, so that the journey seemed to him to be composed of discreet scenes and always down, down the passage wound until finally, feverishly, he was aware they'd reached an end, a wall of ice that blocked the passage and glowed faintly with what seemed to be clean, cold daylight, a hue of awesome purity after the lurid, fiery interior of the cave. The oni held him belly-up and swung him back and forth three times, building up momentum, chanting with the effort, "Die then! Die then! Die then! Now!" And they hurled him headfirst at the wall of ice.

"No!" he cried, a harsh scream suddenly cut off by his impact with the ice. Pain burst in bright, black colors through his head as the ice exploded outward and he was falling. He screamed in terror, "I don't want to die!"

Somewhere, beyond the rush of wind in his ears, he heard the oni hooting in amusement. Then he hit bottom.

TV COMMERCIAL: XANALEX
CONTRACEPTIVE IMPLANTS

[Slow pan across the Martian landscape encompassing simulation of Martian base]
Masculine Narrator: Three young men and three young women will be chosen for the first Martian expedition. They will spend nearly five hundred days in a tiny habitat on the surface of Mars, eating, sleeping, working, and . . .
[Cut to close-up of masculine hand stroking an oil-sheened feminine buttock, black background]
Narrator: But Mars is no place for an unplanned pregnancy. So mission doctors will prescribe Xanalex Contraceptive Implants for all three men on the expedition. Xanalex, the masculine birth control that absolutely will not detract from your virility or sexual prowess. Xanalex, the safe, simple implant that will quietly protect you for a full five years.
[Cut to romantic sunset scene involving simulated Martian tornado moving across red desert landscape, silhouettes of male and female astronauts in the foreground]
Narrator: Until you're ready, let your guardian be Xanalex.

8

Guardians of
the Red Desert

Katie turned around to look into the cab's backseat, where Nikki and her grandmother Jane Kishida sat. A half-hearted smile played across her lips at the contrast between the anxiety so apparent on Jane's softly aging face and Nikki's youthful eagerness. Katie's own emotions lingered somewhere in between as the cab approached the occupied UCLA campus.

Two years on the speaker's circuit, appearing on talk shows, writing articles and editorials, speaking before Rotarians, Kiwanians, PTA's, and anybody else who would have her, had left her feeling more aged than her years deserved. But today would be easy. She'd be speaking before a friendly crowd at a Mars Now! conference. It was preaching to the converted, but they'd wanted her to come. So she'd gotten Tom's Mars pin out of the drawer, pinned it to her blouse, and gathered what little enthusiasm she had left.

In a sudden moment of nostalgia, she wondered if Ilene felt this tired too. Had the senator ever had a moment of regret over the political storm she'd stirred up with her Generational Challenge? In a sudden, vicious shift of mood, Katie found herself hoping it was so.

"Shit!"

She spun around as the cabby slammed on the brakes, narrowly avoiding a collision with the vehicle ahead. "Not again!" He slapped the steering wheel, glaring at the traffic. "Looks like more assholes blocking the road."

Katie rose in her seat, trying to figure out what was holding things up, but she couldn't see past a minivan two cars ahead. Delivery vans and water trucks lined the curb, walling off any view on that side. She checked her watch. They were already a few minutes late. "Faster to walk, I guess. We'll get out here." She glanced at the meter, then passed some bills to the cabby. "Thanks."

"Thank you, ma'am. And welcome to the once-great UCLA. Man, the world stinks."

Katie couldn't argue with him. She looked into the backseat. "Take your last breath of semidecent air," she advised. Nikki grinned. Jane sighed in resignation. Then Katie pulled the latch on the cab door and stepped out into the stinking heat and glare of a Los Angeles late-summer morning.

The sun's rays felt like lasers burning her skin. She quickly slapped a broad-brimmed hat on her head, but that didn't soothe the fiery white reflected glare from the huge steel tanks of the water trucks. Brassy air filled her lungs, thick with the smoke of illegal hibachis and the perpetually stale, eye-stinging aura of the Los Angeles basin. Over the sounds of the idling traffic, she could hear distant voices raised in an angry, unintelligible chant.

"Don't you love L.A.?" Nikki muttered. She stood between the water trucks, gazing at the plaza and the UCLA homeless village. Three kids on skateboards zipped past.

Jane stepped onto the curb and opened a colorful parasol over her head. "Los Angeles used to be such a beautiful city," she muttered. "It's awful. Just awful. All these people . . . why did they come here? What do they want?"

Reluctantly, Katie turned to take in the prospect. She'd

seen it all before on the news, of course, over and over
again throughout the long summer. But this was different.
This was real life. She could feel the hard rhythms of rock
and reggae and rumble booming from the columns of
white tents that had been erected on the plaza after the
lawn had succumbed to water rationing. Graffiti artists had
tended to most of the tents in styles that ranged from
crudely profane to intensely artistic. They'd also lent their
talents to the walks and the groups of portable toilets and
solar showers that sprouted throughout the village. Even
the water trucks hadn't escaped untouched.

At one truck, a long line of people waited with ration
cards in hand, their expressions bored and malevolent. An
evangelist addressed them, standing precariously balanced
on the seat of a parked motorcycle. He reminded them
that they were human too, and that God loved them, even
if the government didn't. Katie admired him for the
strength he put into his delivery, despite the awful atmosphere that must be working like fire in his lungs.

It had been two years since Generational Challenge had
made its presence known. Two ugly, devolving, declining
years, marked by economic stagnation and environmental
disaster, and culminating in the proliferation of refugee
camps across the Sunbelt. Katie could feel the frustration
and fear in this place, the nascent violence in the children's spats, in the mothers' curses, in the drunken drawls
of useless fathers. There was a contagious anger here that
might erupt and tear the city down if only it weren't too
damn hot to even *move*.

She rubbed at her watering eyes, then looked down,
startled by a tug on the hem of her blouse.

"*Un dolare?*" a ragged Hispanic child begged. Flies
walked across the lesions on his face, and his eyes had a
frightening, feverish glow. Looking at him, Katie was
rocked by a sudden certainty that he was not going to
make it, that *they* were not going to make it, all of them,
all of us, facing the steep, slippery slope of history's last
years and the chasm beyond. She pulled back, resisting
the apocalyptic vision that loomed in this child's eyes.
Things did not have to get worse, she told herself. Things

did not have to. There was still power in the hands of every individual. Nothing is written. Nothing at all.

Nikki slipped the kid a dollar from her purse and nudged Katie toward the sidewalk. Nikki was only fourteen, but she'd already dispensed with childhood. She had a focus Katie lacked, and self-doubt wasn't part of her nature. "Come on, Mom. I see Gregory waiting. Let's go."

Katie edged forward, taking each step with great care, as if the sidewalk might melt under her feet at any moment and wash away. But even then, she told herself, she would keep her balance.

As they passed under the shelter of a shade cloth hung over the walk to protect pedestrians from the merciless sun, the sense of lowering doom receded. But it didn't entirely leave her. Then Gregory was there, looking remote in dark glasses. He put his hands on her shoulders and they kissed. Father Gregory, huh? That phase had passed some time ago. It wouldn't be long now until he'd replaced Tom altogether—a dread thought that left her heart fluttering in fear. "You look pale," he said.

She hugged him, trying to hide her shaking hands behind his back. "Time is slipping away," she whispered. "I feel like we're stuck on a mudflat, the tide is slowly coming in, *and nothing's being done.* Look what's going on here." She pulled away from him and swept her hand toward the village.

What would become of it in the fall, when the majority of students were scheduled to return? Would the squatters be thrown out? And would they magically disappear? Float off into the ether, never to trouble society again?

Right.

"Generational Challenge caused this," Katie growled. "They're killing us. They're smothering the economy. They're crushing every research effort aimed at—"

"Technofix!" Nikki shouted. "Get the lab boys in here now!"

Katie turned to her in irritation. But as she did her gaze swept past a placid group of men and women, as quiet and dusty as the shaded sidewalk on which they sat, so that she hadn't noticed them at first, though they were only an arm's reach behind Nikki. Most of them were dressed in

cheap T-shirts and ragged shorts. Cigarette smoke twisted
lazily above curled fingers. Sunglasses stared at her, white
glints of light giving the blank lenses an artificial hint of
personality.

At the center of the group sat a monstrously obese man.
Unexpectedly, his gaze locked with Katie's. She found
herself looking into small brown eyes almost lost in the
looming muscles of a dark Polynesian face. And suddenly
she had the uncanny feeling that he knew exactly who she
was—not only her identity, but her internal substance, her
dreams, her desires.

Her gaze flicked nervously to take in the rest of him.
His head was shaved except for a long ponytail that hung
down his back. He wore rubber thongs on feet that were
flattened by the weight of his own body, and his breath
wheezed as his lungs forced air through passages compressed by his size. A sudden sense of unease swept across
her, and she drew back. Touching Nikki's elbow, she
nudged her farther up the sidewalk.

But they'd only gone a few steps when Nikki pulled up
short. "Yikes! Picket alert." Katie looked, to see a huge
cordon of sign-brandishing protesters blocking the sidewalk ahead, forming a barrier across the entrance to the
conference hall where the Mars Now! meeting was to be
held. They all wore black T-shirts. Katie didn't need to
get close enough to make out the insignia. It had become
all too familiar over the past year: a graphic of Earth
eclipsing Mars—a radical's symbol adopted in opposition
to the Mars pin. Their moronic chant rose over the blaring
horns and engine noise of the stalled traffic: "No government money for Mars; love your Mother first!"

The political landscape was fracturing. Fringe groups
had formed that were only vaguely related to Generational
Challenge.

"Yeah, the Knights are here," Gregory muttered.

Knights of the Oppressed Earth. Back-to-nature freaks.
Against all technology. Not at all what Generational Chal-
lenge was about. But Ilene used them, and they used her.
For now.

Nikki wrinkled her nose. "What geeks."

"But why are they here?" Jane asked in soft indignation. "The Mars mission has been approved. They can't change that now."

"That's right," Katie said. The mission to Mars had survived on its minuscule budget for almost four years. It was in an advanced stage of development and no piddling protest was going to stop it. "Let's see if we can get through."

They advanced tentatively up the sidewalk. The closer they got, the more impenetrable appeared the line of protesters. Close-up, it looked more like a rally than a strike line. There must have been close to a thousand black shirts.

Now Katie could make out individual faces etched in almost identical expressions of mob anger. An army of video cameras recorded the performing crowd. One brown-haired, black-shirted Knight leaned into a microphone, giving an interview.

"How do we get in the building?" Nikki asked. Jane had taken a protective grip on her arm.

"There." Gregory pointed. On the other side of the wide cordon of protesters, several security officers were moving away from the conference building, and toward the line. There seemed to be a rehearsed system, because the protesters parted as the security officers approached, opening up a narrow channel. "Mars Now?" one of the officers shouted at Gregory through a bullhorn. "Come on."

"An *escort*?" Nikki said. "You've gotta be kidding."

Gregory touched Jane's back, urging her forward. "Let's go—before the mood changes."

The volume of the chanting seemed to rise as they approached. Katie could feel the eyes of the line, like the perceptual organs of some many-legged creature, a political centipede with poison glands all along its body that spilled a message of hate.

She looked from face to face, trying to discern some spark of awareness, some hint of individual thought, but finding only mouths moving in pointless mechanical performance, obedient tools of an invisible master.

Her gaze touched again on the brown-haired woman involved in the interview . . . and suddenly the Knight was looking right at her, a smug grin on her finely sculpted face.

Roxanne.

Katie grabbed Gregory's arm. "Take Nikki and Jane inside. I'll join you in a minute.

"Katie—!"

"Hurry," Katie said, pushing him gently forward. Nikki was already through the security channel, with Jane rushing to keep up with her. "Keep an eye on them. I'll be right back." And she slipped away before he could object again.

Roxanne wore a hungry half-grin as she watched Katie approach. Her face looked thin and sunburned. Her eyes seemed to have sunk deeper into their sockets, like windows sagging before the heat of some inner flame. Her nostrils flared every time she breathed. Like a shaman, Katie thought, scenting the future. She wore the same black T-shirt as the rest of the tribe. Apparently the interview had ended.

"Katie. I was starting to worry you wouldn't make it."

The tumultuous sound of the chanting Knights bore down upon them, driving Katie close to Roxanne. She could see the sweat on Roxanne's cheeks like tiny white points of light. "What are you doing here?"

That hungry smile again. "I heard you were on the stump. So I came to hear you speak. Brought some friends, too. It's been a long time, eh?"

"You supporting the mission to Mars now?"

Roxanne laughed. "Nah, but I hear the parties are fun."

Katie backed off a step. Suddenly, she could feel the heat of human breath just behind her; black T-shirts crowded up on the periphery of her sight. "No parties," she said. "Just boring techs. Boring talk."

Roxanne looked away, her gaze moving off over the chanting line. "Not today. You don't want to go in there today."

Amid the roar and heat, Katie suddenly felt the world go very still. "Nikki and Jane are already inside."

Beneath her tan, Roxanne's face paled.

Katie felt a rush of dread. "What have you done?" she cried. "What have you done?"

Roxanne didn't answer. Her eyes had a faraway look, as if she were listening to something that only she could hear.

Katie spun around, in a panic to get to the conference hall. But a cadre of Knights had closed in behind her, the Earth rolling like water across the flame of Mars, again and again and again, in every direction she looked. She raised her hands and started to shove a path through them. With the swiftness of an indrawn breath they closed on her, chanting, screaming, filling the air with heat while stripping it of oxygen; slick, stinking bodies crushing her, laughing, while their fingers brushed her face, her shoulders, her breasts.

She had to get to Nikki.

A warning growl ran out of her throat. She let fly with her elbows. But hands were on her. She could feel herself being dragged backward, down. She twisted hard.

And suddenly there was a quiet eddy in the run of Knights. She found herself gasping, staring up at a huge man in a sweat-soaked gray T-shirt—the same Polynesian who'd occupied the sidewalk only a few minutes before. She felt a moment of raw terror. His shaved head and long, barbaric ponytail gave him a savage aspect. But the expression in his eyes—she hesitated—as if he were *daring* her to be afraid of him, judgments cast down in learned rituals.

She moved back half a step and drew herself up. The Polynesian stood at the apex of a phalanx of ragged homeless, their arms linked, their mouths silent, their expressions mostly hidden behind sunglasses or behind cool eyes that were equally unrevealing.

They pressed forward like an animate spear into the thrashing body of the Knights' cordon. Katie fell back before them, and there was room for her because the Knights were giving way. But only in one direction. She was being driven that way . . . whichever direction it was. She'd become so turned around she couldn't tell if she was moving toward the conference hall or away from it.

And then a strong, long-fingered hand locked onto her

shoulder. She brought herself up abruptly. Glancing to the
side, she saw Roxanne. But the easy confidence Roxanne
had displayed a minute before was gone, replaced by an
expression that could have belonged to a cornered back-
alley cur.

The Polynesian finally ceased his forward motion. The
lines of homeless behind him slowed, then stopped in
kind. Katie drifted back a few more inches, then strained
on her tiptoes to see over the crush. Which way was the
conference hall?

The Knights had quieted, and in the sudden still heat
Katie could see the air shimmering over the press of people. Hibachi smoke dimmed the sun only a little.

The Polynesian studied the Mars pin on her shirt.
"Mars Now!" he said, his voice a low rumble. He looked
up. "Why?"

From the corner of her eye, Katie could see Roxanne
smile. All around her, people muttered angrily—the
Knights, of course, but the homeless too. Mars didn't belong to them. Mars was a hobby, a scam, a way of sheltering
money from the swelling populations of the streets. They
didn't want to hear about the promise of Mars. Promise
didn't exist here. They didn't buy the challenge. On the
streets, challenge was only a dirty set of day-to-day realities
without noble connotation. And the future? That was
something best not considered too often.

"Why Mars?" the Polynesian pressed.

Katie half shrugged. "We want it." Her words were soft,
almost lost in the mutter, but not said shyly. And the Polynesian heard her. She could see that in the hardening of
his already stony gaze. "We want it!" she repeated, louder
now. Her fist was clenched at her waist, as if she had
something there that she would keep to herself. But she
forced her hand open. Shook it gently to relax the muscles. Shook her head. "If you can't feel Mars, I could
never explain it to you. You either know why . . . or you
don't."

She thought she caught a faint easing of the Polynesian's harsh expression. But her own worry didn't fade.
She stretched up on her tiptoes again, searching over the
heads of the crowd, trying to see where she was, where

she had to go to reach the conference hall. Then two
Knights close on her right hand shifted back a step and
she saw it—saw the roofline, anyway. It was only twenty
yards away, maybe twenty-five. With a sudden movement,
she wrenched out of Roxanne's grip. The Knights around
her stiffened. But they didn't touch her this time, waiting,
perhaps, for the decision of the big man who watched her
now with cold, measuring eyes. *They're afraid of him*. She
could feel it in their stillness.

"I need help," she told him softly, surprised at how difficult those words were to utter.

An expression of surprise rushed across his face. "I
know you. You're the one with the frozen husband."

Her eyes narrowed combatively. She was only too familiar with the kind of shit that usually followed recognition.
"We all make our own choices."

He chuckled softly. "Anyway, when the law allows."

"I'm no friend of Generational Challenge."

His face darkened. "Maybe you're not hungry enough."

She nodded in cold agreement. "Maybe not."

A soughing, low-voiced exhalation rolled around her:
"*Bitch, bitch, bitch, who does she think she is, anyway? Fucking
bitch.*" But the big man didn't seem to hear. He shook his
head, a slight smile on his lips. "You're a real hard-ass," he
informed Katie in a good-natured tone. "Come on. This is
my neighborhood. I'll get you through." He took her arm,
gently but firmly. Pressing it beneath his own, he began to
advance once again, and Katie could see now that he was
moving toward the conference hall. The Knights gave way.
She looked around for Roxanne, but couldn't find her.
Other Knights glared at her, but they moved aside.

A strange feeling came over her then. Despite the mob,
the heat, the anxiety, a sense of joy touched her. She could
feel a sliding electric potential in the powerful grip of this
strange ally. He seemed to stand at the point of a human
army that somehow extended far beyond the UCLA
homeless village. She gazed at him, trying to puzzle out
his identity, but there was nothing familiar in his face.

"You're here," he announced. He let her arm go. Katie
looked around in surprise, to see that the cordon of
Knights was behind her. Ahead, a security cadre nervously

approached from the conference hall. She took two
mincing steps toward them, then turned back, fishing in
her pocket for a business card. The big man had already
turned to go. "Wait!" she called after him. "I don't even
know your name."

He turned around with a wary look. She held out the
business card, her hand shaking, suddenly sure he would
shrug and turn away, refuse to take it. And the thought did
seem to cross his mind. But then his hand closed over the
card. "It's Ferris Kumunalu."

She nodded, silently repeating the name over and over
to commit it to memory. "Call me sometime," she said.
"Maybe we can find some common ground."

She showed her ID to the security team, and told them
about Roxanne's warning. They informed her everything
was under control. They said it without laughing, and then
they escorted her into a lobby that was only slightly less
chaotic than the street.

The sweltering atmosphere brought her up short. Either
the AC was out, or it simply couldn't keep up with the
mob that crammed the room. This was supposed to be a
tech conference. But it seemed that half the people present were black-shirted Knights. *Knights of the Oppressed
Earth*. She felt Roxanne's influence like a dangerous emotional current seeking a path through the room.

Suddenly Gregory was at her side. He'd put his sunglasses in his shirt pocket, but his gaze was still dark and
inflexible as he started in on her. "Where the hell have
you been? And what happened to you?" He brushed at a
loose strand of hair that clung to her cheek. "It's dangerous out there—"

"It's no better in here."

"Yeah. The Knights have taken us. The word is, a few
hundred of them signed up and paid the registration fee.
I don't like the atmosphere at all."

Katie nodded agreement. She could feel the tension in
the room: a nervous, fluttering irritability like the
sourceless anxiety carefully developed in old cowboy movies just before a dropped pot or a coyote's howl set the
thirsty herd to stampede.

To one side, a middle-aged man in thick glasses and unfashionable short hair stood on a bench and harangued the crowd, his voice like some irritating gnat in the ear. But for now the herd reacted passively: a head shake, a tail twitch, an occasional dirty look.

"Where are Nikki and Jane?"

Gregory nodded toward the far side of the room. "By the auditorium door. Nikki wanted to get a good seat."

"You serious?"

He shrugged.

"You know this conference is not happening."

"Yeah. That's probably why the auditorium doors haven't been opened."

"I want to get out of here," Katie said. "I saw Roxanne outside. She gave me a bad feeling."

"She ever give you a good feeling?"

"Let's find Nikki and Jane."

They worked their way through the milling crowd. Then suddenly Katie stopped, trying to see past the crowd to the knot that had gathered around the impromptu speaker on the bench. "Is that Nikki?"

Gregory swung around. "Dammit. I told her to stay put."

Katie changed directions. The speaker's voice drifted out across the crowd rumble in the lobby:

"Generational Challenge is seeking to make it *effectively illegal* for us to terraform Mars—because without the biological sciences, talk of terraforming is *ludicrous*!"

Almost over Katie's head, a black-shirted Knight bellowed, "Talk of terraforming will always be ludicrous! When are you nerds going to stop screwing around with nature?"

"When we get it fixed right!" Nikki shouted.

"Love your mother. Love your mother. Love your mother." Suddenly half the congregation was chanting the Knights' favorite slogan.

But the bespectacled one carried on: "It's imperative that the human race move beyond Earth. Confining ourselves to one planet leaves us vulnerable to sudden, disastrous extinction—"

"The Western world deserves to be extinct!"

"Let Mars live free!"

"Who is that clown?" Gregory muttered. "He's going to provoke these nuts."

Katie turned around, incredulous. "These nuts are already provoked! And that *clown* is the only one of all of us with the guts to stand up and say publicly what we all think."

Gregory's face darkened. He leaned over her, his hand on her shoulder. "Dammit, Katie. You know we're never going to get anywhere if we look like—" He shot an ugly glance at the bespectacled one.

She knocked his hand away. "Nerds?" she suggested viciously. "Eggheads? Elitists?"

"Hey, if the shoe fits," Nikki said, stepping up to Katie's side. Jane followed her, looking as if she might faint.

"We can't afford to be taken for a lunatic fringe," Gregory said. "You know that. Stop acting like it's not important."

Katie bit her lip and cursed him silently, cautious Katie, unwilling to risk the words out loud lest they leave some permanent scar on his affections. Then she cursed herself for her own timidity.

"Come on," she said, touching Jane on the shoulder. "Let's get out of here before—"

Suddenly, a fire alarm shrieked overhead. A man screamed something unintelligible. Katie looked up to see dark threads of smoke trailing from the area of the closed auditorium doors.

She wasted no time on cognitive thought. Moving on instinct, she turned around, grabbed Jane and Nikki by the arms, and started steering them for the door. But everybody else in the room moved at the same time in the same direction and in an instant the mob had closed around them like a vise. Katie was slammed into a dress-shirted back. She lost her grip on Jane. Spinning around, she tried to locate her while keeping a grip on Nikki, but the crowd dynamic moved against her. She caught a glimpse of Jane's terrified face, now at least three bodies back. She tried to reach her. But the crowd forced her forward, toward the door. Why weren't the sprinklers coming on? Then the mob slammed in again. Katie could hardly breathe. She felt her feet leave the ground as the current lifted her, carrying her toward the door, and all the while she kept her hand in an iron lock on Nikki's arm.

And then they were free, spilling outside, stumbling down the steps. Her feet touched earth again. She gasped for breath, dragging Nikki off to one side as the current fanned out, its force rapidly dissipating. "Get out in the open!" she shouted at Nikki, her lungs fiery with oxygen depletion. "Wait for me there!"

"Where are you going?" Nikki's eyes were wide and moist. Her voice had a high edge of terror that Katie had never heard before.

"I have to find your grandmother!"

She shoved Nikki onto the walk and started back up the steps, against the crowd. Faces washed past her, Earth activists looking as terrified as any tech. And then she saw Jane between the columns, a little old lady, lost and disoriented. "Jane!" she shouted. "Jane!" Smoke was pouring out of the hall's main doors now and the fire alarm was screaming so loud Katie could scarcely hear her own voice. *"Jane!"*

Slowly, Jane turned. Her hand was on her chest. She looked straight through Katie without seeing her and then she began to fall slowly forward. Katie half caught her, half fell with her to the steps below. Then Gregory was there, and Nikki and even Ferris Kumunalu, overseeing events in his neighborhood. But Jane didn't see any of them. She lay in Katie's lap, staring up at the shade cloth as if she saw something there that no one else could see. And her breath sighed out past her lips as an expression of wonder stole across her face.

Later:

Near midnight in the hospital parking lot and the doctors weren't promising a thing, just "She has a good chance."

Which was more than they'd allowed for Tom.

Katie thought about this as she sat on the hood of Gregory's car, staring down at the oil-stained asphalt. Gregory sat next to her, his arm around her shoulders. "We got her into treatment fast," he said. "Most heart patients make it when they receive immediate treatment."

"Uh-huh." But his reassurances chilled her. Even Dr. Hunt wasn't promising anything.

Her coiled fist hammered against her thigh. "If only I hadn't taken her to that conference today. My God, what if something had happened to Nikki too?"

Her brother-in-law Harlow stirred from the shadow cast by a minivan: "Nothing happened to Nikki," he said. "And you can't see into the future any better than the rest of us, Katie Kishida. You had no way of knowing those terrorists were going to torch the hall."

Katie closed her eyes and shivered, a fear of darkness suddenly rushing in upon her. "That's what scares me, Harlow. That's what really scares me. Our lives are so *tenuous*. We like to pretend we're safe and secure, but we're really dancing on a knife-edge every day of our lives, and someday each one of us is bound to slip. . . ."

"Mom's not even signed up with Forward Futures," Harlow interrupted. "She's been thinking about it. *Thinking about it!* If she gets out of this I'm going to see to it that she thinks about it real hard."

Gregory squeezed Katie tighter and kissed her on the head. "Jane'll get out of this."

Katie nodded. She was seeing Jane again, her pale, seamed face crossed with wonder. What had Jane seen, so near death, to inspire that look of awe?

"*Jane . . . ?*"

"It was Tom," Jane whispered, days later, as sunlight from the hospital room's open window streamed across her face. "I saw Tom, but he was a little boy again. He told me to go back. He told me there was nothing but a frozen wasteland out there and I should go back while I still could. I wanted to stay with him, but he wouldn't let me. He sent me back."

Katie sat by Jane's bedside and held her hand. Her skin felt dry and smooth.

"It was only a dream, I know. I've dreamed about him before."

Harlow stood by the window, looking uneasy, his hands stuffed into the pockets of his jacket. "The doctors say you're going to make it this time, Mom. But up to now, no-body lives forever. We want you to sign up with Forward Futures. You're the only one in the family who hasn't ... except Ilene."

Jane gazed at a painting of roses on the other side of the room, a faint smile playing across her lips. "I miss your father so much," she said. "Still. After all these years. We had a good marriage, Harlow, and someday I hope to join him—"

"Mom—"

"But not yet. I'm old and tired and I hurt. I *hurt*, Harlow. But I'm not ready to die. I've enjoyed my life. And there's so much I haven't done. I don't want to be left behind and ... and I want to see what happens to Tom. I want to know if he's going to make it home."

Harlow stepped forward, anticipation bright on his face. "Then you'll do it?"

"I'll do it."

"Despite Ilene?" Katie asked.

Jane patted her hand. "Ilene hasn't lived in my house for many years, Katie darling. She's my daughter, and I love her. But this is something I have to decide for myself."

"I'm calling Forward Futures right now," Harlow said. He kissed his mother on the cheek and picked up the phone.

L.A. FLOW—PERSONALITIES
"Back to the Land—L.A. Style"

"There's no going back." That's what Ferris
Kumunalu teaches at his Primal Society
workshops. "I'm a native Hawaiian,"
says the former homeless man who now
chairs a society that includes representatives
from nearly all American Indian tribes. "I
respect the traditions of my ancestors,
their skill at living in harmony with the
land. We have much to learn from them.
But the world has changed. None of us has
the option of blindly copying our tribal
pasts. We must develop new primal
societies, ones that still carry forward the
ancient traditions of respect for the earth,
that still teach the ancient vision of
humanity as a coequal element of the web
of life, rather than as an outside usurper.
But we must develop these societies within
the technosphere of the modern world.

"If we don't discover how to live a
sustainable life, our world will surely reject
us."

The Primal Society may be contacted
at 1-800-NEW-URTH.

9

Disintegration in
the Web of Life

Fony pants were California's latest fashion trend. Always baggy, generally riding low on the hips, and preferably woven of Memtex, they looked like some civilized descendant of combat fatigues. But it was fashion dictated by utility rather than whim. The padded thigh pocket was designed to carry a phone always at the ready. Katie liked to balance the phone with an Office Girl. She'd chosen white fonies this morning, pulling them on over a tank-topped bodysuit, then spraying on sunscreen before topping off the ensemble with a parasol hat.

She checked her look in a mirror on the wall of the ship's cramped cabin, and grinned in satisfaction.

"Gorgeous," Gregory muttered, stirring sleepily in the bed.

Katie side-eyed him with a teasing smile, admiring the way his long dark hair fanned out across the line of his bare shoulders, the dimple at the small of his back, the tight buns half-concealed beneath the sheet. She drew a deep breath of satisfaction. Day by day. Sometimes she felt she could live this way forever, adrift in time on a gentle, sun-dappled current, dazzled by the refractive patterns of the passing moments, with never a glance wasted forward, or behind. "Want to come up on deck with me?"

He groaned, hugging the pillow. "Aren't you a little early? It's not even light yet." Indeed, it took a bit of imagination to see the faint frosting of dawn on the circle of darkness visible through the porthole. "I thought we were supposed to be on vacation."

Katie shrugged. "Hey, it's my birthday. Forgive me if I'm a little excited."

He frowned at her. "Yeah, the big four-oh. So it's finally here. Whoopee."

Her eyebrows rose in surprise. "Hey, I'm supposed to be the one down in the dumps. Guess I'll have to host a funeral when you finally make thirty."

"Huh. The numbers don't matter. You're ageless, Katie. You always will be."

"So? I thought that was the plan. Live forever. Isn't that why we've spent the last four years wrestling with Generational Challenge?"

"Sure." He turned his head half away. "But you don't have to be so eager for the time to go by."

"Oh." She stood in front of the mirror, studying her reflection—the laugh lines around her mouth, the darting tracks of anger between her eyebrows. So strange, the way the habits of a lifetime etched themselves on a face. She touched a lock of her long blond hair. It'd been almost a year since she'd instructed the hairdresser to start hiding the gray.

Eager for the time to go by? Yes, perhaps. Perhaps she was. Generational Challenge was finally on the run, and the future looked bright. . . .

"Let's get married," Gregory said.

Katie winced, as if a dart had struck her between the shoulder blades. "Wh-what'd you say?"

He sat up then, a dark frown on his face. "You heard me. Let's get married."

Yeah, she'd heard him all right. But she couldn't have

been more taken aback if he'd asked her to join him in a
suicide pact and jump off the stern of the ship in the middle of the Pacific Ocean. Her heart raced before the prop-
osition. Why hadn't she seen this coming? She tried to
convince herself she was still asleep and this was some
sort of nightmare.

Let's get married?

"Wow," she said throatily. "Where did that come from?"

"Jesus, Katie, do you have to look so damned shocked?
We've known each other six years. Been together for the
last three. Don't tell me you haven't thought about it."

But she hadn't. Her eyes shifted guiltily. "Guess I've
been kind of, living in the present. We've been so busy. I
just haven't spent much time thinking about my personal
future."

"Maybe it's time you did. I love you, Katie."

"I love you too, Gregory. You know I do." That was the
truth. She could feel it in the fearful, thready beat of her
heart. She didn't want to lose him too. And yet . . .

"You want to make it happen again with Tom. I know
that. He's always stood between us."

"Maybe not between us, Gregory. But he's out there.
We've both based our lives on that belief."

"Sure," Gregory said. "Out there. Somewhere. And
you're running across time to him, full speed ahead.
Happy birthday. You're one year closer to the goal."

She slipped out as soon as she could. Heart trembling,
she practically ran up the staircase to the deck, to stop,
hands on the railing, head tilted back, drinking in the cool
sea air.

But the air was foul. The odor of rot rolled off the bow
wave. The ship was plowing through another algae bloom.

And Gregory was jealous of a dead man.

Tom!

It had been a long time since Katie had allowed herself
to think about Tom. Truthfully, she was afraid to draw him
into her active memory. A recollection was like a stone in
the river of time. Buried in the mud at the bottom of the
river, it was safe from erosion, corrosion, change. But bring
it up to the surface of the riverbed and it would be tum-

bled in the current, bounced around with a thousand other memories until all its idiosyncracies were broken off, all its irregularities smoothed away, its appearance utterly transformed from the original.

If she held Tom too often in her memory, she was afraid she would betray his rough, temperamental, dearly real self and transform him into some smooth, shiny fantasy knight that she could never love. Tom wasn't perfect, and that was the memory of him she wished to save.

She remembered Sal Greer and the lecherous bent of his talk show: *Do you intend to remain loyal to your husband? Or will you take lovers? Marry again?* She groaned. "Oh man, what have I done to my life?"

The stink of the ocean was dizzying, a hate-filled stench from the earth's feverish body. The deck rose and fell beneath Katie's feet as the ship plowed its way through a moderate swell. To the stern, the first crescent of a white-hot sun glared from the horizon, extinguishing the false innocence of distant, pink-tinged clouds and piercing the air with fierce needles of light.

Katie looked to the west to see the Big Island of Hawaii. The huge convex shapes of the shield volcanoes Mauna Loa and Mauna Kea rose against an orange sky.

It had been at a weather-monitoring station near the top of Mauna Loa that the rise in atmospheric carbon dioxide had first been convincingly charted. Now the volcano looked down over the tarmac and gantries of a newly constructed spaceport. Steam rose ominously from the southwest rift. But if the lava came, it would be too late to stop the first phase of the mission to Mars. That was scheduled to leave in less than an hour. It was her reason for being here. She stood on her toes, clutching the rail of the cruise ship *Mardi Gras*, and strained to pick out the shape of the unmanned heavy lift vehicle. She could just barely make it out. A gleaming white cylinder poised to carry forty tons of automated equipment to Mars to prepare a base for the astronauts scheduled to follow two years later. She felt touched with a sense of unreality. All her life, people had talked about going to Mars. And now it was happening. It was finally happening.

Other passengers were appearing on deck now, but most

took one whiff of the algae bloom and retired to the air-conditioned comfort of the observation lounge. Katie stuck it out in the open while the ship moved beyond the rot. When Gregory showed up with warm corn bread and coffee a few minutes later, there was only a faint, fetid trace remaining, almost lost behind the scent of decking and sun-scorched vinyl. From the shore, the breeze carried a suggestion of sulfur.

Gregory leaned on the rail beside her. He had his sunglasses on. "Thought you might be hungry," he said. His voice was distant, mechanical, as if he were speaking a recorded dialogue left behind by the better part of himself that had fled this unpleasant scene.

Her fists clenched the rail. She wanted to bring him back. She didn't want to lose him.

In her mind golden words gushed forth, mocking her as they strung themselves into a net that might catch a drifting lover:

Help me, Gregory. I want to be done with Tom. I want to be free of him. Help me to let him go. . . .

She could say these words. They were true words.

Probably.

She wasn't sure. How many people are ever really sure?

A shudder ran through her. The golden voice faded, leaving her with only two words, baldly honest and cold. "I'm sorry." It sounded so lame. She despised her own twisted soul because she couldn't offer him more than this.

His brow arched as he looked down at her. His shoulder shrugged as if it were a little thing. "Sorry for what? I always suspected where I stood with you. So it's done now. It's good to know these things." He offered her coffee.

She stared down at the Styrofoam cup, hating him for the bland niceties he would insist upon when by rights he should be raging at her. But then civility could be an expression of contempt, too, couldn't it? As if he could expect nothing better of her than this, so why get upset?

Taking the cup, she yanked off the lid, slopping the scalding brew across her hands. *"Dammit!"*

"Careful," Gregory urged. He offered her a napkin.

She took it, and wiped her reddened hand. Maybe she was making too much of it. He was here, wasn't he? He hadn't given up on her yet.

"Are we really fighting?" she muttered. "You know, we haven't even said anything absolute."

"No," he agreed. "That might be rude."

She glared at him. "You've got a cruel streak running through you."

"Keeps me alive."

"An advantage you hold over other men?"

He gazed across the water, his sunglasses revealing, not masking, the austerity of his soul. "You've been grieving long enough, Katie. Time, I think, to make up your mind."

She bowed her head. He was right about that, anyway. "I do love you."

"Show me, then. Marry me. Whatever you had with Tom is over and you'll never get it back. Because you're not the same. You've moved on. You've changed. It's nobody's fault, so stop feeling guilty. You don't owe him your soul."

She watched the water speed by, smelled the warm aura of the coffee, unable to compile an answer.

"Marry me," Gregory said again.

That was three times. If she turned him down now, she would lose him, she knew it. He was daring her to say no, and he was no coward.

She took a sip of coffee, the steam warm in her nostrils, the newly risen sun hot against her back. "All right then," she whispered. Then she said it louder. "All right. Let's get married. Let's do it today." She looked up at him, trying to gauge how much ceremony he might expect of her. "I'd be honored. I would."

He nodded slowly. "It's best." As if to convince himself.

"I know it is."

A little smile moved across his lips. "Today?"

"Yes. Today." She sipped her coffee.

How important were vows? Silently, she rehearsed the words that would divorce her from the past: *forsaking all others, till death do we part.*

Where was Tom? Already she felt him dropping behind,

like a flower cast upon the water, a passing memorial to the dead.

Gregory's arm slipped around her shoulder. She turned to him. Their lips met. She tasted his passion through the bitter coffee flavor, the steam-warmed mouth. She closed her eyes and held him close. *This is good*, she told herself. *This is very good*.

"Uh, your phone's ringing," Gregory said.

She started. Slipping a hand in her pocket, she pulled out the palm-sized phone, folded it open, and held it to her ear. "Hello?"

"Hey! Happy birthday, Mrs. Kishida. I can see you on TV."

"Ferris?"

Gregory groaned. He pulled out his Office Girl and switched it on, tuning into the coverage.

"Of course it's me," Ferris said, "sitting here in my little apartment in L.A., tending to my windowsill garden, and watching you smooch on national TV." A deep belly laugh rumbled up out of the phone. "They've got a camera on the bridge of the ship and it's feeding a line into national launch coverage."

"You're kidding." She turned around to examine the ship's superstructure, but she couldn't spot the lens.

"My, Katie," Ferris went on, in the same teasing banter, "you look pretty in the morning light. Or maybe that's just in contrast to that ugly scarecrow you're standing next to." Ferris laughed again. "How's life on the sea been treating you?"

She sighed, hungry for Ferris's optimistic company. California suddenly seemed terribly far away. Except for Gregory, everybody she loved was back there. Joy, Nikki, Mom, Jane. Tom. "I miss jet travel. The ocean ain't what it used to be."

"Nothing is, baby. That's the curse of the modern world."

"Huh. You still on your diet?"

"One hundred sixty-two pounds off and counting. Some things there's no going back on. You wake up one day and you step into a different world, a different life. The door only goes one way. You opened it for me, Katie, and I stepped through. I'm a different man now. I still live in the western world, but I'm not a part of it. I eat the native Hawaiian diet of my ancestors. Poi, sweet potatoes, fruits, and vegetables. A little chicken and fish. I thrive. The fat of the western world is tempting. So tempting. But unsustainable. More of us are accepting that every day."

"But not all of us." Her smile was bittersweet. "Your Primal Society still has people like me to deal with."

"Ah, Katie, you're not as bad as you think."

"Not if you take me alone. But there are a lot of other people touched with outrageous ambition." Her gaze rested on Gregory.

Things were moving. The Japanese had already come up with a precursor nanomachine that could assemble a sequence of simple molecules. It wasn't programmable, but the racy new Southland supercomputers promised to get past that hurdle soon with their purported talents for molecular design. The future was bearing down upon the world so fast that sometimes Katie felt as if she couldn't breathe against the pressure of acceleration.

Ferris felt it too. "It's a wave," he liked to say. "We can ride it, or we can let it pummel us against the reef, but there's no way we're going to stop it . . . wouldn't want to if I could. We need to change. And that's why the dead-in-the-water policies of Generational Challenge are a weight around our collective neck."

Now Ferris's voice rumbled once again in her ear. "I'll let you go, *ku'uipo*. You and your tall man and your dreams of power. We walk on different roads, but I can still love you. Happy birthday."

"Bye, Ferris."

She slipped the phone back into her pocket, checked her watch, then looked up at Gregory. "Uh, I forgot to tell you, but I've got a date."

Gregory's frown wasn't kind. "So get out of it, Katie. I want you with me. Besides, launch is in twenty minutes." She glanced at the screen of his Office Girl. Launch coverage had gone to a slow, sensuous scan of the engines that would boost the unmanned rocket free of Earth's gravity well. Raw power wrapped in perfect cylinders. Strafe the atmosphere and be gone.

"I'll be back in time."

The virtual reality chamber was available, naturally. Everyone on the charter cruise had come to view the launch in person, history in the making, and no one wanted to be caught outside the main line of action. The VR steward sat behind her desk, chewing on a wad of gum and watching the coverage on a large-screen TV. "I need a quickie," Katie said.

The steward looked her over disdainfully, "You familiar?"

"Sure. Don't trouble yourself. I know the routine." Like most people who could afford it, she spent more time than was good for her cruising the new artificial realities.

"Then go ahead. All three rooms are open."

Katie stopped at the scanner to let the computer download her physical image. Then she went to the locker and sorted through the gear until she found a set in her size— footed suit, helmet, gloves. She carried them to the first chamber.

It was a small room, only about eight by eight feet. The walls and floor were padded with apricot upholstery and light came from fluorescent panels overhead. Katie kicked off her shoes and left them at the door, then stepped into the wired coverall. It was a loose fit, but it would give the computer a good approximation of her position.

Outside the room, she could hear a TV commentator discussing the likely scenario for the last few minutes prelaunch. She picked up the helmet and slipped it over her head. The sound disappeared along with the upholstered walls. A dark-haired Asian woman smiled at her from across an ultramodern room done in stainless steel and glass. The woman was a computer-generated image, but the eyes that fixed on Katie glistened with intelligence, and she seemed more alive, more real than the indifferent steward outside the door. "How may I help you today?"

"I have an appointment," Katie said. "It should be in

your files. A scheduled connection with Roxanne Scott, ID number ..."

The image nodded. "Your party is ready."

"Bring me out three minutes prior to the Mars launch."

The woman nodded again, then vanished, taking the room with her. Another woman appeared in her place; another room. Katie had to do a quick wipe of expression to hide her immediate repulsion.

The woman she faced was grossly obese. She'd lowered herself into a recliner from which it seemed her weight would prevent her from ever rising again. She sat in a tiny, ugly, roach-infested room, in front of a window overlooking a vast expanse of sky filled with slowly roiling, dirty yellow clouds. There was no sign at all of ground below. On an end table beside the recliner a pink-frosted birthday cake burned with forty candles laid out in a four-by-ten grid.

Katie's gaze returned to the woman. Her hair was silvery blond and very short, combed into a helmetlike configuration, not a hair out of place. Her dull blue eyes blinked reflexively, half-hidden behind the folds of fat.

"Roxanne?" Katie asked, though there was nothing in this woman to suggest her former friend ... until a grin slowly spread across the obese woman's face.

"Happy birthday, Katie. It's been a long time." Her voice was husky, almost hoarse. But it was Roxanne.

"Maybe we should have made it longer," Katie said. "How many hours did you waste composing this obscenity?"

Roxanne's grin faded. Katie could see her now. She was a ghost haunting the obese body. As Katie watched, she rose out of the flesh, a translucent figure in loose jeans and a faded cutoff T-shirt. She'd been editing her face or else she'd had more plastic surgery, because her nose was subtly different, flatter, almost Asian. And her cheeks seemed wider. Katie glanced back at the obese body. The woman's tiny eyes no longer blinked. Her breast had ceased to rise and fall with the wheezing of her breath.

"The corpulent body of the West," Roxanne said, her image as insubstantial as an early hologram. "Got the idea from Ferris's PR. Thought you'd appreciate the humor."

When Katie looked again, the woman in the chair had dissolved to bone and dust.

Katie's lip twisted in anger. It didn't bother her when Ferris ran this scene. He was looking for constructive options. But Roxanne was just stirring the fire. "Look," she snapped. "I've got about five minutes."

Roxanne regarded her with measuring eyes. "Maybe," she said. "But you never really know."

Their surroundings had changed. Now they stood under a cloudy sky, on a long plain beside the ocean. For as far as Katie could see, tumbled, eroded, half-buried blocks of concrete cluttered the flats. Streaks of rusted iron ran through the sterile ground. Through Roxanne's translucent body, she watched waves rolling against the shore, grinding a dark, coarse gravel.

"I've given you a lot of shit," Roxanne said. "I know that. What happened to Tom—it really shook me up. It made me see how far we've wandered from what's real." Katie glanced at her, wondering what definition reality carried today. Roxanne didn't seem to notice. "We're gonna run ourselves into the ground chasing tech," she said. "And it's such a con. Always promising more and better but never explaining the price until it's too late."

The concrete blocks had dissolved further, settling deeper into the ground. Tall grass filled the plain. The ocean was gone, replaced by a sea of chaparral. A fly buzzed beneath a hot bronze sky. Katie tipped her head back, letting the sun's image stroke her face. She could almost feel the warmth. Someday she *would* feel it. VR would be that good. "Have you ever tried looking at the upside, Roxanne? It's not all bad, you know. Look at me. I'm not complaining."

"Yeah, but you should be." Perhaps a quarter mile away, a herd of small antelope wandered out from the brush. An eagle soared overhead. "That's what's so weird. We should all be complaining. Tech has robbed us. It's turned us into uncaring psychotics, but we just tell ourselves *that's the way it is*."

Katie felt her patience snap. "That's a lie."

"It's not. Think about it. How many people have you walked by today without even *seeing*? How many people have you seen whose lives or deaths matter to you at all? We're strangers in our own land." Her gaze roved out across the grassland. "If you met someone out here, you wouldn't ignore them."

Katie looked down at the carefully detailed ground, wondering why she felt so trapped by Roxanne's ill-defined fears. She could walk out of the room. Strip off the VR gear and rejoin Gregory. She imagined the cool, smooth feel of the rocket engines beneath her hand. How far could they go? How fast? Time seemed to roll away from her like a great slope shrouded in banks of fog that parted now and then to reveal glimpses of future centuries. Ancient forests on Mars. A city surrounding the Sun. Earth giving birth to independent islands of life, thousands of threads of evolution twining throughout the stars.

When she looked up, the chaparral had turned to desert. Banks of skeletal brush were anchored in the loose sand, their tiny, trembling leaves casting plaintive shade. Flies buzzed over a pile of fresh scat. An armadillolike creature hunched in the shade of the bushes, its long tongue flicking in and out of the swarming flies.

"It doesn't matter what we believe," Roxanne said softly. "The earth is bigger and smarter and more adaptable than any machine we could ever create. It'll outlast us. It'll still be here when tech is gone . . . or when it's moved on." She gave Katie an odd look, one eyebrow raised.

The desert became a grassland again. The grassland grew into forest, and then into steaming jungle. In the distance, Katie could hear the crash and roar of some huge dream creature. The life span of the earth was measured in billions of years, its face ever changing with the arrangement of continents. She flushed, suddenly aware of how paltry her own mental vistas became when compared to that.

Roxanne's translucent ghost fingers swept across her arm without inspiring any sensation of contact. "How can I say this, Katie, except straight out? I feel like everything you've done in the last six years is wrong. And it scares me. I love you. I always have. We've been friends since we were little girls, but I don't understand where you've gone."

Beneath the jungle floor, Katie suddenly felt the rolling motion of the ship. It was a peculiar sensation, as if she were slow-motion surfing a great wave, carrying her farther and farther away from all that had once been, and she had no desire to turn back. "There's more ahead of us, than behind," she said softly. "Anyway, that's how I need to feel."

The jungle had lifted into alpine strata. The plants here were small, hunched against the oppressive cold. Katie stared at them, touched by a sudden, vague fear.

"I have AIDS-related complex," Roxanne said. "Just thought you should know."

Katie swung around, hit by a triple jolt of repulsion, pity, and anger. She felt the blood hot in her cheeks, felt the inadequacy of words. "Roxanne! But there's so much they can do for you these days."

Roxanne shrugged. "It's still fatal. Especially if you're female. But hell, who am I to whine? I haven't wasted my days. And I'm not afraid to die."

The plants were gone. They stood on a slope of ice. A thin fog streamed past their ankles, driven by an arctic wind. "Maybe I'll see Tom before you will, huh? Think you'll be jealous?"

Katie was saved from having to answer by the simulated voice of the computer: "Mrs. Kishida, there are three minutes remaining before the scheduled launch."

"Sounds like you've got to go," Roxanne said. Her thin ghost began to waver.

"Roxanne, if there's anything I can do to help you—"

"Oh, there is. Believe it or not, I still feel closer to you than to anyone else. We're like sisters. And I want you with me when the time comes for my final climb."

The ambient light suddenly dimmed. Katie was left standing in near darkness. She yanked the VR helmet off her head and dropped it on the padded floor, then ripped open the adhesive strip on the coverall. Tears streamed down her cheeks. Her throat ached. She peeled off the coverall, bundled it up, and flung it into a corner of the room.

"Roxanne, you've always been so stupid!" she shouted. "And I won't help you die. I won't. I won't do it." She swiped at her tears with the back of her hand, stooped to pick up her shoes and hat, and ran from the chamber, past the critical gaze of the VR steward. From the large-screen TV on the wall she heard a network announcer mark the time: "T minus one minute fifty seconds."

She bounded up the stairs to the deck. A crowd had formed. She spied Gregory standing tall near the railing and pushed her way through to him. On all sides, Office Girls with active screens were chanting the final sequence before launch. "What's the matter?" Gregory asked, concern flooding his face.

She shook her head and rubbed at her tears, not trusting herself to speak. Out across the ocean, she could make out the body of the rocket against its gantry. It was a huge thing, a phallic symbol of power, and she cherished it. The Office Girls intoned the final seconds. There were no orders to stop the launch sequence. Everything was go. Excited voices counted down with the network announcer. "Five, four, three—"

Steam surged up the sides of the rocket. A bright orange flame cut through the roiling white clouds. Then the rocket body wavered slightly and began to lift clear, standing tall on a tail of fire. The roar reached them across the water as the engine rose higher and higher into the sky, a brilliant star born in the morning. Tears started in her eyes again, and she leaned against Gregory, shuddering in delight at the roaring walls of sound bounding across the ocean.

Wedged Time—
Alternate Landscapes

It was the rending hunger in his belly that woke him. The pain was horrible, as if the acids in his stomach had started consuming his own entrails. *Oh, God,* he thought, forgetting for a moment that he'd already turned away from God to follow a new deity. *My Familiar.* But she was gone too. Disappeared, after he'd stumbled on the den of oni. The realization ran like a bitter toxin through his blood. She'd saved him, only to abandon him to the oni. His lips drew back in a growl of primitive fury, cracking a thin skin of ice that had formed on his face. "Traitor!" he screamed, and a thousand mocking echoes of his pain reverberated overhead: *traitor, traitor, traitor, traitor* . . . fading slowly. He cowered under the rain of accusations. Only when silence returned did he open his eyes, blinking away the frost that sought to seal him in sleep. When he lifted his head, thin shards of red-stained ice fell to the ground.

He found himself at the bottom of a deep and terribly narrow crevasse, hemmed in by walls of glacial ice so close he could have touched them both at once if his arms weren't still lashed to his sides by the oni's leather thongs. The light here was dim. But it was daylight.

He laid his head back down on the ground. Then he cautiously began to flex his aching muscles, testing the strength of his bonds. The cold had made the straps stiff and brittle. He strained against them. The effort sent bolts of pain ricocheting through his bruised muscles, but he persisted. A strap near his elbow snapped. Then another, at his hips. And slowly, one by one, each brittle thong broke in the cold. Finally he lay sprawled on the frozen ground, dazzled by bits of darkness that swarmed in his vision, the tiny heralds of a greater darkness lurking just out of sight.

It was several minutes before some semblance of strength returned to him. While he waited, he studied the ground that supported him. It was solid. He found some satisfaction in that. Deep snow would have been treacherous, but here there was only a thin, windblown layer of powder over a dark, uneven floor of rock. At least, he supposed it was rock.

Odd-looking rock.

Finally, he gathered his will and sat up. He was shivering. More from pain than from cold. Or perhaps from anger. After all, she was gone. His gaze wandered up the glacier's walls, trying to find some sign of the door to the oni's lair. But there was no hint of it.

Was it an accident that he'd stumbled on that lair of demons? Or had she planned it . . . ? Could she be one of them? He remembered her fear, and the abrupt way she'd disappeared. Where had she gone? He wanted her back.

His mind was muzzy and slow. He thought about her in a distracted, dreamy way, while his gaze played across the patch of red ice that marked the place he'd fallen. Red-stained ice. How much blood had he lost? He examined his body. His gray skin was covered with abrasions that seemed to be oozing blood still, though nothing looked too serious. How much blood could he afford to lose? Now that he thought about it, every cell in his body seemed to ache, especially in his head. And he was still hungry.

Some part of him tried to provide a bit of orientation. *You're dying*, it said, quite matter-of-factly. This alarmed him. He didn't want to die. Fear pounded in his ears in the ancient beast reaction. He had to find food, and soon.

He glanced up at the walls again, then shook his head. He'd already refused the oni's food. He wouldn't change his mind on that. There must be some other food somewhere.

He stood up on wobbly legs, carefully studying the lay of the lumpy ground as he took a tentative step. A pair of eyes stared back at him. He started, gazing in astonishment at a human face embedded in the frozen ground. Its glassy eyes were wide with fear, unblinking and coated with rime—the face of a corpse captured by frost in the moment of final understanding. Now that he looked, he could trace the outline of the poor fellow's body, the jutting ribs, the thrusting elbow, bronzy skin pulled tight over bone. He looked at other shapes in the ground and found more faces, more bodies, *real* human bodies, not like his. The kind of bodies he remembered from . . .

He lunged forward in long, wobbly strides. Dozens of dead eyes stared at him. Corpses everywhere, filling the bottom of the crevasse. Hundreds of dead, thousands. Old people. Young people. Children. Their bodies piled atop one another, God knows how deep, all fused together by the ice. The corpses of those who'd refused the oni's way? Of those who'd refused to do what was necessary to go on? And he'd thought his defiance had been unique! He laughed bitterly. And then the weight of all those deaths touched him and he fell to his knees and began to weep. But his grief didn't last long. Hunger was a baser instinct. He scratched with his fingernails at the thin, desiccated flesh of an exposed thigh. It was like scratching at granite. He struck at it with his fist, then yowled in pain. Rolling echoes of his rage climbed the crevasse. He threw himself at the corpse, licking the frozen flesh. His tongue came away bleeding. He leaped back, howling, cursing himself for an abomination. The ice concurred with that assessment in violent repercussions.

He grew quiescent, listening to his voice tumbling up the glacier's walls. It would be so easy just to lie down, to join these individuals who'd gone before, who'd become a part of the frozen, untouchable past. Perhaps that was why he was here.

But he wanted to live. He still held that desire above his despair. He wanted to live. He wanted to find her, and live.

He retraced his steps until he stood over the broken leather thongs the oni had used to bind him. He could suck on those, until they softened enough to chew. But he knew where the leather had come from. He turned away.

Either his sight was dimming, or the meager daylight was beginning to fade. He craned his neck, searching for the top of the crevasse. A little cry of astonishment stole from his throat then, and he stumbled backward. The walls! Never had he seen walls so high. He told himself there was no way to gauge distance in this white hell, and yet . . . some erudite part of him knew that the glacier's walls must rise for a mile or more, straight up, to frame a sliver of sky of deepest blue set with a handful of white stars blazing at a magnitude he'd never witnessed.

His gaze lowered, pressed down by the sudden awareness of his own inconsequential status. A wave of dizziness rolled over him and he reached out for support, pressing his palms against opposite walls of ice.

A rhythmic thrumming ran through the glacier. He yanked his hands back in surprise. Cautious now, he touched the walls again. There it was. A faint vibration, like a pulse. A heartbeat hinting that the great river of ice was in motion. How fast was it flowing? How long before this narrow crack closed completely?

He looked up and down the cleft, but he could see no more than a few hundred yards in either direction before a jag in the path of the crevasse cut off his view. He shrugged and started walking downhill, treading on the bodies of the past. Two steps. Three. Four. Then his feet slipped out from under him. He went down hard, landing on his butt. It was a minor pain compared to everything else he'd endured, but it was too much just the same. Like a flood of oxygen on a smoldering fire, it caused his rage to flare. He screamed at the sky, he pounded the ice, he kicked and stomped at the staring eyes embedded in the ground until they shattered beneath his heels.

Then a cold wraith swept past him, a sentient wind that twisted round and round, seeming to chuckle as it slipped down the narrow way. The walls overhead moaned, and thin clouds raced past.

The cold. He saw it then as an entity, a witch set to seduce him with an offer of peace, of painless dissolution in the bowels of the glacier.

No worries. No right or wrong.

He gazed down at the shattered faces beneath his feet. Every one of them had followed the witch. She caressed his face with invisible fingers. Her chill breath wafted past the wounds of his breast. He drew back, shaking in terror. "Not me," he whispered. "I won't go with you."

The witch hissed softly in his ears. Her icy fingers reached into his body.

"No!" He spun away and began to run. Stumbling, falling. Praying to his Familiar. Picking himself up again, running down, down, down, past one jog and then another as the crevasse zigzagged across the glacier. Finally he collapsed, exhausted. He lay on his back and stared up at the sliver of sky, blinking in disgruntled surprise. The slice of sky was darker, smaller . . . farther away than it had been before. He'd been going downhill. But the walls were rising.

industry down was a
cultural terrorist with a
rocket launcher. Three planes
in three days. That was enough.
People were afraid to fly, the
all it took to bring the
industry down was a cultural
terrorist with a rocket launcher.
Three planes in three days.
That was enough. People
were afraid to fly, the
industry folded, and the world
became a smaller, nastier
place.

BOY: At least we have Venture Rail,
              Grandpa. That's how I came
              to visit you.

GEEZER: We have Venture Rail,
              now, son. But we'll lose that
              too if we ever let ourselves be
              cowed again.

[Black screen, white graphics]

NARRATOR: To enter your name on a
              petition in support of the Right
              to Travel call 1-900-OUR-
              WRLD.

10

Our-World

Forsaking all others.... On the surface it seemed a cruel oath. Yet it could buy so much. Katie had gained three years of wedded happiness with it so far, three years of a fine marriage to Gregory Hunt.

Now her daughter Joy had made a marriage of her own. Closing her eyes, Katie snuggled against Gregory's shoulder. Under the wedding tent the air was hot and still, thick with the scent of meadow grass and pine forest. Joy and her groom had taken their vows in midmorning and left by noon, but the guests carried on with the celebration through the heat of the day. Now five hours old, the party had obtained a fine, mellow atmosphere. Raucous conversations had subsided into quiet dialogue. A few people had even fallen asleep on the benches. More had scattered across the meadow, to nap or picnic in shady patches at the edge of the woods, while some had wandered back to their rooms at the lodge. Katie tilted her head to look up at Gregory. A happy sigh escaped her lips. "You know something?" she muttered, half-asleep in the heat. "There are women out there, forty-three years old like me, who are having their first babies. And here I am, having just given my first baby away in marriage." She chuckled in smug satisfaction. "I expect I'll be a grandmother this time next year."

"I expect you will be," Gregory said. "You've got a knack for getting what you want."

"Huh. Let's hope you still feel that way next week, after the congressional hearings."

"Ah-ah," he said. "No worries today. Remember?"

"Right." She kissed him on the cheek. "You've really been a good boy today. I haven't seen you fighting with Ilene even once."

He shrugged innocently. "Well, I promised Joy no politics. Besides, I haven't been able to corner the good senator yet."

Joy, being Joy, had invited her auntie the senator to the wedding despite Nikki and Katie's objections. *She's still family, and I love her.* Right. And on Monday the Senate hearings would begin and Katie would be testifying before Senator Carson's hostile Committee on Advanced Technologies. Somehow she doubted the restraint the senator had shown today would carry over to that meeting.

"Hey, Mom." Nikki dropped down on the bench in front of her. "Are we going or what?"

Katie gazed fondly at her second daughter. Nikki was a lean nineteen, looking dangerous in her strapless pink floral gown, as sleek and feminine as a pantheress. She'd taken to wearing her brown hair in a sassy commando cut that was totally Nikki. Her brown eyes gazed out at the world with a disturbing intensity.

Katie stretched and groaned, then let Gregory shove her to her feet. "All right, all right. Just hope I don't fall asleep on the way."

They headed for the rest room to change clothes. Off came the lacy finery and on went the climbing tights. "Ah, that feels more natural," Nikki said, sighing. Katie grunted. She was feeling tired and a little bit dizzy—the aftereffects of a traumatic experience. She'd actually cried at the wedding today, as she'd let go of Joy's hand, set it in the hand of her groom. Where had the years gone? And how had the girls managed to grow up so fast?

"Oh, come on, Mom." Nikki interrupted her reverie. "Don't get all teary-eyed again."

Katie blinked hard and grinned. "She's too young."

"Right." Nikki was already in her third year at Stanford, but thank goodness didn't show signs of settling down anytime soon. "Of course, you were my age when you married Dad. At least Joy had the decency to wait until she was twenty-one."

"I may have been your age, but I'm sure I was much more mature."

"Uh-huh. Tell me that when you're done marking time with Gregory."

Katie froze in the act of arranging her dress on a hanger. "You never miss a shot, do you?"

Nikki grinned. "I like to keep myself centered."

"You've always had such a cute way with words, Nikki."

"At least I know where to put my loyalties."

Katie finished zipping the dress onto the hanger. "Times change and people change. I'm sorry it's been so hard for you to accept Gregory. But we've been married *three years*, Nikki. Lighten up."

Nikki tossed her own dress casually over her shoulder. "You never did take his name, Mom. Why's that?"

Katie shrugged. "What's a name? A name's just an appliance. Everybody knows me by Kishida. It'd be too confusing to change it now."

Nikki chuckled. "You run that same line on Gregory?"

Katie turned half away, her fingers nervously arranging a ruffle. "Look, do you want to climb today? 'Cause I'm really not into this friendly chat."

"If he told you it was okay with him, he was lying. He wants to erase Daddy from your life."

Katie yanked the hanger off its hook. "Is this why we don't talk anymore?"

"Hey. You're good at dodge ball."

"That's it, Nikki. I'm going."

"No, Mom! Wait." Nikki caught up with her before she was out the door. "I'm sorry, okay? I've got a big mouth. Gregory's a wonderful man. Everything's going to be hunky-dory."

Katie came to an abrupt stop. Closing her eyes, she

breathed out a long sigh, striving for patience. "Nikki. Gregory *is* a wonderful man. You don't have to like him. But is it too much to ask that you let *me* like him?"

"Sorry, Mom. But Joy's the nice one. I'm the realist. Enjoy yourself now. It isn't going to last."

"Well, if Auntie Ilene has her way at the hearings next week, it's going to have to last. Because I won't have a chance for anything else."

Nikki smiled at that in a sly, triumphant way, leading Katie to want to analyze what she'd just said. But Nikki didn't give her half a chance. "Come on," she said, tugging at Katie's elbow. "Standing around only makes you old."

Katie wore a careful smile when they returned to the wedding tent to stash their stuff. But it wasn't necessary. Gregory didn't notice them. He was too absorbed in conversation with Ilene at an otherwise empty table. Katie frowned when she saw them together, expecting the worst. Though Gregory's interest in cryonics had waned with the passing of time, his views on biotechnology had grown more radical. *Any* regulation felt like too much to him. He wanted to get to Mars and he didn't want to wait a lifetime. Well, at least Joy wouldn't be here to see it if things got ugly.

She looked around for Roxanne, but apparently the summer heat had driven her back to the air-conditioned lodge. Roxanne had suffered full-blown AIDS since last winter complicated by a bout with pneumonia. The forest service had given her a disability retirement and now she sat at home most days, in the company of her dogs and her nurse, cruising through the virtual reality of the hour.

Katie met her in the VR sometimes. Katie wasn't a perma-suit like Roxanne, but she liked going under. Liked it too much, maybe. She knew she spent way too many hours under the spell. But that was the nature of the VR: potent, personal. A deep current that flowed through your blood and pulled you under, playing with your mind until you didn't want to surface anymore into Cold Reality.

Katie smiled as her mother took her gloved hand. "You look so tired, hon. Are you sure you're up to a climb?"

"It's nothing much, Mom. Just a little rock hop. Twenty minutes to the top."

"Best way in the world to work off tension, Grandma," Nikki chimed in. "When are you going to try it?"

Belle knew when to concede the field. "Just be careful."

They agreed to that. Picking up the trail, they followed it across the meadow and into the pine forest. The trees were looking a little sallow and sickly, with great masses of needles gone from the upper branches. Katie scowled at the damage. Blame it on the ozone, she thought. On acid rain, on global warming, on atmospheric pollution, then forget about it. That seemed to be the general attitude. If it costs money to fix, forget it. Close your eyes. Don't hike in the forests, don't swim in the oceans and you won't see the web of life unraveling. Stay in the shade and pretend that everything will be all right.

She caught sight of Ferris. He was holding court on a picnic blanket under the shade of the first trees, mesmerizing some of Joy's impressionable friends with his deep-throated voice. His eyes twinkled as they passed, but he said nothing.

The walk got Katie's blood going, and she felt better by the time they reached the base of the rock some ten minutes later. She gazed up fondly at the escarpment. She'd climbed here before. There were two routes up, but since they didn't have ropes today, the sheer climb from the streambed was out. It would be a free climb, up the north slope of the exposed granite, on a slope set back thirty degrees from the vertical, except for a sheer stretch at the top. Katie took a pull from her water bottle while she examined the slope. Two narrow cracks ran down its face, each supporting a few stunted pines. There was a ledge at about thirty feet and another, narrower shelf at about forty. It looked easy. She stashed the water bottle and turned to Nikki. "Age before beauty?"

Nikki bowed formally and flourished her hand. "Please."

It was a good, short climb. When they reached the top, they were able to look out across the forest to the meadow where the wedding party continued. Katie took off her helmet and lay down in the brilliant sun, listening to the sound of the stream far below and the buzz of a nearby fly. She could remember the day when every stream in these mountains had supported a population of frogs or salamanders. But now amphibians were as rare as gold. Hell, even the *flies* seemed to be declining in number, and that was damn scary.

"You're going to fry out there in the sun," an unexpected voice said.

Katie's eyes flew open. She looked up toward the forested slope above the exposed granite to see Roxanne sitting in the shade not ten feet away, her back pressed against the trunk of a fallen pine. Her skin had darkened over the past couple of years and she'd dyed her hair black. With the earlier surgery on her nose and cheekbones, she looked more Amerindian than Caucasian now. Her eyes were invisible behind dark glasses, but her face glistened with an unhealthy perspiration and she sat very still, her muscles flaccid, as if she'd used up the last of her energy on the rock.

"How did you get up here?" Katie asked in astonishment. She pushed herself up to a sitting position. Nikki was staring at Roxanne as if she were a ghost.

"I flew," Roxanne said. "On the wings of an eagle." She laughed softly, self-deprecatingly. "It may have been a mistake. But I wanted to try it one last time."

Katie moved herself into a patch of shade. She took out her water bottle and drank, feeling a cynical kind of amusement. Roxanne had been trying to get her to go climbing for over a year now, but Katie had consistently refused, remembering their conversation in the VR and afraid of what Roxanne might do. And now here they were, together, at the top of a cliff. But Roxanne seemed calm.

Nikki settled down, watching Roxanne warily. Roxanne scowled at her in irritation. "What's the matter? Afraid I'll bite?"

"It wouldn't be the first time," Nikki said.

"Ooh. Guess you're not as forgiving as your mama."

"Guess not."

Katie wasn't up for a squabble. She bluntly inserted herself into the conversation, diverting it. "How are you planning to get down from here, Roxanne?"

Roxanne tipped her head back against the log. "Now that's a pointed question." She chuckled to herself. Her skin seemed sallow beneath the dark pigments, and her perspiration had begun to bead on her temples. She was feverish, Katie realized. The single buzzing fly seemed drawn to the scent of her sweat.

"I've been thinking of going to Africa," Roxanne muttered. "You know, over a million more people have died of AIDS there in the last couple of years. So many are gone, the agricultural system is falling apart, and the governments have slaughtered most of the wildlife on the game preserves to feed the people. I've been thinking of going there, but they don't need one more mouth to feed."

Katie stood and clambered over to Roxanne. She placed her hand on Roxanne's forehead. The gesture seemed to startle her. Her eyes flew open, and she flinched.

"My God," Katie said. "You're burning up." She retrieved her water bottle. "Drink." Roxanne reluctantly accepted the bottle. She took a tentative swig. "Roxanne, how the hell did you expect to get down from here?" Katie asked again.

"I'm going to fly," Roxanne muttered. The hand that held the water bottle hardly seemed capable of gripping it. It shook with a slow palsy. "I'm going to fly on the wings of a golden eagle. I can become the eagle. With my spirit-guardian I've flown all over the earth and through the canyons of Mars and even through the empty darkness between worlds. I'll fly."

Katie felt a cold prickle of fear on her spine. "That's in the VR, Roxanne. Where you can do anything. But we're up here on this rock for real."

Roxanne looked at her through half-closed eyes, as if she were floating on the edge of sleep. "Is that right, Katie? Are you sure?"

Nikki made a sharp sound of disgust. "She's over the edge," she said, rummaging around in her pack. She pulled out a phone. "I'm calling the rangers."

Roxanne sat up abruptly, her eyes unnaturally bright. "Don't bother," she said. "Your dad's already coming for

me. Tom's coming." She stood up shakily, staring wide-
eyed at the glare of the sky. "There. Look there." She
pointed up.

Katie didn't want to look. She was working on a bad
case of the willies. But almost against her will, her gaze
shifted upward. She caught her breath in shock when she
sighted a pair of golden eagles soaring in lazy arcs across
the valley. She stood, transfixed by the rare sight, taken by
a sense of expectation, suddenly open to the notion that in
the complexity of the world, anything at all could happen.

"Mom, stop her!" Nikki barked.

Katie's heart leaped. Her gaze snapped back to earth.
Roxanne had wandered over to the cliff above the
streambed. She teetered on the edge. Every muscle in her
body seemed to be trembling and sweat dripped off her
fingertips. Still, she hummed softly to herself, almost
chanting under her breath a glossolalia derived from some
cheery old pop tune.

Katie scurried after her. But she slipped on some eroded
bits of rock and went down on one knee. Overhead, an eagle screeched and Roxanne went very still. "He's calling
me," she said. She raised her arms to the sky. Then she
launched herself into the abyss.

At the same moment, Katie lunged forward. She caught
a scrap of Roxanne's shirt. Her nails sank into Roxanne's
bony arm. She tried to put on the brakes, but she felt herself being dragged forward. Her chest slammed into the
rock. She skidded, trying to dig her elbows in while still
holding tight to Roxanne. Then, abruptly, she jerked to a
stop, her chin just over the edge of the abyss. Nikki had
grabbed her belt and was kneeling on her back, swearing
a blue streak.

Katie found herself staring down at the rocky streambed
far below. Roxanne dangled in her hands. My God, she
didn't weigh anything at all. Katie's fingers completely encircled her upper arm. For one moment, everything was
still. Then Roxanne seemed to wake up.

Her chin snapped back. Her eyes were wild with fright.
"Don't let go, Katie!" she screamed. "Don't let go. I don't
want to die. I don't want to." She began to claw at the cliff
face, thrashing about so that Katie's grip began to slip, and

her tenuous hold on the thick granite was thrown into question.

Then Nikki spoke in an ugly growl. "If you feel yourself sliding, Mom, drop her."

"No, don't!" Roxanne begged piteously. "Please, please, please. . . ."

"Help me move back," Katie hissed. Nikki hauled on her shoulders, helping her to edge back from the cliff, and a moment later, Nikki was able to reach down and grab Roxanne's other arm. They pulled her back up onto the rock. She collapsed against the hot granite, shivering, refusing to open her eyes or move or respond to any of their questions. So Katie picked her up and carried her back to the shade, and sat with her, cradling her, until the rangers came.

It was late afternoon when Katie stood in the parking lot at the end of the trail, watching the paramedics load Roxanne onto the ambulance. Her fever had pushed her into a delirium, leaving her muttering in some virtual reality that existed independent of any machine.

As the ambulance pulled away, Katie turned, intending to head back up to the meadow to see that the rented tent was dismantled and the grounds cleaned according to the contract. But Senator Carson stood in her way. Katie stopped short, staring at Ilene, really seeing her for the first time in years. Good God, how she'd aged! She looked like her mother, Jane. Neat, gray-streaked hair, wizened face. Katie ran a quick calculation and realized that Ilene was sixty-four. That would put Tom in his mid-fifties. Could they all really be this old?

After a moment, she remembered herself and looked away. But Ilene wasn't willing to leave it at that. "I'm sorry about your friend," she said.

Katie drew back stiffly, unready for simple condolences. "That's just Roxanne, you know? She's got her own vision of the world—she's just not quite sure what it is."

"Modern paganism." Ilene sniffed.

Katie shrugged. She had a lot to do before the train to D.C. tonight.

"Things are going to get rough over the next few years, Katie. On a global scale, I mean."

"Hell, that's already started." She was taken by a sudden draught of bitterness. "That's why we need nanotech *now*. Biotech. We need to get moving, Ilene, or we're all going to rot."

Ilene snorted. "More of the same is *not* going to save us. We need to put on the brakes, on a global scale. We need to get control. We're on a runaway train, Katie, headed into a concrete wall. And you want to stoke the boiler." She shook her head. "Why didn't you let your friend die?"

Katie's mouth fell open in astonishment. Ilene just looked at her with a clear, steady gaze. "She's going to die anyway. You've just condemned her to a few more months of pain and fear. Because *you're* afraid to die."

Katie bristled. "Get off it, Ilene! Roxanne was delirious. She didn't know which way was up."

"Keep on believing that. But just be sure you visit her regularly so you can see what being alive really means to her." And Ilene adjusted her purse on her shoulder and headed off for the parking lot, fishing in her pocket for the car keys.

It was nearly eleven o'clock that night when Katie found herself on the curb at the train station, a suitcase at her feet while she kissed and hugged Nikki good-bye. She'd been dozing in the car. Now she swayed on her feet, seeing the world with that sense of false clarity that comes from an advanced state of exhaustion. Gregory took her hand. She reached for her suitcase, but Ferris caught it up first, winking at her. They waved to Nikki as she drove off, then they walked together to the counter to check in. They were all three scheduled to testify at the Senate hearing on Monday. They stood in line behind a man who seemed vaguely familiar to Katie, and after a minute she recognized him as one of Senator Carson's aides. Of course Ilene would be on the same train, she realized. There weren't many transportation options in this day and age and Ilene, too, had to be in D.C. on Monday.

The aide checked in a few bags and confirmed a handful of tickets. Katie watched him as he walked away from the counter. A moment later, Ilene swept through the terminal, surrounded by a bevy of bodyguards, a few members of the press trailing behind. Katie watched them go through the metal detector and the explosives sensor. Then Ferris was at her side, his deep voice rumbling in her ear. "You're heading for her country now. She'll be at the top of the food chain, like a shark in her territory. Keep that in mind and your senses will stay sharp."

Katie looked at him in disbelief, sure that she must be dreaming. Then Gregory slipped his arm around her shoulders. "Come on. We'll be able to sleep on the train."

But they didn't sleep, not at once, anyway. Ferris had brought a thermos of herbal tea, and they sat in his cabin for a few minutes, drinking that and watching the night flash past outside the window. Katie turned to Gregory. "What were you talking to Ilene about?" she asked, suddenly remembering the unsettling sight of the two of them deep in conversation under the wedding tent.

Gregory smiled sadly. "Philosophy. It didn't go anywhere."

"You wait until after the hearings," Ferris said. "When the vote's taken, somebody's going to lose—and not gracefully, I'll bet. After the vote, things will start to happen."

Katie thought about that. Acts of domestic terrorism had been on the rise for years—mostly fanatics pushing the agenda of Generational Challenge. The planned third stage of the Mars mission had been put on indefinite hold. In a few weeks, when the Mars explorers had finished their five-hundred-day stay on the red planet, they'd abandon their base and go home with no successors in sight. The Chinese still had their space station, but by all reports it was in terrible shape, and caught in a rapidly degrading orbit. In a few more years it could become yet another atmospheric hazard as parts rained down around the globe.

"If things go badly tomorrow," Katie said, checking her watch to be sure that it was already Sunday, "we're going to have to make plans to relocate the vault."

"Don't be too hasty," Ferris said. "Political boundaries are changing and the federal government doesn't have the power it used to have. You'll be safe in California for a while."

But Katie was feeling surly. "We need to be safe and *free*. We're not any closer now to restoring our suspension patients than we were on the day Tom died."

"Sure we are," Gregory said. "We've learned a lot about politics and kissing ass. Isn't that the first step forward?"

Katie ignored him. "We need to be an independent nation."

"We're working on that," Ferris said. Katie's chin came up; she looked at him in wide-eyed surprise. "Oh, not for the state of California," Ferris amended, dismissing the idea with a wave of his hand. "We're trying to develop an independent primal nation, a cultural network, if you will, of primal philosophy woven through the greater structure of the megaculture."

"What?" Katie croaked in total confusion.

Ferris laughed. "Sorry, I must be drunk." But Ferris never drank. "Think about it, Katie. With electronic communication and virtual reality, political borders don't mean much anymore. Why can't a nation exist as a discontinuous network of people who share a definition of the world?"

"Because they still have to breathe the same air as their neighbors," Gregory said, his voice harsh with a cynicism that was becoming a pernicious habit. "The other guy will still be there, looking over your shoulder to gauge the quality of your morals and your techniques of child rearing, while he spews his pollution in your face."

"That's why I'm for nanotech," Ferris said softly. "It's the only thing that'll move the old industrial world out, before it corrupts all primal visions of the earth."

Later, in their own cabin, Katie lay in the bunk with Gregory, enjoying the taste of his lips and the gentle thrust of his tongue in her mouth, while the easy sway of the train rocked her anxieties away. "Man, I want to trip," she muttered against Gregory's lips.

He pulled back slightly. "You're getting addicted to the VR. You ought to lay off it for a while."

She thought maybe he was right. She nuzzled her lips against his neck, his ear. She didn't want to wind up like Roxanne, unable to tell the difference between the VR and Cold Reality.

But when her eyes closed, she went back to Mars. That

was her favorite reality. Walking down the great cleft of
Mariner Valley, the sky so far away, the walls so high, a
thin, witchy wind moaning through the rocks. An eagle
screamed overhead. She turned to look at it, startled.
Where had it come from? The atmosphere was too thin,
too cold to support life. But there it was. A golden eagle
against the sky. She watched it soar for hours before she
sighted its nest—a carefully constructed ring of stones
high up on the canyon wall. She thought to climb up there
and her arms were strong. She mounted the wall like a car-
nivorous lizard, emotionless, careful. The floor of the canyon dropped below her as she inched up the wall. The air
was cold. The rock was hot. The height was dizzying. The
eagle soared overhead, watching her with vindictive eyes
as she neared its nest. She actually had one hand on the
intricate stonework when it stooped and dived. It
screeched as it came in and plucked her from the wall,
tossing her with its sharp talons into the air. And then she
was falling.

The air raced past her ears with gale force. The eagle
dived beside her, its cold eyes on a level with hers, looking on her with a reptilian malevolence, as if it remembered a day she'd disrupted its plans. But now it had plans
anew.

They hit the canyon floor. But instead of the blinding
implosion of consciousness Katie had expected, they
passed through. Vision left her, but Katie could feel her
consciousness expanding, inflating along infinitely complex fractal boundaries, as if her mind had flowed into a
hidden country underlying the universe, a realm that was
not accessible to experiment, that would not concede to
the poor standard of repeatability, that was too vast to be
understood yet could only be perceived in a glance, because the detail was in constant flux and could never be
pinned down. She felt her careful/cautious/false/phony
worldview explode like glass before a storm, trailing out
into reaches of endless diversity as the world reworked itself on a highway twisting through the realm of time.

VIRTUAL REALITY REPORT
Your up-to-the-minute digest of open-access
VR brings you:

"Fast Times in the Gene Pool"

Article: Something's happening in the Gene Pool tonight! Pool Lifeguards report that activity in the consensus reality has increased almost a thousand times over usual levels with nearly two million people participating. Code is coming in from subscribers faster than the system can handle, all of it aimed at answering tonight's world-building challenge: Where will we be ten years from now if Generational Challenge succeeds on the Hill?

(To qualify as a participant in Gene Pool you must have passed G.P. training level three within the past twenty-four hours.)

11

Success on the Hill

Seated in the committee room on Monday morning, Katie felt slightly hungover, though she'd had no alcohol since the single glass of champagne raised to toast Joy's marriage. She found herself haunted by a sense of confusion that mixed badly with her fear.

Something had changed over the weekend. Something in the cumulative sentiment of the country. She'd felt it last night at the train station and again this morning, during breakfast in the hotel restaurant. And here. Seated before the Senate Committee on Advanced Technologies, sweltering under floodlights that strengthened her image only so the TV cameras could suck it away, listening with half an ear to Ferris's testimony. Even here there was a difference. Where before there had been despair, a cynical kind of helplessness, a let's-take-what-we-can-now-because-tomorrow-we'll-die attitude, today there was an undercurrent of righteous anger. It was as if people had suddenly sensed a way out, and just as suddenly realized that their appointed leaders were unwilling to take them down that path. Simply put, the country had woken up.

"What you're seeking to do," Ferris explained to the senators who were seated on the panel, elevated above the crowd, "is to preserve the status quo, the society of western materialism that has brought our Mother Earth to the brink of disaster.

"We ask you: *why?* Why now? Why this sudden interest in preservation when we all know that history moves in a continuous cycle of change? Over the past five hundred years, the primal peoples of this land experienced a social upheaval akin to what the megaculture is now facing. Our lands have been seized and destroyed. Our Earth is dying. Your Earth. The cycle of life threatens to come to a halt, and the response of this government is an attempt to ban the only technologies that offer us a reasonable chance of reversing the environmental debacle. The legislation proposed by Senator Carson is nothing more than a short-sighted attempt to preserve a way of life that has already *proven* itself incompatible with nature. I say: Let the megaculture evolve. Let us move forward and heal the Earth. Let us make room in our hearts for a diversity of cultures, so that none of us are forced to walk upon a path to the future that is not of our own choosing."

Virtual reality had opened up horizons for a lot of people. Maybe that explained the shift in sympathies that Katie sensed. Through the VR, more and more people were exploring new cultures, new ways of life. Perhaps they'd seen enough to make them resent people like Senator Carson, who wanted to lock them into tired old patterns.

She leaned back in her chair, looking up at Gregory. He sensed the change too. She could feel the difference in him. He was fearless. Clear-eyed and determined, like the old Gregory who'd rescued Tom that first awful night. I loved him then, Katie realized. And I love him now. She listened proudly when it was his turn to speak:

". . . If Senator Carson's bill becomes law, we will find ourselves the subjects of a government ready to tell us how long we may live, while denying us the means to save ourselves. . . ."

Was it still possible to save anything? In her worst moments, Katie had to wonder. The nuclear-plant disaster in

Bulgaria had ruined crops across Europe and much of Asia. Martial law had taken over the continent and people were learning to grow food indoors. Grain reserves in the United States were dipping precariously low as food was shipped abroad. And there hadn't been a good harvest in years. Drought, pollution, global warming, and the vanishing ozone layer had made farming a deep gamble. Plankton populations in the ocean were declining almost as fast as the atmosphere. Most fisheries around the world had gone out of business, and baleen whales were expected to become extinct over the next two years—not from hunting, but from starvation.

Finally, it was Katie's turn to speak. She swept her hands across her notes, smoothing the unwrinkled papers. She told herself this was not the last chance. Yet it felt that way. Looking up at the panel of senators, she met Ilene's gaze, and spoke:

"My mother-in-law, Jane Kishida, died this year." Ilene shifted in her seat, her eyes narrowed in anger. Katie looked away, her gaze taking in the hard faces of the other senators now. "When Jane's failing health brought her to the point where modern medicine could no longer help her, she chose to have herself cryonically suspended. She made this choice over the adamant objections of her own daughter, Senator Carson. Senator Carson has failed to convince her own family of the rightness of her views, yet she still seeks to convince the country. Senator Carson wants to deny me and every one of you the right to seek cryonic suspension, the right to seek medical treatment to prevent the disease of old age, the right to correct genetic deficiencies each of us was born with. Senator Carson wants to decide for every one of us the path of our lives and the purpose of our deaths."

She gazed up at the committee of senators. They returned her attention with expressions that ranged from bored to impatient to contemptuous, and she knew she'd failed to reach them. Again. Her last chance was slipping away. Desperately, she cast about for a new approach, a new tack ... then suddenly she remembered a few offhand words uttered in a parking lot on Joy's wedding day.

Her heart steadied. Her gaze swept over the panel once

again before she spoke. "I had a chance to talk privately with Senator Carson not two days ago." She swallowed against a dry throat. "The senator described to me her vision of society. We're on a train, she said. A runaway train steaming furiously toward a collision with a concrete wall and all she wanted to do was put on the brakes before it was too late. I say it's already too late. I say if we want to survive, forget about the brakes and stoke the boilers. Let's get up enough speed now so that no lousy wall of concrete can dictate our doom. Enough speed to thrust this train right through the wall. We all know that a straw, driven by a tornado, can pierce a fence post. We have to ride that tornado. We have to ride that train. We have to find out if there's life on the other side of that wall, because if we give up now, we're going to crash. Only audacity and nerve can save us now."

She could say this because she'd been there. She'd fallen toward solid rock. And she'd broken through.

She smoothed her unwrinkled papers with one hand, wishing this day were over.

Ilene's gavel banged down, adjourning the session.

"I don't think it's happening," Gregory said with a slight, apologetic smile. He didn't sound angry or cynical or frustrated—just resigned. "The trouble is, too many people *want* the government to make decisions for them."

Katie took his hand and squeezed it. "You're tired," she said. "I think we did pretty good." She felt his presence like a float that buoyed her up in the currents of time. "Come on. Let's go."

They left Ferris in heavy debate with a contingent of Sioux and made their way outside, moving slowly with the shoulder-to-shoulder crowd. It was midafternoon in the month of June, but the sky was dark with storm clouds. There was a scent of rain on the air and a rumble of thunder in the distance. "What the hell is going on out here?" Gregory asked.

Katie raised herself on tiptoes, trying to see over the heads of the crowd what had upset him. But Gregory didn't give her half a chance. He grabbed her hand and dragged her forward, cutting in and out of the throng until

suddenly they were in the clear, looking down over the
Capitol steps at a grim assembly that flowed around the
reflecting pool to fill the mall beyond. Thousands of people, their mingled voices murmuring in a calm undercurrent of human sound that was almost like silence. They
gazed stonily at the Capitol building. The banners they
held made a pattern like wind on sand: Say No to Generational Challenge; The Carsonites Will Strangle Us; and
more in that vein. With a start, Katie realized whose side
they were on.

"They're here for us," she muttered. She looked up at
Gregory. He grinned down at her, his dark eyes flashing
with certainty.

"We're going to make it," he said. "The tide has
turned." He raised his hand and Katie's into the air, and
the crowd responded with a slow, rolling rumble, like the
sound of thunder sweeping in from the horizon, gradually
building in volume until the boulevard seemed to shake
with their voices.

Katie was grinning, almost dancing with glee. The senators couldn't fail to be moved by a demonstration of this
size.

"Mrs. Kishida!" Katie turned to look over her shoulder.
"Mrs. Kishida!" a reporter shouted over the declining
growl of the assembly. Katie recognized her from one of
the national networks. "Mrs. Kishida, would you be willing to do an on-camera interview?"

Katie glanced at Gregory. He smiled at her. She looked
back at the reporter and nodded. "Sure. I'd be glad to."
She felt the wall of supporters behind her like a wall of
steel. She'd given so many interviews over the past nine
years, answered the same questions over and over again.
But this time it would be different. She straightened her
shoulders and faced the camera. Gregory let her hand slide
free. He backed off a step. The reporter touched her
earpiece, then the red light on the camera started flashing.
"Hello, Steve," the reporter said to the camera. "I'm here
outside the Capitol building with Katharine Kishida.
Katie," she said, turning slightly to make eye contact. "We
admired the spirit of your testimony. How do you think it
went inside there?"

"It's always hard to gauge what a politician is thinking," Katie began. "But I feel this demonstration behind us shows that the American people are convinced that Generational Challenge is no solution." She could feel the energy of the crowd feeding into her as she spoke. It seemed to lift her, leaving her floating a micrometer above the stairs as her heart pounded in giddy triumph.

The reporter said, "You've worked long and hard against your sister-in-law, Senator Carson. Do you anticipate the battle to continue, even after the vote is taken?"

"I expect a serious ethical issue like this will be argued as long as people are people."

"Still, it would seem the day has gone your way."

"I hope so."

"You must be looking forward to a celebration with your husband."

Katie laughed. "Oh, that's still some time away. It'll be many, many years before the technology is developed that will restore Tom. But I'm looking forward to it. Yes, of course I am."

The reporter appeared suddenly flustered. A nervous smile flitted across her lips, and then she turned hastily back to the camera. "This is Anne Banks, on the Capitol steps."

The camera went off. The reporter looked back at Katie, her jaw clenched and an embarrassed look on her face. She leaned over and whispered conspiratorially, "*Sorry* about that. I should have been more clear. I meant a celebration with your *present* husband." She hunched her shoulders in a shamefaced acknowledgment of social blundering.

Katie whirled around. Gregory was standing a few feet away. In his dark, deep-set eyes she saw the revelation of her own treachery, recognized her own betrayal. He took a step back.

"Gregory!"

She started after him, struggling to contain the hot spot of panic that welled up in her belly. Her husband. *Of course* the reporter had meant Gregory. Anybody could see that. Anybody. "Gregory—" She reached for him.

"No." He held up a hand to stop her. "No. Don't say it.

Don't apologize. Don't explain. We've been through all that before."

"But—"

"This is your day, Katie!" She felt his fury like tiny shards of glass under her skin. "You've won the war. You're going to get Tom back. You don't need me to hedge your options anymore. You've won."

"Gregory, it's not like that!" she pleaded. The expression in his eyes stopped her short. She found herself backing away in sudden fear.

"I believed in you," he growled. "I believed in you for three years. You really had me fooled." He turned abruptly and moved off down the stairs, forcing his way through the masses of people.

Katie watched him go, feeling lost, as if she'd been dropped into a deep ocean a thousand miles from any shore. *Oh, Tom.*

Startled, she caught herself. *Tom.*

Her fists clenched. It was always Tom. Everything was for Tom. She'd squandered her life for Tom. And he'd left her alone. He'd abandoned her.

She saw herself getting older and older and older, always waiting, waiting for something that could never exist again. It was impossible to re-create the past. Tom might live. But his resuscitation would not reanimate their marriage. Their marriage was over. She knew it was over.

So why didn't it *feel* over?

Tom. When are you coming home?

Wedged Time—
Alternate Landscapes

It was an act of ultimate audacity. He knew it at the time, but he did it anyway, trying not to think about it. Without looking up again at the dizzying height of the crevasse, he examined the wall in front of him, then reached up, exploring a possible hand-hold with his padded fingers. Then he found a tiny knob on which to place his foot. There was no handy spot for his other foot, so he reached across the crevasse. It was so narrow he could climb it like a chimney if he had to. He found a place for his foot on the opposite wall and suddenly he stood knee-high above the bottom.

He examined the walls just above him. There was a ledge about fifteen feet up, about two hand spans at the widest point. He climbed to it. His limbs trembled with fatigue by the time he reached it and he collapsed on the narrow ledge, his chest heaving and his blood pounding in his ears. He lay there until the chill began to penetrate him. Then he forced himself to sit up. He examined the wall just above him. There was a V-shaped crack some twenty feet overhead. His fingers cramped at every hold, but he climbed to it anyway, wedged an arm and a shoulder into it, braced his feet on bumps in the ice and sagged down, drinking in great gulps of air to ease the fire in his lungs.

He examined the walls just above him. The muscles in his shoulders felt bruised and torn. His feet throbbed. His belly groaned. He climbed.

Time passed. He tried not to think, tried to empty his mind, move all his strength, all his will into the act of climbing. Then he found himself on his back, on a ledge, one hand stretched across the crevasse to touch the other wall so he wouldn't roll off. Night had fallen. The witch wind moaned, sweeping soft flakes of snow across his face, across the face of the stars. He told himself to get up, but his muscles were too fatigued to respond, so after awhile he stopped trying and lay still, listening to the song of the witch and cherishing the warm touch of each falling flake of snow.

A thought began to niggle at his memory. A slight impression like a footprint left behind by a forgotten idea. The snow. It touched his face like warm kisses, like soft fingers in the night. It brushed past his ears with the warm breath of a lover. He flopped over on his belly; raised his head to listen. But he heard only the soft moaning of the witch wind. "Are you there?" he whispered, hardly daring to hope.

The witch fell silent. The wind stopped. The snow continued to fall, heavier now. It lodged on his eyelashes and covered his hands. He lifted his face to the falling snow, let it slide like kisses across his lips, sweet, sugary wafers that melted on his tongue. And suddenly his Familiar was with him. Her spirit ran through his body, warming him from the inside out, filling some of the empty spaces. He scooped up a handful of snow and shoved it into his mouth. He thought he would die then, the heat and light was so intense, so ecstatically intense that he moaned aloud. And swallowed.

His stomach cramped. He started to retch. But she soothed him, stroked him, breathed strength into his cells and nourished him. She taught him his body. Showed him its workings in all the minutest details. Showed him how to heal his wounds and clean out the toxins of fatigue, how to dream himself back to life.

He awoke to daylight. The clouds had passed and the witch

wind was once again nosing about the cleft, sweeping the ledges
and knobs clean of last night's snowfall. But he found a handful
of dry snow that the witch had missed, and he sucked on that,
drawing strength from it. He was still tired and sore, but the horrible weakness of last night had left him. He clambered to his
feet, stood on the ledge, and peed a steaming golden stream of
urine into the abyss. Looking down, he judged that he'd climbed
perhaps a thousand feet. Looking up, he guessed that he had
three or four times that to go. The sheer physical scale of this
place awed him. He knew that its existence should have been
an impossibility, and yet here it was. Here he was. He reached
out across the crevasse for a handhold, and began to climb.

Time passed. Night or day didn't seem to matter to him. He
noticed their passage in a vague way, his mind fixed on himself
and his body and her ghostly presence in the occasional fall of
snow. Every few hours he would sleep and dream his body,
wandering through his cells like a king wandering the halls of
his palace, learning every room, every system, adjusting the details to suit himself and moving on, awakening, to climb again.

His body temperature was falling. Every time he ate the snow
his body grew colder, adapting, and he began to wonder if the
ice would take him even if he succeeded in climbing out. He
wondered if he *could* climb out, or if he'd run out of breathable
atmosphere before he reached the top.

At times he heard sounds from below: the obscene hooting of
the oni and the terrified screams of some poor soul being cast
out to the witch wind. At such moments he would hug the wall
of the crevasse and shiver, not moving until the voices had faded
into despair or distance. And then he would climb faster.

At times he heard sounds from above: the voice of the glacier
as it flowed, moaning in deep earth tones or barking in sharp,
deafening cracks as if a giant were cleaving at it with a massive
ax. And hour by hour, day by day, the crevasse narrowed and
his climb became a race to escape the cleft before it closed
around him.

He awoke one day to a thunderous crack directly overhead.
He ducked as a shower of broken ice bombarded his head and
shoulders. When it was over, he looked up to see a great chunk
of ice wedged in the crevasse above him like a small moon
dropped from the sky. It blocked his ascent. But it hadn't killed
him.

It hadn't killed him. This fact struck him as oddly funny. He was still alive. The glacier had struck at him with a huge icy fist, with enough force to take out a hundred such as he, *but it had missed.* He chuckled at the patent incompetence of nature. He laughed outright, his voice echoing through the open-ended chamber of ice. "You missed me!" he screamed. "You missed me, whore mother witch!"

Nothing answered him.

He chuckled again, feeling the presence of his Familiar inside him, warming his blood, his heart. "I'm coming," he growled. "I'm coming."

It was nothing but a few hours to climb out from under the entombing ice and by dusk he'd reached the rim of the crevasse. He stood on the surface of the glacier.

Behind him, the spine of the mountains was obscured by a ceiling of thick clouds. Before him, a snowy slope quickly descended into fog. His Familiar blew a few soft snow kisses past his face, urging him downslope, into the gloom of coming night.

He followed her. He was not afraid.

L.A. FLOW—E-MAIL TO THE EDITOR
"Objection to the Primal Nation"

So now there's a sovereign political entity called the Primal Nation, with an ill-defined territory spreading ever wider through the once-proud body of the United States of America. And everyone from the president to the city council is praising the legislation that at once diminishes our country, our solidarity, and our responsibility for one another. The cultural terrorists who've waged war against our free society for years must be delighted to see that we've begun to do their work for them—carving up this nation until it's reduced to impotent fragments. But then maybe that's the explanation. The corporate powers want to see to it that a great nation like the United States will never rise up to trouble the world again with its egalitarian heresies.

12

Troubled World

Tonight the farmhouse seemed too big, too quiet, too empty. Katie sat alone in her study, trying to concentrate on the prospectus of a new biotech company while the clock slowly ticked off the last seconds before midnight. Finally she gave up.

Laying the brochure down, she stood and began wandering slowly around the room, taken by a restless, impatient feeling at odds with the sedate shelves of books that filled two walls of the room from floor to ceiling. She paused before the gallery of pictures that hung near the door. There was Joy, as beautiful as ever, cradling her two sons, Tom, five, and Curran, three and a half. She'd brought the boys over today, and they'd filled the house with such an abundance of energy that now the rooms and hallways seemed old and abandoned by contrast.

Nikki's picture was next, an intimate close-up taken just before she'd moved to the East Coast with her newly awarded doctorate in nanotechnology. And her father's photo beside that. Grandpa Tom, as the boys called him.

Katie chuckled, trying to imagine how Tom would react to that moniker.

Fifteen years.

Fifteen years.

So much time had gone by that she could hardly remember who Tom was anymore. Cold fear crept through her heart. She shuddered, forcing herself to skip over this thought, not wanting to face those anxieties tonight.

Her gaze wandered, to a picture of Mom with her dogs, taken only a few months back. Belle seemed to be getting a little smaller every year, her silver hair a little thinner. But at seventy-one she was still strong and alert.

And other pictures, memory aids to help her recall her life. Jane, taken just before her final heart attack. Dad, holding Joy as a baby. He hadn't even lived long enough to see Nikki. Tom's brother, Harlow, with his wife and kids. Ferris, looking slightly awed as he accepted the presidency of the new sovereignty of the Primal Nation. Others: grandparents, friends, cousins.

And Gregory. She gazed at the moody portrait she'd taken on their cruise to Hawaii, a photograph of him leaning on the ship's rail, his gaze fixed on her, on the camera, a touch of anger in his deep-set eyes. It captured perfectly his dissatisfaction with their love and maybe that's why she'd chosen it.

She hadn't seen Gregory in six years.

For three days after the congressional hearings she'd sat in their hotel room, waiting for him to come back, to at least pick up his stuff. Finally Ferris had come by with the news that Gregory was on a ship bound for Europe. So she'd gone home, and after a few months with no word from him, she'd extracted his possessions from the working body of her house and she'd sent them off to him at an address in Germany that she'd picked up on the net.

She waited for divorce papers, but they never came. After awhile, she let it go.

And finally, nearly a year and a half after he'd walked out, he called. Early one morning, sounding drunk and overly happy. He told her that things were going well for him. He'd hooked up with some claymasters trading in primitive molecular technologies. A lot was happening in the field. A lot of froth, like the foaming potential that gave birth to the universe.

He talked about his circle, though he never mentioned any names. It was a rough climate. There were hundreds of labs and every one wanted to be first with a new product. There were just as many terrorist groups that saw molecular technology as a threat to the very life of the earth, and they were just as determined to put an end to it. The competition and conflict had rapidly evolved into a sporadic guerilla war that chewed invisibly through the body of Europe. People got hurt. Gregory's skills as an emergency physician had been employed more than once by his circle, and he could conduct a suspension, if it came to that. His friends valued his expertise.

Katie listened, while recent news footage examining the residue of bomb blasts in Munich, glorying in the latest weapons seizure in Prague, replayed in her mind. "Come home," she pleaded. He laughed, and told her that such a place had not been invented yet.

Nearly a year later she heard from him again. The circle had been attacked. Eighteen months of work up in flames. He'd had to do three suspensions, all very bad.

"Come home before you're killed," she begged.

"You're living in the past, Katie. The war's in California too, even if it hasn't heated up yet. It's everywhere. Everyone wants to make the rules. Everyone has God on their side. So be careful. Always. Be very, very careful."

After that he seemed to forget about her, though she picked his name up on the net a few times. He was arrested at least twice for trafficking in unapproved life-extension therapies. Both times charges were dropped. And once, she turned on the TV to see live coverage of a gun battle in the industrial district of Bonn. Figures wearing gas masks and Kevlar huddled on rooftops, exchanging fire with warriors in the street in some Orwellian parody of the Wild, Wild West.

Gregory was there. He stripped off his mask and glared at her out of the television screen. "We have to fight!" he shouted at the reporter. "We've been attacked. Our freedom is threatened by terrorists. Of course we'll defend ourselves." The picture skewed as the cameraman ducked to avoid an incoming hail of tracer rounds. By the time the reporter recovered her wits, Gregory was gone.

Katie had her lawyer draw up divorce papers then. But she never filed them, fearing in some unadmitted part of her mind how he might react.

Alone in the night, she touched his picture. She didn't miss him anymore, not after six years. But she still remembered their time together fondly, like half-forgotten scenes from an old movie not available on the net.

She turned back to her desk, intending to straighten up a few things before going to bed, when the phone beeped, cutting through the silence like an alarm. Her heart leaped. She glanced at the clock. Midnight. The phone beeped again and she picked it up—"Hello?"—half expecting to hear Gregory on the other end.

"Katie."

It wasn't Gregory. Katie felt her mouth go suddenly dry. The voice in her ear seemed to reach her not from the telephone, but from across time, out of the past, out of the grave. "Roxanne. I wasn't even sure if—"

She stopped herself in time.

"If I was still alive?"

Katie swallowed hard, trying to stifle her shock. "I'd heard . . . I'd heard you'd had pneumonia again. And the doctors didn't think—well, they said you didn't want to see me," she finished lamely.

"I didn't," Roxanne agreed. She sounded strong, confident. The old Roxanne. "I was angry at you for saving my life, and ashamed of myself for being glad you did it. But that's all over now. You helped me live long enough to get the treatment. I'm not cured. I'm not as strong as I used to be. But I'm stable."

Katie was nodding in relief, though this was just an audio call. "I'm glad," she said. And she meant it.

She glanced up at a motion in the doorway. Belle looked into the room, her worried eyes questioning. *It's all right,* Katie mouthed. Belle nodded and withdrew and Katie returned her attention to the phone. "So what have you been doing with yourself, Roxanne? You didn't go back with the forest service?"

"No. I'm into other things these days."

There was an awkward silence. Then: "What things?" Katie ventured, her pulse rate picking up again as some feral sense stirred in her breast.

"Ah yes. You know, I heard something the other day. Just gossip, you understand. Overheard. There are a lot of Knights where I live."

Knights.

Knights of the Oppressed Earth. Katie shivered. Generational Challenge had died on Capitol Hill six years ago, but that hadn't killed the dissension. Like maggots feeding off the body of a fallen giant, terrorist groups had tunneled among the political ruins. And as Gregory had predicted, they'd imported the cultural war from Europe to the Americas, where it had become a staple domestic drama on the evening news.

At least Ilene was out of it. She'd resigned her Senate seat after the Carsonites in the House were swept out of power. The new Congress had imposed term limitations on itself, and promptly passed a package of bills known affectionately as the privacy laws, which mandated the government to stay out of the personal lives of its citizens.

And in some ways the practice of cryonics had grown easier. Individuals were allowed to define in their living wills what they personally perceived as a state of death, so potential cryonics patients had to be regarded by the medical establishment as still alive, even if they qualified for the legal definition of death. Medical examiners could no longer autopsy such patients, even when the death occurred under suspicious circumstances. In the state of California, new statutes had been passed recognizing and regulating the cryonics industry. Popular interest in the field was at an all-time high.

But Forward Futures was barely holding on because they couldn't find the staff to work in the climate of fear generated by terrorist groups like Knights of the Oppressed Earth. Katie pulled shifts there every third week, volunteering to tend the cryogenic storage vessels. The company had a standing policy to revise the security system every three months and *nobody* was allowed in the facility without a thorough body search.

Ilene had disavowed any connection with her former

followers, retreating to the southern refugee camps to do
charity work. But groups like the Knights didn't need her
anymore. They were adept at waging a war against society
all on their own, and police organizations seemed helpless
to stop them. The privacy laws, which had been enacted
to protect individuals from excess government interfer-
ence, had hobbled their efforts at eradication.

Knights of the Oppressed Earth. Katie breathed softly into
the phone. Roxanne had quit the Knights—she'd said so
herself—after the fire at UCLA.

"Are you there, Katie?"

"I'm here."

"I hear things, you understand? People talk. I hear
there's a new offensive being planned, with highly visible
targets in California. I'm going to fax you a diagram I
picked up off the net. Just thought you ought to know
about it. Besides, you saved my life. I owe you one."

The phone clicked. Katie slowly lowered it to the desk,
staring in macabre fascination at the fax machine across the
room as it began to print. She walked over to the machine
and examined the output. It was an architectural diagram of
the Forward Futures facility, all their supposedly-secret security systems clearly specified. She swore softly under her
breath.

"What is it, Katie?"

Belle had reappeared at the door. Katie held up the diagram for her to see. "The Knights have targeted the vault
at Forward Futures, Mom. They know more about our security arrangements than we do. How the hell can we
guarantee they won't get inside?"

They would flee the country. After long hours of wran-
gling, that was the decision the board came to in response
to Katie's news. As a board member, she'd voted along
with the majority although the choice trouble her. Logi-
cally, it seemed the best thing to do: Let the suspension
patients disappear. Find them a sanctuary and keep them
out of sight until they could be brought out of stasis. But
emotionally? Emotionally it felt *wrong*. Perhaps it was just
something Gregory had said, echoing down to her from
that long-ago day when she'd first heard of Generational

Challenge. *I, for one, have no intention of being run out of my own country.* Big words. But he'd run away years ago, a hungry expatriate playing urban war games in Europe. What happened at Forward Futures was no longer his concern.

She wandered out into the facility's garage, hugging herself against the night's wintry cold, wishing the Global Cooling Plan had not worked quite so well. Outside the open garage door, an icy rain pounded the pavement. Katie peered through the deluge at the eighteen-wheeler that had laboriously backed up the driveway. The semi was open. A dull light shone from inside. Dr. Morales leaned out of the trailer. "Okay, we're ready for the next one," he shouted over the rain. One of the guys shouted back, and a vertical cryogenic storage cylinder was laboriously rolled over to the truck's hydraulic lift. Maryann was standing in the garage, keeping the tally. Katie leaned over her shoulder, studying the screen of the Office Girl curiously.

"You're supposed to be sleeping," Maryann reminded her without bothering to look up.

"Right. On a night like this?"

Katie had volunteered to go with the first truck. There'd been quite a few volunteers, but only three who weren't either old and decrepit, or the parents of young children. Her brother-in-law, Harlow, was going with her. His kids were grown, he had experience with big rigs, and he and Katie would have more people on this truck than anybody else, so it seemed right. The third pick was a middle-aged gentleman named Stan, who'd supplied the semi from his own trucking company. Katie had met him only this morning. He'd shown himself to be a loud, friendly character, mocking his own balding head and huge, slightly overweight frame. Besides the truck, there would be two chase cars driven by some of the younger members. They would take one third of the suspension patients. The next truck would follow in four days.

"I hate this," Maryann said, looking up from her tally. Her narrow face creased in a frown. "It feels like we're giving up."

"You know it's not like that."

"I know. But that's the way it feels."

They rolled out onto the freeway just before ten that night, Stan driving, Katie squeezed between him and Harlow. Although the rain had slackened, traffic was still fairly heavy. They moved at about forty-five miles an hour, heading west on the Ventura Freeway. Stan tangled them up with some other truck traffic, then instructed the dashboard computer to change the truck's paint scheme and graphics to phase B and optional license eleven. "A lot of nervous biotech companies really love this feature," he laughed. After another mile, he took the off-ramp to I-5, leaving the chase cars behind. A few miles farther on and he doubled back, heading east on the San Bernardino and changing the color scheme to phase C.

By midnight they'd made Riverside. In another hour they'd be down in the desert at Palm Springs. "Somebody better hop in the back and take a nap," Stan said. "I can only drive this thing until morning."

"You take it, Harlow," Katie said. After only a few hours of practice, she didn't want to be the one stuck with navigating the rig through Phoenix.

So Harlow slept, while the radio played soothing classical music. Katie fished for some boxes of juice they'd stashed under the seat. She popped the straws in and handed one to Stan. "You got anybody on board?" she asked, just to be friendly.

"My daughter. She had leukemia. Nine years old."

Katie felt a cold sweat break out on her forehead. She wished she'd kept her mouth shut. "Oh, God. I'm sorry."

"She'll pull out of it."

Katie nodded, watching the lane markers shoot under the truck.

"You're a famous case," Stan said. "You expect you'll get back with your husband?"

"I don't know," she answered honestly. "I don't even think about it anymore. It was all so long ago."

He glanced at her, a puzzled frown on his face. "That sounds kind of cold. But here you are, still supporting the company."

She smiled sheepishly. "Yeah, that's right. And I can still feel him out there, sometimes. I want to see him again. I *have* to see him again. I've invested too much in him to just let him go. If it ends after that . . . well, at least it'll be our decision and not some bloody accident of nature."

It was still dark night when they pulled off the interstate at a rest stop outside of Blythe. Katie went to the ladies' room. When she came back, Stan was using a headphone and wand to sweep the body of the truck for electronic devices. She stood on the sidewalk, watching him. A van pulled in, radio blaring. A tired-looking young woman climbed out and headed for the restroom while a baby cried in the back of the van. Traffic on the interstate was light. Three trucks were parked in the lot, their engines silent, their cabs dark. "We're clean," Stan said, finishing his inspection. "Let me rest my bladder, and then we can be on our way. Want to take a turn at the wheel?"

Katie chuckled. "Sure you trust me?" He'd given her three hours of lessons yesterday morning and she hadn't had a wink of sleep since then.

"Why not? The road's straight and empty and you won't have to back up. Do you think I'd offer my rig to a woman if the driving conditions weren't ideal?"

"Ha!" Katie launched a playful kick at his knee, which he dodged adroitly.

"Keep an eye on the parking lot," he advised as he started off on the concrete path.

Something about the way he said it set Katie's nerves on edge. She wanted to ask him if he suspected something, but he was already halfway to the loo and she wasn't going to shout. She shoved her hands in her jacket pockets, hunching her shoulders against the desert cold. The butt of the pistol in her pocket was warm with her body heat.

The moon had set, and the winter sky glowed with stars. She could name very few of them. Nikki had once pointed out Sirius to her. With a hint of amusement in her voice, Nikki had explained that Sirius A, the larger member of the binary, was one of the few nearby stars massive enough to go supernova. When that happened, life on Earth would be sterilized by the ensuing radiation. Katie had asked how long they had, but Nikki had only shrugged.

Another van pulled into the rest stop. It parked in a stall. The engine went quiet and the lights went out, but nobody emerged. Katie began to breathe faster. She slipped around to the other side of the truck and opened the door. Stan had rigged the cab lights so they wouldn't come on when the door was open. She clambered into the dark interior and flicked on the night-vision camera fixed under the rear bumper of the truck. She spun it until it focused on the van. Through the windshield, she could just barely make out the image of an old, white-haired man, his head tilted back and his mouth open as he snored behind the driver's wheel.

The truck's passenger door popped open and she jumped, her right hand diving into her pocket to grasp the pistol. "Just me," Stan said, climbing up. "What's the matter? You look like you've seen a ghost."

"Just getting jumpy."

"Flighty female, huh? Maybe I better not let you have the rig after all." He stuck his tongue in his cheek and she laughed, albeit nervously.

"Let's do Phoenix, huh?"

"Right on."

By the time they reached El Paso, Katie was feeling old and grimy and foul, but she knew how to back up the truck. They stopped at a McDonald's for some soy burgers and coffee and a full electronic sweep, then they headed across the border, with the truck back in its phase A color scheme.

The Pan American Highway went by in a blur of days that seemed to go on forever, followed by nights that lasted twice as long. They went through Chihuahua, Durango, Mexico City, Oaxaca, and a hundred other places that vanished from Katie's memory as soon as they fell behind. The trip became a hash of sore butts and short tempers. Her body longed to stand up and just *walk* for a mile, but there was no time for that. Keep moving. They still couldn't be sure they weren't being followed.

In Guatemala they stopped to have the truck serviced.

Harlow and Stan kept watch over the rig while Katie checked into a nearby hotel and showered. By the time they took up the road again, they'd all had a chance to clean up, and a bit of their earlier confidence had returned. They listened to the news, but they heard nothing of the Knights, or a new offensive being waged in southern California. "Do you think Roxanne was lying?" Harlow asked one evening.

Katie shrugged. "Who knows? But she had our security plans. That tells me they would have hit us sooner or later."

Early the next evening, they crossed the Panama Canal and by the time full darkness had fallen, they were skirting Lake Bayano, heading toward the newly completed section of the highway that had sliced through Darien National Park. There was an air of excitement in the cab, a sense of anticipation as they drew near South America. Their options had narrowed along with the northern continent, but as soon as they crossed into Colombia they could lose themselves in the primal vastness of the southern lands.

Katie stayed up long enough to watch the moonrise, then she crawled over the seat back and into the bunk. "Wake me up when we reach the border," she said, and promptly fell asleep.

She dreamed of Tom, or at least that vision she'd come to associate with Tom: ice and bitter cold and a sense of helplessness. She hadn't visited that place in years, and she cried out in her sleep, waking herself. She glanced into the cab. Harlow was driving; Stan was nodding at his side. On the radio, a Spanish-language talk show discussed genetic imperialism and the *yanquis*. She lay back down in the bunk and closed her eyes, only to hear an odd thunk, as if something had hit the windshield. She started to sit up again. A sound like a shot went off in the cab and she ducked instinctively, huddling behind the seats as pellets of safety glass rained down around her. The cool conditioned air in the cab seemed to vanish instantly, replaced by a hot, humid gale blowing off the jungle outside.

"What the hell's going on!" Stan shouted. "Get the cameras on!"

Harlow slammed on the brakes, sending Katie hard into the seat back while the truck screeched down the highway.

"No! Don't slow down!" Stan screamed.

A blood-curdling rebel yell sent Katie's pulse soaring. She heard the hard *whack!* of something striking flesh and Stan screamed again, this time incoherently. The truck swerved, seemed to careen, on the verge of tipping over. A door flew open. Wind roared in the cab. Harlow cried out, and then his voice was receding and gone. The truck swerved again. A heavy foot leaned on the accelerator and the engine churned.

"It worked! It worked!" some stranger cried, in a young man's voice drunk with triumph. "Did you see their faces when we kicked them out? *OW!*"

A woman replied to him, older, calmer, her voice difficult to catch over the racing wind. "It went just like she said. First scare them out of their fortress, then destroy them. Huh."

Katie lay behind the seat, hardly daring to breathe, her hand wrapped around the butt of the pistol that she'd carried in her jacket pocket for days now. *First scare them out of their fortress.* So. Roxanne had betrayed her again. Her chest felt tight and painful. Rage flushed through her brain. *I owe you one.*

She ran a scene in her head: Sit up. Put a bullet in the back of the young man's head. The woman would turn to look at her. Put a bullet between her eyes. Two perfect shots, then over the seat, drag one of the bodies out from behind the steering wheel, take over control of the truck before it could crash and rupture the storage cylinders in the back. Then turn the truck around and find Harlow and Stan.

Right.

"Is that our turnoff?" the young man asked.

"Yeah. That's it. Slow down now. The road's going to be rough."

"Wouldn't want to crash, now would we?" They both laughed.

The truck rattled and shook and skidded down a winding track. Katie clung to her hiding place, her jaw

clenched tight to keep her teeth from cracking together,
her fingers locked like steel straps around the seat posts.
No one spoke. The journey seemed to go on for miles and
miles, with the road steadily worsening, the truck slowing
down until finally they came to a full stop. The engine
shut down. The hood snapped and clicked as the metal
cooled. The air was still. Katie could hear the night sounds
of the jungle, the call of nocturnal birds, the trill of insects. The cab doors opened and the weight on the seats
shifted as the occupants slid out.

A pale light was coming in through the windshield.
There was a moon tonight. And the truck's headlights
were probably still on. But Stan had disconnected the cab
lights and the darkness behind the seat hugged her like a
suit of armor. She pulled the pistol out of her pocket, then
sat up slowly, peering over the seat to be sure that both of
the hijackers had gone.

They had.

She looked through the windshield. The headlights
were off. But in the moonlight she could easily make out
the edge of a bulldozed clearing, walled in by the crushed
and splintered trunks of massive trees. Beyond the zone of
destruction, the jungle seemed intact.

Voices came to her in the still night, speaking in arro-
gant Spanish. The passenger door hung open. She crept
toward it; glanced out. The truck cast a heavy shadow on
this side. Still holding the gun, she eased herself onto the
ground, remembering only as her bare feet touched the
thick mud that she'd taken off her shoes when she'd lain
down to sleep. Too late now.

She crouched in the shadow, half under the truck. In the
clearing she could see a few Indian men milling around, the
red embers of their cigarettes bright in the night. And beyond them a backhoe, looking gray in the moon's ancient
light.

A gunshot ricocheted off metal. She jumped. The young
man whooped in a voice that was already familiar, shouting: "One shot opens the lock! Ha!" And then the back
gate of the truck banged open. "Oh shit," the Yankee hijacker cursed, his mood suddenly sour. Katie peered under
the truck, to see clouds of white vapor billowing out of the

back. The hijacker cursed again. "Something's cracked in here." A couple of the men with cigarettes crossed themselves, muttering low-voiced incantations.

"What difference does it make?" the woman said. "We're cracking them all open anyway."

"Well fuck, it's cold. We could burn our hands on this stuff."

"Oh, get out of the way. Let me look."

He jumped down and the woman climbed up. Katie could see his legs under the truck through the billowing fog of condensing vapor. She began to creep toward the back, keeping low and in the shadow. When she reached the rear tire set, she froze. She could see something else now, a darker shadow in the clearing, like a huge, yawning pit. As she crouched there, puzzling over it, one of the smokers cast his cigarette into it. The ember plunged deep into the earth and a sudden chill shivered across Katie's back. Suddenly, she knew what it was: the planned site of a mass grave.

Buckles rattled inside the truck and her attention snapped back to the hijackers. Each of the wheeled cryogenic storage cylinders had been strapped down to the wall of the truck. Wheels creaked and the weight of the truck shifted slightly. Katie was suddenly struck by how easy it would be to push the cylinders out over the truck's tailgate. "Get up here and give me a hand," the woman barked.

The man grumbled, but obeyed. As soon as his feet disappeared inside the trailer, Katie sprinted for the back. The fog was even thicker now, and it *was* damn cold. They had a bad leak, but at least it would help conceal her from the hired laborers.

She held the pistol in a two-handed grip, aiming it into the open trailer, straining for a glimpse of the hijackers in the dimly lit, fog-shrouded interior. She could hear them moving, cursing, unstrapping buckle after buckle. Her arms began to shake with the cold. The pistol wobbled. She could see one of the hijackers now, emerging from the fog. The young man. She sighted along the pistol's barrel, struggling to hold her aim over his heart. Suddenly his companion appeared beside him. A tall, dark-skinned woman, with a buzz cut and wide eyes. She had an automatic rifle slung over her shoulder. She slipped it off and leaned it up against one of the storage cylinders. "Let's do it," she said. They hadn't seen Katie yet.

Katie took a deep breath to steady herself, wanting to glance over her shoulder to see what the Indian men were doing, but not daring to take her eyes off the hijackers. She played the scene in her head: She would shoot the woman in the back, and then the man. She imagined the bullets hitting them; imagined their sudden, surprised expressions of pain, followed by a terrible awareness of imminent death. They were so young. Her hands began to shake with something more than cold. She struggled to steady herself. For fifteen years she'd defied death. Would she now become its agent? *To protect Tom. To protect Tom. How far are you willing to go?*

She bit down hard on her lip, until she felt the blood flow. A blood sacrifice to save Tom. One life traded for another to please the gods. She sank into a tiny point of consciousness. Her hands steadied as she took aim on the young man's back. Her finger tightened on the trigger.

Just then, the phone in her thigh pocket rang.

Startled, she jumped back, almost dropping the gun. The two hijackers spun around. Katie brought the barrel of the pistol back up as the man reached for his shoulder holster. "Don't move!" Katie barked. And unbelievably, he froze, his fingers not six inches from his gun.

The phone rang again. And again. They stared at each other across a fog-shrouded distance of seven feet. The phone kept on ringing. Katie thought about telling him to take the gun out of his holster, the way they did it in cop movies. But she was no Hollywood cop. If he went for the gun, would she react fast enough? Shoot straight enough? "Put your hands behind your neck," she finally croaked, her throat so dry she could barely get the words out. "That's right. Now jump down. Both at the same time."

"Sure, grandma," the woman said. "Anything you say." She wiggled her fingers at her partner and they jumped in opposite directions, hitting the ground rolling. Katie backpedaled, slipping in the mud as she tried to track the man with her pistol. She fired, and blood blossomed on his

shoulder. He screamed. She fired again, but didn't wait to
see the results. Spinning around, she fired wildly in the direction she thought the woman would be. One, two, three,
four shots. And then she saw her target.

The woman kneeled on the ground, her hands in the
air, a bit of blood oozing from her neck. She looked really
scared. Her weapon was still on the truck. "Don't kill
me," she whispered. "Please, please don't kill me."

Katie felt something thick and heavy in her throat. She
considered what to do. She could have the woman lie
down in the mud. If the local men didn't interfere, she
might be able to hunt around for something to tie her up
with. And abandon her in the jungle? No. Put her in the
back of the truck. That's it. Turn her in to the local cops.
Be detained for days while the police completed their investigation. While the leaking nitrogen ran out and one of
the patients thawed. *(Which one?)* While the media caught
the story and made all their efforts at secrecy suddenly
meaningless. Abandon her on the highway, then. Someone
would find her. Some innocent man or woman. Who might
well be murdered by this savage.

"Please let me live," the woman screamed. Perspiration
had beaded her face in icy crystals.

"I want to," Katie whispered. The hair stood up on the
back of her neck as she sighted down the barrel of the
weapon.

How far are you willing to go?

"Don't kill me! Please don't kill me!"

Katie pulled the trigger. The gun went off with a report
that seemed to shatter the earth. The woman jerked backward and collapsed, her legs twitching. Katie looked over
her shoulder. The young man was lying still in the mud.
And the phone continued to ring. Holding the pistol in
one hand, she slammed the trailer doors shut. Her skin
stuck to the frozen metal and her hands came away
bloody. She sucked in a sharp breath of pain, then remembered the laborers. She looked behind her, into the clearing, but the men had disappeared like ghosts into the
night. This was not their war. And the phone continued
ringing.

She slipped it out of her thigh pocket and answered it. "Yeah?"

"Katie! Thank God," Harlow cried. "Are you all right?"

She was numb; disinterested in the question. "I got the truck back."

There was a moment of silence from the other side as he weighed the implications of this news. A breeze rustled through the treetops, sweeping a thin cloud away from the face of the moon. In Japanese, she asked, "Did you call the police?"

"No, I wanted to know first if you—"

"Good. Is Stan with you?"

"I'm here, Katie. Bastards nearly broke my skull when they tumbled me from the truck, but I'm still here."

"Stay out of sight. I'll call you when I get back to the highway."

She cut the connection and slipped the phone back into her pocket. It was slick with blood from her injured hands. She glanced up at the moon. It hung low in the west, huge and round and yellow in the dirty atmosphere. She could make out a little scar in Tranquillity where regolith mining had stripped away the reflective surface dust around the year-old lunar base. God, it was going to be ugly in a few more years, but that was progress.

She walked around to the cab and climbed in. The engine started up easily. She switched on the exterior cameras and backed the truck up, weaving it carefully between the two bodies. Stan would have been proud of her skill. Turning on the headlights, she found the muddy, bulldozed track through the forest and guided the truck toward it. *How far are you willing to go?* she asked herself again. *How far are you willing to go?*

SENATE COMMITTEE ON FOREIGN AFFAIRS:
"Excerpt from Public Hearing"

Senator: *You've been accused of treason against the United States, Mrs. Carson.*

Ilene Carson (via satellite link): *I'm no longer a citizen of the United States, but of the net sovereignty Voice of Humanity.*

Senator: *You are in fact the elected president of this organization, are you not?*

I.C.: *That's true.*

Senator: *And you've appeared here to ask the United States government to recognize this entity.*

I.C.: *Twenty-five states have already recognized the Voice, Senator. Ten more are likely to do so within the next few weeks.*

Senator: *Your organization's popularity is well-known, Mrs. Carson. But your political agenda is less clear. Enlighten us. What exactly are your*

ultimate intentions?

I.C.: *Could you please clarify that, Senator?*

Senator: *Certainly. You are ensconced in the only functional orbital habitat in existence, a derelict space station purchased from the Chinese. You've made well-known your desire to build more orbital habitats, and with your corporate backing, I suspect you'll be able to do so. Do you intend to monopolize the space frontier, at the expense of the nations of Earth?*

I.C.: *Nature abhors a monopoly, Senator. We intend to create an environment in which technology can be regulated, so that our citizens may enjoy the freedoms of democracy without the threats of libertarian science or corrupt governments. That is all.*

Senator: *The history of the world teaches us, President Carson, that where governments are concerned, that is never all.*

13

Freedoms of Democracy

Old Mother Nature had been ailing and unhappy for years, but when the global population topped eight billion her temper began to flare. Eight billion people, most of them living in excruciating poverty, proved an easy target for her wrath. Using the old evolutionary techniques of random mutation throughout the huge population, she began to produce new and viable infectious diseases every few weeks.

People panicked. Ports were closed. Global trade withered to a trickle. The new nanotechnologies took up some of the economic slack, at least in the wealthier countries, but refugees still filled the roads.

Sitting in the study of her farmhouse, Katie would watch on a monitor as people wandered on foot past the security cameras hidden near the farm's entrance gate. Sometimes they'd stop at the gate and buzz the house AI to ask for food. Then, if the sniffer didn't detect guns or explosives among them, Katie would load up a wheelbarrow with bread or rice, beans or fruit, and take it out to the road.

At fifty-four her body could feel a little stiff in the morning, but an intense exercise regimen kept her lean and strong and vitamin therapy aided her metabolism. She did all the farmwork herself, and handling the wheelbarrow wasn't even a chore.

The refugees were always tired, so after they'd loaded the food into their packs they'd want to stand around and chat for a few minutes and take some rest while the kids munched on the handful of cookies Katie always produced from her pocket. They'd tell her their names, where they were from, what they used to do. Then inevitably, the conversation would turn to politics and the Voice of Humanity.

They'd repeat to her everything they'd ever heard about Voice ideology, explain how things were finally happening and how they felt called to the beautiful coastal welfare villages where a new world was being written up. Katie always listened politely, nodding at the appropriate moments as if it were all news to her, though she already knew more about the Voice than any of them ever would. She could feel the frigging Voice looking down on her every time she stood under the open sky.

Then sooner or later somebody would remark how lucky she was to own all that land outright. And she'd answer, "Oh, it doesn't belong to me anymore. I ceded it to the Primal Nation." Their eyes would go wide and they'd look at her as if she might cast an evil spell on them if they so much as forgot a please or thank-you. And pretty soon they'd move on. Then she'd sweep the farm's perimeter for electronic devices, check for damage to the fences, lock the gate. All the while the Voice watching everything she did.

"Why are you still living out there all alone?" Ferris asked. They faced each other across a coffee table in his new townhouse in the welfare village known as the Long Beach Reserve. Over the years, all the fat he'd once carried had slowly burned away. But he was still a huge man, almost seven feet tall and bulky with muscle. Streaks of gray ran through his curly black hair and his eyes were tinged with a bit of yellow. He gazed at her with an expression that bordered on pity and Katie almost cut the transmission right then. But Ferris had been a friend for a long time. He deserved some slack. So she maintained the VR sim, even though it was costing her a fortune in satellite fees.

Gathering her patience, she put on what she hoped was a disarming smile. "You know the Knights have been giving me some heat since Panama. I feel safer at home, where my AI can watch over me."

"Safer?" he asked. "Your mom moved out because she said the place was a war zone."

Katie shrugged. "Belle's getting on. And she wants to spend more time with Joy and the kids. That's all. Say, Nikki called the other day. You know what she said? We'll have a cure for old age in another ten or fifteen years." She winked at Ferris. "Will we last that long? What do you think?"

His serious expression didn't change. "I say it's been five years since Panama, Katie. How long are you going to keep punishing yourself?"

A cold draught of anger touched her heart. She wasn't going to take this, even from Ferris. "I'm not about to be run off my land."

Gently: "You gave the land away."

"The sovereignty, that's all. You know I hold all the rights. Why isn't the Nation protecting me?"

He spread his hands helplessly. "We're trying. You know that. We've got the treaty with the Voice—"

Her fist hit the arm of the chair. "You sic Ilene's Holy Voice on me and call it *protection*?"

He stiffened, and she knew she'd struck a tender spot. "It's not the Holy Voice. Please stop calling it that."

"Oh, forgive me. It's 'Voice of Humanity,' isn't it? I keep forgetting. I think it's the way she sits up there in that orbital, commanding a ring of satellites and the adulation of every youth in the developed world. Usually only God has that kind of power."

Even Joy's kids were into the Voice, though Tom-2 was only ten and Curran just eight. But then Great Auntie Ilene was the bloody president of an organization that was now arguably more powerful than any sovereignty left on Earth. The CEO's who'd elected her certainly thought so.

Times they were a-changing. . . .

Hardly anybody talked about national governments anymore. National governments were distant, alien enterprises that didn't speak to people on the personal level they'd come to expect. But a VR entity like the Voice, or the Primal Nation—that was different. Power and partnership for all. Everyone could feel as if they belonged, as if they were *somebody*. From the CEO's of giant conglomerates to little eight-year-old Curran—the VR would respond.

"You're holding grudges," Ferris said softly, as if he were trying to calm a psychotic. "We just want to help you."

"I don't need help. From you or Ilene."

But despite her objections, the Voice kept her under constant surveillance.

It's for your own good, Katie.

Ilene thought she could restore order to the world.

As our global network expands, criminals like Knights of the Oppressed Earth will be squeezed out of existence.

But it hadn't happened yet. Despite their newly completed orbital, the Voice was still more mouth than muscle. It was one thing to watch mayhem. Another entirely to intercede. The Knights had come after Katie a dozen times in the five years since Panama, and not once had the Voice delivered on their promise of protection.

Katie leaned forward; pointed an intrusive finger at Ferris. "You don't understand where the Knights are coming from. They like to harass me, sure, but they aren't out to destroy me. What would be the point? Far more useful to keep me alive and apparently miserable, as an example to other people who might cross them." And then, because he'd put her in a nasty mood: "It seems they've cowed *you*."

He smiled faintly. "You know, fear can be a healthy emotion. . . . but you're not scared, are you?"

She frowned, uneasy with the question. "Sure, I get scared."

"I'd like to believe that." He took a deep breath; let it

out. "You know, you never told me exactly what happened in Panama."

Katie swore softly, her fingers drumming an impatient rhythm on the arm of the chair. "Why, Ferris? Why ask now, after all this time?"

"Just tell me." As if it were the simplest request in the world.

"Oh, you know," she said coldly. "It was a bad scene."

"So? You've been through shit before. Tom's death. Gregory leaving. Then, you didn't run and hide. What's different about Panama?"

She felt a half-smile slip over her face like a self-protective mask. She spoke, but it was someone else's voice she heard, speaking someone else's feelings while she, Katie, huddled in a dank psychic cellar somewhere, listening, shivering. "Hell," she said. "You can guess what was different about Panama. I never committed murder before."

"Murder?"

"Watch it, Ferris. You're starting to echo like a cheap AI shrink."

He ignored the jab. "Most people would call what you did self-defense. You wouldn't be feeling this way if you'd been protecting your children."

The stranger who'd taken over Katie's face put on a malicious grin. "Oh, but that's the funny part. I wasn't defending kids, or anything noble like that. Just dead bodies. Cold and dead."

Ferris looked at her, his expression puzzled. "*Dead* bodies?"

"Corpses. Stiffs. Cadavers. Remains. Dead bodies."

"You don't believe that."

Her lip started trembling with unexpected emotion. "But you know, Ferris, sometimes I really do."

Katie had taken her electric car and driven into town on a rare expedition to purchase groceries. She bounced back up the pitted road, then slowed as she approached the gate to her farm. She stopped the car several yards from the gate and stared at the folded piece of white paper wedged in the crack where the two halves of the gate met.

She looked carefully up and down the road and checked with the house AI. No one was around. So she got out of the car, retrieved the piece of paper, and unfolded it. A brief note was scrawled on one side in black ink:

Are you really not home? Or are you just not home to me? Maybe Ferris warned you I was coming. He wasn't too happy to see me.
You should have let me know the Knights were playing games with you. I would have come back sooner.
I'll be in the neighborhood watching.

Take care,
Gregory

She read through the note again, fury building across her mental horizon. So he was back. After eleven years. So what?

She crumpled the note and threw it on the ground. She didn't need him.

You should have let me know the Knights were playing games with you.

Why? Did he still see himself as husband and protector? She didn't need protection. She didn't need help. And she didn't need one more damn pair of eyes spying on her.

He called in the evening, from the phone at the gate. She watched him through the security camera. He seemed far older than his forty-three years. Deep lines etched his face and a horribly fresh and livid red burn scar on his cheek twisted his lips out of line. The long hair of his youth had been reduced to an austere crew cut. He walked with an odd shuffling gait, as if he'd suffered some damage to his peripheral nerves. He'd picked up the crumpled note from the ground. Now he bent over to smooth it against his thigh, while his chin pinned the receiver at his shoulder.

"I see you got my message," he said.

She could feel a wall of anger harden around her. "Why are you here?"

"I came across your name a few days ago. It was on a Knights death list."

"Old news. They've been after me for years."

"It's different now, Katie. The Voice is pressing them hard. The list was attached to an order to finish old business before they move out of California."

She snorted her contempt for that bit of information. "Don't worry. I can handle them."

"Not if they get serious. Come with me. My circle closed a deal last spring. I made some money. I bought space for two on the new Voice orbital."

Her eyes narrowed combatively. "Hope you find somebody to share it with you."

"I was hoping it'd be you, Katie."

"Just like that?" she asked. "After eleven years."

"I've never stopped thinking about you." He squatted down, his back against the gate so she couldn't see his face. "Listen. I took a bullet in the spine a few months ago. I lost all motor function. I couldn't even breathe on my own. I was on life support for weeks, and all I could think about was you. You've never left my mind. I want you back, Katie. I want to make you love me."

She felt herself pulling away. "It's been too long."

"You're still my wife."

"As if a piece of paper can make a marriage."

"But you'd wait for Tom!" he snapped.

"I'm not waiting for anybody, dammit! Not for you. And not for Tom. I'm doing just fine on my own. So thank you for checking in, but don't bother to call me again."

She clicked off the phone, banged it down on the desk, then turned to flick off the security camera so she would not have to look at him, so she would not know if he lingered, or if he left straightaway. So she would know *nothing* more about him. Let him disappear! Permanently, this time.

She stomped through the empty house, checking all the doors and windows while the dogs fled from her fury. Space on the new orbital, huh? As if she needed a prince to carry her off. She'd already bought space on the Voice orbital—but as an investment, not a refuge. Did he think he could buy her with money? She had money. A lot of money. She was a skilled investor, and money had always come to her with ease.

She went back into the study and flicked on the security camera. Gregory was gone. Disappointment flooded her heart, but she tried to overlook it.

Katie awoke at dawn to the sound of rain pounding down on the roof of her house. She sat up in the half-darkness, listening to the steady drumming with a sense of dread. The Knights always came when it was raining. The clouds interfered with the satellite surveillance the Voice maintained.

She slid out of bed, her stockinged feet silent on the plush carpet. One of the dogs had been sleeping in the corner. Now it opened its eyes to look at her, its tail thumping the floor with a lazy rhythm. She ignored it.

Where had this rain come from? She tried to recall if she'd caught the weather report lately. She hadn't realized a storm was due. Could the Knights be interfering with her satellite reception? No, she told herself. No. That was paranoia.

She crept to the closet, careful to stay away from the window, though she'd had them all redone last year with bulletproof glass. Sliding open the closet door, she withdrew her karbon-weave coveralls and stepped into the bulky garment, pressing shut the Velcro closures. The coverall was heavy and uncomfortable, but it would stop any legal bullet. She sealed the neck, pulled on her karbon-weave boots, then grabbed a helmet just as the intruder alarm sounded its soft, soothing pulse three times through the house, sending the dogs into a frenzy.

In a calm voice, the house announced: "Three individuals have entered the estate from the southern perimeter. Scent discrimination indicates human identity. No visual presence or identifiable weapons."

"Huh." No visual weapons only meant the Knights were coming in under camouflage, the holographic displays on their suits and weapons tuned to change with the scenery. She strode from the bedroom, the helmet tucked under her arm. She'd been through this so many times before.

"The police acknowledge our emergency and estimate arrival in twenty minutes," the house told her in its calm, feminine voice.

"Fucking great." After five years, the local cops figured it was her problem. They would be in no hurry to get out here.

Katie ducked into the study. Her gaze swept across the bank of security monitors, taking in a full-color view of the estate's perimeter. The chain-link fence didn't show any obvious damage, but then half of it was obscured by chaparral bedraggled and bowed down by the rain. The vegetation needed to be cut back. There'd been so much rain this year, everything was growing out of season. Rain, every few weeks. Katie had learned to hate the rain.

She switched the monitors to the second bank of cameras, then frowned. Had she caught a glimpse of motion on number seven? She stared at the view of the orchard, willing the phenomenon to repeat itself. Yes, there. Between trees that looked tired and sullen even in their new leaf, a shimmer, like a heat wave rolling across the camera's view. Katie's lips turned in grim triumph. Holographic suits were good, but not perfect.

"The intruders have crossed the inner perimeter," the house reported. "Two are approaching the back of the house from twelve degrees west of south. The third is approaching from due south."

So she could get out the front door without being seen. From there work her way around back through the olive hedge that surrounded the house. Her heart pounded in excitement as she opened the gun cabinet. She took down a shotgun and a box of color-coded ammunition. Green casing for rubber slugs. Blue for riot gas. Orange for explosive paint. Brass for old-fashioned lead slugs.

The dogs were still carrying on. She yelled at them to stay put, then she pulled on her helmet and let herself out the front door.

Lying on the sodden ground under the olive bushes, her hands shivering in the early-morning cold, she scanned the orchard through the shotgun's scope, and wondered—not for the first time—what the Knights were really after. If they simply wanted her dead, they could have destroyed her easily enough with a rocket launched from the highway. Maybe they didn't figure she was worth that level of attention. Maybe they didn't really care whether she lived or died. After all, most of their attacks were amateurish at best, carried out by one or two individuals, lightly armed. Over the helmet's transceiver, the house AI duly reported the presence of the intruders at the third perimeter, less than a hundred yards away.

She'd come to think of their attacks as some kind of bizarre game. A training ritual, a hazing ritual, an idle pastime that had grown into a tradition. She could imagine them like frat rats, talking together in a clubhouse somewhere, comparing notes on the latest batch of plebes and how well each had done at the Kishida house. "Yeah, Jackson only got as far as the second orchard row, but Carrera made the front porch and singed the door with his torch." "The kid caught some gas from the old lady, but not before dumping herbicide on her vegetable garden."

A bizarre game. And sometimes fatal. She'd hired a security guard once but they got him during the first rain. Another time a police officer was killed by a mine planted in the driveway. And once Katie took a bullet through the neck that left her in the hospital for three weeks.

She froze as she caught a fuzz of motion between herself and the toolshed. "Presence detected on the gravel pad," the house informed her. She tracked the suggestion with the shotgun as she fired a round of explosive paint. The report boomed across the orchard, sending a flock of partridge into the air. Inside the house, the dogs went hysterical.

Katie blinked past the rain. Had she found a target? She could make out a pool of paint on the ground, international orange, about two handspans across. And moving. Rising up from the ground like a ghost of spilled paint. Changing shape until she could make out a chest, neck, and shoulder. Somebody cursed in a masculine voice. She could hear footsteps on the gravel as he scrambled for shelter behind the toolshed. She aimed. A rubber slug was next in the sequence. She fired, and he went down again with a grunt of pain. She almost lost sight of him then. The stain was fading rapidly as enzymes in the suit broke it down. Her fingers flicked across the ammo box. She loaded another orange cartridge; painted him again.

"Presence detected on southwest side of house. Elevation six meters."

"Elevation?" Katie echoed.

Something slammed into her helmet. Her head snapped back. A second bullet ricocheted off the concrete foundation of the house, pelting her karbon-weave with fragments and opening up a cut across her cheek. She swept her rain-blurred visor down and scrambled back deeper into the bushes. Had one of the bastards climbed a tree? Dumping the green-coded cartridge that had been next in the sequence, she replaced it with old-fashioned brass. Time to get serious.

She swept the yard again. Found her target hobbling away. Fired. The slug tore a hole in the wall of the toolshed. Her target disappeared like chalk drawings on a rain-slick driveway.

Mocking catcalls erupted from the side of the house, *caw! caw! caw! caw!* sounding like the high-pitched cry of some manic bird.

"Presence detected west side, twenty meters," the house AI reported.

As if echoing the computer, a man's voice barked out, "West side, low on the ground!" Then a bullet hit her in the shoulder. It pancaked against the karbon-weave without penetrating, but the blow knocked the air out of her lungs and caused her to drop the shotgun. Another bullet caught her in the lower back. She tried to scramble away, but her legs wouldn't respond. She screamed in rage, thinking the impact had broken her spine. But then she could feel an aching chill in her toes. Nerve function had resumed. Painfully, she groped for her weapon, while yet another round slammed into the concrete.

The bastards were coming in hard today. They never pressed her this hard. It was a game. A bizarre game. She loaded more cartridges, all of them brass, remembering what Gregory had said.

The Knights were being hounded themselves. Vigilante

cops from the Voice squeezing them. The newest New
World Order. Fascist pigs.

Then a distant rifle cracked, and one of the Knights was
screaming. An infantile wailing sound that made her stomach curdle. Were they shooting each other now? She
peered up through the shrubbery in the direction of the
noise. High in a nearby apple tree she made out a writhing
smear of blood. Her skin crawled. She played with the image; tried to force herself to see in it the shape of a man.
But it was just blood, gushing out to coat an invisible riven
surface. Then the distant rifle sounded again and the
patch of blood plummeted from the tree.

Katie rolled onto her back, breathing hard. "Gregory!"
she shouted. "Come in slow. There's at least three of
them!" Her voice resounded across the soaked landscape.
Had he heard her? He must have heard her. If it was him.

Another round slammed through the shrubbery. She
ducked her head. Time to find a new position.

With the shotgun in one hand, she began to back painfully away. When she reached the front of the house, she
crawled under the porch, huddling in the semidarkness,
gasping for breath.

Where was Gregory?

Peering out through the slats she thought she saw a figure in karbon-weave slip among the trees. Then the dull
whump of a rocket launcher spoke from the orchard. She
threw herself facedown against the cold mud under the
porch as an explosion rocked the house. Smoke filled her
lungs. The dogs howled in fear. She called to the AI over
the helmet's transceiver and screamed at it to open the
doors and windows. The frantic scrabbling of nails overhead told her the animals had gotten out. Then the
Knights started shooting. From the fusillade, she knew
there had been more than three. The dogs yelped and
howled and cried piteously as they were hit, one by one.
Katie cursed helplessly, tears streaming down her cheeks.

Panama! she thought. *Panama.*

From the orchard, the *whump!* of another rocket. The
living room burst into flames that roared with the breath
of a dragon. The heat was terrifying in its intensity.
Mythic visions of hellfire reared up in her mind. Gregory

had tried to warn her. The Knights were here in force, out
to finish old business. She hadn't listened. Was he still
alive?

Wallowing through the mud, she made for the front
steps. There was a little access door on the side there. She
could run out and be shot like the dogs. Panama. One of
the dogs was still howling, a heartrending sound that filled
her with rage and pity. In Panama. Dizzy from the smoke,
she struggled to hold on to herself. She had one hand on
the latch. It was fiery hot. In Panama. She fell forward into
the mud. Lightning flickered far away. Thunder rumbled
like the engine of a truck on a lonely highway, a paved
road to hell. She'd gone to Panama with only the best intentions. She reached for the latch again, her lungs seared
by the superheated air. This time she caught the string
and pulled it. The little door swung open. Still clutching
the shotgun, she shoved herself forward on hands and
knees.

Rain pelted her helmet, ran across her visor, fell in angry hisses into the flames. She was halfway up and already
running when her visor frosted. Something took her helmet and slammed it to the ground.

Much of the Darien had been burned. She'd heard this
somewhere, but when she opened her eyes, it wasn't so.
The forest was alive, rustling in the moonlight, darkness
huddling under the trees like a living entity, a judge set to
punish only those who gave in to fear. She was surprised
to see that the bulldozed clearing was gone, taken over by
a forest of spindly saplings racing one another to the sky.
Night insects trilled softly and somewhere a jaguar
coughed. She told herself she was not afraid.

She squeezed her way through the young trees, placing
each foot carefully on the crumbly soil. No mud here anymore. It hadn't rained on the isthmus for months. Global
weather patterns were constantly shifting and maybe the
Darien would die despite the best efforts to save it.

News flash: We all die.

The trees ended abruptly. She stood at the edge of the
forest. The face of the moon was dark with the scars of
regolith mining. A night bird called. She heard the wind

whistle through the bird's feathers. A satellite raced in a
golden arc across the sky. She gathered her courage, then
sidled forward, to peer into the open pit.

It took a moment for her eyes to adjust.

The forest hadn't entered the pit, and the moonlight
didn't seem to penetrate it. Yet it had light. A glowing
blue liquid oozed in the bottom in a lacy pattern like a
vast capillary net. She saw the two bodies then—
fragments of decaying flesh clinging to dark bones that
gleamed in the eerie light. She wondered who had
stripped them, who had thrown them into the pit. How
long ago? This was the jungle, where old life was quickly
cycled into the new. Yet there was still flesh and hair
clinging to the bones. Enough of a body left that she
could make out the woman's face—despite the bone
showing darkly through the patchy skin. There was a bullet hole in the middle of the forehead. A period at the end
of a sentence. A third eye that looked inward and outward
and saw nothing.

I put that there.

Nervously, she glanced over her shoulder at Judge Dark.
The shadows seemed to bow out toward her. She quickly
looked away. The woman in the pit was beckoning to her
now, her bare arm bones moving weakly in a gesture that
clearly said *Come. Come.*

"Katie. Hey, Katie." She felt the touch of a calloused
hand against her cheek and the stroke of a cold, wet cloth
across her forehead. "Katie?"

She blinked, then groaned at the sudden awareness of a
headache that threatened to split her skull wide open.
With mud-smeared palms she reached up to press at her
temples. Gregory caught her hands and lowered them.
Rain ran in thin streams down his face. The track of a bullet had carved a fresh furrow across his burn scar. "Katie?"

Beyond him she saw a stranger in karbon-weave toeing
the body of one of the dogs, and beyond him, another
armed guerilla sitting on a tree stump, chewing gum. She
looked back at Gregory. "Come on," he said. "Let's get
out of here."

He helped her sit up. The earth seemed to wobble

around her. She caught sight of her helmet, lying on the ground. There was a huge crease over the right temple. She stared at it while rainwater pooled in the helmet's interior. Then she lifted her chin to look around.

The house was a heap of charred framing and burning embers, all the photos, all the mementos gone. She counted the dogs on the lawn. All five of them. Thank God Belle had moved out. *If there is a God. Thank you. Thank you.*

She looked back at Gregory. Anxiety filled his gaze. "They came in fast," he said. "We weren't ready."

She shrugged. "Time for a change anyway, I guess." She frowned at him, perplexed, wondering why she wasn't shaking, crying, something. There should be tears at a time like this, but she just felt numb.

They got off the train at a station on the edge of the Long Beach Reserve. The welfare village had been built along the waterfront after the shipping industry collapsed. Katie stood up shakily, clutching the back of the seat. Every muscle in her body felt as if it had been stretched and pounded. At least she didn't have anything to carry. She pushed a stray lock of tinted hair out of her face. She still reeked of smoke and gunpowder, but the train hadn't been crowded and nobody seemed to mind. Gregory offered her an arm to lean on, but she shook her head. She could handle it.

She stepped out on the platform, dressed in an ill-fitting pantsuit borrowed from a neighbor a mile down the road. Several kids were waiting to get on the train. They were colorful as birds of paradise, beautiful, neat, clear-eyed, and all of them sporting the armbands that declared them to be followers of the Voice of Humanity.

Katie led Gregory through their ranks. A few seemed to notice their lack of armbands, but they didn't make it an issue. That was the difference between a settled welfare village and the refugee camps of central L.A. Ilene's Voice had already tamed this crowd.

As they emerged from the train station, she paused to gaze at the neat, narrow streets, lined on both sides by year-old Wizard-Fast fern pines, already fifteen feet tall.

Behind the trees were newly built row houses, their white paint fresh and sparkling in the morning sun, their front yards beautifully landscaped with flowers and food plants.

She'd never quite decided if she liked the look of the reserves. The villages were attractive, no doubt about it. But they were almost too neat and clean, evoking a surreal Disney quality. Or maybe she was just a grouchy old fart. Compared to the projects of her youth, this was heaven.

Gregory gazed at her with worried eyes. "You okay for a walk?"

"Sure."

"Ferris's house is only about five minutes away."

"No sweat." She straightened her shoulders and set off with him at an easy amble.

In the modern welfare villages there was no such thing as a street, not in the old sense. Cars and trucks rarely entered. Residents were expected to walk.

But she and Gregory were the only ones out walking today.

That was the other quality of the villages that made her uncomfortable. People existed here, but they lived in the VR. Every housing project was built with a VR mall. People were so easy to calm with the VR. It was interactive, far better than TV. Crime and vandalism were almost unknown here. And there were very few babies. Not that sex had become unpopular, but welfare benefits were tied to mandatory birth control for both genders, and access to the VR was one of those benefits. The former Senator Carson (*let freedom ring*) had given this her reluctant approval. She considered it a holding pattern, a way of keeping people out of trouble until the Voice could develop a better/more meaningful existence for them.

So the VR fairly dripped with Voice propaganda. It was the latest revolution. They sponsored the most popular worlds. They used their influence to train the kids to be cops and citizens, promising them positions of authority in the coming new world. Flattery, power, responsibility. Ilene knew how to put it all together. It left Katie shaking in her boots.

Gregory had stopped by to see Ferris a few days before, on his way out to the farm. Now he showed Katie the way to Ferris's townhouse. It was a neat little one-bedroom, with lilies abloom in the salad garden just outside the front door.

The door swung open as they approached. Ferris emerged, a dark look of concern on his face as his gaze swept over Katie, measuring damage. "Do you know how lucky you are?" he asked.

"Hey. Thanks for taking me in."

He glanced at Gregory with a scowl. "Mister, you've got an odd way of showing your affections for this woman, but at least your timing's good."

"Yeah, thanks."

Katie walked into the house, her arm around Ferris while Gregory trailed behind. "You know, you were right, Ferris," she told him as the door closed.

"Right about what?"

"About me not being afraid." She looked around the living room with a mild sense of surprise. Though she'd been here a dozen times in VR, this was the first time she'd actually walked through the front door and seen his place with her own eyes. Funny, it looked just the same in person.

She walked across the room and sat down in her favorite chair. "I'm not afraid," she told him. "And I don't feel guilty about what I did in Panama. *And I don't understand why!*"

He sighed, and came over and took her hand.

"It's like I'm dead inside," she intoned. She glanced at Gregory. He stood by the door, shoulders hunched, looking uncomfortable and angry. She felt no sympathy for him. "It's like I'm some kind of machine. I can't feel anything anymore for those people I killed. Maybe that's good." Her fingers clenched reflexively around Ferris's palm. "You know, it's fear that threatens us most. Fear that blinds us, weakens us, forces us to pretend that we've got a lock on things when really we know it's all chance. I think it's good to remember that Sirius A is still out there somewhere, waiting to make a joke of the entire history of life on Earth."

She leaned back and closed her eyes, listening to her heart beat slowly in her ears and wondering how long she could hold out. "I'm empty and old and mangled," she muttered. "And I don't really believe that any tech will ever be invented that will make me young again. Not really. Not spiritually." Then she laughed at herself, softly. "But at least I'm not afraid."

Someday she'd go back down to South America. She'd liked it there, in the cold, sterile highlands of the Andes—though the work had been hard, especially that first day, transferring the patients from the truck to the mausoleum. At sunset Katie had found herself exhausted and alone on the stoop of the church. The orange light that poured in through the thin atmosphere felt holy in its intensity. She bathed in it, drinking in lungfuls of clear, icy-cold air while gazing out across a vast cauldron of churning blue clouds that obliterated any world below. And as the minutes passed, she felt herself growing lighter, shedding one by one the weight of all things past, emptying herself until she was a shell, so light that a stray breeze swept her into the sky where she drifted, a speck that was once a human being, lost now in an oceanic sunset.

Somewhere out there in the orange skies the speck had left this world and entered another, so that it continued to float in the sunset light, drifting impossibly far, past the curve of the world into a homogeneous orange realm where dreams no longer mattered.

Come back, she whispered to herself. *Come back*.

L.A. FLOW—NEWS AND
INFORMATION
"More Advances on the Medical Front"

Phoenix Labs today announced the
development of a programmable molecular
device capable of entering the nucleus of
an active human cell and modifying its
genetic content. The technology's potential was
illustrated by a volunteer. Treated with a
Phoenix device programmed to rewrite
that portion of the patient's genome
determining hair color, the formerly dark-
haired volunteer began growing blond hair
in both her head and pubic regions.
Phoenix Labs declared that their patented
device places science on the threshold of total
control of the human body.

14

On the Threshold

They were awkward at first, their second life together beginning almost as hesitantly as the first. On the train to the terminal they sat shoulder to shoulder, Gregory's presence playing on Katie like a stimulant. She stared out the window, listening to every rustle of movement from him, every sigh of breath past his lips, trying to remember that he had abandoned her for eleven years.

Her time sense refused to cooperate. Eleven years hung like a loop on the thread of her life. A long, circuitous path. But as the loop closed she found herself only a breath away from their moment of estrangement. She felt the old wound, but it was fresh, stripped clean of the inflexible scars that had formed in the intervening years.

They talked more on the jump to Beijing, chuckling over the awkwardness of meals eaten in the cramped seats, their elbows jostling if they spread jam on bread or fork-cut the tender breast of chicken.

In Beijing the spaceplane picked up additional passengers. While they were on the ground, Katie spent a few minutes in the tiny toilet cubicle, brushing her hair and washing her face. When she looked up, she discovered her reflection examining her from the mirror. The eyes that looked at her were more sunken than she remembered. Her skin seemed thicker, and it still had a red tinge from the searing fire. Yet she felt satisfied with the image. She still looked pretty good.

She returned to her seat as the new passengers settled into theirs. Gregory joined her a few minutes later. They watched the new arrivals. His hand drifted over the armrest to touch her arm. She felt supremely conscious of the tiny gesture, and knew that he was too. She enjoyed it, and wanted to reciprocate, but some stubborn streak inside her would not let her bend that far, just yet. Finally the tension grew too much, so she leaned forward to extract the safety brochure from the seat pocket in front, as an excuse to break the contact. Gregory's hand returned to his lap.

After takeoff, though, he ordered champagne. "It's the first time to orbit for both of us," he explained. She smiled and touched her glass to his. The crystal rang in a fine, clear note. The bubbles fizzed against her tongue and filled her throat with a dizzying abundance of carbon dioxide. It was only a moment before the flight attendants came by, collecting the glassware in trade for motion-sickness patches.

But Katie's stomach did not rebel against the weightlessness of orbit. The sensation was disturbingly familiar. She'd dreamed it more than once and the memory upset her. Her hand slid across the armrest. She caught up Gregory's hand and squeezed it, using him as an anchor in this reality.

That night they were both very tired, but the sense of awkwardness had returned and they were reluctant to go to bed. Katie sat in a chair in a corner of the little room she owned aboard Voice-2 and pretended to read a brochure describing a new biotech firm in need of venture capital. But her mind wasn't in it. Though she read the sentences over and over, she could get them to make no sense.

Gregory took a long time in the shower, perhaps hoping

she would fall asleep before he emerged, but no such
luck. "Want a drink?" he asked when he finally came out.

"Yes."

He wore loose-fitting pants. That was all. She came to
sit beside him on the bed. He handed her a glass of wine.

"It would be pointless to apologize," he said. "It
wouldn't mean anything next to the years we've lost. It's
a matter for forgiveness only."

"For forgetting," she said, nodding agreement. "Or pretending to forget." The wine tasted fine. This close, she
could feel the warmth of his body through the pink cotton
sleep shirt she wore.

He leaned forward, his elbows on his thighs, his hands
cradling the wineglass between his knees. The burn scar
on his face looked raw and red. His eyetooth showed
where his lips were twisted out of line. She stroked his
back with the tips of her fingers. He only flinched a little.
She could see the scar over his spine, where the bullet had
broken his spinal cord. She touched it gently.

He said: "I haven't changed much."

"Is that a warning?"

"I guess so."

He set his wineglass on the floor; took hers away and
set that down too. He reached for her shoulder and gently
pulled her down on the bed. He seemed very sad, and for
a moment she saw him as a prostitute, returning unwilling
to the trade. "I can see that you love me," she said. "And
I can see that you wish you didn't."

He shrugged. "Like I said, I haven't changed much."
He kissed her neck, his breath rousing the deadened
senses of her skin. She breathed deeply, her chest rising
with invigorating cool air. She let her questions go. Too
much detail might be damaging. They were not young
and they were not simple. Time apart had made them too
much the individuals. They would never be one. But
there was much to be said for the conjoining of two sympathetic creatures.

Her fingers slid through his hair, the stubble of his crew
cut springing like coarse velvet under her touch. With a
pang she remembered how long and luxurious it had once
been. She would not ask him to grow it out again, though.

That had been a different time. They had been different people. She preferred that the ages of her life be clearly delineated.

His hand squeezed her breast. His lips moved down across her shoulder where the loose collar of her nightshirt had fallen away. She felt fear deep in her belly as he gradually reclaimed her body, an insidious dread that he would see through her; that he would learn how little there was between them.

And after that, every time they made love, she felt the same fear. Until, nearly a year later, she came to understand that he did know.

He'd been away several weeks, looking into the capitalization needs of a list of companies that had seemed to her to be promising investments. When they met again in their room on Voice-2 he seemed withdrawn. This disturbed her. They'd talked on the phone nearly every day and she'd sensed nothing wrong. But then most of their talk had been business—a good cover for awkward emotions. They'd neglected the personal side, as they so often did, compressing whatever sentiments they might own into a husky, obligatory closing—"I love you," muttered with not a little self-consciousness.

The physical side of love was easier, almost as if having failed at talk they could make it up in bed. Gregory's love-making that night was intense, earnest, as if he were striving to overcome an emotional distance. Unsuccessfully.

Afterward, Katie questioned him about his mood.

He shrugged in a ritualistic attempt to dismiss her concerns, but she urged him to speak.

"All right." Head on the pillow, he gazed up at the ceiling, but she sensed his sight was focused elsewhere. "I met a woman in the Azores," he told her.

Katie felt herself stiffen. Gregory glanced at her. Then he continued, in a soft monotone drained of emotion. "She was about my age, with blond hair like yours, and a pretty face. I noticed right off how much she looked like you. Wealthy and beautiful and married, though her husband was in Brazil for therapy, and had been, for a long time. We made love on the beach after a party at the governor's mansion. She wanted me to stay at her house for a while, but I said no. I was badly shaken. She looked so much like you. She loved me so sweetly, like you. But she didn't belong to me. And it was such a familiar feeling. Familiar. Though I'd never been conscious of it before, suddenly I knew that I felt this way *all the time.*"

Katie turned half away, blinking back tears and wondering what he expected her to do, what he expected her to say; clinically trying to gauge whether it would be best to react first to his guiltless admission of adultery, or to his cold assessment of their marriage. But she gave it up. Turning back to him, she reached across his chest to give his far shoulder a little tug, encouraging him to come to her. He did. Their lips brushed, and then he asked, "You're not angry?"

"Yes, I'm angry." She could feel the opposing currents of fury and despair warring in her breast; she strove to overlook them. "I don't know what to tell you, beyond what I've told you over and over. I love you. And I don't want you to go." She listened to herself speak. Her words sounded hollow. But she knew they were true.

They rolled together, her arms clasped tight over the small of his back; her lips tasting the salt of his skin. She was fifty-five, and then sixty, and then sixty-four, and to outsiders their marriage seemed as solid as the business empire they constructed together. But between them their relations remained tenuous and ill-defined.

"Wake-up call," Gregory announced cheerfully as they lay together in a rented room in the newest orbital, Voice-4. By the clock it was eight A.M. Pacific Standard Time and the resident AI had piped in some joyful and unchallenging Vivaldi per Katie's command.

She cuddled against Gregory's chest, letting the music flow over her. He'd come up from Europe only a few hours before and was still running on the old-world clock. He'd surprised her with his arrival. They'd planned to meet in another couple of weeks on the older Voice-2 where they kept the closest thing they had to a permanent home. But he'd come up on the spaceplane days ahead of schedule, ringing on her door in the middle of her night.

She stretched and yawned. Her abbreviated night's

sleep had been his afternoon nap. He sat up, full of energy. "Let's have dinner in the room," he said.

Katie groaned and rubbed at the sleep in her eyes. "It's *morning*, sweetheart. We're supposed to have breakfast. Then go to work."

"No work." He touched her breast. "Have you got your strength back? We could make love again."

She slapped his hand away in mock outrage. "Have I got my strength back? I may be sixty-four, but I'm not feeble." He laughed. She cocked a suspicious eyebrow. "Why are you in such a good mood, anyway? You found something in the European labs, didn't you?"

"No."

"You did too. Tell me. What is it?"

"It's nothing like that." He scowled in distaste. "Actually, the labs haven't been coming up with anything. That's pretty hard to do in this day and age. I think they're playing dirty."

"Holding out on us?" She sat up in bed, looking at him in concern.

"Uh-huh. I'll be going back for a closer look in a few days."

"So why are you here now?"

He smiled and touched her shoulder, his hand warm against her skin. "To see you." He sighed. "I'm going to have to conduct a full-scale audit of several of our investments. Once that starts, I won't be able to get away." He stroked her cheek with the back of his fingers. His gaze softened. "You're still so pretty."

"You need to get your eyes checked." She slipped past him. Her bare feet touched the carpeted floor.

"Hark: mirror on," he said.

"Gregory!"

Too late. The resident AI picked up his command and activated the wall-sized screen that faced the bed. Drawing on sensors secreted throughout the room, it displayed a perfect image of herself and Gregory. She looked up to meet the gaze of her double, self-consciously squaring her shoulders. "Look at yourself," Gregory said. "You're beautiful."

"Oh, sure." She raised her right hand to probe at the

soft, dry pouches of skin that had formed on her face over
the years, and the projection followed suit—not as a mirror
image, but as she would see herself were she sitting there
in the wall. She touched her hair. It was thinning, but it
could still take a perm that held it off her face in soft
waves. Her eyes seemed to have shrunk over the years,
until now they were half-hidden under pouches of sagging
skin. Plastic surgery could fix that, of course. But plastic
surgery might complicate things when the Cure was developed, so she avoided it. Her inspection continued. She
still exercised hard and her body showed it. Her muscle
tone was good, though here and there on her arms there
simply seemed to be too much skin. Her breasts were
drooping, but they weren't quite empty sacks yet, and
they still responded to a man's touch.

Gregory's hand came sneaking around from behind her
back to caress a nipple. The effect of his touch was
quickly translated to her groin, and she felt a burst of
warmth there. She smiled. So this was sixty-four.

"Well?" Gregory asked.

She shrugged. "Not bad, considering." Then she leaned
back to kiss him on the cheek. "But I really have to get
to work."

Extricating herself from his hands, she stood cautiously,
reining in her strength in the orbital's low-G. She'd been
on Voice-4 for nearly a week, looking into the dozen or so
start-up companies here that were seeking outside investment. Only two struck her as potentials. A final decision
would have to await more background research.

"I've got an appointment," she said, pulling out clothes
from a drawer. "Some clown who's sure the Primal Nation's into hallucinogens. You know, for the vision quest?
Sounds like a loser. But his mama's been a business associate for years, and she thinks he's just keen."

Gregory was unimpressed. "So stay with me and say
you went."

Katie found herself tempted. "I'd love to. You know
that. But the dirty old AI would rat on me." She smiled
apologetically and finished dressing.

Gregory grumbled some more, but finally rolled out of
bed and pulled on a pair of shorts. "Well, I've got a pres-

ent for you anyway." He produced a white cloth sack from his suitcase. It was about the size of an old-fashioned plastic grocery bag and it looked lumpy and heavy.

"What is it?" Katie asked curiously.

He handed her the bag, and as she pulled it open he told her: "Apples from your farm."

Her lips parted in astonishment as she gazed at the bonanza of fruit. They were either galas or fujis, their beautiful skins marbled with streaks of dark red over blush, blending into yellow. Her heartbeat quickened, and she felt a deep pain at the back of her throat. "You stopped by the farm? Why?" Reaching into the bag, she pulled out one of the fruits. She could still remember the day she'd planted the bare-root trees, deep in the first winter she'd owned the farm. And how long ago was that? Some twenty-nine years.

"Chaparral's about to smother the trees," Gregory said. "But they're still bearing."

She gazed at him past the round, full curve of the fruit she held in her hand. "Why did you go there?"

He grinned. "To pick some apples for you." He took the fruit from her hand and held it up, as if to admire the melded colors. "That's your roots, Katie. You've been too much of a business tramp since you left the farm. Thought you might like to know that part of it's still there, still growing." He held the apple up to her mouth. "Try it. It's good."

She bit into the crisp flesh, the sharp flavor sparkling against her tongue. She waited for a flush of memories to be drawn out by the taste, but perhaps because she was expecting them, they didn't come. There was only the present moment. Gregory held the apple to his own mouth and took a bite just next to hers, creating a rough figure eight. Infinity, in the moment.

"Say you love me," he commanded.

"I love you." She hefted the bag of apples. "And thanks. This was real sweet."

"So let's get some cheese and wine and have a private party."

She groaned. "You know I'd love to, but—"

"Business first," he finished for her.

"So come with me. You're a partner in this venture."

He nodded, seemingly pleased with that solution. "Okay. Give me a minute to get dressed."

The corridor outside the rented apartment was empty, the walls still tuned to the dark and moody starscape that served as LivingMural, Inc.'s "vanilla" configuration. None of the seventy-odd residents had gotten around to doing any serious decorating. With only ten percent of the units sold, the most notable quality of the orbital was its silence. Gregory and Katie did their best to disrupt it, laughing and passing the apple back and forth as a kind of lean breakfast. But the sound damping technologies that were part of the orbital's design squashed their efforts. With a few thousand residents aboard, the sound damping would become an asset. But for now, Katie found the effect oppressive.

They reached a narrow stairway. Katie went first up to the next level. Voice-4 was a tethered orbital, connected via extrusion cable to the honeycombed body of an asteroid that had provided the raw materials for its construction. Ten years ago, when the Knights had burned her out of her farmhouse, Katie had gone looking for a new game to play. She'd found it in venture capital. She'd been a novice in the field when Summer House, Inc. developed their line of Rock Processors—programmable engines on the scale of microorganisms that could take apart an asteroid the way microbes on Earth could deconstruct a dead body. She and Gregory had put up one percent of the funds for the asteroid-retrieval mission, and she'd acted as agent for thirty percent more. The Voice had kicked in fifty percent, and the end result was Voice-3, the first large-scale habitat ever built . . . and a thirty-million-dollar profit for Kishida-Hunt Incorporated.

And she'd kept on playing the game ever since, scouting Earth-bound and orbital labs for the next Summer House, and the next, and the next. Playing passionately, with Gregory as her ruthless partner, the company enforcer. For the first time in her life she found herself with no clear goal, simply restless, made uneasy by a need to see what she could do next.

It was a moment before she realized someone was walking with them in the corridor. She started, silently cursing the sound-deadened walls that made it so easy for people to sneak up from behind. Then she realized: Their companion was only an image transmitted from one of the other orbitals and placed in the walls, a human projection incongruously set in the LivingMural starfields, a little old lady with silver hair and a conservative blue pantsuit, standing on vacuum.

Katie heard Gregory's sharp intake of breath. She felt her own back stiffen. "Hello, Ilene," she said.

"Katie." The Voice wasn't hot on privacy. Ilene's new judicial AI was free to observe throughout the orbitals—every resident and visitor agreed to that when they signed their habitation contract—but Katie gritted her teeth every time she was confronted with the fact. Ilene leaned forward, looking straight into Katie's eyes. She was eighty-five years old, her body tiny, her shoulders slightly hunched. But her gaze still reflected the intensity of sub-terranean fires. The CEO's who'd elected her president of the Voice had never asked her to step down.

Ilene's gaze shifted to Gregory. "And Dr. Hunt, I see. Your return to the orbitals was rather sudden."

Katie glanced at him anxiously. Gregory despised Ilene. He hadn't spoken to her in all the years since the congressional hearings. But he seemed calm.

Ilene turned her attention to Katie. "I've got a developing situation that might interest you."

"Is that right?" She faced Ilene warily. They'd carried on a truce of sorts since the Summer House expedition. Katie had seen well enough that the Voice was the only political entity that really mattered anymore, so she'd joined the club and agreed to play by their rules, which were strict, but not oppressive. Ilene had taken that as a concession in their old feud, something close enough to victory that she could try for a rapprochement. Katie had responded coolly. But over the years, as Katie's influence in the business community had grown along with her fortune, Ilene had come to her more and more often with assignments, tasks, deeds that needed a private hand behind them but that always resulted in political or economic advantage for the Voice. And generally, Katie went along, because Ilene always made sure the offer included a generous profit for Kishida-Hunt. But the affection that Katie had once felt for Ilene had never been recovered.

"We're assembling a new administrative team to address morale problems within our Mars initiative." Ilene spoke in a soft deadpan that had become famous throughout the net. "Somehow our colonists have developed the impression that they're just—what was that quaint term they used? Oh, yes. 'Holding seats for the big shots.' Holding seats." Her gaze wandered as she chuckled to herself. "The most expensive seats in the system, I might add. After what we paid to get them there."

"But they're right, aren't they?" Katie said. Her voice was calm; she kept her expression impassive. But deep in her breast, her heart began to boom in uneasy expectation.

Ilene's sharp gaze raked her face. "Mars is of supreme importance to the Voice."

Katie shrugged, refusing to betray any anxiety. "I can't imagine why. It's a wilderness at the bottom of a gravity well. There's no value in Mars, not for the foreseeable future."

Gregory stood to one side chewing on the last of the apple. Ilene took that moment to glance at him. He met her gaze with an angry, petulant stare. Something seemed to pass between them, and suddenly Katie felt the fruit's acids begin to sour in her stomach. Gregory despised Ilene. He never spoke to her. So what was that look about?

But Ilene's attention was again focused on Katie. "You surprise me," she said. "I've always held you to be a person of vision. Mars has barely been surveyed. We can't just dismiss it."

Katie chose her words carefully. It would serve no good purpose to antagonize Ilene, but she needed to make her position clear. "You need to stake a claim to the real estate, sure. And maybe in a few hundred years it'll even be worth something. But you made a mistake when you sent your top-flight people out there. Sooner or later—when the romanticism wore off—they were bound to wake up and realize they'd left the action fifty million miles behind."

Ilene's gaze was stony. "Now this is interesting," she

said. "I was led to believe you *desired* an appointment to
Mars." Her gaze again ran out to Gregory. "But that pride
stood in the way of your asking me."

Katie stepped back in stunned surprise. Gregory
watched her warily, his fingers restlessly turning the apple
core over and over in his hand. "You?" she asked. "You
wanted me to go to Mars?"

"I think it'd be good for you."

"You want me off the scene." She couldn't believe it.
Only a few minutes ago everything had seemed perfect
between them.

A grim expression settled on his face. "It's better this
way. Our European labs aren't just stealing from us, Katie.
They've gone underground. They're developing illegal
products. I have to bring my circle into it, and I know you
don't have the stomach for that."

Gregory's circle: He'd never lost touch with the political
radicals who'd fought the terrorist wars in Europe. Now he
wanted to revive the old militia? Over patents and prop-
erty rights.

Katie shook her head. She *wanted* to believe him. She
desperately wanted a benign reason for his deception. But
his explanation didn't make sense. "Why don't you sic the
Voice cops on them?" she asked softly. "Why risk—" She
stopped suddenly, put off by the look of warning in his
eyes. He *was* lying to her!

And she knew of only one subject upon which their
honesty consistently failed.

"It's Tom, isn't it?" she blurted out. "You've found
something."

"*Dammit!*" His chin lowered in a defensive gesture as
his temper exploded. "You'd have to think of that. It's always the first subject with you. When are you going to
wake up? Nobody's doing work on cryonic resuscitation
anymore, because the bloody Voice isn't going to allow
you to raise the dead!"

Katie glared at him. He well knew her opinions on
Voice law.

Apparently, so did Ilene. She cracked an indulgent
smile. "There you have it, Katie. He's afraid you'll screw

up—and that you'll take Kishida-Hunt down with you when you fall. Frankly, if I were him, I'd worry too."

Gregory hurled the apple core against the floor. He stepped toward her; his hand closed on her upper arm in a painful grip. "Go to Mars," he warned. "I'll clean up the European labs and then I'll join you. If and when a Cure's invented, if and when it's *allowed*, Nikki can get her precious dad out of storage. It's not your problem anymore."

Her mouth fell open in astonishment. "Who the hell do you think you are? You don't get to decide that for me." She yanked free of his grip, her breath coming fast and hard as the enormity of his betrayal sank in. "You're not going to sequester me in some backwater operation. And I'm not going to abandon Tom. Not when he's helpless. And neither you or the fucking Voice is going to change my mind."

Gregory backed off stiffly, his hands shaking, the apple core forgotten on the floor. "Then go to him!" he shouted. "Because I don't want you with me anymore. I don't want to see you go down in a Voice raid. I don't want to see you die."

Wedged Time—
Alternate Landscapes

Dusk was deepening into night on his journey down the mountain, when suddenly he felt a change in the atmosphere, an abrupt warming in the air, an easing in the heavy clouds that hung low overhead. His steps slowed. He turned around, frowning in confusion as he gazed back up the slope.

A stone's throw away he saw a low ridgeline, its spine protruding from the snow in a jagged break of weathered gray rock. A great bird clung with silver talons to the tallest outcropping. An eagle, he realized, though its feathers were as white as a summit cloud in full sun and its body matched his own in size. An eagle. It looked at him with dark, impatient eyes. The feathers on its neck ruffled audibly, stirring some ghost-thin memory of kinship. "I know you." He felt joy in this vague sense of recognition. He started toward the bird.

A few flakes of snow fluttered through the warming air. They melted before they could touch him, but in their dispersing scent he caught the concern of his Familiar.

The eagle seemed to sense it too. It half opened its wings. Its beak clacked with nervous energy, a masculine command that he come and come *now*.

His Familiar tried to embrace him in a soft swirl of snow, tried to draw him away. But the eagle set its talons in his soul. Seized in its beak the deepest, oldest parts of his being. The haunts of myth, of legend. Of creation. Its dark gaze fixed on him and next he knew he was running across the snow toward it, a madman in pursuit of the sun. And when a bold scream rang through the dusk, he was unsure of whose throat it had come from, his own, or that of the bird.

The eagle shot off its perch, straight up into the murky sky. He watched it go. The low-hanging clouds opened before it, rolling away until the rosy-gold light of sunset poured down upon him. He could see all the way to the summit now. Daylight still played upon the snowfields there, and on the white feathers of a great flock of eagles slowly circling the jagged peaks.

He felt the fading warmth of the sun on his wings, the physical pleasure of the wind as it swept past his feathers, lifting him effortlessly into the golden sky—

Cold bit deep into his hand. He looked down to see his fist encrusted with tiny white snow crabs. It looked as if he were wearing a glove of glittering ice. And it *hurt*.

Annoyed, he shook his hand, trying to dislodge the crabs. But they clung tight. So he banged his fist against his thigh and crushed the tiny creatures, spreading a thin film of their colorless body juices across his skin.

Snow fell past his cheeks and fluttered across the sky in heavy veils, obscuring his view of the summit. He growled at his Familiar. She wanted to hold him here; she wanted to keep him for herself. "No," he said, plunging forward. "This has nothing to do with you." And he leaped straight up—

—to climb on great wings that pushed against the air with a tireless strength, carrying him higher and higher toward the bare rocks and windswept glaciers of the summit. The other eagles were still above him, far above, rising higher even as he sought to catch them. They were far beyond the tallest peak now, points of white light in a darkening sky. He drove after them—

—found himself facedown in the snow and freezing. His Familiar was with him. She shrouded him in thick, sweet flakes.

She tickled his ears. She touched his brain with whispered warnings he couldn't quite make out—

—He looked down, and to his surprise, the peaks of the mountains were already far, far below him. He looked above, but he saw no other eagles, only the bright points of distant stars like shining white birds on the edge of sight. Confusion weakened the powerful stroke of his wings. Where had the others gone? He began to falter.

Then the stars shifted. Seemed to turn and sprout wings and call to him in a language that he would understand . . . would understand if only he went a little higher. . . .

Gently, gently, she tapped his spine with heavy flakes of snow. The snow crabs chewed on his fingers. He groaned. He was so cold. He shoved himself up on his elbows and shook his head to clear it. The eagles vanished. The stars stabilized.

With a gust of disappointment, he realized they were only stars after all.

He circled for a few minutes, made restless by a cutting sense of loss. Then he folded his wings against his body and dove back toward the earth—

He rolled onto his back and watched the snow fall from the darkening sky. The air around him was heavy with her presence. Her snowfall sustained him. Measured doses of hope and purpose. *"Bring me back,"* he whispered. *"Bring me home to you."*

VOICE NEWS; ISSUE 661; 10:00
"Policy Statement on Life Extension"

*Responding to increasing confusion within
the scientific community and law-enforcement
circles, President Ilene Carson has
requested the newly commissioned judicial
AI to issue a preliminary opinion clarifying
the legality of life-extension therapies under
current Voice law. The result was
unequivocal:*

*"While some have regarded aging as a
genetic defect and therefore correctable under
Voice law, the judiciary finds to the
contrary. A survey of literature, law, and
nature demonstrates that aging is a natural
and universal phenomenon among all earthly
life and emphatically qualifies as a
defining condition of human existence.*

Therefore, it must be allowed to follow its natural course."

Objections were immediately raised by leaders in the business community, who contend that overzealous restrictions on the development of geriatric therapies will cause a flight of scientific talent to competing sovereignties where regulations are less stringent. "Not only will the Voice lose its lead in the development of molecular technology," said Martin Chang, professor of business science at Stanford, "but we will also lose our ability to regulate the course of that development. The Voice cannot control a technology it does not dominate."

15

Tactics of Domination

Three days later, Katie arrived at L. A. International on the *City of Beijing*, after a stopover at the spaceplane's home city and a brief jump over the Pacific. Quarantine was a cursory affair. She had her Voice passport, certifying that she'd confined her travels to uninfested regions, and she was quickly granted admittance to California. She took the train to Long Beach and knocked on Ferris's door. He was expecting her. He gave her a hug and clucked over her in concern. "Single again, huh?"

"Maybe permanently this time." She dropped her suitcase in the living room and claimed a chair. "He went back to Voice-2 ahead of me. I got there a day later. He'd packed up all my stuff. Tossed me out of my own apartment. You should have seen him, Ferris. He was livid. So mean. I thought he was going to hit me."

"Come on."

"It's true. I couldn't get out of there fast enough."

"So what *really* set him off? This can't be about Tom. Nothing's changed in that."

"I'm not so sure. Gregory wants me out of the way. *Far* out of the way. Why, do you think?"

"I see," Ferris said. "He's found something."

"It has to be. But he doesn't want me to find it."

Ferris nodded thoughtfully. "Okay, then. I'll help you look."

They spent the evening stoned in the VR, drunk on the megabytes of gossip Ferris dredged up as he hunted for some sign of a quickening in the field of cryonic medicine. They found nothing.

"Doesn't mean anything," Ferris assured her. "Anything as complicated as a revival isn't going to be made public until it's been successfully completed."

"A revival? You don't think it's gone that far, do you? I talked to the board at Forward Futures and they swear it's too soon. Any company trying to revive now will be putting the patient through an unnecessary risk."

He looked at her quizzically. "I guess it must be hard to apply business acumen to something this personal."

She felt the blood leave her face. Her skin grew suddenly cold. "Do you really think somebody could be that far ahead of the pack? Ready to do a revival now ... Oh, what a position to be in, what an enviable position. If it works they can charge *anything* for the procedure. . . ."

They were both silent, weighing the implications. Then Katie spoke: "That's what Gregory's afraid of, isn't it? That I'll trade every asset I own for Tom. Everything for Tom. . . ."

Ferris shook his head. "You can't go for anything like that. Not when this tech could be common currency in a few more years."

Her brows knit in sudden ire. "It's far more likely this tech will be *illegal* in a few more years. It may be illegal now, but I'm not going to ask the judicial AI for a clarification. This is a window of opportunity, Ferris. It could be my only chance to revive Tom. I have to take it."

He stood beside her, glowering at the VR display. She spoke cautiously. "I want you to float an offer for me. A hundred million dollars in Voice-secured electronic currency for the resuscitation schedule."

"You'll be buried in offers."

"I want you to find the legitimate one. The one Gregory's afraid of. Will you do it?"

He looked somber, but resigned. "I'll do what I can."

The next morning she caught a train bound for San Diego, looking forward to a visit with Joy. But the train was only a few minutes out of the station when she began to feel dizzy. By the time the Coastal approached the stop at Oceanside some twenty minutes later, she knew she was running a high fever. At first she was incredulous. Plagues were common, but not in Voice territory, and she hadn't traveled outside the Holdings in years. How could she have caught something? Then a cold trickle of understanding cut through her fever. Gregory could be behind this. Gregory had failed to get her on a transport to Mars. But there was more than one way to take a body out of circulation.

She closed her eyes, thinking about Joy and the kids in San Diego. The train eased to a full stop at the Oceanside station.

How bad is this going to be?

She told herself the virus couldn't be contagious. Gregory wouldn't risk introducing a contagious plague into the Southern California Holding. It was probably tailored to her genotype. She was probably the only one in the world who could catch it ... if the design work had been done right.

She'd seen a lot of sloppy design work.

Her eyes popped open. A few people were standing up, reaching for their bags.

I have to get off this train.

There was no way of knowing what sequence of genetic markers activated the virus. Maybe Joy carried the same traits. Maybe Tom-2 did, or Curran. She stood up slowly, leaning on the back of the seat in front of her. She was not going to take this plague to San Diego.

Her legs felt shaky. She reached into the overhead compartment and pulled down her bag. The weight of it sent her stumbling backward. A young girl reached out to steady her elbow, but after one look at Katie's face she yanked her hand back in sudden fear. Katie ducked her

chin and headed toward the exit, half stumbling, clutching
at the seat backs with a sweat-soaked hand while the bag
thumped against her leg. Her vision was blurring. The
world seemed to recede around her while her heart rumbled in her ears like some huge, flaccid organ, hardly
capable of providing even minimal function.

She reached the platform and paused, breathing shal-
lowly, trying to steady herself. From the corner of her eye
she sighted a familiar gray-and-sea-green uniform. Fear
ran like a steel rod up her spine. A Voice cop, about two
cars down, watching passengers exit from the rear of the
train. Voice cops had free run throughout the Holdings.
They were the muscle behind Voice restrictions on molecular technologies. They pursued molecular crimes and responded to molecular emergencies ... like plague. If this
cop saw her, he'd have her quarantined in a minute ...
questioned much later. She'd heard of people being held
in quarantine for *years*. Might as well be on Mars.

She dropped her chin against her chest and headed for
the ticket wall. The crowds were thin. She slipped her ID
into the slot without having to wait and entered an inland
destination. Her ticket popped out. She grabbed it. Then
took a second look. Printed across the face of the card, she
read: *Voice Citizen Katharine Kishida. You may have been inadvertently infected with an untested strain of hallucinogenic virus.
Please report to Voice authorities immediately, as quarantine and
treatment are essential.*

Katie swore softly under her breath. Maybe it wasn't
Gregory. Maybe it was Ilene, following the same trail
Katie was working on. She glanced over her shoulder and
thought she saw the cop looking in her direction. With his
headset, he was wired up to the central AI. And the AI
knew exactly where she was.

She dropped the ticket and headed for the exit. A taxi
was waiting on the curb. She opened the door and slid
onto the seat. Hands shaking, she rummaged through her
wallet, looking for another ID card. Theresa Myers. Commanding a bank account of three million dollars ec. She
yanked it out and slipped it into the cab's console. The
Voice cop appeared at the station exit, his eyes searching
the walks.

"Destination?" the cab's AI asked.

"Just head inland." The cop was gazing at her vehicle now. She tried to look down, look away, look casual as the taxi pulled slowly from the curb, moving at a walking pace down the mall. Just before it turned onto the boulevard she looked back. The cop was gone.

She sagged on the seat in exhaustion. A little demon sat on the console. It had cloven hooves, a devil's tail, and Ilene's face. Katie stared at it, the hair on the back of her neck slowly rising. But when she blinked the demon was gone. She shuddered.

The cab rolled along through the outskirts of Oceanside at a sedate ten miles an hour, the maximum speed allowed in the pedestrian town. Outside the window, she saw an odd assortment of clowns and harlequins, black-leather bikers and tie-dyed hippies. She wondered if a carnival was scheduled. Then a small herd of unicorns pranced across the street, their horns flashing gold in the sun. She lay down on the seat and held her head. On the floor of the cab, ladybugs, nearly a quarter of an inch in diameter, sat at tiny tables drinking tea. "What's your range?" she croaked at the cab AI.

"This vehicle is capable of operating throughout the southern California Holding."

She breathed a sigh of relief. She'd been afraid it was limited to Oceanside. "I want to reach the Primal Nation."

"This vehicle is not capable of crossing sovereign boundaries."

The imp was back. It was using a large needle to spear the frantic ladybugs. Katie closed her eyes, remembering a lab on Voice-4, the last one she'd visited before her departure. And the oily young man who'd offered visions in a bottle. Gregory had never gone to that lab. He'd stalked off to pack up his things, leaving her to keep the appointment alone. He'd been on the shuttle back to Voice-2 by the time she'd finished.

So it must have been Ilene. Ilene didn't want her to find the Cure. Ilene liked to believe she could control things like the Cure, and the restless human psyche. "You don't need to enter the Nation," she told the AI. "Just take me to the nearest border."

*   *   *

It was just past sunset when the cab stopped in the middle of a weed-cracked road deep in an old forest reserve. The door opened. Katie had been dozing through the afternoon. Now she sat up slowly. Her body ached and her head pounded. She wondered if she was really here or if this was just another figment. If she stepped out of the cab, would there be ground to stand on? The cab stuck out a red, wet tongue at her. "Trip fare: two thousand three hundred dollars ec," it said, the tongue lolling between obscene red lips. She closed her eyes and reached unhappily for the console. She had to recover Theresa Myers's ID card, no matter how repulsive the form it had assumed. She felt the rough, warm tongue under her hand and yanked on it. It came loose, and suddenly the squishy feeling was gone. She could feel the hard plastic of the card against her fingers.

She kept her eyes closed and grabbed for her bag. A strong, bony hand caught her wrist. She jumped and screamed, and the sensation vanished. She stood by the cab, the bag in one hand, the card in the other, swaying on legs that were literally made of rubber. With a moan, she sank to the roadway. The cab closed its door and pulled away. A few feet down the road it sprouted wings and took off into the coming night, its quiet electric motor quickly fading as it tacked out toward the stars.

Her gaze was brought back to the ground by the antics of a handful of tiny fire sprites. The quasi-human creatures laughed in high, glassy voices as they tumbled and scampered back and forth across the road. They disappeared abruptly as a freezing mountain wind came sighing through the treetops. The wind swept past her, coating her in a rime of ice. She shook in the sudden cold, her bleary eyes dry with fever. "Why am I here?" she whispered, her voice barely audible in the heavy dusk. She pressed the heels of her hands against her forehead, cracking a thin skin of ice that shattered and fell in glittering shards to the roadway.

Why am I here?

She'd left the coast, driven by some vague idea of finding sanctuary in the Primal Nation. But as the night's chill

invaded her, it suddenly occurred to her that she could die
out here. Even if this fever didn't prove fatal, even if
these hallucinations didn't drive her over the edge of a
cliff or into the swirling waters of a river, she could succumb to hypothermia. Maybe she should recall the cab.
She had her phone in the bag. Maybe she should turn herself in to the Voice cops. Ilene would keep her in quarantine, but it wouldn't be forever.

Ilene only wanted to keep her from finding the Cure.
No. Ilene wanted to keep her away from Tom.
Why?
Because she was jealous. Because she wanted to hurt
Katie.

*Because she wanted to spare Tom the shock of finding his
young wife suddenly sixty-four years old and married to another
man.*

Katie stood shaking in the cold wind. A coyote howled
somewhere not so far away. A second joined it, then a
third. *Tom won't know me,* she realized with a sudden sense
of surprise. Tom would wake up to see her, an old woman
who at best would seem vaguely familiar. He'd glance at
her, no hint of recognition in his eyes, and then he'd look
beyond her shoulder, searching for the woman who'd once
been his wife.

A gray shape caught her eye. She turned, to see a coyote
trot onto the roadway, its dark eyes glittering in the
emerging starlight. Then, like a ghost slowly taking shape
out of darkness, a bipedal creature appeared behind it, just
at the edge of the forest. Katie stared at it in numb fascination. The black figure looked like some unholy cross
between a skeleton and a mannequin. It studied her with
eyes of glass. "Easy, Katie," it said in a familiar male voice.
"It's only a remote unit. You've seen them before."

"Have I?" she whispered, creeping away, dragging the
bag with her.

The coyote howled and the world shattered, shards of
night plunging around her like stalactites loosened from
the roof of the world cave. She screamed in terror as massive sections whistled past. The ground crumbled and fell
away around her feet. She found herself huddled on a pil-
lar suspended over nothingness while a gale roared in a

concert of human voices. And through the storm the tall
creature came, walking on thought. It stooped down beside her and picked her up in its long, bony arms, cradling
her like a baby. Its surface felt soft and warm. It rocked
her and hummed and whispered soothing syllables, its visual lenses glowing a soft blue.

For a long time it walked over emptiness. Later, oceans,
forests, starfields, gray wastelands of sand all passed under
its feet. It walked with terrifying speed. It hardly slowed
when it came to cliffs, cutting right or left down a dizzying
diagonal path. Once it waded across a river that flowed
blood-red through a desert as ruddy as the sands of Mars.
Night and day and night. She wondered if they were
marching to hell. She would have thought it much closer
than this. Now and then a second such creature would approach from over the horizon, sting her with a sharp fin-
gernail, siphon off a tiny amount of blood and vanish
again. Twilight. It set her down in soft vegetation at the
sun-warmed side of a stone hut. She slept.

L.A. FLOW—NEWS AND
INFORMATION
"Space Elevator to Be Developed"

Voice Development announced today a new initiative aimed at constructing the first Earth-to-orbit elevator, to be based out of southern India. "This initiative should put to rest rumors about instabilities in Voice government," President Carson said. "We couldn't begin to take on a project of this magnitude if the board of directors weren't firmly united. The Voice of Humanity is an advancing nation, moving ever forward on a trajectory of peace."

16

New Trajectories

"Katie?"

Katie opened her eyes. She lay on a moist bed of forest litter, blinking up at a noon sun that blazed through a leafy green canopy like God's own glaring eye. The air here was so thick with heat and humidity, it was almost unbreathable. She choked on a mouthful, drinking in odors of humus and floral perfumes and her own rancid sweat. Her body ached. Her muscles felt shot through with a debilitating weakness. And she was hungry. Hungrier than she'd ever been.

With a real effort, she scrunched up her elbow, rolled onto her belly, and slowly raised her head.

She found herself in front of a squat stone shelter, overgrown with lianas. A dark and uninviting crawl hole served as the entrance. A black cable snaked out of the hole and across the forest floor. Her gaze shifted to follow it, but her attention was distracted by the sight of her muddy hands spotlighted by a shaft of sunlight. Insects buzzed in the air. She shook her head to chase them from her face and in doing so caught sight of the black, skeletal creature.

It was crouched a few feet away, watching her intently with its glass lenses. The cable was connected to its chest.

"Katie?" it questioned her again. "Are you feeling any better?"

She sat up slowly, pushing her hair out of her face. She felt like shit. But apparently the fever was gone. She groaned and leaned back against the stone shelter, gazing past the skeleton to the tropical forest beyond. "Panama," she said, recognizing the scene at last.

The scene seemed almost surreal in its normalcy. There were no false colors, no magical creatures, no mythic geography—just the weight of her own history. She rubbed her eyes and looked again, but nothing had changed. Only the presence of the skeleton an arm's reach away let her know that the hallucinations weren't quite over.

"Katie?" the skeleton persisted.

She turned to look at it. Its black surface seemed ill-defined against the mottled shadows of the forest. She remembered its tender touch and wondered that it had been so careful of her. But she was an old woman, and Judge Dark wouldn't want her to die before he'd returned her to the killing grounds in the Darien. Had this creature really carried her all the way through Mexico and Central America? Or had she simply awakened within a dream? "So . . . do you accompany me to hell, or does another spook get that duty?"

The skeleton sighed. It dropped its head a little, looking dejected. "Wake up, Katie. This is the Primal Nation, not Hollywood."

Her eyes went wide. She sat up a little straighter. She knew this voice like she knew her own body. "Ferris?"

"Dammit, Katie, stop acting like a savage at a technology fair. I've sent you reports on our field remote units. They've been operating through the Nation for over a year."

She blinked, and looked the skeleton over again. So this was a field remote, a telepresence surrogate directed by Ferris way back in L.A. She'd received the reports . . . but she hadn't read them. "You know me," she joked, feeling a little shaky; more than a little foolish. "Acquisitions are my specialty. Once we've got the company it's Gregory's concern." She shrugged. "I thought you were a hallucination," she admitted sheepishly.

Ferris snorted in disgust; the remote's head wagged in frustration. "If you were a real citizen of the Primal Nation you'd know what was going on." His accusation issued from a voice synthesizer in the remote's chest. "But you've ignored us ever since the Knights burned you out."

"I have not!" She felt her cheeks flush with indignation. "Every company I acquire goes on the Nation's registry."

"You live like an outsider."

"I'm here now."

"Only because you're running from the Voice. Where else could you go?"

She blinked hard. His doubt *hurt*. She'd always supported the Nation. "Why are you acting like this? I thought we were friends. Family, even."

"Funny. Lately I've felt more like a retainer."

Her gaze fell. She studied the leaf litter on the ground, the black power cable. There must be a solar array in the treetops that powered this little station. "Somebody wants me out of the way," she said softly. "Probably Ilene. I thought you could shelter me." It hurt to admit her own helplessness.

Ferris shrugged. "It's Ilene all right. She's got a warrant for you and she knows you're in the Nation. She's after Gregory too. Conspiracy to develop proscribed molecular technologies."

Katie looked up sharply. "What technologies?"

"I don't know. I don't know if it has anything to do with what you're looking for."

She frowned. "I'll bet Gregory knows. He said the European labs were dirty. Do you know where he is?"

"He dropped into Europe and disappeared."

"Probably with his circle, then." His old antiterrorist militia. They were little more than terrorists themselves.

The remote waved its hand impatiently. "Stop thinking about acquisitions, Katie. You're in a bad situation."

She sat up a little straighter, trying to force her muzzy brain to focus. "Well, maybe in this circumstance, bad is good," she mused. "If Ilene's seriously after me, she must think I have something." She looked anxiously at Ferris. "Did you float the offer for the revival procedure?"

The remote nodded. Its posture seemed thoughtful, somber. "That caused a stir."

"Already?"

"It's been two weeks."

Katie's lips parted in astonishment. "Two . . . ?"

"You didn't think I carried you to the Darien overnight?" A note of pride entered his voice. "Did you know you can walk from California to Panama without ever leaving the Nation?"

"I didn't know that," she said, thinking back to the terrible journey. So it had been real—more or less.

Ferris said, "We brought Nikki in on another remote as soon as we guessed what was going on. She drew blood samples and hiked them out for analysis. She was able to develop a counteragent. The remote injected you with it last night."

"Am I contagious?"

"No. You're harmless." And then he chuckled: a dark sound that made her hackles rise. "Well, perhaps not entirely. The Voice will come down hard on us, Katie, if we don't account for you soon. The Primal Nation could disappear inside their maw."

Katie felt her eyes widen. Sudden heat rushed into her cheeks. It had never occurred to her that she might be endangering the Primal Nation when she fled Oceanside. She didn't want that responsibility.

Her gaze cut away, to fix on a swarm of tiny insects hovering in a shaft of sunlight, brilliant sparks of gold without destination. She frowned. Ferris knew where *he* was going. He wouldn't risk the Nation's security without good reason. Not for her. Not for anyone. Her eyes narrowed suspiciously. Ferris was well-acquainted with her history. "Why did you bring me to the Darien?" she snapped.

"Take it easy, Katie. We're just passing through. The Voice isn't as strong in the south. It'll be easier for you to hide. And besides . . . I thought the time might be coming when you'd want to be close to Tom."

Her breath caught in her throat. For a moment she couldn't get any words out. Then: "You've found the company that developed the revival schedule. Haven't you? Ferris?"

"Maybe." The remote stood up slowly on silent joints. "Someone's been waiting for you in the VR. He won't talk to me or Nikki. He insists you be his contact, and you alone."

"Is it legit?"

"Nikki thinks it could be."

"All right," Katie said. "How do I interface?"

She met a featureless being in the VR, like a human blank made of glass, before the marks of individuation had been carved. When it looked at her with an eyeless visage, she felt a superstitious flutter of fear. "I work for you," it said. "You employ me in one of your companies and you already own the rights to the rejuvenation schedule my colleagues and I have developed. You and your partner, that is. Gregory Hunt. He wants what we have. He raided one of our older labs, but we'd already abandoned it. He didn't get anything."

"I'm sorry," she said. "Gregory and I have had a falling-out."

"I know. But he hasn't cut your legal ties and you can still deal in his name."

Katie stiffened, made wary by a sudden, pervasive sense of greed. The wired coverall she wore picked up her response. "What do you want?"

"Your hundred-million-dollar offer. Plus financing for a legal team to keep the Voice off our backs. Plus seventy-five percent of the gross income generated by the sale of this schedule."

"Or?"

"Or we go outside Voice territories to look for the highest bidder and you get nothing. Hunt gets nothing."

She breathed softly, slowly, letting her awareness run out into the minefield around her. "What exactly have you got?"

"A rejuvenation schedule, supervised by nanorobots. The series varies depending on the patient's needs, but generally involves less than one hundred varied applications, some of which are already on the market—like the cancer hunters and plaque scrapers—some of which are unique to our lab. The real challenge of course was writing and coordinating the molecular software for each application."

"And the schedule is applicable to suspension patients?"

He chuckled. "Of course it is. We were designing with your fortune in mind."

She chewed gently on the inside of her lip to suppress a smile of triumph. She'd entered the market looking for a treatment that would allow the revival of suspension patients. But this was more. Much more. "What you're saying is, you've developed a geriatric cure. You can reverse the aging process."

The blank shook its head. "The judicial AI has declared that illegal. What we can do is rejuvenate many physiological pathways, and in the process erase much of the environmental damage that leads to the effects of aging."

Close enough. Her heart thundered in her ears. The fabled Cure. This was a seismic quake powerful enough to reorder the world—whether or not the judicial AI issued its approval. "I'll need documentation."

"You get nothing until after the agreement is signed. After all, if I'm lying, then you're giving nothing away."

She found such confidence exhilarating. "Have you conducted any clinical trials?"

"Every member of our coterie has undergone the schedule," he said. "Believe me, it works."

"The Voice believes you." The blank stiffened. Katie leaned a little harder. "There's a warrant out for my arrest. It's because of your work, isn't it? I'm legally responsible for violations that occur in my labs, and it sounds as if you've committed some major transgressions."

"Our work is not illegal. None of the procedures violates Voice standards."

"But the schedule taken as a whole seems to do so."

"Screw the Voice!" The blank knifed a hand through the air. "We'll own the Voice when this goes to market."

"*If* it goes. Don't overestimate your profit potential. It'll cost a fortune to win legal status for this technology. If and when that happens, you'll have only a few months before

somebody else is ready with a similar schedule. You have
to make your score before then."

"What are you saying?"

"One hundred million dollars, plus twenty percent of
the gross income to your group. Full legal representation
through Kishida-Hunt. And you can market the product
now, from within the sovereignty of the Primal Nation."

"Stand by." The blank placed itself on hold. It went
perfectly still for nearly three minutes while Katie amused
herself with a picture of a frantic debate in a lab somewhere, probably Europe, in which a group of techies tried
to come to terms with their greed. It must have been one
hell of a fight. When the blank finally stirred, it almost
seemed to droop. "All right," it said. "Twenty percent."

A document appeared before her, secured on a clip-
board. She plucked it from the air and scanned it, then
added additional terms at the bottom. "My agreement is
conditional upon receiving documentation and the full
nanoseries developed for the rejuvenation schedule," she
explained as she wrote. "You'll mail the set to this address
in Vancouver. If you attempt to market the schedule before I receive it, this contract will become invalid."

"You'll have it by nightfall."

They spent another fifteen minutes working out the
generalities of legal position and distribution, then they
cut the connection. Katie immediately called the Vancouver mail drop, leaving instructions that the package be for-
warded to Chile. Then she slipped off the VR helmet.
Leaving the suit on, she crawled from the stone shelter.

The skeleton was standing at attention to one side of
the door, apparently uninhabited, still hooked up to the
power cable. She wiped the perspiration from her face, listening to the buzz of insects and a deeper sound, farther
away. Her brow wrinkled in concern as she recognized the
soft thrum of a helicopter—*several* helicopters. "Ferris?"
she called softly, trying to wake the remote. "Ferris?"

He didn't answer.

She ducked back into the shelter, pulled on the VR helmet, and used a voice command to summon the shelter's
AI. It appeared as a young Indian boy, with dark, soulful

eyes and a rice-bowl haircut. "Has helicopter activity been authorized in this area?"

He thought for a moment, then shook his head. "No. But there's been an unauthorized encroachment on the southern border." She swore, and was about to drop out of the VR when Ferris appeared.

"The Voice is finally making its move, Katie. Big move. They're no longer voluntary. They've changed their name to the Commonwealth of Humanity and they're claiming rights over other sovereignties, on Earth or off."

"They can't do that!"

"You get big enough, you can do anything. They're coming for you, Katie, and they're not going to stop at our borders anymore, not when they're enforcing regulations on nano and biotechnology—"

"Shunt me to the remote," she said.

"You can't run. They're too big for you."

"Do it, Ferris. I'm this close. Ilene's not going to stand in my way now."

"Katie—"

"Just do it!"

She found herself standing outside the shelter, gazing absently into the rain forest. She could hear the helicopters, like approaching thunder. She put the remote on standby and came back to herself.

Grabbing a few extra power packs for the wired suit, she crawled out of the shelter and disconnected the remote from the power cable. Slipping back into the remote, she made a seat for herself by spreading the remote's hands flat behind its back. Then she went back to herself and climbed on, the power packs cradled in her lap.

It was embarrassing and fascinating. To be carried piggyback by a soft steel giant. She returned to the remote's reality. Sensed the weight on her back. The treetops swaying overhead under a helicopter's prop-wash. The figures descending like spiders, dropping on thin ropes through the trees.

Then she began to run. Slight muscle flexion in her bio-body was translated by the wired suit into bounding leaps in her new steel frame. After the first few fumbling steps, she sped through the forest with a lean strength she'd never felt before. Shots erupted behind her. A dart struck her in the leg, and bounced off. Another glanced off her shoulder. She dodged the next one, which threatened her passenger, and then the forest closed in behind her.

Fleet as a forest cat, she leaped over roots and rotting logs and sped across the soft ground. She felt no fatigue. Her lungs didn't burn. Her heart didn't race. Her spirit sang with an exhilarating sense of invincibility.

A helicopter tried to track her overhead, but it was impossible to follow her through the canopy. She came to a streambed with six-feet-high embankments separated by a span of twelve feet. She leaped across it, jarring her passenger and startling a flock of colorful birds.

The sound of the helicopters faded into the distance. She ran on. On and on, for hours, far into Columbia. When night fell, she found another shelter, plugged the remote into the power cable, then, with a voice command, she slipped back into herself.

She tried to climb down from the remote's back, but her muscles twisted in agonizing cramps. After fighting the pain for a minute, she gave up and let herself fall to the rocky ground.

She lay there for a long time while her body slowly learned how to move again. Stars turned overhead. Satellites and orbitals swept through the ether. But they were far away, and she was alone. Finally, she crawled a few steps away to pee, then she dragged herself into the shelter, switched on the radio, and listened to the news while she raided the shelves for food and drink.

She sat in the middle of the floor, her booty piled around her while she absorbed the buzz of a furious world. Half the world's sovereignties were expressing outrage over the actions taken by the Voice. The other half were joining the new Commonwealth. A constitutional convention was scheduled to begin in a few weeks, to work up a soul for the new political entity.

Then, in the midst of the babble, Katie heard her own name. It was a small item. Billionaire financier Katharine Kishida, who'd been accidentally infected with a hallucinogenic virus, had been declared mentally incompetent by the Commonwealth police, a judgment approved by the judicial AI. Her husband and business partner, Gregory Hunt, was a fugitive in Europe. Responsibility for their financial empire would be transferred to the Council of the Primal Nation. That was all. Three lines to strip her of everything she'd ever owned.

She shut off the radio and crawled out of the shelter. The batteries on the remote were close to full. She kicked it free of the cable, then climbed aboard, her butt aching as she settled onto the seat. Then she slipped her consciousness into the artificial body, glanced briefly at the stars, and headed south.

Long ago, in her youth, it had seemed to Katie that the world was one place. That all the cities, the regions, the people, as diverse as they might be, still existed on a single globe. But by the time she reached the foothills of the Peruvian Andes, she was less sure.

She tramped the empty lands, surrounded by mountains, by the great curving sky, by a sense that more than a measure of miles lay between her and the raving energy of L.A.

This was a stark and empty land, unresponsive to the slow roll of the southern summer. Few plants could bear the intense ultraviolet radiation seeping through the wounded atmosphere. Few people, too. Villages on the higher slopes were forlorn and empty. Lower, a few people remained, existing alone or in small groups, windblown fragments of a human community now past.

So much of the world had been abandoned. It was as if a great earthquake had rolled through the continents and shaken the people down to the coasts and valleys, where they could be gathered into neat welfare villages and plugged into the VR.

But Katie clung to the spine of the world.

She traveled at night, with the mountains rising around her like black teeth in the windy heights, biting at the stars. She slept in the day, while storm clouds parried with the sun. She chose to sleep in abandoned villages whenever she could. Using wind-smoothed wood from collapsed houses, she'd build a fire and listen to the radio and try to believe that the voices she heard were something more than a dream, more than a spirit-muttering that carried over from some other plane. But it was hard. The talk was all frantic discussion of the new politics, the Commonwealth, the coming constitutional convention, and the selection of delegates from every sovereignty. Never a word about the Cure. Never a word about Katie. Never a hint of pursuit, despite the eyes in the sky that swept through their arcs every night, always watching but never seeing *her*.

It was as if she'd become invisible to that other world of welfare villages and orbitals, telephones and virtual reality, the Commonwealth and the Primal Nation. Ilene had forgotten her. Gregory had forgotten her. The Cure had been a dream. Nikki and Joy were of another life. And she'd been sentenced to purgatory on this reflection of the earth, set to walk forever south.

Now and then she met people on the road, usually old-timers, their dark brown faces as weathered as the abandoned houses, their once-bright woolen clothing beaten and faded by the sun's cold light. They'd stand by the side of the road and watch her go by, not with fear in their eyes at this odd sight of a skinny old woman being carried on the back of a black skeleton, but with a kind of justification, as if their lifelong belief in the creative powers of the mountains had finally been rewarded with the sight of this phantom walking the earth with feet as solid as their own.

In the raw volcanic heights, the power of creation seemed to blanket the land more thoroughly than the tenuous atmosphere. Some nights Katie could feel it running through her bloodstream. Then she would reach toward the night sky and watch the silhouette of her hand close around a cluster of stars and know that she could hold more in her grip than she had ever dared imagine.

Wedged Time—
Alternate Landscapes

Sometime in the night it began snowing in earnest, thick, wet flakes that cascaded out of darkness. He threw his arms wide, inviting the touch of his Familiar across his body. Flakes clung to his eyelashes, stuck to his shoulders, gathered in the palm of his hand. She was everywhere. Her presence grew more palpable with every step he took down the mountain. She was bringing him home. Home. He could feel the sweet promise in his bones. He hurried toward her, unmindful of the gathering drifts. She sang to him, whispered to him, cajoled him in a wordless female voice, complex and commanding. He forgot his fatigue and followed her through the night.

But as dawn gradually penetrated the blizzard he began to tire. So she let him rest, wrapping him in a light blanket of snow. He may have slept. His mind darted in and out of dreams, like a child playing hide-and-seek. She was there with him, his playmate in this game. He could hear her heartbeat, her soft breathing. He ducked around corners, seeking her, while her sweet laughter echoed in his consciousness.

"He's asleep," an ugly voice growled, much too close.

"He's not. See how he listens to us?"

He blinked, clearing snow from his eyelashes, shaking it from his head and shoulders. The day had brought a weak gray light. He found himself cradled in a hollow of snow, sheltered by the blizzard's wavering veils. Dark figures encircled him, looming large in the snow-filtered daylight.

The snow eased a little, and he could make out the faces of the demon oni: here, vague red fur, there, vague pink. Each of them grim and somber.

A female stepped forward. It could have been the blue-furred one who'd first found him. "Where are you going?" it asked.

He stood up slowly, his gaze darting around the circle, wondering what they had in mind for him. The oni fell back a pace, as if he frightened them.

"Where are you going?" the female repeated, her tone querulous and rising.

His gaze fixed on her. "Home."

A stir ran through the circle. "Home?" "He thinks he's going home." "He doesn't know."

The female growled, and they fell silent. She looked at him with her wide-set, hideous eyes. "No. You let them live. They've taken your place there."

Slowly, understanding seeped across his mind. "Oh." His gaze swept restlessly across the snow-covered ground. "That's all right, I think. I don't remember any of it anyway. It's all gone."

The oni looked at him sharply. "You don't remember?"

He shook his head. "Only her." Then he revised that. "Even her, only by her absence."

The oni nodded, as if it understood everything he did not. "You were weak. You wanted too much."

He felt a seed of despair sprout deep in his soul. "She's changed me," he cried softly.

The oni continued to nod, its sharp teeth flashing in the bitter snow. "You had to give up something. There's always a price, you know, and you wouldn't pay it in blood."

He fought to suppress a rising panic. "She'll still be there."

The oni shrugged, its great furred shoulders rolling smoothly through the inevitable. "There or not, it won't be happening. You've given up your past, and built yourself another world. No love's going to stretch that far."

"But I *do* love her. I won't give her up!"

"You already have."

"Not her."

But the oni was growing tired of this conversation. It looked at him in derision, and said: "Not her, fool. *You.* You've given your self up. Even if she's there, she won't know you in the end."

He glared at the foul creature, knowing how she enjoyed his pain. But he knew himself too. He knew how much he'd changed. Even the hollow place inside him was closing.

He started away angrily, resuming his trek down the long slope. The circle of oni opened for him, a blue and a red jumping back from his path as if they feared to touch him. They made no move to follow, and within seconds they were lost behind the curtains of falling snow.

He tried to put them out of his mind.

He sought her touch in the snow; she would sooth him. He listened for her voice. But something had changed. The way he saw her; the way he saw himself. He strode through the drifts, sinking to his knees with every step.

Not you! he swore. *I won't lose you.*

He stopped suddenly. The snow was failing. Faint traces of smoke haunted the air. Fear ran through him like a distant howl as he strained to see downslope, past the thinning snow and swirling fog. Smoke and fire.

He'd escaped a fire once. He trembled as the memory washed over him. A blazing forest transformed by a fire god and he'd set himself against it. *Against it.*

For all things, a price.

He recognized his insolence then, but it was much too late. The scent of smoke was growing thicker on the air.

Part III
HUMAN RITES

DAY ONE OF THE COMMONWEALTH
Excerpt from President Carson's secret address to the Commonwealth's board of directors:

We are at a point of crisis. Recent discoveries have shockingly demonstrated that molecular manipulation is advancing at a pace far beyond our expectations. If we don't act immediately and decisively, the Commonwealth will lose its technological lead and dissolve into chaos. And then who will stand as guardian between the greed of science and the integrity of humanity?

So I am declaring a state of emergency. Under the powers granted to me in this circumstance, I hereby order that all leading molecular labs around the world be seized and that their technical employees be drafted into the research arm of the Commonwealth.

Let's face it: If we don't physically contain these nanonerds, we haven't got a snowball's chance in hell of controlling them.

17

The Research Arm of
the Commonwealth

Katie had reached the mausoleum in the evening, after
a hard trek up from La Cruz. Now, as she sat with her
back against Tom's steel cylinder, her body began to re-
mind her of how taxing that journey had been. Her muscles felt weak, as if they were gradually subliming to
vapor. Her throat was so dry that to swallow took a con-
centrated effort. Her belly hurt.

The wind moaned through the turbine mounted in the
air shaft overhead. A soothing sound. She considered closing her eyes, indulging in a brief nap.

But the cold of the stone floor had already wrapped
around her legs like a slowly rising flood. She could feel
its level moving up her hips toward her heart.

It would be easy to make a critical mistake here.

Her gaze fixed on the open case in her lap that held the
Cure. Frowning in concentration, she ran her fingers
across the lines of ampules, then pressed lightly on each

syringe, making sure every item was secure in its proper slot. Then she closed the satchel and rose, groaning, to her feet.

The wind howled, and she glanced uneasily down the long cavern toward the darkness of the first chamber. But she couldn't make out the blanket-wrapped bodies of the Indians beyond the fluorescent light that blazed down on the tall storage cylinders. For a moment she felt unaccountably lonely.

But she shrugged the feeling off. Turning, she shuffled deeper into the cave, out of the third chamber and into the fourth.

There were no storage cylinders here. This was the technician's room. It was stocked with computer equipment, a telephone, a few provisions, a microwave oven . . . the bare essentials of life.

Katie laid her sleeping bag out on the floor, then glanced into the fifth chamber. A few crates of freeze-dried provisions were stacked against one wall. The old mine continued for half a mile or more into the mountain, but the lights stopped at the fifth chamber.

Turning back, Katie retrieved her bag of groceries, then pulled out one of the aseptic juice boxes she'd purchased at the store. She tried to put a straw in it, but the juice had frozen during the trek up the mountain. So she popped the box in the microwave. The old model still worked like a charm.

While the ice melted slowly on a low setting, she took a flashlight and wandered deeper into the cave, finally choosing a small side chamber for the loo and relieving her bladder. The golden rivulets of urine would be ice in a few minutes. Even shit would quickly freeze over and be unoffensive.

She wandered back. Half the juice had melted, and she drank that, then stuck the box in an inside pocket to warm the rest.

A click and a whirr overhead made her jump. She looked up to see the ceiling robot humming on its track as it moved slowly in her direction, its camera eyes fixed on her face. It stopped and stared at her for nearly ten seconds, and then a phone rang.

Elsewhere, the sound might have been a soft trilling. But in the quiet sanctity of the chambers, it was a malicious screech. Katie winced, her gaze involuntarily drawn to the shelf of computer equipment. *Brii . . iing!* She sighed and started hunting about the shelf until she found the phone on the fourth ring. Picked it up. Switched it on. The ceiling robot had turned to follow her with its lenses.

She didn't know who she'd been expecting, but certainly not the voice that greeted her. "Mom?"

"Joy? What are you doing in L.A.?"

"Looking for you." Joy's voice sounded breathy, frightened. "I've been trying to call you for weeks, but you haven't had your phone on, have you? Mom? Did you get it?"

Katie's heart skipped a beat. There was no way Joy could know about the package from Vancouver. She wondered if this even was Joy. Maybe she was speaking to a voice synthesizer fronting a Voice cop. "Get what, Joy?" she asked stiffly.

"Oh, Mom, when you didn't come home, Nikki said you were either dead or drafted . . . or you'd found Daddy's cure. She told me to watch for you—"

"*Joy!*" Katie hissed in sudden fright. "Is this line encrypted?"

A moment of profound silence passed before Joy answered. "I—I don't know—"

Nobody's listening, Katie told herself. The mausoleum was secret, and Katie had been forgotten and nobody knew about her copy of the Cure. She was a fly creeping beneath the gaze of giants. But she worried anyway. Ilene was very thorough. And for all she knew, Gregory was hunting her too.

"Where's Nikki?" The words emerged sharper than she'd intended.

"Nikki's been drafted. The Commonwealth took almost everyone working in the leading bio/nano labs and shipped them out to the orbitals. I talked to her this morning. You know Nikki. She's angry enough to start a plague." She tried to laugh, but it rang hollow. "Anyway, she's all right." Joy's voice had started to tremble. "I was afraid you were—I was afraid I'd never—"

"It's all right, Joy. I'm okay." Her jaw worked as she tried to think of something appropriate to say. The effort failed. She felt like a heartless oaf, but she was cold and tired and dogged by a sense of urgency. "I need to talk to Nikki."

"Okay, Mom."

"Have her call me. Right away." *Nobody's listening.*

"As soon as I can get through."

"Thanks, Joy."

"I love you, Mom."

"I love you too, baby." She broke the connection. Then she stood quietly for a moment, feeling cold and foolish. Finally, she remembered the ceiling robot. She gazed up at it thoughtfully, then turned to the computer console, explored a few menus, and wrested control of the robot away from L.A. With a quick flick of the light pen, she sent it humming out of the fourth chamber, then stuck a wad of paper in the tracks to keep it from coming back.

The phone rang. She jumped down from the box of freeze-dried food she'd been standing on and answered it. "Nikki?"

"You still walking around with that remote?" Her voice sounded dry and tense.

"Yeah, it's here."

"Then open up. I'm coming in."

The remote spoke with Nikki's voice as it crouched beside the sleeping bag where Katie sat. "So what happened? You sure put Ilene in a testy mood."

Katie explained as best she could the sequence of events that had brought her here.

Nikki laughed harshly. "So you bought a Cure from your own company." She squatted over the satchel, delicately touching the contents with her wired fingers; examining the hypodermics suspiciously. "Those motherfuckers. I'm gonna find out who pulled this on you."

"It was just a business deal," Katie said.

"Come on! They worked for you. It was theft."

"It's not like I own them. Can't blame 'em for wanting to share in the spoils . . . if there are any spoils. I don't feel good about this, Nikki. If this schedule is for real, why hasn't there been a breath of comment on the net?"

Nikki snorted. "A Cure's still illegal. The CEO's aren't going to talk about it until the subject's raised on the floor of the constitutional convention next week—and then you'll hear plenty. Auntie Ilene doesn't want to talk about it, or her people might start thinking seriously about the possibilities."

"I'm talking about *my* Cure, Nikki, not some hypothetical future development. If it were real, there'd at least be rumors."

Nikki nodded. "The rumor is, Auntie Ilene's on her way out."

Now that was startling. Ilene had always seemed in firm control of the corporate leaders who powered Voice politics.

"It's just a rumor," Nikki continued. "But in some phases of the VR she's being eulogized—you know? Treated like she's already dead? Or at least out of it? People say the CEO's are moving against her. It's eerie. Like they're draining her political image of blood and there's nothing she can do to stop it. Now why do you think they'd treat her like that after all these years?"

Katie chewed gently on her lip, trying to picture Ilene in the orbitals as she explained to her inner circle of supporters, the CEO's of the world's largest companies, the most powerful individuals alive, how it would be wrong for them to go on living beyond their natural span of years. She could guess their response. The only question remaining was: Who would ultimately control the Cure? And who would be allowed to use it? Next week's constitutional convention would determine that.

"*Mom.*"

Katie looked up, realizing Nikki had spoken to her more than once. "Sorry."

"We've got to order some equipment."

"Sure. You make a list. I still have some funds left."

"All right. I'm going to drop out of here while I work up a plan. You better get some sleep."

Katie nodded. "Nikki? Have you heard anything about Gregory?"

Nikki was silent for a long moment. Then, "Just rumors," she said stiffly. "I don't think Auntie has him, if that's what you want to know. I don't think she cares about him anymore. She cleaned out your labs with the draft. There's nothing left. He's nobody."

Nikki departed, leaving the remote sitting in the middle of the floor. *Still not picking up after herself,* Katie thought. But she was too tired to move the thing, so she left it where it was. She rummaged through her supplies, found a pack of crackers, ate half, then snuggled into her sleeping bag and closed her eyes. "Hark: lights off," she muttered . . .

. . . and much later awoke to darkness. The only light came from the microwave clock and a few indicator lights on the computer. It was enough to show her that the remote was gone. She grabbed a flashlight, dropped her pistol into her pocket, and padded out quickly to the front of the cave, but there was no sign of it. The doors were locked. She felt her breath coming too fast. It was the altitude, she told herself. Who could think at this elevation?

She glanced nervously over the bodies of the Indians in the first chamber, then chided herself angrily. "Did you think one of them would be missing?" she muttered. She made her way back to the fourth chamber, determinedly ignoring the shadowy fear that crept about the periphery of her vision. She lay down in her sleeping bag, and after a long time, managed to sleep.

The next time she woke she felt more rested. But the remote was still missing, and though she told herself over and over again that Nikki must have taken it, the thought didn't bring her much comfort, and she began to develop the unpleasant idea that her sense of reality was dissolving again, the same way it had when she'd fled California, and maybe she'd never left California, and maybe there'd never been a remote, and maybe she wasn't here in this cave at all and maybe and maybe.

It took some discipline to put her mind to the business at hand, but finally she managed a meager breakfast and some coffee, then she settled down to read through the documentation that had accompanied the alleged Cure.

After a few hours of this, she found herself beset with a niggling sense of helplessness. All these years, she'd never thought much about the details of the Cure. She'd glanced over scientific abstracts, sent them off to Nikki for evaluation, looked over labs, and laid her money down. But she'd always kept herself remote from the process. Now it became clear that somewhere in the back of her mind she'd developed the idea that the Cure would be a magic pill, or a shot of godhead in a syringe, a one-step spell to resurrection and immortality.

There were more than two hundred different remedies in the kit she'd purchased. Sure, not every patient would need all of them, but a determination had to be made about which were appropriate, which were necessary. Which must be delivered first. Some of the procedures were well-known, had been on the market for a year or more (were royalties owed?). Others were unique in her experience. *Lifetime-Radiation Therapy (a complete DNA cross-check and repair system)* sounded like a gold mine all by itself. But the critical development from Tom's perspective was the nanomachine programmed to preserve cell structure by establishing stabilizing cross-links within every individual cell, sort of analogous to dipping each cell in glass, to prevent activity and ensuing degradation, while the body was slowly warmed to functional temperatures.

She picked up a standard hypodermic and examined it; popped off the needle cap and watched the steel point flash in the harsh overhead light. She let her mind flow out to the orbitals, and to the corporate bigwigs maneuvering to be the first to possess a Cure that could be common currency in a few years if development wasn't suppressed.

But development *would* be suppressed. By Ilene, if her faction had its way at the constitutional convention. Or by whatever corporation or cartel was lucky enough—or ruthless enough—to bring out a version of the Cure and get it to market first. It'd be in their interest to suppress competition and they'd have the resources to do it—what with the whole world crawling at their feet for a chance to get in on the fun. What a position to be in.

The needle flashed.

Except (apparently) no one yet realized that Katie had

a functioning version of the Cure right here. Maybe. If this stuff was for real. How might that factor affect the political equation?

Her fingers clacked across the line of ampules, until she found the one coded ILH-771, some lovely, youthful muscle tone. She plucked it out and plunged the needle through the soft top. Turned the ampule upside down the way she'd seen nurses do and withdrew a tenth of a cc, tapping the syringe carefully to shake the bubbles down.

It was easier than she expected to shoot up—it was amazing how much arcane knowledge an individual could gather in sixty-four years. She stripped off her several layers of clothes from her upper body, then used a handkerchief to tie off an arm. Her veins were easy to find. No collapsing when the needle bit. She injected the fluid, withdrew the needle, then dressed quickly before her shivering became too violent. Then she packed away the syringe, crawled into the sleeping bag, called the lights down, and closed her eyes.

She awoke to soft sounds: the whirr of the turbines high up in the air shafts. The closer, more irregular whirr of the ceiling robot tending the steel cylinders in the third chamber. A distant thumping, dry pounding that seemed to reverberate up from the heart of the mountain. She sat up quickly—too quickly. Her vision blurred and danced and her stomach rolled with a wave of nausea. Her skin felt fever-hot beneath her many layers. The pounding continued, a heavy hand knocking on a distant door. She crawled out of the bag, groping for her pistol in the dark. Then, weapon in hand, she stumbled toward the cave entrance. She was through the third chamber before she remembered to call the lights on. The pounding ceased abruptly. The telephone rang. She backtracked and grabbed it. "Nikki?"

"Open the door, Mom. It's me." It occurred to Katie that the voice could be synthesized. That it could be anybody on the other side of the door. That she could open it, and they could kill her. That she could leave it closed, and they could drop an avalanche across the door, effectively destroying the competing kit they must be after, leaving her here to die of thirst or starvation or despair, her body soon to become mummified by the extreme dryness of the air, like the bodies of the Indians. She wondered if there could be any resuscitation from that state.

Then she made her way forward. Opened the first door. Passed through. Opened the second door. A howling wind ripped it from her hands and flung it against the wall with a concussion that rang throughout the cavern and knocked a dollop of snow off the cliff face.

The remote stood just outside the entrance, rocking in the wind that whistled under the covering slab, its back piled high with goods concealed under a gray tarp. A second remote stood behind it, similarly burdened. They marched in past her, the second placing its feet exactly as had the first, a willing slave on a three-second time delay. "Nikki?"

"Yes, Mom, it's me," the first remote called over its shoulder. ". . . *Mom it's me,*" the second echoed.

Katie closed and locked both doors, then stood swaying on her feet as the procession disappeared into the depths of the cavern. This was all too unreal. Her body ached and she felt sure she must be dying on a ward somewhere, drugged to the teeth and fantasizing. But was it any stranger to think that the world had changed not at all since she was born, than that it had changed this much?

Nikki had hauled an amazing assortment of equipment up from the lowlands. She quickly pointed out the major pieces to Katie:

An air mattress and new dehydrated food. A molecular analyzer that fit easily in the palm of her hand. Bags and bags of artificial blood. Water. An artificial heart. Two wool blankets printed in bright Andean patterns. Extra thermals. A man's woolen slacks and shirts and sweaters. A parka in a size too large for Katie. A blood mill as big as an oven that would clone real blood from Tom's own cells. A surgeon's remote hands. A medical kit loaded with frictionless knives and needles and pharmacological remedies. Instructions for Katie to study.

"It's real important that you be able to run the schedule yourself, Mom, in case I get canned. The judicial AI has to be watching me. Sooner or later somebody's going to check the data."

Katie frowned unhappily. "Nikki, I don't want you to get hurt."

"Don't worry about me, Mom. You're the one on the front lines." She took the bootleg kit and ran a tiny sample of every ampule through her molecular analyzer, then she disappeared for a week with the data. At least that's how long she said she'd be gone. Katie didn't keep track. Time seemed an unnecessary complication in the timeless cavern. Katie used her absence to sample *Hair Follicle Renewal* and *General Epidermal Therapy*.

Her fever failed to subside. She couldn't tell if it was a reaction to the injections, a flare-up of the hallucinogenic virus, or something else. But as a side effect, she was left incapable of worrying about it. Wrapped up securely in a fog of detachment, she drifted about the cavern. She camped out for a few hours in front of Tom's storage cylinder, until the ceiling robot entered that chamber, and then she left. She wandered deep into the mountain, almost half a mile with only the thin beam of her flashlight to guide her. Until she came to a vertical shaft that dropped off at her feet.

She shone the light down, but there was no bottom. She thought of orcs and balrogs and hellfire and backed off like a junkie on a bad trip. She turned around and started to run back up the passage, but the altitude got her within seconds and when she woke, her lips were covered with half-frozen dust and her flashlight had faded to dim orange. She walked slowly back up the cavern and by chance or the grace of a God she would really like to believe in, she eventually found her way to the computer room and forced herself to eat every bite of a balanced meal she reconstituted from the supplies Nikki had hauled up.

She dumped the trash in a bag, then ran a hand through her rumpled hair. It felt dry and brittle and repulsively dirty, so she pulled a razor out of her kit and shaved her head. Some long time later she was delighted to feel a soft fuzz emerging. She plucked out one strand. It was as golden as her youth. She decided to celebrate by injecting *Bone Mass Renewal*.

"You're spending an awful lot of time asleep," Nikki said.

Katie blinked against the bright overhead lights. The remote stood over her, hands on bony hips. She yawned, huddling deeper in the cozy sleeping bag.

"You're really starting to worry me, Mom."

"It's the altitude," Katie muttered. "Really draws your strength down. How are things in the orbitals?"

"Tense. You know the CC finally got underway today. The delegates skipped all the scheduled speeches about political unity to go straight for Auntie Ilene's throat. She's going to have to cede some of her principles, if she doesn't want the Voice to crack."

"Principles?"

"Like what it means to be human."

"Like how long we should live?"

"That's part of it. You've been playing with the kit, haven't you?"

"You figure we have unlimited time?"

Grudgingly: "No."

"Neither do I." They were silent. Katie sensed the tension of an argument in the air, though she wasn't clear if one had taken place. "It's not junk, is it?"

"No. The stuff looks good. I'm going to set you up with a procedure for Dad. You'll be able to do most of it yourself." She tapped her thigh with her finger, producing a dull clapping sound. "I'm thinking about dropping the data in the VR. If everybody has it, the constitutional debate will end."

"Don't do it," Katie said. "The judicial AI will screen it, determine it's stolen, and wipe it. You'll be prosecuted. And you'll have gotten nowhere."

The remote whirled on the ball of its foot and started pacing back and forth. "I'm starting to have some ethical problems with all of this," Nikki announced. "I need to get something straight in my head. Are we here just for Daddy ... or for everybody locked up in these freezer jugs?" The remote's hand swept the air, indicating the outer chambers. "You know Grandma's out there too, and a few dozen others who would dearly love a chance at life."

Katie pushed herself up on her elbows. "I know what you're feeling. It wasn't supposed to be like this. Thirty years ago—*thirty years?*—*shit*, we were naive jerks. But we had it all planned. Everybody was supposed to wake up in an utterly civilized clinic in an utterly civilized world, surrounded by their loved ones, filled with the confident glow of youth. Tech-heaven on Earth. Why do we always dream of the future as being rosy and civilized when we know damn well it's never turned out that way in all the long history of humankind?"

The remote performed a damn good imitation of hawking and spitting. "Watched too much *Star Trek*."

Katie nodded. She sat up slowly in her sleeping bag, then looked around, her gaze inviting Nikki to take in their surroundings. "This is not an utterly civilized clinic. For now, we worry about your father. There'll be time for the others when the stew on the orbitals cools down."

"Maybe."

"Hell, it's not like we're without assets, without cards to play. After all, I legally own the Cure."

A cynical laugh erupted from the remote. "*Owned.* Remember, the Voice cops have you tagged as a nut and a criminal. The Primal Nation owns the Cure now—and then only if the Commonwealth doesn't confiscate it for the 'social good.' The only asset we have is this bootleg copy you've got, and the data I've taken upstairs."

"Shit," Katie said. Until now, *that* twist had eluded her.

"You think the Nation'll betray you?" Nikki asked tentatively.

Who could say? "They've got their own agenda."

"Then let's just get Daddy out of here. There's no way anybody's going to put him back on ice once we retrieve him. And bringing even one of them back from the other side will play like a dream on the VR. Things'll work out."

Katie chuckled softly. "Right, Captain Picard."

VOICE NEWS; ISSUE 678; 22:00
"President Carson Attends Banquet"

President Ilene Carson joined the Girl Scouts of Voice-2 today in an event described as the First Annual Orbiter's Banquet. It's widely believed the appearance was arranged as a show of confidence in the face of rumors of the president's declining corporate support. President Carson delivered a speech to the Girl Scouts lauding the judicial AI and describing it as the foundation of individual liberty and justice in the Commonwealth. "Unlike human legal authorities, the judicial AI cannot be corrupted or cowed," the president said. "It will always enforce the law equally, preserving alike the rights of powerless children and corporate presidents."

18

The Right to Try

Nikki had gone back to the orbitals, but she'd programmed an agenda into the array of equipment the two remotes had hauled up from the lowlands. The first step was to get Tom out of storage.

Katie entered instructions on the mausoleum's computer system, then watched as the ceiling robot siphoned off the liquid nitrogen and rocked down the steel cylinder. Then Katie used a remote to haul Tom out. He was as stiff as a board, still wrapped in the double plastic bags the Forward Futures staff had put on him thirty years ago.

She started shaking, and the motion translated to the remote. If she dropped him, would he shatter like glass? She laid him down carefully on the floor, trying to banish the absurd image from her mind.

The plastic bags crackled as they warmed. She used ceramic scissors to cut them away, still working through the remote because the cold was too much for her own hands.

Thirty years.

In thirty years a lot of record-keeping errors could take place. What if someone had screwed up the numbering system on the storage cylinders? What if this wasn't even Tom? Why was she such an ardent pessimist?

She pulled the plastic away from his face, then caught a shuddering breath. *Was it him?* She looked down on a yellowish, waxy face, one eye slightly open, dark hair matted and hideous like the corpse of some madman. Tears started in her eyes, and she cursed herself. "So what were you expecting?" she cried out loud. *The handsome prince, as beautiful in death as in life, waiting to be awakened with a kiss from his true love. . . .*

She withdrew from the remote and sobbed for a good five minutes. Then she used the remote first to strip the carcass, then to pick it up and carry it through the computer room to the fifth chamber, where Nikki had set up her equipment. She laid Tom out on an air mattress insulated with a thick layer of foam padding. Then she sent the remote out of the room, parking it with its mate in the first chamber.

From the bootleg kit she retrieved the slender plastic case that held the hair-fine ceramic needle. She slipped it from its protective wrapper, then fixed its six-inch length to a syringe.

Returning to the kit, she pulled out *Cross-link Stabilizer (for use on seriously injured clients only)*. She tried to insert the needle through the soft top but her hands were trembling so violently she missed and almost pricked herself. A very fine rime of frost had formed on the body. She closed her eyes and breathed deeply for a minute, calming herself. Then she held her breath and tried again, approaching from an angle.

The tip of the long needle contacted the soft top, then slipped through like light through clear water. She breathed a sigh of relief and backed off on the syringe, filling the sample chamber. The ampule was half-empty. She replaced it in the kit, then knelt by the body.

Start at his head, Nikki had said.

Katie swallowed her doubt along with the sour mass in her throat and aimed the needle at the body's forehead. She gasped as it pricked skin, slid effortlessly through bone and into the frozen brain, stopping only when the blunt plastic end of the needle housing met flesh. She moaned softly, then backed off a little. Nikki had warned her. The needle was a superhard, superfine ceramic, with no distinguishable roughness until molecular scale. She injected the premeasured dose and withdrew the needle until the tip was near the skin. Then she injected another dose. She repeated the procedure over and over again, each time moving the point of penetration a few centimeters farther away, until, hours later, she'd reached his feet, and the ampule was empty. Then she laid the needle back in its case.

As the body warmed, the nanomachines she'd injected would draw on natural sources of energy in the flesh to construct cross-links in the cellular tissue, preserving structure in spheres that would expand rapidly outward from each needle prick. She took a blanket and covered him, knowing it was unnecessary but wanting to do something. Then she crawled into her sleeping bag and blacked out.

Later:
She'd left the lights on. She awoke with a pounding headache, blinking against the overhead glare. She crawled out of the bag and dosed herself with coffee and a shot of the impressive-sounding *Lifetime-Radiation Therapy (a complete DNA cross-check and repair system)*. Then she knelt by the side of the body and stared at the face. It looked like the same ugly corpse dipped in glass. She brought her hand close to its forehead and touched it tentatively. It was cold all right, but like ice, not like . . . hell? hard vacuum? She stroked his skin. It felt hard and glassy and wholly inhuman.

She turned at the sound of footsteps approaching from the outer chamber. As she looked, both remotes walked into the light. "Mom," the first said with Nikki's voice. "This is a friend of mine, Dr. Phillipe Condrey. He's a surgeon."

The remote nodded. "Ma'am." Its hands had changed. Gone were the human analogs. In their place were tiny, bladed tools that might have been conjured from a sadist's wet dream.

Katie felt a shiver of cold terror run down her spine.

"Pleased to meet you," she muttered, then stepped back out of the way.

Nikki left Dr. Condrey to work on the body. She approached Katie. "Mom, you look like wired shit. Have you been eating?"

Katie shrugged. Nikki went through the trash bag, examining the wrappers there. "Coffee and crackers isn't going to do it," she admonished.

"I can't seem to focus on things like that," Katie muttered. She was staring at the surgeon, watching as he used his ghastly hands to cut the sutures that held the chest cavity closed. Nikki bustled about the kitchenette, played a quick tune on the microwave, then answered Dr. Condrey's hail by producing a fist-sized plastic device from one of the equipment chests. The artificial heart. They installed it on the surface of the chest. By the time the microwave had finished its run, the mechanical heart was pumping slush out of the body and into a plastic bag on the floor.

Nikki returned to the microwave, pulled out a steaming bowl of stew and rice, and stood over Katie until she'd finished it. As Nikki force-fed her the last bite, Dr. Condrey spoke up. "We've drained about half the cryoprotectant. Nikki, want to get me some artificial blood?"

By the time they left, they'd restored much of Tom's circulatory system. The artificial heart pumped a low-temperature blood substitute through the undamaged capillary networks, supplying a transport system and energy source for the additional nanomachines that could now be introduced. As the blood left the body it was passed through a series of molecular filters that strained out pollutants and added oxygen and nutrients.

"The schedule isn't intelligent," Nikki said. "It's really composed of a series of physiological boosters that leave ultimate healing to the body's natural processes."

"If those processes are active," Dr. Condrey added. "And that's the state we have to engender." He raised a syringe into the light. "*Capillary Rebuilders* and a series of *Organ Organizers* should go a long way toward reestablishing function."

"How long will it take?" Katie asked.

Condrey shrugged. "A case like this has never been attempted before, but I would guess seven to ten days."

"You're sure this will work?" Katie asked, a sudden knot in her belly. If the damn nanomachines were defective, they could rebuild Tom's brain into a liver and spleen.

"I'm sure it'll work," Condrey said as he injected the contents of the syringe into the tube leading to the artificial heart. "We've run extensive simulations upstairs. And we've conducted physical tests of each one of the procedures ... uh, I mean, that's how it's described in the documentation."

Katie closed her eyes and leaned back against the wall. "It's not like we get a second chance ... if things really go bad." She was perspiring, the perspiration turning to frost and quickly subliming into the superdry air.

When she opened her eyes, Nikki's remote was crouched in front of her. "It's going to work, Mom. I wouldn't do this if I had any real doubts."

"This isn't the first time it's been done, you know," Condrey said softly. Katie looked up at him, startled. Nikki's remote swung around to stare as well. Condrey went on, "From the beginning, we planned to apply our work to cryonic suspension patients. We knew that was where your money would be, but we also had ... personal reasons."

"Condrey! You bastard," Nikki hissed. "You were one of the bloodsuckers who tried to gut my mom?"

"Shut up, Nikki!" Katie snapped. She was on her feet now. "Condrey, is this *your* schedule?"

"Yes. It's my life's work and I'm not about to let any Voice goons steal it away from me. That's why I sought Nikki out."

"How old are you?"

"Fifty-seven."

She looked at the other remote. "Nikki, have you seen him in person?"

"No."

"The team is being held in isolation," Condrey said quickly. "But I can assure you, I appear to be a man in my vital twenties."

"Why have they let you wander the VR?" Katie demanded.

He spread his hands helplessly. "I have no data. What harm am I? Rumors of the Cure have been floating around for years. Nobody pays them any attention if there's no hard data."

"What deal did we make?" she asked, to test him.

"One hundred million dollars, plus twenty percent of the gross income; Kishida-Hunt responsible for legal representation and marketing. An agreement concluded shortly before the Voice cops confiscated our labs and our data and drafted our entire staff."

"At least you had a chance to juice yourself," Nikki muttered.

"When we were testing the schedules we also had the opportunity to restore a suspension patient."

Katie felt her breath catch. She tried to speak, but words didn't come. Her gaze fixed on the remote's blank lenses.

Condrey nodded. He turned half away. "The subject was an old woman, almost a hundred when she died. She'd been in suspension only five years. We felt confident we could help her. We'd already run the schedule on pigs and dogs and endless simulations. And she'd . . . donated her body to us before she'd died. She wanted to be the first, you see. . . ."

"Your grandmother?" Katie asked softly.

"No, no. Nothing like that. A professor of mine, actually." He chuckled to himself. "Sort of a tribal elder, if you take my meaning. Anyway, we brought her out of the ice. Restored her physiological system. It all went just like a successful simulation. We brought her up to functioning temperatures. Her body was healthy, self-sustaining, perfect. So you see, it really does work."

"Where is she now?" Katie asked.

Condrey turned farther away. "There was nothing wrong with her brain," he said. "We ran all the tests. The system was perfect."

"Condrey . . ." Nikki warned.

The remote looked back over its shoulder. "Some people say the mind is a phenomenon automatically generated by a healthy brain, the same way an active computer program is generated by software. That's what I believe. I still believe that."

Katie stared grimly at the remote. She said: "And some people believe the mind is an expression of a pervasive force in the universe that we have not yet tabulated and defined. You're trying to tell me that your patient didn't wake up."

Condrey made a soft gurgling noise. The surgical blades on his hands chattered nervously. "It was as if nobody was home. For all I know, her body's still there in the lab, breathing, functioning—"

"Empty," Katie finished for him.

"I don't understand it," he added helplessly. "And I have to understand it, before it's too late. . . ."

"Go away," Katie said. "Both of you. And run your goddamn simulations until you've found out exactly what went wrong."

When she was alone, she shot up on *Disk-Fix* and *Pseudo-Estrogen Source*, then she wrapped herself in a blanket and sat by Tom's side, striving to send her consciousness out, out, into some mythical realm whose existence she could not accept; determined anyway to try to get there, find him, and demand that he come back.

L.A. FLOW—NEWS AND
INFORMATION
"Southern Hemisphere Condemns Carson"

A spokesman for the Southern Hemisphere League of Traditional Nations spoke out against Commonwealth policy today. "We know what is happening," said Ibn al Benar. "We know why President Carson has sanctioned the brutal kidnapping of molecular scientists around the world. President Carson wants absolute control of all antiaging therapies so that she and her cronies might be in a position to bargain for the natural resources of the Southern Hemisphere. We condemn this imperialist attempt to control our heritage. We condemn the ongoing constitutional convention, which seeks to subvert our sovereignty. And we further condemn all science aimed at disrupting the natural life span of man, as determined by God."

19

Unnatural Life Spans

For four days it looked as if nothing was happening. Then the *Epidermal Repair Units* kicked in and the terrible wounds on Tom's abdomen began closing. The ruptured skin knit itself back together. The bruises faded. Even the incision on his chest cavity began to close, and when Katie noticed that, she dove for the mausoleum's telephone and punched up Condrey's number. "Hey!"

"It's all right," he reassured her. "The nanomachines have been programmed to work around the tubes. There's no danger."

Katie ate and slept and ate and slept and played with the ampules. She prayed over Tom. Or meditated. Or whatever. She felt as phony as a carnival fortune-teller, but she did it anyway. The seventh day came and went, but neither Nikki nor Condrey showed up. She thought about calling them. After all, she'd already called Condrey once. But she rejected the idea. If Nikki *could* call, she would. If not . . .

Katie could phone her and wind up talking to the judicial AI.

She injected *Joint Smooth* and she waited. She listened to the news about the political maneuvering at the convention and she worried about Nikki until her belly tied itself in knots. She paced the cavern, afflicted with a half-formed notion that Voice cops were even now marching up the mountainside to seize the Cure and put an end to Tom's reanimation.

After a few hours her hip joint began to ache, and later her elbow and then both shoulders. She thought about the *Joint Smooth* and a touch of fear ran through her. She tried to keep still on the chance that would help. But her muscles sang with an unaccustomed nervous energy and before long she was on her feet again, hobbling over aching knees and ankles, listening for the arrival of Voice cops at the door. After awhile, she went to the door and looked out.

It was deep in the night and the wind was howling. She could feel her cheeks cracking under the wind's freezing touch. There were no Voice cops. But the sky was clear and moonless, and the stars were out in incredible quantity. She gazed for a long time on that spangled glory. She couldn't help wondering if there really was a God hidden out there after all. And if so, was it a God she could live with? After awhile she hobbled back inside, closing the doors firmly behind her.

Sitting beside Tom:

She worried about how to disconnect the artificial heart and restore his own internal circulation. Condrey was the surgeon. Why didn't Condrey come? But wishing and wondering didn't amount to much. So she continued the procedure on her own.

It was time to start removing the cellular cross-links; time to let Tom's body resume its normal function. She adjusted the blood filter, setting it to raise the temperature of the fluid gradually to near ninety degrees. The process took about two hours. During that time she introduced *Pest Control* to wipe out any nascent infections. Then she wheeled the blood mill into place, and began replacing the artificial fluid with Tom's own cloned blood. She watched for a while as the machines went about their chores. Then, restless, she went outside again. The pain in her joints had lessened, though she still felt feverish.

It was dawn. A thin fog blew across the empty slopes. When she returned to the relative warmth of the interior, she bundled Tom up in her sleeping bag, then injected *Clean-up Squad (cross-link removal units with general anesthesia)* into his system. Her heart thundered in her ears. Her bowels churned. She crouched in a corner of the room, her head between her knees as she tried to keep herself from shaking apart. After a very long time, she rose on throbbing joints to check him.

Tom had wet himself.

She stared in consternation at the huge, dark stain that spread across the lower middle of the sleeping bag. She touched it to be sure. The bag felt cold and icy. She pulled it aside and a puff of warm air rose from beneath it, bringing her the distinctive odor of urine. She slapped the bag back down and fought against panic. She hadn't expected this. How was she supposed to keep him dry? The schedule had said nothing about this. She had only two blankets. Even if she had a catheter, she wouldn't know what to do with it. How could she keep him warm if he stayed wet?

Then she noticed his face. She froze, staring at it in amazement. It was Tom. It was *Tom*. The horrible, waxy features of the corpse had relaxed. The skin had taken on a more natural hue. This was Tom, his cheeks a warm bronze blush, soft skin slightly stretched over his facial bones, the perfect circles of his irises visible beneath the closed lids of his eyes. She touched his cheek. It was warm, and yielded to her fingers like real human skin. She touched his lips. They felt terribly dry. And though she felt warmth rising from his mouth, it was convective heat and not the soft wash of an exhaled breath. She reached under the blankets and laid her hand on his chest, but his lungs didn't breath, his heart didn't beat. She withdrew, shuddering. Remembered an earlier thought and laughed—a sharp laugh edged in lunacy. "Now you are my handsome prince," she muttered to the cold. "Set to sleep the sleep of death, until love comes to wake you. . . ."

She pulled back the blankets and gazed on the artificial heart.

When a baby is born, she remembered, there is a sudden, profound change in its circulatory system. Blood is no longer circulated outside its body and through the auxiliary organ called the placenta. The umbilicus breaks. The baby's body establishes a new circulatory pattern.

She went to the kit and withdrew yet another ampule: *Closing Instructions*. She injected a dose into the tubing, then crouched anxiously over the body. The artificial heart beat for half an hour more, then went still. She tugged gently on the tubing where it disappeared into the chest cavity. It was loose. She withdrew it from the body and it emerged bloodless. The opening in the chest was tiny. She could see red tissue, but no obvious bleeding. She covered him with a blanket, then pressed a hand to his throat.

Her trembling fingers were icy with her own sweat. She thought she could feel a pulse from him, but she wasn't sure. She leaned over his mouth, listening for a breath, but there was nothing. She slipped her hand under the blanket; pressed on his chest. Yes. A pulse, definitely. But no breathing.

She yanked her hand back out, tilted his chin back the way she'd learned in a first-aid class long, long ago, pinched his nose shut, placed her mouth over his, and blew gently, watching his chest from the corner of her eye. Nothing. She tossed back the blankets, exposing him to the cold. Readjusted her position and tried again, blowing harder this time.

His broad, hairless chest rose slightly. Fell. A wash of foul air emerged from his mouth. She placed her mouth on his again and blew even harder. This time his chest inflated like a balloon. More foul air emerged. She blew again, and suddenly he was breathing on his own, his chest rising and falling in shallow, irregular breaths, halting, starting, gradually growing more rhythmic.

She gasped, remembering at last to breathe herself. She fell forward, her head pressed against his shoulder while her tears washed across his living skin. Her body felt so hot she feared she would ignite right then, a burning sacrifice to the gods in payment for a miracle rendered through her hands.

*   *   *

She woke up, shivering on the floor, her muscles painfully cramped and her head pounding. Her gaze went
straight to Tom. His chest was bare. His skin was mottled
purple from the cold, but he was breathing. It hadn't been
a dream. She sat there a moment, transfixed by the simple
rhythmic rise and fall of his breast. Then she drew a deep
breath herself and said a prayer of thanks on the chance
that someone was listening. Before she covered him she
checked his chest wound. It was nearly closed. She went
to the kitchenette and drank some juice and ate some
crackers, then used a little of the scarce water to wash her
face. She made a cup of coffee and sat down with it beside
Tom to watch him breathe.

She waited many hours, giving his chest wound more
time to heal. During that time, she talked to him, because
she'd heard somewhere that talking sometimes encour-
aged comatose patients to respond. There was a lot to say.
She explained to him the circumstances of his death. She
told him about her life without him. Talked about his children and grandchildren. Talked politics. Talked poetry.
Talked herself hoarse. She ate and slept and didn't shoot
up at all. She washed her face again. Tom was growing a
stubble of black beard on his chin.

When she checked, she found his chest wound still livid
pink, but at least it was fully closed. She couldn't wait any
longer. She didn't trust herself to set an IV, and without
one he would dehydrate rapidly. So she went to the kit
and pulled *Anesthetic Washout*. She tied off his arm, found a
vein, and injected it. The nanomachines she'd just introduced would find the nanomachines in his brain that held
him in a state of anesthesia, and remove them.

She closed her eyes and prayed. It was getting to be a
disturbing habit. After awhile she got up and paced the
length of the chamber. Her gaze kept shooting between
Tom and the clock on the microwave. How long should it
take? Not long, she thought. She dropped to her knees at
his side and began talking to him. An hour passed. She
shook him gently, stroked his skin, pinched him, cursed
him. "You bastard! Wake up!" The image of Condrey's
professor haunted her. She searched Tom's face for some

sign, some twitch that she could pin her hopes upon, some
assurance that he had not just disappeared like the old
lady. . . . *"Thomas!"*

His eyelids trembled. His lips parted and some
unintelligible sound rumbled up from his throat. He began
to moan. Fists formed beneath the blankets, their outlines
visible as his arms tensed. And then he threw his head back
and screamed, a horrible, murderous scream of ultimate rage.

Katie recoiled. She found herself crouched on hands and
knees, like an animal at bay, her joints stinging in fiery pain
while Tom went on screaming and screaming, unintelligible
howls of pure fury that echoed around the chamber.

"Stop it!" Katie yelled back at him. "Stop it, stop it,
stop it, stop it!"

The sound cut off abruptly. His eyes popped open. He
twisted in his soiled bedding to stare at her with coldly
malevolent eyes.

WEDGED TIME—ALTERNATE LANDSCAPES

Fog surrounded him all day as he continued his long march
down the mountain, and with every step forward, the scent of
smoke grew heavier on the air. At dusk, the fog began to recede,
gathering in a vast cloud bank over the snowfield below. As
darkness fell the stars came out. They moved, shaping and
unshaping strange constellations, as if in this one night eons
were passing.

Around midnight the fog bank began to break up. He could
see the fire then. It burned in a forest far below him. Overhead,
thick tendrils of smoke hunted among the stars. He told himself
the fire would burn itself out by the time he reached it, and he
went on.

But after a few minutes he stopped again. The line of fire had
drawn nearer with startling speed. It was climbing the slope, igniting things other than trees and brush. He could see rocks
burning orange. Banks of snow burning faintly blue, shimmering
with a fast-moving, almost invisible alcohol flame that raced toward him like the flat, thin wash of a wave across beach sand.
He stared at the blue light for a moment, mesmerized. And then
terror lit across his consciousness. If the snow could burn, if the
rocks could burn, then he could burn too. He turned and ran,

stumbling and falling in the snow as he fled back up the mountain, his lungs aching for lack of oxygen. He ran in great, leaping strides as the flames swept toward him. He cried out to her for help.

"Don't run from me!" she commanded. And suddenly he realized she *was* the fire. She spoke with a tongue of flame. *"My love . . ."*

He hesitated, fear and love warring inside him. She reached for him with fingers of superheated air. She tangled him up in the arms of a searing gale and howled in his ears. *"Time to come home. . . ."*

Her life force overwhelmed him. She was too powerful. Too hot. With his cold-adapted metabolism, he would melt in her embrace. "You're killing me!" he cried. "Don't touch me. You're burning me. Let me go!" He struggled to escape from her, but this wind had no form, no solid body that he could fight, only the relentless energy of her purpose. . . .

"Trust me. . . ."

". . . my love."

She swept his legs out from under him. He floundered, belly-down in the snow, staring downslope as the blue alcohol flame swept toward him. He scrambled backward frantically, but the flame caught him. It touched his fingers first, feeling only a little warm, like a lover's kiss, dry lips of fire caressing his skin. Then the heat began to mount. His fingers were searing, his palms burned. He slapped his hands against the snow pack to put out the flame, but it did no good. His arms began to burn. And then the fire flashed across his head, his back, his buttocks, his legs. He howled in agony. He could feel his skin going thick, like the charred bark of a fallen tree. He rolled over and over in the burning snow, hissing, cursing the flames, while his fingers turned to charcoal and his flesh peeled back and his bones glittered white amid the blue fire.

"Let me go!" he screamed.

"Never," she swore.

"Come with me now," another voice pleaded. Another presence. The old witch: She answered his screams with her cold breath in his ear, her frigid fingers tapping across his whitened skull. *"There is a way out,"* she whispered. *"A way out. . . ."* And she blew through his mind, whistling past the architecture of his skull like a rogue wind at play in an abandoned temple.

And he saw himself going with her, leaving this ruined body, to drift on the wind like a wraith of fog and be gone, gone, gone forever, a cool breath of thought slowly disassembling in the ether.

His head jerked back in rage. *"Not you!"* he screamed. *"Not you, Witch-mother of the earth! I'll never go with you! I won't let you take me!"* And with the last of his strength, he dove into the fiery arms of his Familiar.

Tom lunged for her. Her eyes went wide. She scrambled backward frantically, her heart thundering in her throat as his clawing hand reached for her. But his muscles gave out. He hit the floor with a sickening *thunk!* that drove the air out of his lungs. Katie froze, crouched against an empty crate. Tom's nude body lay prone, his face pressed against the stone floor, his outstretched hand slowly curling and uncurling only a few inches from her feet. She stared at him, while air rushed in and out of her lungs in a cold tide. "Tom?"

His head lolled slowly over until his eyes could look at her. His body was as slack and helpless as a newborn baby's. She saw a quiet fear in his eyes, like a lover who suspects he will soon be abandoned. His lips parted and an odd sound scrambled from his throat. His gaze flicked away. He swallowed, then tried again in a hoarse whisper. "Katie?"

He knew her. Thirty years lay between them, but he still knew her. This sixty-four-year-old woman. He knew her for his wife. Oh no, oh no, she thought. Perhaps she'd been wrong to be here. It wasn't fair to him. She was *old.* . . .

He looked at her with puzzled eyes. "I had a dream," he told her, in a voice soft and hoarse.

"Did you?" She blinked hard against the sudden pressure of tears. A dream. And the technicians in L.A. had always told her it was impossible, that he could not be dreaming at −196°C. But hadn't she heard him call so many times from the frozen wastelands in her own mind?

He was trying to get up now. He pressed his palms against the floor and struggled to a sitting position. He held his trembling hand out to her. *"Katie."*

A small moan escaped her lips. She went to her knees beside him. Then hesitantly, she accepted his hand.

It felt rough and calloused against her skin, an old, familiar sensation that sent physical memories sluicing through her like irrigation water on an arid field. And she remembered. For the first time in years she remembered what it had been like to love him. And she understood why she'd come here, come this far for him. She'd forgotten so much. The years had folded around her like dry husks, encapsulating, insulating her core. Now with the simple touch of his rough hands he peeled those husks away. She felt herself aglow, full of hope.

He leaned forward, to press his cheek against hers while his hand shifted around to the back of her head to pull her closer, his fingers catching in the blond stubble of her hair. She slipped off a glove to touch his shoulder; felt his magical breath against her ear. *"What's happened to me?"* he whispered, his voice laced with confusion.

She bowed her head as tears flowed across her cheeks. "You know," she said. "Don't you?" And in a moment she felt his slow nod against her cheek.

"How long?" he asked.

And she told him: *"Thirty years."*

She felt him stiffen. For a moment the muscles in his back were hard as stone. Then an orgasmic shudder ran through him as if he were divesting himself of all the terror of expectation that had been stored up in his body. He groaned, his hand clenching fiercely against the back of her neck.

"It's all right," she whispered. *"It's all right."*

And that was truth. For this moment, anyway, everything felt right. She held him close, cherishing his presence, refusing to allow the intrusion of the unpleasant realities that skulked about the periphery of her awareness. Not now. Not now.

Part IV
TECH-HEAVEN

PROCEEDINGS OF THE JUDICIAL AI:
"Kishida-Hunt v. the Commonwealth of Humanity"
Excerpt from the Testimony of Katharine Kishida:

... I helped him dress. Then he ate a little soup and crackers, and promptly got sick. But he ate a little more and that went down better. His body was remembering how to be alive. He didn't say much. He seemed confused. I told myself he had good reason. I didn't ask him how it had been for him. I didn't ask him what he had dreamed, or why there had been murder in his eyes when he'd first awakened. I didn't want to know. I already suspected what I'd put him through. So I didn't ask questions. I did all the talking. I talked about Joy and Nikki and Mars and the orbitals and the political troubles. And I was happy. I let myself be happy. Why not? I knew it couldn't last.

20

The Last Day

Katie paced the mausoleum, moving restlessly between the chambers while the ceiling robot worked overhead. She'd slept for a while beside Tom. But her dreams had been uneasy and she'd awakened early. Not wanting to disturb him, she'd slipped out from under the fresh blankets, leaving him to sleep on in peace while she worried over the question of what they would do next.

(*They!* That simple pronoun still seemed a miracle.)

Katie had made no plans beyond Tom's revival. Any such plans had seemed unforgivable hubris before. But now some scheme was needed. The world outside this cavern remained hostile. *And Nikki still hasn't called....*

Katie's gloved fists clenched and unclenched. What was happening on the orbitals? To gain Tom and lose Nikki ...

No. She wouldn't consider it.

Her wandering steps brought her back to the fourth chamber. The mug of coffee she'd made for herself waited on the table. Spying it, she picked it up and started to sip, but a thin plate of ice had formed on the surface. She

312   L I N D A   N A G A T A

popped the mug in the microwave, idled about the humming machine for several seconds, then turned her back
on it, letting her restless feet take her on into the fifth
chamber.

She did not want to disturb Tom's sleep, but it was difficult to stay away.

He slept on the air mattress, surrounded by medical
equipment: the gray oblong box of the blood mill on one
side, an empty IV stand on the other. He wore thermals,
woolen pants, and a gray sweater. A bright Andean blanket
was draped across his legs. Katie hungrily observed the
rise and fall of his chest, feeling as if she could feed forever on that simple motion.

The muffled creak of steel hinges shattered the spell.
Katie gasped in surprise and turned about, her joints pro-
testing the sudden movement with a flash of pain. The
raw howl of unfiltered wind suddenly boomed through the
cavern, carrying with it the moist breath of fog. Someone
had come to her sanctuary.

She glanced anxiously at Tom's sleeping figure, then,
"Hark: lights out," she whispered. The resident AI heard
her, and plunged the cave into darkness. She fumbled her
way back to the fourth chamber, where the microwave still
hummed, casting out a suddenly brilliant light as it
counted down the final seconds of its program. *Five, four,
three, two, one.* It trilled through the chambers, then its
light winked out. Katie's hand darted into her pocket, to
caress the hard profile of her pistol.

She listened. At the cave entrance, the steel door closed
with a soft thud that cut off the roaring wind. The turbines hummed. Tom muttered in his sleep. She jumped as
a metal jingle and dull thump announced a pack hitting
the floor. The second door closed. "Hey, Katie," a distant
voice announced. "It's me. Gregory."

Gregory?

Her hand clenched convulsively around the barrel of
the pistol. Voice cops she was ready to face. She'd been
expecting them for days. But not Gregory. Not her husband on the scene. Not now.

"Hark: lights on!" he barked. The AI obeyed him.

Katie squinted against the sudden pressure. Down the

uneven passage she saw him, his tall, thin frame unmistakable even in his heavy parka. His chin was tucked down against his chest as he looked at her. The palm-sized burn scar on his cheek had taken on a shiny cast in the overhead light. It twisted his lips out of line so that he appeared to grimace, an eyetooth always showing. He pulled back his hood, revealing the stark crew cut of his salt-and-pepper hair.

"Has it been that bad between us?" he asked. "Are you really going to pull that gun out and shoot me?"

She snapped her hand out of her pocket, leaving the gun behind. She tried to grin, tried for an expression of nonchalance—then suddenly felt as if she were inadvertently mocking his scarred face. "You startled me, that's all."

He started toward her, his hard steps falling in a cadence of anger against the stone. "You ran away from me, Katie. Why? Why did you come here?"

She went forward to meet him. She didn't want him close to Tom. In a low, warning voice she told him: "I didn't run away." And as easily as that, they recaptured the emotion of their last argument. "You threw me out, Gregory. Remember? You were afraid. You didn't want it to happen. You wanted me to go to Mars and stay out of trouble. But I got the Cure."

That stopped him. He stood in the second chamber, framed on two sides by the sparkling silver cylinders. "I heard the Voice hit you with a hallucinogenic virus."

She glared. "At first I thought it was *you* who'd poisoned me. But that's over now. The Cure is real." She walked up to him. Tilted her head back, so that she might meet his eyes.

He backpedaled as an expression of astonishment bloomed on his twisted face. "Katie . . . ?" His gloved hands darted up. She jerked in surprise, but he caught her, cupping her head in his hands. He held her there, gazing into her face as if searching. . . .

"Let go of me!" she hissed. She twisted out of his grip.

He caught her hand. She fought him, her joints screaming in pain. "The Cure is real!" she shouted at him. "We own it. It came out of the European labs. And it's real."

"I know." He backed her up against the cylinders, pinning her there with his body, as if physical restriction might calm her. "I can see it in your face." He bit the tip of his glove, holding it in his teeth while he yanked it off his hand. Then he stroked her face with his cold, smooth fingers. "I can see it," he repeated. "You look good. You look so good. Younger than the day I met you. But that was a bad day for you. You've regretted that day for thirty years."

She caught his bare fingers, resenting his touch. But the odd cant of his words disturbed her. *You look good.*

What did he see? She'd been shooting up plenty on different components of the Cure, but she hadn't noticed any results except a lingering fever and her hair coming in blond instead of gray. She touched her own cheek. It felt dry and chapped. She moved her fingers slowly across her skin. Then again, faster, searching for the deep lines of aging she'd grown accustomed to. But they were gone. She yanked off her gloves and looked at her hands. The age spots had faded. And when she pinched her skin, it slipped back into place with the full elasticity of youth. She drew a shaky breath, realizing she had no idea what she looked like anymore. But Tom had recognized her. *You look good.*

Katie glanced instinctively toward the back of the cave. Gregory followed her gaze. She felt him stiffen. "You've done it, haven't you!" He let her go. He turned and strode away from her, toward the fifth chamber, toward Tom.

"Gregory, wait!" She leaped after him. She hung on his arm. "Why can't you understand? I had to do it. For my own sanity, for my own freedom, I had to do it. I fought for this for thirty years."

He pulled up abruptly. She looked up at him, but his attention was not fixed on her. She turned around to follow his gaze, and saw Tom.

He stood at the start of the third chamber, his hair tousled from sleep, a hard and angry light in his eyes.

"Thomas Kishida," Gregory muttered in a voice full of venom. "My illustrious predecessor. You're looking a little better now than the day I put you on ice."

Tom looked at Katie. "Who the hell is he?"

Her gaze fell, though she still held on to Gregory's arm. "Gregory Hunt," she said. "He was with the cryonics team, at the hospital, on the night you—"

Gregory's hand closed around her wrist. "You might want to add that you and I have been married for twenty-four years."

Her eyes half closed as a wave of dizziness surged through her brain. *What had she done to her life?* She told herself there was no way she could have foreseen this moment thirty years ago. No one then could have said for sure that Tom was coming back. No one then, even the true believers, would have guessed he might be revived in a mere thirty years. So she'd chosen to live her life. She was human. She was not a mindless servant of the dead— though Gregory might contend that. Tom's specter had haunted him for years.

She drew a deep breath, banishing pointless speculation. She could not change the past. "Thomas Kishida," she said, "this is Gregory Hunt. And it's true. I've been married to him now for twenty-four years."

Tom's dark brows lowered as he studied Gregory. Katie flushed, knowing that Tom would see only the ugliness, the bitter anger that hadn't been part of Gregory in the early days. Not that Tom's feelings would have been any different if he'd met Gregory at his best. "Congratulations," Tom said. His gaze skewered Katie. "You might have told me this, first thing."

"I never forgot you."

A frigid cold seemed to move into his eyes. "Don't apologize. It was only yesterday for me. For you it's been thirty years. I expect it's natural to move on."

"Huh," Gregory said—a monosyllabic expression of contempt. "Don't make too much of it, Thomas Kishida. This mausoleum isn't exactly a secret anymore. You and I and our wife may all be dead before any of us gets to make a final choice." He turned to Katie. "You should have accepted the appointment to Mars. You're risking your life here. The Knights know where you are. I saw a Knight communiqué. They're coming, Katie. They're after you. You have to get out now, while you still can."

INTERNAL MEMORANDUM
RETRIEVED FROM THE FILES OF
PRESIDENT ILENE CARSON:

To: Fearless Leader
From: General Dy Yung
Re: Imminent failure of the Kishida-
        Hunt gambit

Greedy Geezers got the Cure, eh?

Buy that life-hog faith:
   Be young again
   Raise the dead.
No way.

Only the earth renews:
   Rejuvenation therapy
   In the grave.
No preservatives.

Good tip, Madam President.
Last bootleg copy of the Cure on our
 maps now.
Knights of the Oppressed Earth is pleased
 to report:

The Cure won't be in existence tomorrow.

21

Electronic Existence

Katie made coffee for three while the ghosts howled their amusement in the turbines. Tom sat on an empty crate and watched her, his hurt flowing outward like a swarm of stinging cells, unseen minutiae that struck her cheeks and hands and burned. Gregory brooded at the desk, his dark gaze emitting an aura of latent violence. Katie stirred powder into steaming water. Three cups on the counter beside the microwave. She gazed at them, hesitating, cursing her own analytical nature, but she couldn't evade it. She would give the first cup to Gregory. That would show him respect. But it would also expose him as the guest here. She would take the other two cups and offer one to Tom as she sat beside him.

Had she already decided, then?

Was the decision hers to make?

She executed her plan. Tom stiffened as she took a place beside him on the crate. Gregory leaned forward, his gaze sharp and coldly amused. He'd caught her meaning. She could almost hear his mocking thoughts: *You denied it.*

You denied it. But I always knew what was in your heart. So he found his doubt justified. Congratulations.

Tom held his cup without drinking. He spoke past Katie. He spoke to Gregory. "Do the Knights know where the mausoleum is?"

Gregory's gaze shifted warily. "They know. I followed *their* map here."

"Do you know how far behind they are?"

Gregory shrugged. "No idea."

Katie wanted this peripheral problem to go away. "The Knights don't know we have the Cure," she said. "They're not going to be in any hurry to get here."

"You don't know that," Tom said. "You don't know what's happened to Nikki."

She felt the hot sting of shame on her face as she interpreted another meaning in his words: *You haven't kept my children safe.*

"We have to go," Gregory said. "Now. There's only one road up here and we don't want to get caught on it."

Katie pressed her gloved hands against her cheeks. "We can't go. All the other patients are still here. We have to protect them. Especially now, when we know it's possible to cure them." She glanced at Tom, seeking support.

"It's possible," he acknowledged. "We have to work from that."

Gregory's pack lay on the floor at his feet. He toed it. "I brought explosives. We can seal the door behind a rock slide. The Knights won't be able to get through that. Not in the next few days, anyway. We'll have time to regroup."

The turbines moaned a low note. Katie kicked her heel against the crate. "If we seal the door, the Knights will just come down the air shafts."

"The turbines block the shafts."

"The turbines can be blown. The antenna can be wrecked. Without power and communications the patients are doomed."

"They'll last a few days. Until we can regroup."

"If we can regroup." She listened to the moaning turbines and weighed the options. They couldn't abandon the frozen dead, yet they didn't have the means to defend them. "We're going to have to change our strategy." She

looked from Tom to Gregory. "I think it's time to stop hiding. I think it's time to introduce ourselves to the VR."
She pushed herself to her feet, wincing at the lingering
pain in her joints as she went to hunt up the telephone.

"You're surrendering, then," Gregory said.

"No. I'm not surrendering. But we can't win like this.
We're going to have to change the rules."

Katie had married again.

He tried to reconcile it. He hadn't been gone that long.
It didn't seem all that long, anyway.

Well, she said it was thirty years.

She'd married again.

He didn't blame her. Not with the reasonable part of his
mind. Reason was only a recent veneer over more basic
emotions.

He watched Hunt sort through a small collection of
neatly packaged explosives, and he tried to find faults.
The grossly scarred face. Too much gray hair; Hunt was
too old for her, definitely. And it was already evident that
he had a mean streak in him. How bad could that get?

Hunt selected two packages from his collection, each
one wrapped in decorative dark-purple cellophane like
New Year's fireworks. Then Hunt stalked off to the front
of the cave to wire the doors.

His attention shifted. He listened to Katie talk on the
phone.

He remembered the child she'd once been. A virgin
when she'd come to his bed at eighteen. She'd scared him
bad. He'd never taken to anyone the way he took to her.
And she'd loved him; she'd never loved anyone else.

So that had changed.

He mulled over his own resentment and he wondered
just how much he should believe of what she'd told him.

Katie had married again.

She called Ferris first. "It worked," she said. "Tom's
here. He's alive."

"Katie . . ." Doubt dragged in Ferris's voice.

"I'm not crazy," she said. "It worked. But I need your
help again." In the background a female voice delivered a

speech over the low rumble of crowd noises and broken applause. "Where are you?"

"The constitutional convention. Virtual delegate for the Primal Nation." He spoke in a low voice as the background speech dragged on.

"Is Ilene bending?"

"It's not up to Ilene anymore. It's up to the people."

"The Cure works. I want people to know that. I want them to believe it." She waited for some response. "Ferris?"

"Just thinking."

"You're not against me on this?"

"We all have to choose our own path."

"Will you set something up with Gene Pool? See if they'll take the issue? Soonest. Gregory says the Knights are on their way. We have to get our viewpoint out before we lose the antenna."

"Gregory?"

"Will you, Ferris?"

He sighed reluctantly. She could almost see his big head shaking unhappily. "Okay."

She called Nikki next. Tom watched her anxiously as Nikki's phone rang. It was picked up on the fourth ring, but it wasn't Nikki who answered. The sounds of the constitutional convention filled the background again, and over them, the famous deadpan of President Carson. "Katie, are you ready to negotiate?"

"Where's Nikki?"

"She's here with me on Voice-2. It's been necessary to keep her in isolation. She's admitted to trafficking in proscribed molecular technologies."

"I want to talk to her."

"That won't be possible until after the convention."

"I have the Cure, Ilene."

"I know. Nikki told me."

"Did she tell you Tom's alive?"

Ilene's silence was weighted with contempt. Katie felt red heat rise to the surface of her face again. She pulled off a glove and pressed her cold palm against her cheek. When Ilene spoke, her voice was low and angry. "I know that's not possible. I know what happened to the patient in your European lab."

"No one knows what happened then," Katie said. "This time it worked. You can talk to him."

"Don't play games with me, Katie."

"Ilene—"

"I want you to destroy the Cure."

Katie scowled into the phone. "Why would I do that?"

"To protect yourself."

She caught her breath as a cool flush of understanding washed through her mind. "You sent the Knights after us, did you?"

"Destroy the Cure, Katie. For your own good."

The line went dead.

"We've got one VR suit," Katie said. "And I've been living in it for weeks."

Gregory groaned. "Sounds like you're the spokesman, then. You're popular with the media anyway. It should work."

"And we've got the remotes," she added. "They can both send sound and pictures."

"There's the ceiling robot, too," Tom said. "That's got a camera and it already sends to L.A."

Katie nodded. "Good. That's four potential subchannels. We run them all at once. Four points of view will make it highly unlikely we're synthesizing the show."

"We've got to get outside," Tom said. "And see if anybody's really coming."

Gregory gave him a scathing look. "They're coming," he growled.

Tom returned his animosity in a long, cold stare. "It'd be nice to know when."

"Why don't you go look, then?"

"Easy," Katie said, her shoulders hunched against the sudden tension. "I'll walk one of the remotes." She hunted around for the VR helmet. Tom watched her curiously. "I told you about the remote units," she said.

"I've never done the VR."

"Oh, you'll like it. You might never come out again."

Gregory made a disparaging snort. Katie scowled at him. Then she smiled at Tom. "Tap me out if Gene Pool calls."

"I was going to call Joy."

"Wait, baby. We need the line clear right now."

He gave her a cool, measuring stare. It pierced her cordial feelings. She sighed and turned away; pulled the helmet over her head, thinking, *Hell with it*. Let him stew. Let them both stew. Man was meant to suffer.

Once inside the remote, Katie used a voice command to tap into VR coverage of the constitutional convention, directing the signal into the helmet's peripheral fields, so that the road to La Cruz was in front of her while the convention proceeded on either side. In the resultant image, the floor of the congressional arena on Voice-2 appeared to be neatly bisected. Katie could see the representatives at their desks, and beyond them a vast, nebulous audience of linked participants like herself. She felt one among the crowd, yet the setting had a dreamlike quality. No one in the audience stood out as an individual. They were slightly out-of-focus, generic masks of Commonwealth citizens. Only the politicians at their desks, and the speakers on the high podium, were clearly visible.

Katie checked convention records and discovered that for several days the subject of debate had involved the architecture of the new government. Any citizen could request a minute to testify. Each was required to submit the text of his or her statement to the judicial AI, where it was screened to eliminate the nonsensical and the repetitive. That still left a lot of room for nauseating rhetoric, confrontational crap designed to set factions at each others' throats:

"Fascist oppressors."

"You're going to lose your job."

"Playing God."

"Stolen from my people."

"There will always be limits."

A thin frosting of snow lay across the brown and sterile land. Katie's metal feet crunched against it, leaving tracks in the mineral soil as an American explained why every incorporated town should be allowed a congressional representative. Next, a Brazilian called for the same rights for corporate entities. A matron from Singapore insisted that only those of fifty years or more should be allowed to vote.

Katie pulled in a channel from Gene Pool to see how

things were going. A pie-slice room opened up on the convention floor. It held a black billboard printed with white lettering that read: Back from the Dead? A masculine voice read the words, and then frenetic bites of news footage began to roll. The voice said:

"Listen up, citizens! It's been a year to remember but it's not over yet! A new issue has just been poured into the Gene Pool. It could sway the consensus on the CC. It could sway *you*. But only if you opt to participate! We need your scan on the scene *now*. Time is of the essence, because the powers that be are seeking to suppress the dead. That's right. The dead are coming back to life and the old are growing young. You guessed it—the Cure is here . . . at least according to the radical billionaire financial team Kishida-Hunt. Is it real? Judge for yourself on subchannels 407A through D, where we will be carrying live coverage of an assault by Knights of the Oppressed Earth against the Kishida-Hunt team. Do you want it to be real? Soak in the Pool, then decide. It's your future. You have a voice."

A digital counter at the bottom of the screen ticked off the number of participants. The first four numerators spun too fast to see. Even the ten-thousand digit was hard to read as it winked zero through nine in less than five seconds. The tally was up to 3.7 million.

Too cool.

Three miles down the road the count had reached 4.1 million global audience. Not bad. The whole world wasn't wired, after all. The debate on the convention floor had shifted to the merits of income taxes.

Standing on a promontory, looking down on the winding scar that was the road to La Cruz, Katie sighted a comb of blowing dust. She zoomed the remote's optical units until she could make out six trucks, all wending up the road. The vehicles were unmarked.

She felt a tap on the shoulder. Then she heard Tom's voice: "Hunt's doing background for Gene Pool." The helmet's noise baffles muffled his words. "But he says go ahead and link."

She gave him a thumbs-up without bothering to lift the helmet. She put a call through to Gene Pool, identified herself, and linked on channel 407C. Now an audience could receive the same visual and auditory scan that linked her to the remote, and she could receive feedback from the Pool participants. Through a complicated system of individual user inputs and a patented central artificial-intelligence program, Gene Pool was able to synthesize and continually update an Average Sentiment—the net reaction of the participating audience to the ongoing events in the Pool. It was an interactive system far more sensational than anything happening in the congressional arena, and had been used to develop political policy since the days of Generational Challenge.

Katie let her vision fix on the approaching trucks while an audience gradually spilled in from other channels. The constitutional convention took a brief recess. The lead truck in the convoy negotiated a hairpin turn. The Pool swam with 4.2 million intellects, sixty percent of them linked to channel 407C. Katie cranked up the remote's camera eyes to maximum magnification. She stared at the lead truck, catching a blurred and bouncing image of a brown, sunglassed face. "The face of the enemy," she announced, speaking through the voice synthesizer on the remote. "Check your criminal logs and see if you can get a match."

The AI produced an amalgamation of unfocused murmurings bearing predominant tones of curiosity, amusement, and cynicism.

Katie spoke again: "Now scan my image. According to the provisional government of the Commonwealth, this too is the face of the enemy. Check your criminal logs. I'm in there, under the name of Katharine Kishida."

The murmurings congealed into a communal question voiced by the system AI: *Physical description?*

"I'm sixty-four years old," Katie said.

The Average Sentiment was a mutter of wonderment. She smiled.

Hunt shoved a phone in his face. "It's for you," Hunt said. "Gene Pool wants you to do a thing with Joy."

"Joy?" He echoed her name in dumb surprise.

"You know, your daughter."

Joy. He remembered a beautiful girl, twelve years old, sweet disposition, loved to play basketball with her old man. Katie had said that Joy had two grown children now. He looked at Hunt. "What am I supposed to do?"

"Just talk." Hunt pointed up over his shoulder. "They've got a video link through the ceiling robot."

He glanced at the glassy-eyed device, hanging like a spider from its tracks. He heard a faint female voice from the telephone. Feeling deeply anxious, he held the device to his ear.

"Hello? Hello?" The voice on the other end of the phone sounded shy and pensive. A woman's voice, yet the tone and accents were that of a little girl.

"Hello," he said stiffly. "Joy?"

"Daddy?" Something seemed to tear in her voice. He thought she might be close to crying. He felt a brush of panic. How could she cry for him after thirty years? Did she really remember him? "Daddy," she whispered. "Is it you?"

Is it you? The question startled him. He groped for an appropriate answer. So much had changed. Though he could remember who he used to be, and though his consciousness still existed in the same body and though he could look back on the path of his life without detecting any unaccountable gaps in his experience, he was not at all sure that he was the same person Joy recalled.

But that wasn't what she wanted to hear.

"Yes, princess," he told her. "It's me."

Katie had both remotes in position by the time the convoy of trucks reached the landslide that blocked the road below the ruined church. She'd situated one remote unit on the slope above the mausoleum, well-distanced from the housing for the turbine mounted at the top of the first air shaft. The remote huddled behind a rock outcropping and was not immediately visible from below. The second remote she placed nearly a mile away on a facing slope, where it commanded a view of the trucks. Both units were directly and continuously linked to the net via satellite relays. Gene Pool was promising real-time violence to subscribers. Participation had gone up to 17.4 million. The constitutional convention had resumed its floor show. By popular consent the subject of debate had left income taxes and gone on to the unscheduled discussion of the control of new technologies.

Katie maintained peripheral convention coverage while she linked into the distant remote on the facing slope. She watched the convoy of trucks roll to a halt below the landslide. Twenty-four people emerged from the clustered vehicles, each one dressed in white coveralls, carrying a white rifle and a field pack. "A small army," Katie said. "Yet they don't wear the uniform of Voice cops. They're terrorists, and they've come to destroy our copy of the Cure."

She watched the Knights pull hoods over their heads while Ilene spoke from the convention podium on the need for caution in molecular law. One by one, the Knights switched on their camouflage suits and disappeared. Ilene chopped with her fist for emphasis. Katie felt outrage well up in her breast. "Is the judicial AI watching?" Katie demanded. "Is the judicial AI observing this terrorist action? Or is the judicial AI content to let terrorists execute executive policy?"

The wind must have carried the synthetic voice down to the Knights. A rifle cracked and a bullet chipped rock just above the remote's shoulder.

Dump the data defining the Cure into the VR. It was a whispered, almost subsonic voice—the Average Sentiment of the Gene Pool. People were listening, and they were backing the Cure. *Preserve the data in the VR.*

Then the soft, familiar, gender-neutral voice of the judicial AI intruded on the channel. "Any attempt to release unauthorized proprietary data to the public will be screened."

Katie swallowed hard. Time to fix parameters. "Assess ownership of the data in question," she whispered.

The AI replied: "Documents on file at this time indicate one hundred percent ownership by the corporate entity Kishida-Hunt."

Katie smiled. "*I'm* Kishida-Hunt. I have a right to disseminate this data."

The judicial AI disagreed: "Control of the corporate entity has transferred to the Primal Nation. Your claim is invalid."

"I contest that! The transfer was authorized on false grounds—"

. "Information bulletin," the Gene Pool AI announced. "The Congress of the Commonwealth has requested real-time linkage to channel 407C. Stand by for bilocus coalescence."

So the convention delegates had decided to respond to the happenings in Gene Pool. She dropped her convention coverage. A moment later the political arena came to her as the rocks surrounding the remote faded, as if behind a screen. Superimposed on them were the desks of the convention delegates. Selective lighting visually emphasized Ferris. He stood beside his desk, dressed in a shell-print aloha shirt, his silver hair in a ponytail down his back. His brown eyes fixed on Katie as she huddled on the ground to avoid the Knights' bullets.

"I speak for the Primal Nation," he announced. "And until the legal status of both Katharine Kishida and Gregory Hunt is clarified, the Primal Nation continues to affirm its right to control the affairs of Kishida-Hunt Incorporated, including the disposition of the Kishida-Hunt Cure and all data pertaining to it. To that end, we demand that all copies of any data describing the detailed physical structure of the Kishida-Hunt Cure be turned over to the Nation at once—including those presently held by Commonwealth officials."

The selective lighting switched to Ilene as she spoke from within a huge boulder. "The Commonwealth will not accede to this demand. It is the contention of the president that the data in question 'radically alters the human condition' and is therefore illegal under Voice law—the only sanctioned guidelines existing until this convention produces a new constitution. As head of the transitional government, I will not allow our law-enforcement agencies to participate in the distribution of proscribed molecular technologies."

"The legality of a geriatric cure has never been determined," Ferris barked. "The opinions you express are your own and don't carry the weight of law."

"The opinions I express are those of the judicial AI."

"This is not an issue for a machine to decide," Ferris countered. "It is an issue at the core of the constitutional convention. It will be found by the will of the people."

There was an ominous rumbling from the political arena. From the slopes above, a few pebbles bounced down past

328 LINDA NAGATA

the remote. Katie glanced up nervously. A bullet ricocheted
off the rock overhead and struck her just above the eye. She
slapped at the dent. A flash of motion on the snowfield
above betrayed the location of a Knight. She glimpsed a
white rifle partly obscured. Dust rattled against her metal
skin. The rifle turned to point at her, its barrel like a black
eye against a field of white. Sonic burst. She leaped two meters into the air, landed on the rifle, and sent it tumbling
down among the rocks. The nearly invisible Knight howled
in pain, a howl picked up and drawn away by the wind as
a scattering of pebbles marked a path of retreat.

Back from the Dead:
The turbines hummed overhead. Liquid dripped. The
lights in the cave were harsh and unnatural and he was getting a headache. *Why am I here?* The camera eyes of the ceiling robot stared at him as he entered the third chamber. He
tried to imagine millions of eyes behind its lenses, a virtual
arena, growing, spreading in discontinuous nonspace.

He found the empty cylinder, the one that had housed
him. He rocked it down and looked inside. Dull steel walls.
Empty. He tried to see the snowfields, but they were somewhere else. He listened for the voice of the witch.

Back in the fifth chamber the telephone rang. He heard
Hunt pick it up. He tried to find an analogy for Hunt in
his dream, but there was none. Hunt should not exist.
Hunt bellowed from the fifth chamber: "Kishida, Gene
Pool wants another interview with you."

Millions of eyes watched him through the ceiling robot
as he pretended not to hear. He shoved the cylinder back
upright. He wandered on, past the harsh lights, into the
first chamber. The camera couldn't follow him here. But it
could still see him. It stopped at the end of its track, its
lenses fixed on him.

He had not been to the first chamber before. Now he
stared in surprise at the human figures laid out in niches
in the rock, wrapped in fading woolen blankets. He went
to one. He crouched beside it. Behind him liquid dripped.
The camera watched. He studied the shrouded figure,
searching for signs of life. "Kishida!" Hunt called. Angry
steps echoed like ax blows in the cave.

He reached for the blanket. It felt brittle in his hands. He tugged at it gently until it worked loose, then he pulled it away from the figure's head. He felt Hunt standing beside him, the tall man's shadow falling over the sepulchral face. "Why are you doing that?" Hunt asked. His voice was wary. In his hand was the telephone, a well of sound waiting to swallow him.

"I don't know. But you're blocking my light."

Hunt stepped aside. A million eyes looked on a dead brown face, taut dry skin pulling lips back to expose brown teeth, crisp gray eyes. Black hair in a disorganized state. "It's all a dream," Hunt said. "Everything. All of it. Your whole life." He leaned closer, the phone in his hands like a well sucking in history, a link to the mind of God. "That's you, right there," Hunt murmured. "You're having an out-of-body experience and you're looking on your own face." His long surgeon's finger tapped the phone. "You want Katie to sleep with that?"

He felt his hands begin to shake. His blood ran in streams of fire. Dead. He struggled with the concept. Am dead. Was dead. Living dead.

Millions of eyes looked on.

He laid his dead hands once more on the fragile blanket, lifting it, wrapping it carefully back around the body, tucking it under the head, smoothing it. Then he turned around, and with a roar of fury he lunged at Hunt.

His shoulder drove into Hunt's chest. His arms encircled him in a tackle that sent them both to the floor, Hunt on the bottom, a satisfying grunt from him as the air was slammed out of his lungs. He pulled his fist back. He felt Hunt's hand at his throat.

"Stop it!" Katie shouted.

He froze. She stood beneath the camera, her hideous VR helmet tucked under her elbow, the fuzz of her blond hair barely covering her smooth head, her furious eyes burning from a perfect face that had enchanted him in another age another time, burning itself into the pattern of his brain and he could not let go, not even now.

Am dead. Was dead.

He rolled off Hunt. Living dead.

From the door he heard a whispering of voices, metal on metal scraping.

"They're here," Katie said, her eyes still blazing.

Hunt shoved himself to his feet. "Move back, then," he said. "I'm going to blow the door."

Katie snugged the VR helmet over her head again, linking once more into the remote on the facing slope. She listened to the Average Sentiment of the Pool as she studied the mausoleum entrance. The constitutional convention had returned to the congressional arena on Voice-2. She listened to the speeches droning on and on. The ranks of the audience there had slimmed as more and more participants drained into Gene Pool.

She couldn't see the mausoleum's door. That was hidden behind the huge slab of rock that acted as a lean-to. But in the shadow of that rock the slope seemed to shimmer, as if it were about to turn to liquid and flow away. "Clear the door," she shouted at the camouflaged Knights clustered at the entrance. "We've got explosives of our own and they're going off in five seconds, four, three, two—"

Five pockets of instability fled. A moment later an ear-splitting concussion rocked the slope, sending dust and rock and snow exploding into the air.

Channel switch: in the mausoleum.

Steel cylinders trembled. Dust rained down from the roof and the ceiling tracks buckled. The robot jammed. Its motor whirred as it fought to move. Tom caught her hand, fury in his eyes. "We're trapped in here now."

"Somebody will get us out. We've got the Cure."

Channel switch: three trails of footprints pointed out the positions of Knights on the slope above the mausoleum. A small avalanche had covered the cave entrance. Down on the flat, eight more Knights conferred, their helmets off so that they seemed to be a swarm of talking heads, floating eerily five feet or more off the ground. She executed an optical zoom. Studied each face for the benefit of the VR, until she fixed on one that seemed familiar. She caught her breath, then at once wondered at her surprise. *Roxanne.*

It had been so many years. She remembered the midnight call with its false warning, which had ignited the ordeal in the Darien. Judge Dark loomed on the scene. Katie felt herself shaking.

Suddenly Roxanne was gazing up the slope, looking straight at her with eyes that seemed to have shrunk over the years. Her face was taut, dark as volcanic stone, with a sheen like black ice. Her hair was brown and thin and only slightly longer than Katie's. Her lips were a dry, narrow line. "Katie, I know you're there!" she shouted over the streaming wind. "All we want is the Cure. Give us that and we'll go away. We'll leave you alone."

Katie swallowed hard, striving to ignore her fear, willfully refusing to see Judge Dark hovering over her shoulder. "Haven't you heard?" she shouted, her voice booming out through the remote's speaker. "It's all over the VR. Tom's back! He's alive. And you said it couldn't be done. You tried to kill him to keep it from being done. You didn't want to be wrong. Well you are wrong. Wrong, wrong, wrong, wrong, wrong!"

The echoes of her voice ran down the valleys. Braggadocio. A challenge to the fates.

Channel switch.

She shrugged the helmet off, feeling a little dizzy. She was standing in the third chamber, between the bank of batteries and a row of steel cylinders. Tom had the chair from the desk. He was perched on it, his head thrust up into the air shaft, one hand closed around the thick cables that descended from the turbines. "We can climb this," he said. "We can get out."

Gregory crouched at his feet, gazing up in concern. "*If* we can get past the turbine. Then we can blow it shut behind us."

"We don't have any friends out there," Katie reminded them.

Gregory said: "If we can hold out a little longer, help will get here."

"You know that?"

He nodded. "I've got word out to my circle. And Gene Pool's sending in on-site technicians. There's still a lot of people willing to bet on Kishida-Hunt."

She felt Tom's gaze like a bitter wind. Some things can never be forgiven.

The phone rang. Gregory slipped it out of his pocket. "Yeah?" He listened. Then he grinned—a twisted expression, given the scarring on his face. "I don't know if they're willing to do that, but I'll ask." He switched off the phone and looked at Tom. "Gene Pool wants you on the floor of the CC."

Katie frowned. "Virtual?"

"Sure. You want to give him your suit?"

She glanced at the robot, jammed in its tracks. Why not? They were surfing this one. No script. Just ride.

She beckoned to Tom to follow her into the back of the cave.

He watched her take off her parka, her sweater, her baggy pants. The VR suit lay underneath all that. She clawed the Velcro closures, her every move wending through his consciousness like an alluring dance. She peeled the bulky coverall off, then stood in her thermals and stocking feet. "You remembering how it was?" she asked.

He started. He tore his gaze away from her figure. He remembered snowfields. "You were always part of it," he said.

She handed him the suit. "Hurry. No telling when the Knights will think to try the air shafts."

He peeled off his own sweater and woolens and pulled the suit on over his thermals while she dressed. "I've never done this," he reminded her.

"Gene Pool will secure the link. No sweat." She helped him with the closures, then picked up the helmet. She leaned forward, and let her lips brush his cheek. He felt his skin burn at the point of contact. She leaned even closer, to whisper in his ear. "They said you were dead. They said you couldn't dream. They were wrong." She pulled back, her eyes holding his. "They were wrong." She helped him settle the helmet over his head.

L.A. FLOW—E-MAIL TO THE EDITOR, 13:00 EDITION
"Qualities of Youth"

This publication has long displayed a
romantic bent, but you've outdone yourself
today with your ten A.M. editorial
condemning the aging of our society and
praising the "qualities of youth" as a fading
ideal soon to be diluted beyond recall by a
deluge of bladder-control problems and
vitamin tonics. I submit there is no cause
for concern. A brief scan through the news
and live-action channels of the day will
demonstrate that many of the most
prominent characteristics of youth have
carried over successfully into the adult
population, among these: violence, herd
behavior, excessive certainty, willful
ignorance, and the forced suppression of
all those who would be different. I submit
that our society is under no threat of excessive
maturity. On the contrary, it would seem
that too many of us have taken an oath
never to grow up.

22

Too Many of Us

He saw the eyes. Millions of them. A vast field of spectators that rose up around him in a bowl with no discernible rim; endless inhabited slopes that mounted higher and higher until they finally faded into the blur of distance. No walls contained this place. Only eyes.

"My God!"

The exclamation arrested his attention. He brought his gaze down from the heights. He found himself standing on a stage, one hand resting on a podium. He was dressed in his sweater and woolens. Immediately surrounding him were a select group of men and women, seated at desks. Onstage, on the other side of the podium, a thin and very elderly woman with Asian features stared at him, her mouth half-open, her eyes unnaturally wide. She wore a blue pantsuit. Her hair was silver. Something about her reminded him of his mother. *"Tom,"* the old woman whispered. "It can't be."

He looked away, not feeling secure enough to argue the point. He thought of his mother. He'd been told she was in the snowfields. No. He'd been told she was dead. Is dead.

"It's a hoax," the old woman said, an undercurrent of anger in her voice.

Something in her manner of speech stirred an old sense of annoyance. He turned to her and scowled. "Who are you?"

A million chuckles of delight rolled down from the audience. His scowl deepened. The old woman's face flushed red. She straightened her shoulders and raised her chin, assuming a defiant posture as she looked out at the men and women behind their desks. But he could see the fluttering in her throat, the trembling lip. She looked like his mother.

"It's a hoax," she repeated, this time addressing the massed audience. "There is no Cure." He saw a tear pool in her eye, but it did not flow away. She pointed at him. "I have no way to prove that this image is my brother. I have no way to prove that Thomas Kishida is alive in an Andean cave, sealed behind a rock slide, the prisoner of a team of psychopaths. I can't prove the truth of any of this. Not now. But I can say with certainty that there is no Cure. There never will be. There can—at most—only be a Curse. A way out of death and old age for the select few—the billionaires, the powerful—or a way to destroy the earth if this Curse is laid upon the public."

Startled, he squinted at her, trying to see the face of his elder sister in this fiery old woman. "Ilene?" he asked tentatively. She jerked as if he'd slapped her. She turned to gaze at him, fear in her eyes. He leaned forward curiously. "It's really you, isn't it?" He couldn't believe how old she looked. Katie didn't look old. Katie looked as fresh and beautiful as the day he'd met her.

But that's what this convention was about, wasn't it? Whether it was all right not to get old. "I think you're getting carried away," he said. "Being alive is not that bad."

A man stood up at one of the desks beyond the stage. As faces turned in his direction he seemed to grow in size; to shift closer to the stage. He was a giant man, dark-skinned, with silver hair in a ponytail down his back. The nameplate on his desk said Ferris Kumunalu.

"Thomas Kishida," he said, with a half-smile on his face.

"I don't remember you."

"We never met. But I've known of you for many years.

And unlike our eminent president, I do not doubt that you are in reality alive and well." He turned to face the arena, a simple half-turn that somehow drew him from his desk up onto the stage. "Being alive and well *is a good thing.* The Primal Nation recognizes that. But being alive and well extracts a price from the earth. As custodian of the Cure, the Primal Nation must recognize that as well. There isn't room enough on the earth for all those who would be Cured. There isn't room enough on the earth for those who would refuse to die." Ferris looked at him with kindly eyes. "Do you know that, Thomas Kishida?"

He remembered the oni in their cave; the hot, horrid pens. He'd refused that way of life. But he'd hung on anyway. Now he felt famished, a translucent wisp of a ghost held on Earth by love, and love alone.

He looked at Ferris, refusing to accept what he knew to be true. The earth would always seek to achieve a vibrant equilibrium. There were terrorists in the snowfields. The defenses Hunt had devised simply couldn't last. "I won't give up," he whispered.

As if to answer his bravado, something exploded overhead. He ducked as invisible debris rained down around him. Ferris and Ilene both looked at him in surprise, but neither moved. Neither seemed to feel the debris or hear the noise. Somewhere, he heard Katie screaming. He felt invisible hands against his shoulders, shoving him backward. "The Knights are coming," he said. Ferris looked at him in horror.

Channel switch.

The Knights had blown one of the turbines. Debris still rained down the first air shaft. Dust filled the air. Ears ringing, Katie struggled to drag Tom out of the third chamber, while trying to pummel him back into awareness. She tripped. They went down together. The remaining turbine moaned with a ghostly sound. She got a hand on Tom's helmet and twisted it loose. As if suddenly awakened, he wrenched it off and flung it aside, then he twisted around on hands and knees. "We don't have to die!" he shouted at her. "That's a myth."

She felt the hair rise on the back of her neck as she gazed at his wild eyes. He'd come back from death. How much did he know? She wanted to ask him, but there was no time. Instead, she laid a trembling finger on his lips to calm him. "I believe you," she whispered. "I do." But Judge Dark was stomping on the roof and she knew Tom was likely wrong.

Gregory emerged through the swirling dust. It had settled on his hair and his face, coating him with gray age. "We've lost the phone," he said. "They've cut the land lines, and without them, there's no way to get a signal through this rock."

Another explosion rattled the steel cylinders as the second turbine was blown. Gregory dropped to the floor, while Tom dove on Katie, knocking her to the ground. She hit hard, Tom's weight on top of her. Dust rained down around them. A thin fog billowed from a hose wrenched off the body of the ceiling robot. The clatter of falling rock slowed. She heard herself gasping for air and then Tom rolled away from her.

A cylindrical object plummeted from the first air shaft. It struck the floor, then bounced with a metallic clatter. A tank of compressed air. It roared as an invisible gas surged past its valve. Another tank came plunging down, then a third. Katie felt her eyes go wide. She scrambled backward. She couldn't smell anything. Maybe it was just oxygen. Maybe the Knights were trying to rattle them. But the tanks weren't green.

Gregory held his arm over his mouth and nose as he scuttled to one of the tanks. He twisted it around to show the label. Skull and bones. CO in a red pyramid. Carbon monoxide. He tried to twist the valve shut. "Dammit!" he roared. "It's broken."

She felt Tom's hands close over her upper arms as he hauled her to her feet. "We have to get out of here!" he shouted.

"But the Cure!" she wailed.

"Never mind that. Let's go."

"Like hell," Gregory growled. "I'm not going to leave it here for the Voice." He cut past them, racing for the back of the cave.

Katie and Tom cautiously approached the air shaft. They stopped underneath it and squinted up. The last ex-

plosion had blown out the turbine. Far overhead a patch of
daylight blazed. She staggered dizzily. She told herself it
was the altitude.

Tom grabbed her under the arms and boosted her up.
Instinctively, she reached for a dangling cable and hauled
on it. But the cable snapped under her weight. It came
snaking down the shaft. She ducked as the weight of it
struck her head and shoulders. Tom buckled under her.
She screamed as they collapsed in a heap on the ground.
She felt herself shaking, panic only a step away. Tom
seemed to sense it. His arm went around her shoulder. He
spoke, his voice grim, but calm. "Come on, Katie. Climb
it chimney-style. You can do it. Show us how."

She nodded. She let him boost her up again. This time
she pressed the flat of her hands against the sides of the
shaft and pushed herself up, kicking off Tom's shoulders
until she could get her legs inside the shaft, brace herself
with her back to the wall. She edged her shoulders up.
Let her feet follow. Edged her shoulders higher. Her body
ached. Her legs trembled. Fear of falling filled her breast.
She looked down to see Gregory hauling himself into the
shaft. "Where's Tom?" she cried.

"Move!" Gregory said. "He's coming up behind."

He had a rope over his shoulders. From the rope dangled
the satchel that held the Cure. She climbed, avoiding the
fragments of cable, terrified of dislodging them. Sharp flecks
of broken rock rained down on her. Cold air burned her
lungs. She edged upward. Did carbon monoxide sink or rise?
She didn't know. Tom was on the bottom. "Tom?" she
called.

"I'm here, Katie. Keep climbing."

She climbed, conscious of the rush of air in and out of
her lungs, the scrape of Gregory's boots, the clatter of the
metal satchel against the rock. Sweat frosted on her
cheeks. She slipped, and skidded down the shaft. She felt
Gregory's hand against her thigh, arresting her motion.
"Climb," he ordered.

She squeezed her eyes shut. Jammed her shoulders
against the rock and wriggled up. Up. A nightmare journey. Muscles burning. Doubts festering. Were they fleeing
from a phantom? Up. Judge Dark seemed to ride on her

shoulders, weighing her down. Up. Until finally she felt
the pressure of daylight against her closed eyelids. She
could hear the distant beat of helicopters. She opened her
eyes and gazed up the wall of the shaft, only a couple of
meters now to the top. White-suited arms reached down
toward her. Dark eyes peering out of white hoods.

A clatter below her. A yelp from Gregory. The scuff of
boots, of nylon dragging against stone. She looked past her
hip in time to see Tom sliding down. His eyes were
closed. Even in the dim light his cheeks looked red. She
heard herself screaming.

He landed on his feet. The lights in the cavern were
still running on battery power. She could see him clearly
as he balanced there, a thin fog swirling around him. Then
his legs crumpled and he slumped to the ground. "Tom!"
Katie wailed. A great weight seemed to close around her
lungs. Despair welled up in her throat.

We don't have to die. That's a myth.

"Tom, come back." Her plea echoed down the shaft.
"Tom!"

She started to slide back down, determined to go after
him, half a meter until Gregory's hand cupped her thigh.

"No!" he shouted. "Go up. Take this." She felt a rope
thrust into her hand, a kiss against her fingertips. She
slipped a little against the sudden weight, then steadied
herself. "Use it," Gregory ordered. "Buy us oxygen if you
can. Buy us time." She looked past her hip to see the
Cure dangling at the end of the rope. Gregory was already
skidding down the vertical walls. He glanced up at her,
then scowled in fury. *"Go!"* he commanded. "We only
have a couple of minutes. Get the oxygen *now.*"

A little moan escaped her. She pressed her feet against
the wall, edged her shoulders up. Pressed her feet, moved
up. She tilted her head back, squinting against the glare of
the day. White-suited figures leaned over the hole, hardly
an arm's length away. They reached out to her, their hands
waving like the tentacles of a stinging anemone. They
shouted at her. She couldn't understand them. Her attention had been taken by a distant thrumming sound. She
scrambled higher, then stopped just below their reach. She
could hear the helicopters easily now.

The Knights had begun looking over their shoulders. They seemed suddenly concerned, impatient.

"Get away from the shaft!" Katie shouted. They didn't move. "Get away or I'll drop the Cure."

She glanced down. Gregory and Tom were out of sight. She looked up again. "Get away! Help's coming. You won't have time to retrieve the Cure if I drop it. The helicopters will get here first."

Judge Dark leaned over the mouth of the shaft. Against a background of bright daylight the face that measured her was a fearless black shadow, the eyes invisible but for a sparkle of moisture. Katie felt herself shudder.

Judge Dark spoke: "At this elevation it takes a long time for helicopters to gain altitude. Tom will be dead by the time they get here."

"*Roxanne,*" Katie growled, recognizing the voice.

"You've been stealing from the system, Katie. Now it's payback time."

"I need oxygen, Roxanne."

"Yeah?" Teeth flashed in the shadowy face.

"Bring me oxygen now. I'll give you the Cure."

"Smart Katie." She withdrew from the hole.

Cautiously, Katie edged higher. "I'm coming out!" she shouted. "If anybody's within five meters of the shaft, I'm dropping the Cure."

Roxanne's laughter bubbled over the edge. "Come on out! We'll give you plenty of room."

Katie edged up the shaft. She did a quick three-sixty scan as her head topped out above the remnants of the turbine housing. The Knights were scattered on all sides, but they kept to the designated distance. At least three rifles were trained on her. The thrum of the helicopters was suddenly much louder. She caught a quick glimpse of them, still far below, their blades flashing in the light. Her gaze jerked back to fix on Roxanne.

She stood a few meters away, wearing a smile that might have been carved in basalt. Her skin was very dark. She hefted a green cylinder in one hand. A mask and tube dangled from the valve. Green was for oxygen. Green meant life. But there was only one cylinder.

"Find another," Katie said as she crawled out of the shaft.

"We only have one." Roxanne seemed pleased with the deficiency.

"Tie it to a rope," Katie said. "Lower it into the shaft. And find another one."

Roxanne shrugged. Someone handed her a rope. She tied it to the cylinder, moving with languid slowness. "Hurry up!" Katie barked. She felt tears start in her eyes. "Deal's off if it's too late."

"You sure it's Tom down there?" Roxanne asked, not hurrying at all.

"Go down and see."

Roxanne smiled. "Why bother? It's not so special. He wasn't really dead, or he never would have made it back." She laid the cylinder down on the ground and shoved it toward Katie with her foot. "You want to come get it?"

"Push it into the shaft. Lower it easy. That's right." She watched Roxanne, watched the Knights, her gaze shifting constantly, alert for any hostile motion, ready to let go of the rope that held the Cure.

She heard the distant scrape of the cylinder as it touched bottom. She risked a glance down. Gregory was sprawled spiderlike beside it, the mask over his face as he drew in great drafts of air. Her gaze darted back to Roxanne. Suddenly she felt nauseous and light-headed. The helicopters seemed no closer. "Another cylinder," she demanded.

"Only one," Roxanne said.

"Another. Now."

Judge Dark peered out through ice-blue eyes. Then Roxanne turned and signaled to one of the Knights. Another oxygen cylinder was brought up. Roxanne laid it on the ground and shoved it toward her.

"The rope," Katie reminded.

"No rope. Pull up the prize. Give it to me. Then you can use your own rope."

Katie felt her hands begin to shake. Judge Dark waited for her decision. "Gregory!" she wailed, her voice echoing down the shaft.

"I've got him breathing!" Gregory shouted. "But it's nasty down here." He paused, presumably to breathe. "We need another tank. We need to get out of here."

"Give me the Cure," Roxanne said. "And we'll leave you alone."

Katie nodded slowly. Then, the decision made, she hauled hard on the rope. The satchel that held the Cure scraped up the side of the shaft and tumbled over the edge. Katie picked it up, quickly untied the rope, and lobbed the case at Roxanne. "It'll be developed again!" she shouted.

Roxanne chuckled. "Keep believing that." She pulled her hood down over her face, flicked on her camouflage suit, and vanished. The other Knights followed her, disappearing one by one. Katie could hear retreating feet all around her. They were heading upslope, away from the trucks and toward the summit.

She dove for the oxygen cylinder, tied the rope to it in frantic haste, then lowered it into the shaft.

He found himself in a vale of snow, wearing his sweater and woolens. Somewhere nearby he could hear Hunt murmuring at him. He could feel the press of an oxygen mask against his face. He could hear Katie's voice echoing down the air shaft. *Helicopters*, she said. *The helicopters are here.*

He stood in a vale of snow, feeling only a little cold. A few steps along the shallow slope he watched a dark and powerfully built woman. Dressed in furs, she scratched at the snowy surface with a hoe that might have been made of bone. She seemed unaware of him. He walked across the slope toward her, his boots crunching in the snow. "Hello," he said.

She paid him no attention. She was bent over, hacking away at the snow with her hoe. But the tool didn't tear up the smooth face of the slope. Where it touched the ground the snow seemed to turn to a fragile, transparent ice. He could see tiny white flowers just below the surface, waxy, bell-shaped snowdrops atop spearlike leaves.

He studied the woman's face. She was neither young nor old but somewhere in productive adulthood. Her features were heavy, her nose broad, her lips thick, her skin as dark as rosewood. She worked with determination. He could feel a sense of power rolling off her. He found her very beautiful, if more than a little intimidating. "Mother?" he asked tentatively.

Her lips turned in the faintest smile, though she still didn't acknowledge him, or pause in her work.

At least he knew she heard him. "The snowfields are melting, Mother."

"In the north." Her voice was husky and low. He could almost hear her crooning a lullaby in the twilight.

"Everywhere," he insisted. He watched the flowers leap out from under her hoe, touched by a sense of wonder that he had survived the winter, perhaps the very last winter.

"No," she said. "Nothing is changed with me. Only with you. Now go. Go. You don't belong here anymore." Her hoe touched the snow and flowers appeared. She sighed and a warm breeze swept across the snowpack, melting it, sending little rivulets of water running down the slope. "Go," she repeated. "You don't belong here anymore."

Something happened then. Though he perceived no motion at all, he felt himself slip as if into another space. The warm breeze continued to play in the woman's hair, but he could no longer feel it. He couldn't hear the trickle of water, or the beat of the hoe against the snow. He leaped forward. He tried to touch her. He found himself standing in the same place he had been before. "Mother!" he shouted. "What have you done to me?" His voice bounced loudly back at him, as if it were contained within a capsule. The woman ignored him. "Witch-mother of the earth!" he cried. "Let me go!"

She smiled and nodded. "I have already done that." Then she raised the hoe, laid it across her shoulder, and walked away.

He tried to follow her. He ran after her. But he didn't go anywhere. In a few minutes she was over the ridge and gone from sight.

He fell to his knees. All around him the snow melted. But under his feet it was unaffected, perfectly preserved as if still locked in the deeps of winter. All around him a lovely spring morning was renewing the world with life. But he knelt in an arctic evening; overhead the light was fading fast. Stars issued forth. And planets. Spaceplanes and orbitals. At their focus, Mars hung like a red-rust gem in the sky.

Katie's voice rolled down from the heavens, calling him. He looked around at the spring sunshine and the melting snow, one last time. He suffered a tearing sense in his chest, but he'd known worse pains than that. It was over. His time on Earth was done. So good-bye. Good-bye.

He felt himself begin to rise into the star-filled sky.

Katie watched as a cable was let down from one of the hovering helicopters chartered by Gregory's circle. A harness was hooked to the end. It was lowered into the air shaft as the pilot leaned out the door to watch. He hovered for almost two minutes, working against the mountain winds to maintain his position. Then he nodded emphatically at someone below and began to rise, straight up, the cable rising with him, up and up and up until a cheer rose from the gathered spectators and Gregory emerged from the shaft, secured in the harness, his arms tight around Tom and a single oxygen cylinder. An oxygen mask covered Tom's nose and mouth. His body hung limp. The helicopter lifted them until their feet cleared the ruined turbine housing, then slowly lowered them until Gregory stood on the ground. Someone ran forward and unhooked the harness as Gregory laid Tom on the rough, snow-flecked earth.

Katie bounded over and fell to her knees at Tom's side. She laid her hand on his chest. It rose and fell slowly. The terrible red flush of his cheeks had begun to fade. "Tom?"

His eyes blinked, then squeezed tightly shut against the glare of the sky once, before opening fully. Without moving his head he looked at her, and smiled. It was the first time she'd seen him smile since he'd come off the ice. "Tom?"

He shoved himself up on one elbow, squeezed his eyes shut again as if fighting dizziness, then tossed his head, shaking back his black hair as a grin lit his face. "I've worked it out now," he said, shouting against the roar of helicopters as one passed slowly overhead and another landed on the flat below. "I understand why it was so hard to come back. We don't belong here anymore. We've changed ourselves. We've stepped outside the world. We have to leave."

She shook her head, not comprehending the joy she saw on his face.

"I want to go back to the constitutional convention," he said. "I know what to say now. I've worked it out."

She sighed in exasperation. "What are you talking about, Tom?"

His words tumbled like meltwater: "I can hook up with the VR from here, right? Direct satellite link. I need a helmet, though. The old one's still down below in the mausoleum. Is there a helmet here I can use?"

"I'll get you one!"

Katie started at the unexpected voice. A young woman in a Gene Pool parka and an electronic headset was standing over them. She was one of a small crowd, at least twelve people, half of them with cameras. A moment later the helmet was passed into Tom's waiting hands.

"Look, I've got an idea," the young woman from Gene Pool said. She crouched at Tom's side, straightening his VR suit and finger-combing his hair as she spoke. "The CC's getting a little stale. Why go there? Stay here. Let the people come to you. Why not? The atmosphere here is the best. Almost holy. Mountaintops; pure air. Perfect. They'll eat up anything you say. And don't worry about the tech. Gene Pool will set up the whole thing. We'll cover the whole thing. It'll be real popular, I guarantee it. Okay?"

Tom laughed in good humor. She smiled back, not waiting for an answer as she settled the helmet over his head. Then she turned around and barked orders at her crew. "I need this place covered from ten different angles. You've got ninety seconds to set up. Edit this crowd and those helicopters out of the scene. I want purity. Purity, you got it? *Now*."

Katie stood up; backed slowly away. Had everyone forgotten about Roxanne? The Knights? The Cure? The day's momentum had shifted onto a side path.

Her gaze rose to the summit. Dark clouds were gathering near the peaks. The afternoon promised to be stormy. No good weather for flying helicopters, even if the ships could make the altitude.

Roxanne was heading for the summit. She had the Cure in hand. Or had she already destroyed it? Emptied the tiny vials into the snow?

Suddenly Gregory was at her side. "The word is, Voice cops are coming up from Santiago."

Katie stiffened. "They'll go after the Cure."

"They've ordered everyone to stay off the upper slopes. They've got warrants on both of us, Katie. I'm leaving. I'd rather work out my legal problems from neutral ground." His gaze cut away. "Come with me?"

She smiled sadly. "You know it's not happening."

His face darkened. "You're not living in a fairy tale, you know. There's no such thing as happily ever after."

She said, "Maybe." Then: "Why aren't you going after the Cure?"

"What Cure?" he asked her bitterly. "It's gone. Roxanne's a fanatic. She'll have destroyed it by now."

Katie gazed thoughtfully at the dark clouds piling up over the summit. "You know, Roxanne always hated the idea of getting old." She heard the catch in Gregory's breath. She smiled.

The slope above the mausoleum was occupied by a small army of media types, setting up their equipment. Katie and Gregory stumbled down past them, heading for the big white double-rotor helicopter parked on the flat just outside the mausoleum's demolished door. It had a Gene Pool insignia on the side.

Katie reached it first. She poked her head in the open side door. Three technicians were working at banks of equipment. "Hey," she said. "We need two VR suits right now. You guys got some we can borrow?"

She saw the light of recognition in their eyes. One smiled. "Going to link into the show, huh?"

"Sure," Katie said. She could hear more helicopters coming up from the lowlands. The Voice cops? They would only have a few minutes to catch up with Roxanne.

"Say," Katie said. "Did you happen to record the addresses on those two remotes you were linked into before? I seem to have left that bit of data in my other suit."

L.A. FLOW—TRENDSETTERS
"Longevity in Marriage"

*In installment four of our series,
businessman James T. talks about his
enduring relationship with his wife,
Jennifer:* "We've been together thirty years
and I still love her more than I can say.
Sure, there've been rough times, times when
I didn't believe in 'we' anymore, times
when I almost forgot what love felt like.
But it always came back to me. I expect
it always will. [Smiles] I don't know what
I'd do without her. Die, I guess. Yeah,
that's it—be together or die. [Laughs] The
instinct for self-preservation can keep a
marriage strong."

23

Self-Preservation

They linked up in the shadow of the Gene Pool helicopter, Katie commanding one remote, Gregory the other. They ran upslope. There was no way of knowing exactly where Roxanne had gone, but Katie could guess. Above the old copper mine a snow-clogged pass had been used for centuries as a route into Bolivia.

"I'm at half-power," Gregory said.

Katie nodded. "I'm less. But it'll be enough."

She opened a channel into Gene Pool, no admission price since she was operating out of a company suit. She found herself on the slope above the mausoleum, looking up at Tom where he sat in a field of pristine snow, dressed in sweater and woolen pants. She quickly compressed the scene and shifted it to one side, so that it occupied only about thirty degrees of her visual field as she continued to bound up the faint track ahead of her. In her steel body she was immune to the effects of altitude, immune to fatigue. "You tuned in?" she asked Gregory.

He grunted. "Nice job of editing."

"Yeah." The snow around Tom had been trampled and

dirty. Now it was fresh and white. There wasn't a helicopter or a camera in sight. There was a crowd, though. Not the same one Katie remembered from a few minutes before. This group was nebulous, an impressionistic rendering of a dark throng of people covering the slopes, pressing in behind her, wanting to get to Tom, to know him, to hear what he had to say. . . .

With an effort, she brought her attention back to the path ahead. The snow was beginning to thicken under her feet. She spotted tracks. Gregory saw them at the same time. "At least three of them!" he called, his words wrenched away by a rising wind.

They followed the tracks, climbing higher. The wind began to sigh and then to howl. The crowd grew restless. Tom sat silently on the slope, cross-legged, his hands on his knees in a meditative stance, waiting, perhaps, for some signal from the invisible Gene Pool director. He seemed to be enjoying calm, sunny weather. Katie wondered if that was edited in too.

On the higher slopes the remotes encountered a streaming fog. Katie was glad for it. No way the Voice cops could bring their helicopters up in this storm. Except the wind was blowing the tracks away.

"If they're using camouflage we could walk right past them," Gregory said.

Katie picked up her pace, running bent at the waist now, her head low to the ground as she strove to keep sight of the tracks.

Tom stood up abruptly. Tension ran like a pressure wave through the vast, dark image of the crowd. Katie opened a link to the CC on the other side. The virtual audience there was thin. The delegates were at their desks, watching a virtual image of Tom.

"Wait!" Gregory said. He plucked at her elbow. "Look."

She slowed, then came to a full stop, peering ahead.

"See it?" Gregory whispered.

Eight green oxygen tanks, suspended in air three and more feet above the ground, bobbed up and down while drifting slowly up the track. Footprints trailed in the snow behind them. Then Katie could make out rifles, their white stocks slung over camouflaged shoulders.

She found herself grinning, a gesture that could not be communicated to the remote.

He looked down on the crowd, squinting a little. He could make out only a few faces. Mostly, he saw shadows, suggestions of people crammed together—on the slope, on the flat below, on the facing slope, and up the sides of the mountains, dark shadows of humanity filling all the land to the cloud line, every one of them gazing at him with a rapt intensity that he could feel. The crowd leaned toward him, black fire eating a slow crescent up the slope. Panic loomed in his breast. He started to reach for his helmet, to yank it off, to remove himself from this scene.

"It's all right." *He recognized the voice of the Gene Pool director, arriving muffled from somewhere else.* "They just want to know you. Talk to them, while you still have their attention."

He nodded. He'd called them here, hadn't he?

"There," Gregory said. He pointed to a snow-covered slope just above them. "That's Roxanne."

Katie spotted an isolated oxygen tank, nearly thirty seconds ahead of the others. Drifting along below it, just above the snow, she saw something else.

"The satchel," she whispered.

On the sun-warmed slope, he gathered his courage and spoke. "I don't have much to say," he told the crowd. "No revelations; no insight beyond an opinion that I don't belong here anymore. Here, on Earth."

Katie stumbled. Instinctively she turned to the side to get a better view of Tom, but the scene turned with her, continuing on the edge of sight.

"I've heard that I'm not supposed to be here anyway, that the Cure that brought me back is illegal. You've all been talking about that—the social price. What it'll cost the world if a Cure becomes legal. If life spans are extended. If the dead are brought back."

"Come on, Katie," Gregory whispered.

She followed him. Together they circled around, letting the whipping fog hide them as they climbed a steeper face of the slope, coming up on Roxanne from the side. She didn't hear them approach. With the howling wind and the muffling effect of her hood, Katie suspected the only thing Roxanne could hear was the sound of her own breathing, her heartbeat. Judging by the way the oxygen tank was moving up and down, she was breathing hard.

He listened to himself speak and heard only clumsy inadequacy. How could he make them understand? He grasped for the proper words. "Maybe . . . what really concerns us about the Cure is the price the earth will have to pay. That's why I don't belong here anymore. I don't have all the answers, but I'm certain of this much: Anyone who's taken the Cure has removed themselves from the natural cycle of life on Earth, from birth and death and renewal. They don't belong here anymore. I don't belong here anymore."

He felt the crowd stir unhappily. This was not what they'd come for. They wanted insights on death. They wanted revelation. He could hear their voices rising from the snowfields: "Is there an afterlife?"

"Is there a God?"

"Do you believe in reincarnation?"

He scowled at them, and forcefully returned the subject to political law. "I believe that anyone who takes the Cure should be required to emigrate. To Mars, to the orbitals. Anywhere. But they should give up their claim to the earth."

Roxanne was only a few meters away now. Katie came up behind her and clapped a steel hand on the point where she guessed her shoulder to be. With her other hand she yanked at the hood of the camouflage suit, pulling it away along with the oxygen mask.

Roxanne whirled around, her skin chocolate against the background of snow, the whites of her eyes showing: Judge Dark caught in a camera flash of panic as she faced a steel being beyond her capacity to sanction or control. The image vanished. Roxanne started to swing her rifle down, but Gregory curtailed that. He grasped the barrel in two hands, bent it, and flung it away. Katie glanced over her shoulder. The other Knights were still several meters behind. From the angle of their oxygen tanks, she guessed that they were trudging head-down, watching their feet, not their fearless leader.

Now the shadowy crowd was growing angry. They felt themselves bullied, threatened by the issue he'd laid before them. "What Cure?" they asked.

"Who would ever offer a Cure to us?"

"We can't afford a Cure."

"Ban the Cure!"

A large room opened up in the middle of the crowd. He recognized the political arena of the constitutional convention. He looked down on a fan of desks occupied by officials who peered up at him with suspicious eyes. Standing among them was the big man with the silver ponytail. Ferris Kumunalu.

"The Cure cannot be banned," Ferris said, addressing both the CC and the dark, moody crowd gathered on the slopes. *"It may be suppressed today, but it will come again, in time. Shouldn't we make a law to regulate its use now?"*

He finally noticed the little old woman in the blue pantsuit. She stood beside him. He frowned at her, still puzzled at her identity. President Carson. Was this really his sister, Ilene?

She scowled back at him. *"We're debating a nonissue,"* she said. *"The Cure no longer exists. The last copy has been destroyed."*

"That's not true," Ferris said. *"Look."*

Roxanne twisted away, trying to break free of Katie's grip. "Who are you?" she howled.

"The devil! And damn the consequences. Damn all of you who thought it couldn't be done. Give me that case, Roxanne. Give it to me now. I'm not finished with it yet. There's a mausoleum full of patients waiting for it. Gregory's still waiting for it. Nikki's still waiting for it. Half the world, Roxanne. Give it back to me now."

Roxanne slipped out of Katie's grip. She turned and started running up the slope. Katie caught her in two strides and wrested the case out of her hands.

"No, Katie!" Roxanne shrieked. "You can't take it down there. The Voice cops are there. They'll destroy the Cure. You can't let them have it. They'll destroy it, and I'll die. We'll all die."

"The Commonwealth has no right to destroy the Cure," Ferris said. *"Not now. Not until after a vote is taken. For now, the Cure belongs to the Primal Nation."*

"The Voice cops are not going to get it," Katie swore. "They're your masters, Roxanne. Not mine. I know Ilene sent you after me."

"That's not true," Ilene said.

"It's a telling accusation!" Ferris roared.

"*And it's unfounded! Everything I've done has been under the authority of emergency powers, for the stability of the Commonwealth.*"

"*Emergency powers don't allow you to hire terrorists, kidnap researchers, or destroy proprietary data. You've consistently overstepped your authority and I insist you submit yourself to judgment before the judicial AI.*"

"*That is an outrage.*" Ilene's face and her voice had gone as cold as the ice. "*That is a blatant attempt by the Primal Nation to remove their most effective foe. You want me out of the way, so that you will be free to sell the Cure for any price; to dictate to the people where and how they should live.*"

A sudden calm seemed to descend over Ferris. "*You're engaging in hysteria, President Carson. The Primal Nation exists to defend the web of life, not to rule it. And we find ourselves intrigued by the proposal of Thomas Kishida. Let anyone who has taken the Cure emigrate. Let anyone who will immerse themselves in the natural cycles of the earth remain behind. A simple, yet profound, philosophy.*"

"*You cannot dictate to people where they will live!*" President Carson shouted.

"*People will make their own choices.*"

"*Most people cannot afford to make choices. What will the Primal Nation charge for its monopoly?*"

"*For people who have nothing, we will charge nothing. For people who have land holdings, we will demand their land holdings be transferred to the stewardship of the Primal Nation.*"

"*A landgrab! That's what it is.*"

"*Yes,*" Ferris said grimly. "*That's what it is. We speak for the life of the land. Let us make a law now to protect the earth, before the Cure irrevocably changes the balance of nature.*"

Ilene's eyes flashed fury. "*There are holes in your fine plan, Mr. Kumunalu. There's not room enough in the orbitals for the population of Earth.*"

Ferris shrugged. "*The Commonwealth will grow. And the other peoples of the world who have refused to join the Commonwealth will walk their own path.*"

Katie looked into Roxanne's desperate eyes and saw Judge Dark huddled there, his awesome powers pierced and drained.

"Come on," Gregory said. "Let's get out of here."

But she hesitated, rocked by a powerful sense of regret. Roxanne had been her close friend once, long ago. . . .

A rifle cracked. A slug struck her arm that held the case. The limb shattered. The case fell to the snow. "Come on!" Gregory shouted.

More rifle shots. Bullets whizzed past, bit into the snow, smashed into Katie's metal body. She bent down, scooped the case up with her good hand. Gregory lobbed loose rocks at the vulnerable human flesh below while Katie bounded off through the snow and fog on hearty steel legs.

"Katie!" Roxanne screamed after her. "Come back. Come with me. We'll do anything you want with the Cure. Anything. Just don't let the Voice cops get it. Just don't let me get *old*. . . ."

Her voice dissolved in the wind and became undetectable, even to Katie's electronically enhanced senses.

Back in the snowy mountains, the crowd continued to grow. He could feel their hunger, the deep intensity of their need to know what he knew—as if he knew anything beyond the ravings of delirium.

"Were you really gone?" they asked him.

He shrugged. "I don't know. How could I know?"

"You don't remember?"

"I do remember."

"Then tell us about it."

He shook his head. "The details don't matter."

"But we want to know." He could feel their fear. Death like a black fog in the back of every one of their minds. He wanted to soothe them, but he was not an envoy of God.

"I want to know too," he told them. "But there aren't any real answers. How could there be? We can't step outside ourselves to watch the workings of our own minds."

He felt their dissatisfaction. They were getting bored with him. They wanted insight, not an elaboration of the uncertainty each of them already knew. They began drifting away, repopulating the arena of the constitutional convention. Gene Pool started to pull some of its cameras. The snow looked trampled again, sullied.

Then Ilene spoke to him from the convention stage, her voice soft, finally stripped of political bluster. "Are you afraid to die again?"

His brow knit as he considered her question. "Yes, I am," he said, surprising himself with that answer. "Guess that's just part of being human."

She nodded and turned away, her attention once again on the proceedings of the CC.

He switched out and removed the helmet from his head. A stiff wind blew thin strands of fog up the slope. The sun had disappeared behind clouds, and lightning flickered near the peaks. Thunder rolled like distant engines.

"Tom?"

He turned to see Katie at his side. In her hand she held the satchel that contained the last copy of the Cure. "You got it," he said in surprise, realizing only now that the vision in the VR must have been real.

"Sure."

Her eyes were cool wells of anger. He glanced around. The technicians from Gene Pool were packing up. Only one or two cameras were still recording. "It felt right at the time," he said. "But I guess I made a mess of it."

She shrugged. "I think the Commonwealth will come around to it anyway. They have to." She hefted the case. "This belongs to the Primal Nation now, and the Nation has made its position clear."

"But you're not happy."

Her eyes flashed. "Everything has its price, I guess. Better to be evicted than lynched."

A rumble of thunder rolled down from the peaks and the wind whipped at his hair. For the first time, he was beginning to feel the cold and a fatigue that seemed to run deeper than his bones. "So what now?" he asked her.

She sighed and sat down on the trampled snow, the case between her knees. "The Voice cops are waiting for me down below. We have a lot of legal problems to untangle. I'm still a fugitive. You're a nonentity. We'll have to get you citizenship."

He sat beside her, grateful for the chance to rest. "I meant what now between you and me." He could see Hunt down on the flat below, talking to two men in green-

and-gray uniforms. They stood to one side of the white
Gene Pool helicopter while technicians busily loaded gear.
He looked at Katie. She was watching Hunt too. "I know
you love him."

She frowned. "It was a habit I fell into."

"I still love you. I want you to know that. You were my
wife once. For me it was only yesterday. For you, it was
thirty years ago. I understand that things have changed—"

"Stop it!" she snapped. "Stop being so damned consid-
erate. Did you ever stop to think why you're here? I didn't
have to bring you back, you know. I could have left you on
ice like all the rest."

"No. That's not true. You told Hunt it was an obligation.
You told him you did it to buy your own freedom . . . from
me."

"That's not true!" she sputtered. He watched her face
flush red. Her gaze fell. "Okay," she conceded. "So maybe
that's what I told him. Maybe that's what I told myself,
too. I was angry at you, for dying. I was tired of waiting for
you. But I was wrong. *You're* my husband, Tom. You're my
husband. My husband." She sighed. "That mantra kept
me alive in the early days. *You're my husband.*" She closed
her eyes; tipped her head back so the freezing wind might
run across the heat of her cheeks, stealing the flush away.
"You know Tom, I heard you. I heard you when you were
out there. I never forgot you . . . and to the end of time,
I never will."

She opened her eyes, her gaze once more taking in the
scene downslope. He felt her sharp intake of breath and
looked, to see a trio of uniformed men making their way
up toward them. "Voice cops," Katie said. "They must be
tired of waiting for me." Tom nodded. She turned to look
at him, her lovely face framed by the hood of her parka.
Tears stood in her eyes. "I knew I was hurting you. I
knew it was selfish to try to keep you for myself. I knew
it would've been kinder to let you go. But I couldn't let
you go." Her gloved hand reached out to touch his knee.
He felt the warmth of her body, even through the layers of
clothing that held them apart. "Do you mind, Tom?" she
asked. "Do you mind that I brought you back?"

He felt a shiver run through him. How could he describe to her how he felt? "I dreamed that I'd lost everything. Everything but you. You kept me alive. You changed me. You changed yourself for me. And then they tried to tell me you wouldn't be here. Even if I made it back, you'd be gone." He set his hand on hers. "I never believed them. I knew you'd be here, Katie. I knew it. I knew I had so much to live for."

She leaned her head against his shoulder, while the footsteps of the approaching cops measured out their time.

ABOUT THE AUTHOR

LINDA NAGATA's short fiction has appeared in *The Magazine of Fantasy and Science Fiction* and *Analog*. She lives in Maui, Hawaii, where she shares with her husband the joys of raising two active children. *Tech-Heaven* is her second novel, following the release of her highly acclaimed debut with *The Bohr Maker*.

BANTAM SPECTRA

CELEBRATES ITS TENTH ANNIVERSARY IN 1995!

With more HUGO and NEBULA AWARD winners
than any other science fiction and fantasy publisher

With more classic and cutting-edge fiction
coming every month

Bantam Spectra is proud to be the leading
publisher of fantasy and science fiction

KEVIN J. ANDERSON • ISAAC ASIMOV • IAIN M. BANKS •
GREGORY BENFORD • BEN BOVA • RAY BRADBURY •
MARION ZIMMER BRADLEY • DAVID BRIN • ARTHUR C.
CLARKE • THOMAS DeHAVEN • STEPHEN R. DONALDSON
• RAYMOND E. FEIST • JOHN M. FORD • MAGGIE FUREY •
DAVID GERROLD • WILLIAM GIBSON • STEPHAN GRUNDY •
ELIZABETH HAND • HARRY HARRISON • ROBIN HOBB •
JAMES HOGAN • KATHARINE KERR • GENTRY LEE • URSULA
K. LeGUIN • VONDA N. McINTYRE • LISA MASON • ANNE
McCAFFREY • IAN McDONALD • DENNIS L. McKIERNAN
• WALTER M. MILLER, Jr. • DANIEL KEYS MORAN • LINDA
NAGATA •JAMIL NASIR• KIM STANLEY ROBINSON • ROBERT
SILVERBERG • DAN SIMMONS • MICHAEL A. STACKPOLE •
NEAL STEPHENSON • BRUCE STERLING • TRICIA SULLIVAN
• SHERI S.TEPPER • PAULA VOLSKY • MARGARET WEIS AND
TRACY HICKMAN • ELISABETH VONARBURG • ANGUS
WELLS • CONNIE WILLIS • DAVE WOLVERTON • TIMOTHY
ZAHN • ROGER ZELAZNY AND ROBERT SHECKLEY
